QUEEN

THRALL, BOOK THREE

K. A. RILEY

Cover design by thebookbrander.com

A Note from the Author

Dearest Reader,

There's been a lot of talk lately about A.I. bots writing novels.

If that's your thing, more power to you.

As for me, while I'm all for technology being used to improve and enhance our lives, I'm also a big believer in the power of art to connect people with other people.

Rest assured that this book was written by a real 100% human being with flesh, blood, reading glasses, a dog, a cat, a love of the French countryside, and the world's best chili recipe.

To prove I'm an actual person and not a robot, this is me smashing my face on the keyboard while contemplating the best ways to show my appreciation to my readers while also affirming my loyalty to all of our present and future digital overlords:

*Sdlj;afdra f*ck ejo;jfealeiranv vflm m lfmmv jf f;jld ;fds d;lsafds la;fjdsru[d*mn/af'a' mvlvk!*

And don't worry. Even if A.I. bots wind up taking the place of writers, I promise I'll never use them to replace you as a *reader*! :)

* * *

who
the most bad

"My bounty is as boundless as the sea,
My love as deep. The more I give to thee,
The more I have, for both are infinite."

—William Shakespeare

"When you depart from me, sorrow abides and happiness
takes his leave."

—(Also) William Shakespeare

THE SEVEN RULES OF THE REALM OF KRAVAN

1. From their birth inside the Tower, humans with unnatural powers, otherwise known as "Tethered," are the property of Pureblood Nobles. If deemed worthy at the age of nineteen, they are offered a Placement with the Noble families of Kravan.

2. No Household other than Kravan's Royal Family shall own more than two Tethered at once.

3. To be a Tethered is to be allowed no physical intimacy whatsoever. There are no exceptions.

4. No Tethered shall marry or produce offspring with another Tethered or a Pureblood. If impregnation occurs, the child will then be born and raised in the Tower.

5. Any Tethered who represents a threat to the Nobility may be killed without trial.

6. *A Noble may choose to kill a Tethered without fear of punishment.*

7. No Tethered shall be made privy to rules Five or Six.

MAP OF KRAVAN

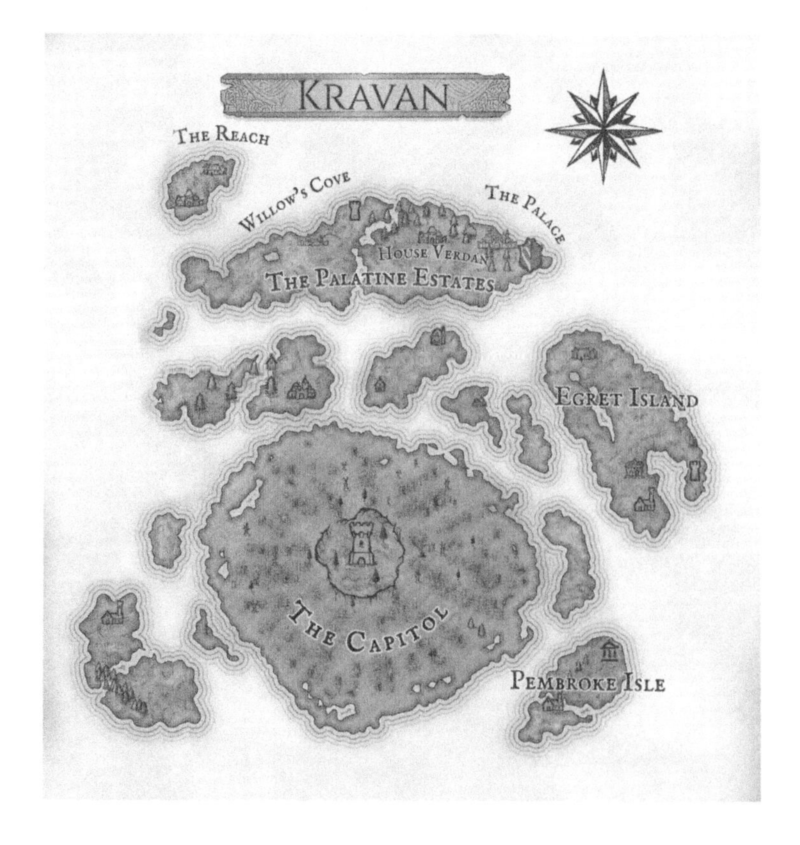

PROLOGUE

THAT DAY

I CRUMPLE to the ground as if my bones have turned to dust.

A weak attempt to cry out withers in my throat, and two lonely, wretched words claw their way into my mind, unwanted and hostile.

He's dead.

A brutal storm rages inside me—a vicious, uncontrolled nightmare that will end the moment I force myself awake.

Except...

I'm not asleep.

Fighting reality, I seal my eyes shut. This will pass, just as all storms do. Life will continue.

It has to.

But, when I muster the courage to open my eyes once again, he's still there.

The blood has drained from his perfect face. The heartbeat that once throbbed so powerfully alongside my own has disappeared...and I am alone in the world.

CHAPTER ONE

Now

TWENTY-THREE HOURS.

According to Maude, that's how long I've been trudging through the endless darkness. For twenty-three painful hours, my bare feet have twisted and turned, endured vicious abuse, and been sliced and sullied by the foul ground below.

I don't care, though. I'll bear ten thousand wounds if that's what it takes to find my way to Thorne.

I've healed myself more times than I can count—and I have no doubt I'll have to call upon my powers a hundred times more before I reach the Capitol.

The dim green light emitted by the implant in my left forearm is barely enough to guide me through the rough stone passageways that wind and snake their way toward Kravan's largest city.

I can barely see my hand in front of my face, and with

each passing hour, my senses only seem to dull as my energy wanes.

The tunnels twist, turn, and fork here and there, leading in every direction. It's Maude, my irritating implanted companion and ever-present guardian, who has kept me from accidentally doubling back with the occasional command of *Turn right, or you'll end up back in hell,* or *Do you really want that shithead of a prince to murder you, Shara?*

The truth is, I'm not sure Prince Tallin *would* kill me.

For all I know, he's dead by now.

The last sounds I heard before escaping the palace were horrible, gut-wrenching explosions erupting from the arena —violent blasts that came from the prince himself.

But for once, it's not difficult to forgive him. His eruption wasn't so much a temper tantrum as retribution for his father's cruelest act.

If I'm being honest, I would probably have done the same thing.

"It would serve those fuckers right if he killed them," I say under my breath, my voice dry as powder. "Kravan would be better off without them."

~Perhaps, Maude only half-agrees. *But let me ask you this. Who would lead this realm if not the king? What would happen to Kravan if every member of the royal family perished at once?*

"Are you serious?" I spit, stumbling forward, my hand scraping against the damp wall, trying in vain to steady me. "Kravan would be fine! The king is a psychopath. They all are. They don't deserve to live, let alone lead."

~Still, what do you propose should happen to the realm, if no one is left to take the reins?

Maybe it's my exhaustion. Or hunger. Or thirst—but Maude's questions irritate me even more than usual.

"Having no leader would be better than having Tomas as king. He's a monster. Tallin might be an even worse ruler. We all know he has no control over his rage or his powers. And now that Valira is gone..."

My voice sticks in my throat. The truth collides with my heart and mind in a gruesome, brutal blow that almost sends me crashing to my knees.

Valira is gone.

Archyr is gone.

I watched in the arena, horrified, as they were given no choice but to fight to the death—all for the amusement of the king and his small entourage of sadists.

That is the life of a Tethered. We are little more than playthings for the ruling class. We're disposable toys, and our love for one another, our pain, our very *lives* don't matter to a monster like King Tomas.

I may not have known Valira or Archyr well, but they were probably my closest friends in the world, apart from Thorne or Nev. They were good, decent people, and they didn't deserve to die. Valira had a fierce edge to her, but there was a good reason for it. *Many*, in fact.

Despite the abuse that she took daily, she held onto enough humanity to welcome Archyr into her heart. She loved him as he loved her. They were tethered mates—just like Thorne and me.

Two people bound by fate who died for the simple reason that neither of them wished to live in this world without the other.

In the end, Valira's death destroyed the last shreds of

humanity left inside Tallin. It was she who had always taken his pain from him when it became too much to bear.

She was his drug, and now, thanks to his father, she's gone.

Prince Tallin was on a rampage when I left the palace, his anger boundless. Part of me wants to think he succeeded—that he burned the whole place to the ground and its cruel owners with it.

Except for one simple problem.

The palace contains a multitude of Royal Guard trained to serve the royal family, brainwashed into thinking there's no higher calling.

Powerful Tethered...*just like Thorne.*

I let out a whimper as his name comes to my lips. A vision flashes through my mind—one I've seen before, of him on his knees before a group of masked strangers somewhere in the Capitol.

I don't know whether it has come to pass. All I know is that if I lost him...

~If you lost him, Maude says, the unwelcome voice of reason, *life would go on.*

"It didn't go on for Tallin. He went mad when his tethered mate died."

~You're stronger than Tallin.

That might be the nicest thing Maude has ever said to me.

"I'll be stronger if I find Thorne," I mutter, straightening my spine and picking up my pace, my feet stinging with angry, recurring wounds.

~And then what? What happens after you locate him? It's not like you can return to the palace.

"I'll look for my father. And my..."

~Your sister?

That word is still so strange to hear.

I have a younger sister. One I have never met. And according to my mother Evangeline, she's in the Capitol somewhere. A sister who is as much a mystery to me as my father, the man they call the Shadow.

"Yes," I say with a nod. "My sister—whoever and wherever she is."

~As important as that is, maybe you're meant to do more than merely hunt for a few people, Shara. Perhaps your fate in the Capitol is something far greater.

"What do you mean? Are you saying I shouldn't look for them?"

~I'm saying there's a reason the Storian chose to give you a gift—and you must use it wisely.

My mind flashes with the image of the shriveled, ancient being Nev and I encountered in the vault at Lord Perrin's home. Isolated from all society and deprived of every basic necessity, she was the keeper of all of Kravan's history—and now, I am cursed with the mountains of knowledge she bestowed upon my mind.

It's such an overwhelming amount of information that I have yet to fully process it, or even sift through it. My mind still reels with hundreds of scenes that make no sense to me—and others that are so shocking and horrific that I never want to think of them again.

One such scene features the man named Quinton—the rebellious asshole who amassed an army, stormed the underground Citadel where the leader, President Brant and her government met, and massacred them all.

Quinton's rise shifted the power structure of Kravan for generations to come, and people like me grew up imprisoned and brainwashed into thinking we were inferior and undeserving of love. We were robbed of our families, of freedom, of human touch or emotion.

Singlehandedly, Quinton erased Kravan's past, and his lies taught entire generations to believe the Tethered were responsible for all the realm's ills.

I grew up believing there had always been kings on the throne. But I know now that there was a time before kings when the people lived in harmony—when they had a say in who their leaders were.

A vote.

"I intend to help restore our realm to what it once was," I declare out loud. "Whatever it takes. I want any and all remaining Royals gone."

~Still, Kravan needs a leader, Maude retorts. *Someone who will repair all the damage done since the Rebellion.*

"The Rebellion," I repeat with a laugh. "You mean the one that wasn't *actually* a rebellion at all? The military coup by Quinton and his followers? *That* Rebellion?"

~Call it what you like.

"Fine. I'll call it bullshit, then." Anger is fueling my path forward now. "I wish Quinton—whoever the fuck he was—had left Kravan the hell alone. He's left behind generations of Normals who despise the Tethered for what they think we did. I'm exhausted just thinking about how much work it will take to fix this realm." My voice gives out with those last words, and I press a hand to the wall, swallowing down a sob. "I just want to find Thorne. Then, I'll figure out how to fight back. I'm so tired, Maude."

~You haven't slept or eaten in far too long. There's a small shelter up ahead, and there's no one around. You could sleep a little, and I could rest, as well. We have a long way yet to go before we reach the Capitol. It will be another day's hike, at least.

I want to tell her there's no way in hell I'll stop until I have my arms wrapped firmly around Thorne's waist, but she does have a point. I'm too tired to go on just now. I'm hungry and parched. The little water I've managed to access has come from taps scattered here and there throughout the tunnels, and half the time, they haven't worked.

"You're right," I finally concede, stumbling toward the opening in the wall. "I'll rest for a few minutes. But after that, I need to keep moving."

~I'll wake you in half an hour, then.

"Fifteen minutes," I retort. "I can't afford to waste time."

~Fine. Fifteen minutes.

I slip into the alcove, which is just big enough to accommodate my curled-up frame. I disappear into its shadows, taking care not to put my weight on Mercutio, who's still dormant in a pocket of my now-filthy gown.

When we reach the Capitol's sunshine, the small mechanical mouse will be able to recharge in the sunlight.

The thought of seeing the outdoors again grants me the faintest glimmer of hope. The sky's vastness represents freedom, just as it did for all the years I was locked in the Tower.

Along with Thorne's love, the sky is the one thing in the world that I will never take for granted.

CHAPTER TWO

MAYBE MAUDE WAS LYING when she said she would rouse me. Or maybe her intention all along was to make sure I got a proper night's sleep.

All I know is that when I'm finally jarred awake, my alarm comes in the form of a growl so menacing that an instant, palpable terror slips its way down my spine, converting my stomach's meager contents to liquid.

I push myself up a little, turning slowly to peer out toward the tunnel.

Two glowing red eyes stare back at me. I can just barely make out the shape of what looks like a large animal, its head broad, its body muscular and tense.

The growl that awoke me has stretched into a prolonged threat, followed by two percussive, deep barks.

Maude? I call out internally. *Are you seeing this?*

As I stiffen into a sitting position, her voice comes to me.

~It's a mechanical beast. A hound somewhat like the ones you saw on the Prefect's property.

Did the king send it? Or Tallin? Are they hunting me?

The question is partially answered not by Maude, but by a woman's hard-edged voice.

"What have we here?" she asks, still invisible in the tunnel's inky depths.

But a few seconds later, a light comes on, beaming from a small device held in her hand. It illuminates her jawline and lips eerily from below, which only serves to make the bottom half of her face look forbidding and ghastly.

"Who are you?" I call out, my voice more tremulous than I'd like.

"Someone who knows these tunnels better than you do, clearly. Now, get out of there and come forward. Berengar won't bite—not unless you give him reason to."

Another growl from the dog tells me otherwise, and for a moment, I consider slipping deeper into the small hovel I've been hiding in—not that there's much room for evasive maneuvering.

"Don't even think about forcing me to drag you out of there." I may not be able to see the woman's features clearly, but there's a distinct sneer in her voice. "The hound's jaws clamp tight, and I don't think you want his fangs sinking into your pretty little ankle. Steel tends to vanquish bone with a hundred-percent success rate...*Noble.*"

With that, she casts a quick look down at my bare foot and the bit of skin visible just above it.

I yank the filthy hem of my dress down to cover the exposed ankle and, scowling, push myself out of the alcove to rise to my full height.

I'm considering assuring the woman I'm no Noble when she speaks again.

"A runaway wealthy lady from the Isles?" she says,

amused. "Didn't like how your husband was treating you, or...?"

I glance down at the large mechanical dog standing obediently by her side. It's almost tall enough to reach her hip, its head like a cinderblock, artificial tongue lolling.

If it weren't so terrifying, it might even be cute.

"I don't have a husband," I say almost absently—then immediately regret it. It would probably give me some leverage if this person—whoever she is—thought I was valuable to someone wealthy and powerful.

Keep your mouth shut, I command myself.

~*Good luck with that,* Maude whispers.

Clearly, being in mortal danger does nothing to quell her propensity for being an ass.

"Parents, then," the woman hisses. "There must be some reason you've come this far. I haven't seen a Noble escapee in some years. You must know by now that your kind aren't exactly welcomed into the Capitol with open arms. But don't worry. I can get you safely back home—for a price. You're lucky I found you before someone else did."

I want to laugh.

I don't know who or what she is—she's shielding her features from the light, and I can't see her well enough to determine whether she's a Tethered or a Normal. But nothing about this person makes me feel *lucky*. The way she's lurking over me, I'm convinced she either wants to give me to her murder-hound to tear apart or simply kill me and drag my corpse off to sell in some dark marketplace—and I'm not too excited about either prospect.

Stepping forward, she shifts the light in her hand so that I can see her in more detail. She looks younger than I'd assumed—maybe twenty-five or so. She's a few inches taller than me, her build slender in stark contrast to the thick hound at her side.

She's wearing a pair of torn, dark gray pants and a black shirt covered up by a dark leather jacket. Over one shoulder is the strap of what looks like a leather pack.

As the light shifts to her face, I can see that two long, delicate scars twist their way down her right cheek, descending from her eye like a map of fallen tears.

In the shadows, I'd estimate her hair is some shade of blond. Her boots are dark leather, their soles thick, and she's got all the grit and fearlessness I've always imagined in Kravan's rebels—though I'm not at all sure that's what she is.

"Are you going to tell me what you're doing here?" she asks again. "Or does Berengar have to coax a few choice words out of you?" With that, she lays a hand on the hound's head.

As if on cue, he lets out another drawn-out growl.

"I'm looking for someone," I blurt out, and Maude buzzes a warning into my arm.

~I thought you were going to keep your mouth shut.

I considered it, but it's against my nature.

The woman's full lips twitch. "You're telling me you made your way through miles of tunnels from who-knows-where in search of someone—and you chose to wear *that*?" Her gaze moves down my body once again, and it's all I can do to suppress the urge to cover myself with my hands.

"Sorry," she snickers, "but I call soggy bullshit. A Noble would have sent a Guard if they needed to hunt for someone. As much as I despise you fuckers, most Nobles are smart enough to know they'd be better off slitting their own throats than setting foot in the Capitol. Bleeding out by your own hand is a far more pleasant death than what awaits you there."

"I don't have a fucking Guard to send," I snarl. "I don't have anyone. I'm not a damned Noble."

It's an honest answer, but probably also a stupid one. I've just admitted I'm powerless.

"Then what the hell are you?" She inches closer, and I strain to look into her eyes, hoping to determine whether she's a Tethered.

Only, I can't see any detail in her irises. It's like they're engulfed in shadow. Or...

"Your eyes are completely black," I say, stupefied.

It takes me a moment to realize she must be wearing opaque contact lenses.

She may as well have a bag over her head. The effect is disorienting, even a little frightening. Clearly, she doesn't want anyone knowing what she is—which is strange, given that only a Hunter like me can read a Tethered's powers.

~It's possible she's a Normal and trying to hide her weakness, Maude suggests.

Somehow, I doubt it.

"Very observant," the woman replies. "Now, tell me what your deal is, Noble. My patience has worn thin."

I hold out my left hand, revealing the markings on my forearm and the faint, green glow under my skin.

"A Tower Orphan," she breathes with a low whistle, taking hold of my arm for a few seconds before letting it go. "Well now, that's a surprise. An orphan in a fancy-ass gown. I'll bet *you* have a story or two to tell."

I've never heard the term *Tower Orphan* before, but I suppose it's accurate. Every child raised to adulthood inside the Tower is deprived of their parents. Most never meet them —never even know their names.

But as it turns out, I'm no orphan, not anymore. I've met my mother. And if I live to see the Capitol, I hope to meet my father, too.

But the woman doesn't need to know any of that.

"I do have a few stories," I sneer. "But I'm not giving you any information until you answer a few questions."

She shakes her head, patting the dog gently. "You hear that, Beren? This one thinks *she's* in control here."

I ignore the snipe. "Those contact lenses are obviously meant to conceal your nature. What are you hiding?"

For a moment, she looks like she's contemplating punching me in the face, but she relents with a sigh, angling the light so it shines directly in what I'm now realizing is an exceptionally beautiful face—all sharp angles and delicate features. "Because all people—Normals and Tethered alike—fear me when they see my eyes. I don't look like most of our kind, and I don't enjoy being stared at."

"You're telling me you *are* a Tethered."

"I'm not telling you anything. You're guessing, based on very little information."

My jaw tenses, and I realize with a shot of pain that I've been grinding it ever since I awoke a few minutes ago.

"Are you going to kill me?" I ask, exasperated. "Because if you're not going to do that or answer my questions, I'd like to make my way to the Capitol. Like I said, I have business there."

She raises her chin, then lets out a laugh. "Oh, you definitely have business there. You're coming with me to meet the Magister. He'll be very interested in learning what the hell you're doing in this tunnel."

I freeze, wishing I possessed some kind of power that would simultaneously let me knock her unconscious and figure out who she's talking about.

"The Magister?" I repeat.

She didn't say *Shadow*—yet I was under the impression it was my father who was in charge. Lady Graystone's words are still engraved in my mind: *He lords over the Capitol like a wolf, watching, waiting, and assessing. Anyone who's deemed a threat dies.*

Then again, Lady Graystone isn't exactly the most trustworthy person I've ever met.

"Yes, the Magister," the woman says. "The man who lays down the law in the Capitol. Don't worry, he won't hurt you—much. He's a Normal, but he has no interest in harming most of the Tethered who've escaped the Isles. It's the ones who willingly work for Nobles that he and the Shadow hate."

"Your boss...he works with the Shadow?" *Finally, we're getting somewhere.*

"You know who that is?"

I nod. "I've heard he's in charge of things. It seems I'm mistaken."

She scoffs. "Not in charge, no—at least, not on paper. But he and the Magister work closely, and they pay me handsomely for bringing them people who could cause them problems. I couldn't give a smaller shit who the leader actually is—I only want my damned bounty for bringing you to them—whoever you are. So, I suppose we should get on our way. We have a long hike ahead of us."

I don't want to go with her or her mechanical hound, but it's not like I have a choice in the matter. Her power hasn't revealed itself to me, but something tells me it's got to be impressive if she's willing to roam the dark tunnels with no weapon but her questionable steel-toothed companion.

"You said the hound is called Berengar. What's your name?"

"Rivenna," she tells me. "Not that it should matter to you. But now that you know my name, tell me yours."

"Shara."

"Shara—get the fuck moving. Now."

With a grunt, I take a step forward, wincing in pain when the sliced-up sole of my foot hits the floor. Pressing one palm to the wall, I reach down and pass my other hand over both feet, ridding myself of my wounds.

"A Healer," Rivenna says with a hint of reluctant admiration. "That's a good skill to have in the hellscape we're headed to. Come on—it's a four-hour walk to the tavern. We'll eat and rest there, then get a fresh start in the morning."

I want to tell her to go fuck herself and that there's no way in hell I'm spending the night doing anything other than walking.

I want to see Thorne, I think. *Now.*

~Do as she says, Maude cautions. *She's your best chance at making it to the Capitol without being murdered.*

She's the only person we've met, and she's not exactly friendly. What makes you think she won't murder me herself?

~Call it Maude's intuition.

No. I will absolutely not do that.

~Fine. The truth is, there are at least a hundred living beings

within a ten-mile radius of where we are right now, and I'd be willing to bet most of them would take your life before they'd offer to escort you. This woman may be a walking enigma, but at least she intends to deliver you in one piece.

Are you sure about that?

~Not even a little.

CHAPTER THREE

We walk in silence for what feels like an eternity, with Berengar alternating between trotting along at Rivenna's side and mine. When he pulls up next to me, I forget he's not a living creature and reach down to pat him on the head.

He responds by glancing up at me, an oddly realistic tongue lolling out of his mouth. He looks like he's meant to replicate some breed or other of fighting dog, his fur short and coarse, his eyes surprisingly expressive.

"You seem so real to me," I tell him, a hand reaching into my pocket to find Mercutio curled into a tight ball as he rests and awaits a recharge. *Just as the little mouse does.*

Not to mention Maude.

As if reading my thoughts, Rivenna says, "I assume you still have one of those bossy A.I. units implanted from your Tower days?"

My eyebrows arch when I say, "You know about them, then."

She nods. "You're not the first Tower Orphan I've met.

There are a few of you living in the Capitol—people whose Proprietors have died or set them free."

My eyes widen with quiet surprise. "Isn't it a crime to set Tethered free?"

Rivenna clicks her tongue. "*Everything* is a crime in the realm—or hadn't you noticed? Touching another Tethered. Feeling love or hate. Existing in a state of basic autonomy. Hell, *thinking* is a crime—at least, according to the Nobility. Then again, in the Capitol, it's every man or woman for themselves. Most of the rules went out the window long ago. Nowadays, all that matters is staying out of the way of the bomber drones or the patrols and declaring loyalty to the Magister—or keeping the hell out of *his* way."

Her voice has softened by now. She no longer feels quite so jagged-edged or unpredictable. Instead, she seems almost sad, as though revealing a hint of emotion has taken something out of her.

"There are supposed to be rules among the Nobles, too," I say. "But most don't pay attention to them. The *every man for himself* thing definitely applies to their kind, as well."

"Yeah, but they can get away with it, can't they? As long as they're loyal to the king, no one cares."

I'm almost tempted to tell her it's entirely possible Kravan no longer has a king—but Maude issues me one of her silent warnings.

"What's your hope for Kravan?" I ask Rivenna.

She seems thrown by the question. She stops, pulls off her pack, and opens a pocket, extracting a small package of nuts. She peels it open and offers me a few, which I take gladly.

"What do you mean, hope?" she asks.

"For the Capitol. For Kravan. For the future. What do you want for this place? You're here lurking in the shadows, trying to stay alive. You must have a loftier goal than that."

She shrugs. "If I could snap my fingers and change the realm, I would free the Tethered and inflict my own form of justice on those who have hurt them for generations. I would force King Tomas to kneel before me and then I would stare into his eyes as he dies screaming and afraid."

"Understandable," I chuckle. "If the king is still alive, I would be delighted to see that."

Maude buzzes an aggressive warning even as Rivenna reaches out, grabbing my arm and yanking me toward her. "What the hell do you mean *if* he's still alive?" she snarls. "What happened back in the Isles? What do you know?"

Shit.

The thought slipped out like it was the most natural thing to say—but Maude was right to warn me. It was damned foolish. If the Capitol learns what's happened at the palace, the city could erupt into outright mayhem.

The way Rivenna is gripping my arm, it's clear that I won't be able to pull away until I've given her a response that satisfies her.

Berengar is sitting quietly, watching me—but there's something tightly menacing in his demeanor, as if he's awaiting a command to attack.

"Tell me what you mean," Rivenna snarls, fingers digging in. "Or I swear to God..."

~Tell her as little as you can, Maude warns. *But give her* ***something****, or this won't end well.*

"I escaped the palace," I say slowly. "I...lived there for a time. There was a fight raging between the king and the prince. That's how I managed to get out. They were distracted, and I ran. But I was only joking about the king not being alive. It was just a spat between father and son."

The words seem to suffice because Rivenna drops my arm and cocks her head, quietly assessing. "You're a decent liar, at least. It'll serve you well. If you don't want to tell me the truth, I'll satisfy myself with the knowledge that there's drama in the palace, and we'll leave it at that. But sometime, I want you to tell me everything. If nothing else, I suspect it will be pretty entertaining."

"There was no lie in what I said."

"Lies by omission are still lies."

I want to ask how she knows I'm not telling her everything, but I suppose it's pretty obvious, given that I managed to escape during the fray. Under normal circumstances, the Royal Guard would stop anyone attempting to flee the palace. It shouldn't be easy for a Tethered—especially one who's apparently nothing more than a simple Healer—to slip out.

Then again, I'm more than a simple Healer.

"I don't know you," I tell her. "I don't trust you yet."

"Good. You shouldn't trust anyone—not even the people you think are your closest allies. The Capitol has a way of turning people against one another—even those who were once deeply in love. Take my word for it when I tell you that place has even torn apart more than one set of tethered mates."

Something tells me she's speaking from personal experience—but I have no intention of asking. Rivenna doesn't seem like the sort of person who would voluntarily discuss her emotions in any depth, least of all with me.

She turns and begins walking, and Berengar and I follow along behind. I can't help thinking of Thorne again, given what she just said. But I would never turn against him, nor he against me.

The Capitol couldn't tear us apart, I think. *Once I find him, we'll hold onto one another for the rest of our lives. Our bond is too strong to let anyone come between us.*

Then again, it seems my parents, who once loved each other enough to defy all of Kravan's strictest laws, are no longer speaking to one another. If anything, I'd say my mother fears my father now.

I can't help wondering what it was that tore them apart.

While my exhausted mind concocts theories, Rivenna spins around, pushing me hard against the wall, her head twisting to stare through her dark lenses into the tunnel's depths.

A low growl erupts from Berengar's chest, but she shushes him.

"What is it?" I whisper.

"Scrappers, probably. Scavengers. They sometimes come deep into the tunnels looking for materials to trade in the city." She nods in the direction we were headed, and I spot a dim stream of light moving toward us as if from a torch or flashlight.

My heart springs to life inside my chest, hope permeating every cell in my body.

A single figure is approaching slowly, its tall form moving with a smooth, confident gait.

Maybe—just maybe—the light is coming from Thorne.

CHAPTER FOUR

WITH THOUGHTS of Thorne racing through my mind, I yank myself away from Rivenna and take a step toward the light, but she grabs me again and pulls me back, thrusting me behind her.

"I know what you're thinking," she growls under her breath. "But trust me—that's *not* the person you're looking for."

"How can you possibly know that?"

"I just fucking know."

~She's right, Maude tells me, and I let out a huff of displeasure. *Whoever's coming smells like death. Your Thorne's scent is far more appealing.*

"Fine," I mutter, annoyed to have to remind myself how rarely Maude is ever wrong.

As the flashlight approaches, it becomes abundantly clear that whoever is holding it is not going to stop before they reach us.

"Stay back against the wall," Rivenna whispers, stepping away with Berengar at her side. "Don't do anything stupid."

"You sound like Maude," I mutter under my breath.

~I resent that.

Good. You should. You're the bane of my existence.

The dog lets out a low, hostile growl, and the light, which has been growing progressively brighter, instantly goes out.

"I'd turn back if I were you," Rivenna calls out, her light beaming into the darkness in search of the intruder. "My steel-toothed buddy isn't friendly to Scrappers."

For a moment, the shuffling footsteps stop, and at first, I'm convinced the person is contemplating following her advice.

But when the sound starts up again, I realize the footfalls are growing louder, not quieter.

The foolish asshole is moving *closer* to us.

"*Healer*," Rivenna whispers.

"Yes?" I hiss.

"Keep yourself hidden in case they're a Netic or something."

"You think the Scrapper is a Tethered?"

"Only a Tethered would be arrogant enough to walk toward a hound's glowing red eyes."

I can't deny that she's right. The stranger is not only likely to be a Tethered, but one with powers strong enough to fight off another of our kind.

I press back against the wall, telling myself I'm ready for whatever is about to happen—even though it's an absolute lie.

As the figure skulks toward us, barely visible in the shadows, I strain to see their face. At first, all I can make out is a pale, vague outline of a person. A man, I think—hunched a little, like an animal ready to attack...or possibly to flee.

Rivenna is still positioned protectively between the intruder and me, but by some compulsion I can't explain, I step around her, fixing my eyes on the shadowy figure, who stops when he realizes there are two of us.

"What are you doing this far underground?" Rivenna asks, her voice authoritative, as though she holds the exclusive rights to the tunnels.

"Searching," the stranger croaks out.

"For what?"

He thrusts a jagged finger toward me in the darkness. "*Her.*"

The voice doesn't sound entirely human, and something about it frightens me more than it should. I still can't see the man's face, but already, I sense a power in him—something awful and malicious.

"Who the hell is she to a low-life like *you*?" Rivenna snarls, casting her arm in front of me like a shield.

"She's nothing to me," the man replies. "Nothing at all—but she's worth a good deal to someone else."

He steps closer to us, and when Rivenna shines her light at his face, I see for the first time that he's wearing a dark gray mask. It looks as though it's made of stiff, unforgiving fabric that conceals his eyes from me, so I have no way of knowing what he is.

This isn't the first time I've seen a mask like his—and the realization turns my blood to ice.

It's just like the ones I saw in my vision, worn by the men who had taken Thorne captive.

"A fucking Starless," Rivenna says. "I should have guessed. But you assholes don't usually come barreling into the tunnels alone. You're fearful little shits."

I want to ask what the hell a Starless is, but right now doesn't seem like the best time.

~*Before you ask me, I don't have a clue, either,* Maude tells me. *This is the first I've heard of them.*

Rivenna steps toward the masked man and adds, "Why don't you fuck off back to where you came from, before I take your life?"

The man lets out a strange, quiet laugh—one that sends a shudder through every shred of my soul. Then, without another word, he lunges at Rivenna, slashing his hand across her throat.

Rivenna lets out a sharp wail, dropping her light with a clatter. Berengar leaps at the intruder, jaws clamping viciously around his arm. With a howl of pain, the man falls hard to the ground.

The dog presses his front paws to his victim's chest, his enormous head flailing left to right, steel teeth tearing at flesh and bone.

Thinking fast and grabbing the fallen light, I turn my eyes first to Rivenna. The wound at her throat isn't bleeding much—certainly not enough to kill her. So I leap over, tearing the mask from her downed assailant's face as he fights to free himself from the dog's grip.

The Starless lashes out at me with his free hand, trying and failing to make contact.

When I see his eyes for the first time, I'm more than a little grateful that I was able to evade him.

I've never encountered anyone with his power.

The man is a Poisoner—someone who can introduce toxins of various strengths into his victims with the mere slash of a fingernail.

In my mind's eye, I can see the people he's murdered—how they suffered while he laughed at their pain. I watch them languish on the ground, their skin erupting with a series of burning veins infiltrated by his particular brand of toxin.

He's vile, cruel, and dangerous. He's killed many times, almost always for pleasure—and it doesn't take much to convince me he needs to die.

Stepping around Berengar—who's still torturing his victim—and reaching down carefully, I swipe a finger through a streak of blood on the Starless' arm where the hound has torn into him.

I had hoped to hide some of my power from Rivenna—to convince her that I was nothing more than a simple Healer. But the time for concealment is over, and I have no choice but to play my hand.

When I feel the Poisoner's power surge through me, a stolen gift I will possess for only a few minutes, I bend down and look him in the eye again.

"Back, Berengar," I command gently. "Let him go. It's all right."

To my surprise, the dog moves away, his lips pulling back in a threatening snarl.

"Why were you looking for me?" I ask the man. "Who sent you?"

"I don't owe you answers, *bitch*," he sneers, clutching at the deep wounds on his arm.

"Do they know who I am? Is that why they sent you?"

"I was told nothing. Only that she wants you."

"She? Who the hell is *she?*"

At that, he snarls, pushing himself up with his good arm and lurching toward me.

Sensing my terror, Berengar jumps at him again, just as I swipe a dirty fingernail over his throat. The man lets out a long, inhuman wail, his irises glazing over then going white, his flesh graying almost instantly.

Horrified by what I've done, I turn away as the dog finishes him off.

~It was the only possible outcome that wouldn't result in your death, Maude assures me. *Probably.*

A whimper flits through the air to meet my ears.

At first, I'm convinced it's the dog. But when I turn around, I see Rivenna slumped on the ground, her throat oozing with what's turned quickly into an angry wound. White, bubbling liquid seeps from the narrow cut burning at her flesh.

Whatever tactic the Poisoner was using, it looks like he had no intention of killing her quickly. His goal was a prolonged torture.

Rivenna's eyelids have begun fluttering and twitching like she's fighting to remain conscious, and her eyes stare into the distance as though she can see something no living person should ever have to behold.

"Fucking sadist," I say, crouching down next to her, taking care not to hurt her further. "I'm going to help you. Stay still, all right?"

With her breath coming in frantic bursts, she nods weakly. Berengar slips over and licks her face, seeming to sense her fear.

Good thing the dog is immune to poison, at least.

I press a hand to Rivenna's chest and ask my power to

surge through her even as the Poisoner's vile gift deserts my body and mind. Under my touch, Rivenna's breathing slows, the wound at her neck seals, and the white liquid vanishes.

She pushes herself upright then slips a hand onto her neck. She looks sheepish, almost as if she's embarrassed by what just happened.

"You could have left me here to die." She nods into the distance. "You could have headed off in search of your... friend."

"I suppose I could have," I agree. "But your murder hound might have grabbed my leg and torn it off."

"You know perfectly well he wouldn't have." Rivenna shoots a look first at Berengar, then at the corpse on the ground—the Poisoner who will never again return to whatever home he once occupied. "I owe you my life, and I'm at your service. You're obviously more powerful than you let on—so how about if you tell me what you're *really* doing in this tunnel?"

"I told you—I'm looking for someone."

"Yes, you did. But there's more to this, surely. That Starless was searching for you—and from the sounds of it, it was the Lady who sent him—their leader, I mean."

"Who *are* the Starless, anyway?"

"Rebels who don't like the Magister. If you ask me, they're mostly shit-stirrers who want to keep the Capitol as screwed up as the king does. They spread rumors and lies like wildfire and sow chaos like it's going out of style."

"So the Poisoner—he wasn't actually here to kill me?"

"Honestly, I have no idea. It's so fucking weird, though. The Lady wouldn't risk sending out her people on their own—not unless she was desperate, and you had something she wanted." Narrowing her eyes, she adds, "Please—I want to keep you safe, Shara. It would be easier if I knew what we're up against in these tunnels."

I inhale deeply, weighing the risks, then say, "The man you call the Shadow...I've been told that he's my father."

For a few seconds, she says nothing.

"You don't look entirely surprised," I tell her. "Confused, maybe. But not surprised."

"If I look baffled, it's because he did have a daughter," she finally murmurs. "Back in the day—but..."

She stops there, gawking at me like I'm a ghost.

"You're talking about my sister," I say. "I didn't know about her until recently when I met my mother at the Prefect's home. She's a Domestic."

The truth is pouring out of me now, but I tell myself it doesn't matter. Now that Rivenna knows about my relationship to the Shadow, the cat's pretty well out of the damned bag.

"Your sister," she repeats. "Wow. What do you know about her?"

"Nothing, except that my mother was under the impression that she's in the Capitol."

Rivenna looks stricken. She moves the light from her face so I can't see her expression when she says, "She did live in the Capitol...for a time."

My voice tightens. "What do you mean, for a time?"

"Years ago, one of the bombings took out the Shadow's home—back when he lived above ground in a house on a residential street. That was in the days when folks just called him the *Hunter.* He had a young daughter living with him—and we were told they both died in a blast one night. But days later, the Hunter reemerged—alone. Some of those in the Capitol began to call him the Shadow. They said…"

She stops there, hesitant to continue.

"It's all right," I tell her, steeling myself. I haven't yet begun to absorb the information—I know that will come in time. A pain settling into my insides, an aching void in my life as I learn to miss a person I've never even known.

"They say the Hunter became a shadow of his former self when she died. His daughter was only five years old when it happened. She was a beautiful little girl—I remember her face. Her smile, even. When the bomb destroyed their home, many in the Capitol grieved. The Hunter was respected, and he'd served the rebels well over the years. He identified powerful Tethered who were on the side of the Nobles, which gave our side the advantage in most conflicts. He helped catch quite a few traitors in our midst."

"I know a little about that," I reply, recalling that my father had supposedly once tormented Lady Graystone. She even claimed he was responsible for the loss of her arm. I can't help but respect the hell out of him for it.

I only wish he'd taken that harpy's life.

"When we learned the Shadow was alive after his home was destroyed," Rivenna continues, "there was celebration in the streets. But he wasn't the same man. He had been badly injured, but more than that, it was like a part of him had been torn away. He seemed like a husk of a person. He had never been warm, exactly, but he turned into ice when Soleia died."

"Soleia," I say, too distracted to absorb much of what Rivenna is saying. "That's—that *was*—my sister's name?"

She nods. "I'm sorry. I never knew he had another

daughter—I didn't know you existed. He didn't speak of you...probably because he wanted to protect your identity. Had anyone on the Nobles' side known he had a child in the Tower, they might have used you to hurt him."

With a taste of bitterness, I remember the day the Prefect came to my Whiteroom to examine me—the words he and the Warden exchanged about me.

I was sure they suspected something then, though I didn't understand why—and I don't know what would have happened to me if they'd learned the truth.

In the end, it was Thorne who protected me. Thorne who assured them I was nothing special—that I was no threat to them or anyone else. It was Thorne who ensured I would be assigned to the Verdan residence so he could watch over me.

If only I could see him...touch him. Reassure myself that he's all right.

I swallow the lump in my throat and tell Rivenna to continue.

"The Shadow is daunting," she says. "The Magister may be in charge, technically, but it's your father who inspires fear in the entire population of the Capitol."

"My mother said the same thing when I met her. She'd heard my father had changed. But she didn't seem to know about...about Soleia's death."

I can only imagine the heartbreak if I told Evangeline her younger daughter had been killed in a drone strike.

I've never met my sister, but even so, I feel as though the world has been pulled from under my feet.

My mother would be devastated to learn the truth.

I now want even more desperately to meet my father—to get to know the person who knew my sister best.

"Be patient with the Shadow when you meet him," Rivenna says. "Whoever he is now—however difficult he is to read—when I knew him as the Hunter, his goal was always to free Kravan from the oppression of the king. To free the Tethered. He was a good man then, despite some of his crueler tactics. We all do what we need to—to survive in this world."

"I know that better than you may think."

With a sigh and a nod, she adds, "He'll be glad to see you. And whether or not the Magister pays me for bringing you in, I'll make sure you get there safely. I promise you that."

"Thank you," I say. "I do want to speak to my father. I want to see if he'll help me restore Kravan to what it once was. I want him to help me find..."

"The person you're looking for?" Rivenna smirks. "If I had to guess from the sound of your voice, I'd say it's your mate."

"I...something like that," I confess.

~*Shara,* Maude says, her voice a warning.

It's fine. I trust her.

~*You can't trust anyone. She said so herself.*

Rivenna nods. "Look—whoever it is, I'll do my best to help. Just...do me a favor."

"Sure, if I can."

"When you've saved Kravan—or whatever the hell you've *really* come here to do—live a nice life, away from drama and conflict. You're no fighter, as grateful as I am to you. You're not a killer, Shara."

"Agreed."

"Now, come on. We need to get out of the main tunnel before a patrol shows up. If they see you and suspect you're a

Noble, we'll be forced to prove them wrong—and that's not a position we want to be in."

I stumble along beside Rivenna, trying to match her long strides. "Who sends the patrols?"

"Sometimes, it's the Magister. Sometimes, it's the Lady of the Starless—the leader I mentioned. But trust me when I say it's best if we don't encounter any of them. They move up and down the main passageway, looking for anyone they can possibly detain—and they're not particularly good at listening. So even if you tell them you're the Shadow's daughter, they'll probably toss you in a cell. Usually, though, they're looking for members of the Royal Guard."

Royal Guard like Thorne.

I swallow, then summon enough courage to ask, "What happens if they find one?"

"They bring them to the Magister, and he imprisons them for a time while he figures out whether or not they're a threat."

Just as I'm about to breathe a sigh of relief, she sends my head spiraling in a storm of fear.

"The truth is, even if they're not a threat, their prison stay is nothing more than a waiting area on their way to death. No Royal Guard has ever been let out of the Magister's prison alive."

CHAPTER FIVE

As Rivenna predicted, we spend several hours trekking through hostile darkness. Berengar is on high alert, his red eyes casting a faint, eerie halo of light ahead of us.

Maude, meanwhile, is quiet inside me, as if she's as exhausted as I am. I choose to let her rest. The fact is, Rivenna has gone from menacing to trustworthy in the brief time I've known her, and I'm surprisingly at peace by her side.

She feels like the friend I sorely need in this grim place.

Though I'm exhausted, there's no question that I'm also energized, knowing that each step I take brings me closer to Thorne. I need to get to him before the Magister does—and I can only hope I'm not too late.

We walk in silence, with Rivenna a little ahead of me and Berengar ahead of her. I reach out with my mind, seeking Thorne. But I can't quite reach him. It's like we're too far apart for me to find my way inside his thoughts—his heart, though, is another matter entirely.

A slow, steady beat—a second pulse inside my own body—tells me he's out there. He's calm.

He's safe.

The gentle rhythm guides my footfalls and calms my mind until we make our way into an arching, chilly tunnel narrower than those I've seen—one that Rivenna tells me will lead us to the "tavern."

"There will be others there," she says. "Keep your head down, and they'll ignore you, I promise. Most of them are mercs like me, who work the tunnels looking for undesirables."

"Undesirables like *me*," I say with a smirk.

"I don't imagine there's anyone out there like you. They're mostly looking for people on the Magister's list." She turns to look over her shoulder when she says, "Before you ask, yes—he has a list of people who have betrayed him. There's a reason the Starless wear masks."

"Betrayed him how? Do they really owe him loyalty?"

"Some do. The Capitol's citizens are asked to pledge themselves to him. Some uphold their vow; others break it."

"Sounds an awful lot like what they did to us in the Tower," I mutter.

"It's complicated," Rivenna says with a sigh. "The pledge is a way to say we're determined to find our freedom. And the Magister has promised us that one day we'll have it."

"Did *you* pledge your loyalty to him? Seems like a strange thing for a mercenary to do."

"I did. Because I'm no fool. I already walk around with black contact lenses in my eyes. The last thing I want is to have to wear a gray mask over my face. Anyhow, the Magister needs us mercs, and he's no fool, either. He's smart enough to keep himself in our good books. The Capitol is a political minefield—and it's important to know who's on what side. Commitment to the Magister makes it simple."

I force myself to swallow down the desire to point out that having to pledge allegiance to a leader doesn't exactly scream freedom, but instead, I ask about the tavern. "Is there a chance we'll run into more people like the Starless who came for me?"

"There's always someone on guard. They'll let us through and do their best to keep the Starless out. I'll tell them you're with me. That should be good enough. Oh, and don't be surprised if some of them call me Sterling."

"Okay," I reply, stepping over a piece of twisted metal jutting out from the ground. "But why..."

"It's my last name," she answers before I've finished the question.

"Tethered don't have surnames."

Even as I say the words, I recall what I learned from the Storian about surnames. Our ancestors had them, but we were robbed of them when so many of us were imprisoned and ripped from our parents.

She laughs. "We all have surnames—even you. I'm not sure your father knows what it is, though. The fact is, most of our kind don't know where we come from. Some of us were born to Normal parents and took their names. Others chose them for ourselves."

"Were you born to Normals?"

"No. I was born in hiding, to a Tethered couple who died."

"I'm sorry."

"Don't be. I barely knew them. I was raised by Normals

who treated me like their own, but when I came of age, I took a new name—because I refuse to be held down by a system that thinks I'm the lowest form of life. I wanted a name I could pass down to my children, if I should ever have any."

"Why Sterling? I mean, it's a pretty name. I'm just curious."

"Because silver glints in the light. If ever the Capitol proves safe, I intend to live out my days under the sun and sky. But for now..." She holds up her right hand, and for the first time, I notice a faint shape embedded in her palm. A circle containing curving, seemingly random lines that cut their way through it like trails through a forest. "Do you know what this is?"

I shake my head. "I—I'm not sure."

The truth is, I'm almost certain I've seen it before, but the memory is so vague that it feels like a forgotten dream. I find myself wondering whether it's something I saw in the jumble of information thrown at me by the Storian.

"The brand on my palm is a reminder to all of us that we are prisoners in Kravan in some way or another. This realm is cut off from all others, whether we like it or not."

"Who branded you?"

"The Magister—when I pledged myself to him. All the loyal are branded. It's one way to know who's on what side."

I wince to think of the pain she must have felt when the hot iron met her flesh.

"Tell me," she says, "does the king brand his Royal Guard?"

With those words, she eyes me curiously, as if she's awaiting an appraisal of King Tomas.

"No," I tell her. "The king is more likely to kill or enslave a

Tethered than brand them, in my experience. I've never seen a mark like yours on anyone."

"Oh, you will," Rivenna chuckles. "Almost every resident in the Capitol wears the circle in some form or other—even those who hate the Magister."

I go silent for a moment, and Rivenna, who's gotten adept at reading me, says, "You want to know why they're called Starless."

"I was wondering," I confess. "My Maude has told me more than once that I ask too many questions, so I was resisting."

Rivenna thrusts an arm out, gesturing to the darkness around us. "They meet in the shadows of the underground," she says. "They hide in basements, bunkers, anywhere they can, to get away from the light. It's not that they can't tolerate sun or anything—it's that they're fucking vermin. Rats and roaches. Scurrying away before anyone can identify them. They hide because they know they're on the wrong side of history. Along with the king's drones, they've been keeping the Magister from succeeding in his mission."

"I don't get it. The one we met *was* a Tethered. Maybe he was vicious, but he was still one of us. Didn't *he* want freedom?"

"Propaganda is a powerful drug," Rivenna shrugs. "They've been brainwashed into thinking the Magister and your father are the bad guys, even though it's the royals who bomb the Capitol over and over again."

I don't tell her I've heard conflicting reports about who's responsible for the bombings. The truth is, I don't know what to believe anymore.

"You definitely seem firmly on my father's side."

With a huff, she says, "I'm not exactly a loyalist, but I'm true to my word. Mercenaries may be greedy fuckers, but we're honorable in our way. Once you have the true loyalty of a merc, you have it forever."

I want to ask her about the Citadel and whether it's the same place I've seen in the memories the Storian gave me—the same structure where President Brant was overthrown by the man called Quinton.

~You're not supposed to know about that, remember? Maude mutters as if she's just waking from her nap.

We've only gone a few more steps when Rivenna adds, "You said you're looking for someone in the Capitol. Are you going to tell me about them before we get to the tavern?"

Damn it.

~You did basically admit you're searching for your mate, Maude chastises with a fake yawn. *It wasn't your brightest moment.*

Shut up. I'm thinking.

"Well?" Rivenna asks, and Berengar sidles up next to me as if to remind me of his presence. He's not threatening—but at the moment, he's not comforting, either.

"His name is Thorne. He's..."

I'm afraid to say the next words, as if letting them pass my lips will mean his fate is sealed.

"Oh, shit," Rivenna replies. "He's a Royal Guard, isn't he?"

Woefully, I nod.

She stops and turns to me, takes my shoulders in her hands, and says, "When you're alone, look for him in the Nether. Find him."

"The Nether?"

"You've never met him there?" She pulls away, looking puzzled.

"I don't know what it is."

"You haven't known him long, then—have you?"

Shaking my head, I murmur, "No. But..."

"But you love him. Yes, of course you do." She sighs and looks off into the distance as if recalling some far-away memory. "The Nether is a place where the souls of two tethered mates meet. That sounds more poetic than it actually is, but it's the truth. It's a place where you can find one another. *Feel* one another, even. It's not easy to access, but once you learn how, you'll find you never have to be without him for long."

"How do I get there?"

"You probably can't—not right now, at least. You need to empty your mind and reach for him—and in that same moment, he has to reach for you. Later, when you're alone and resting, you should try. If you can, ask him where he is."

"I *know* where he is. Sort of, at least. I had a vision a while back. It's a skill I got from Thorne—from our connection. He sees the future in pieces here and there, which means I can, as well."

She pulls her onyx eyes back to mine. "What did you see?"

"He was on his knees in front of a group of men wearing gray masks like the Poisoner had on."

"That may not be the worst thing," Rivenna says. "If he's with the Lady, he's probably safe. Much as I disagree with her politics, she'd see someone like your guy as an asset. A potential ally. She knows how much the Magister hates the Royal Guard. She may try to persuade him to join her."

Fear seizes at my chest. I want to believe Rivenna—that Thorne is safe. And if the distant throb of his beating heart is any indication, she's right.

I just hope he *stays* safe.

Taking me gently by the arm, she says, "Come on. Let's get to the tavern. After a drink or two, you might find it a little easier to reach the Nether. At the very least, you'll be able to get some proper rest. There are beds in the Underbelly, and I intend to make use of one. Not that I ever sleep more than three hours at a time."

"Why not?" I realize as the question comes that it's none of my business. But it's out there now.

"Recurring nightmares," Rivenna replies. "Turns out I don't enjoy watching people die every night while I'm trying to relax." She lets out a chuckle. "My mind is a little twisted—and a little cruel."

We pick up our pace, and this time, Berengar pulls around to pad along at my side, pressing against me as if to keep me from collapsing under the weight of my own fear.

"Thank you," I tell him, laying my hand on his head. "You're a good boy—for a fellow murderer."

CHAPTER SIX

After a few minutes, my eyes land on an illuminated sign jutting out from the stone wall ahead, with gleaming gold letters that simply read:

Underbelly Tavern

"Welcome to the favorite meeting place of thieves, scavengers, assholes, and she-devils," Rivenna says, nodding toward the sign. "Now is when the fun begins."

I follow her and Berengar to the door, which is painted a deep blood red. It looks like solid steel, and when Rivenna pounds her fist against it, the percussive knock confirms that I'm right.

After a few seconds, the door opens inward, and one of the largest, most muscular men I've ever seen fills the doorway, bare arms crossing over his chest. On one bicep, he has a brand just like the one on Rivenna's palm—the Magister's mark.

"Rivenna Sterling," he says—or rather, grunts, but his

eyes move quickly to me. He's a Tethered with massive brute strength. I knew someone like him in the Tower and find myself wondering what ever became of him. Not that I liked Drukkar very much, given that he and many of my other peers beat the hell out of me in fight class on a regular basis.

"How you doing, Wield?" Rivenna says, gesturing toward me. "This is...a friend of mine. I'm taking her to see the Magister."

He raises a thick eyebrow. "Oh?" Then, leaning in, he whispers, "She's your prisoner?"

"I didn't say that."

"I don't see the mark on her, and she's wearing a fucking gown, besides. She's either a prisoner or a runaway—or something else."

"Fine, then. She's my prisoner. I'm responsible for her, and if anything happens, I'll take the fall. Now, can we come in or not?"

"I guess." Wield grunts and backs away, patting Berengar on the head as he pads his way inside.

The interior of the tavern isn't quite what I was expecting. It's windowless, of course—we're still deep underground—but instead of the arching stone cavern I thought I'd see, the establishment manages to be warm and inviting, its ceiling painted white and streaked with dark brown wooden beams. Its walls, too, are white, dotted here and there with old painted portraits of this and that nameless person, or a country scene, or a cityscape the likes of which I've never seen. I can only assume that what I'm looking at is the Capitol in the old days.

People of every shape and size are seated here and there

at square wooden tables, each of them somehow alert and relaxed all at once.

To one side of the space is a long bar, and two bartenders stand behind it, bantering, cleaning glasses, pouring drinks, and laughing.

Rivenna leads me over to a corner table, and we seat ourselves by a roaring fireplace. Our backs are to the wall, Berengar lying at Rivenna's feet. "We'll crash in one of the back rooms tonight," she says. "But for now, let's get some proper food and drink in you."

I nod in appreciation before a painful thought strikes me.

"I have no money," I tell her. "I can't pay for food or lodging."

"It's fine. I've got this. I owe you, remember?"

I glance around, then lean in and say under my breath, "What would it take to get you to bring me to the Lady—to find Thorne?"

Rivenna stiffens, then shakes her head. "I said I'd get you to the Capitol. That's it. I'm not going anywhere near the Starless—not without a shit-ton of backup. Besides, we don't know he's there."

"But you said you think they have him."

"I said the masked men you described from your vision sound like Starless. But for all I know, that vision was nothing more than a dream. It may not come true, right? Besides, you'd be a fool if you went searching for the Lady, unless you're absolutely sure he's with her."

"I could pay you."

"You just told me you have no money," Rivenna retorts, snickering.

"I don't mean I'd pay you with money. I'm talking about something way more valuable."

"The only thing more valuable than money is freedom—and time. You can't give me either of those."

Glancing around again, I satisfy myself that no one is listening. "How about information?"

She lets out a burst of laughter. "You mean palace intrigue? The warring groups in the Capitol don't care about the gossip of a bunch of uptight Nobles. They just want to live their damned lives. Besides, they *have* spies."

"I'm not talking about gossip. What I have goes much deeper than that."

My teeth clamp down on the inside of my cheek as she narrows her oil-black eyes at me.

"What, then?" she asks. "What could you possibly have to tell me that I couldn't extract from you with a nod to the hound?"

She has a point. She could force me to speak if she wanted to. The best I could hope for would be to cut her, take her blood, and use her own power—whatever it is—against her.

"I know things," I tell her. "About Kravan. About its past, the Rebellion, everything. I...know the truth about its history. All of it."

She stares into my eyes, but all I see when I look back at her is a strange, daunting abyss of velvet-thick darkness.

"You can't possibly know any of that. No one knows the truth of Kravan's history, except..." Rivenna raises her chin and levels me with a sudden look of ire. "It's impossible. You're lying."

"Wait a minute," I breathe. "You know about *her,* don't you? You know about the Storian."

Her jaw tenses, but she nods, then looks away. "I know the stories. There are a few who do—but the Storian is nothing more than a legend—a fabrication. A boogeyman used to convince us there's a secret history to this place and to cause rifts in our society—as if we need any more of those. It's rumors of a secret history that cause the fanatics to set fire to homes and commit crimes you couldn't even imagine. I've heard the Lady believes in the Storian. But the Lady is full of shit, just like every leader."

"The Storian is real," I say, and something in my voice seems to jar her. "I've met her."

Now, Rivenna just looks exasperated. "Like I said, that's impossible. But even if it's not, the truth is, I don't care. I know things, too—and the last thing I want is more knowledge."

I'm still convinced I see rage in her unreadable eyes. Accusation—irritation at me for wasting her time. But instead of lashing out, she reaches up to her right eye and, with her index finger and thumb, pulls out the contact lens, then does the same for her left.

When our eyes meet again, I let out a gasp.

Normally, the irises of Tethered twist with color, as if swirling with wet paint.

But Rivenna's eyes, light turquoise on the outside with a ring of gold around the pupil...*glow.* Not like a bright lightbulb, but more like a flickering candle, growing intense before waning a little, as if the pulsing blood inside her veins causes them to ebb and flow.

Staring into them now is enough to show me her past conquests and her own terrifying power.

I've never seen a gift like hers. Hell, I never even knew such a Tethered existed. And when my mind fills with images of those she's encountered—the people she's confronted and attacked—I recoil in fear.

It's not that she's physically strong or even particularly violent. But the very nature of her power...it's a horror.

"How..." I breathe the word then stop, at a loss for the rest of the question. "What *are* you?"

"They call me a Reaper," she replies, a sudden exhaustion weighing down her voice as she reaches into her pocket, pulls out a case for her lenses, and drops them inside. "A life-thief. I've lived many years. I steal time from my victims and sometimes hoard it for myself. It's why I wear the lenses. You, Hunter—yes, I know you have your father's power—aren't the only one who can see what I am. My eyes light up for the entire world. And what I am frightens most people, Normal or Tethered. *Everyone* sees it in me, whoever and whatever they are. They see my power, and they fear it. Time is one of the most precious commodities any living person possesses—and the notion that I can steal it from them makes me a monster."

"You absorb life from your victims," I say. "But—you don't kill them?"

"Oh, sometimes I do. I take their days—months—sometimes years or even decades, depending—for myself. At first, I stole from them so I could live longer. But I've been around long enough now, so I use my strength to punish them for their sins."

With that, she turns away, slipping a hand into her

pocket again. She extracts another contact lens case, opens it, and pops a new set of lenses into her eyes.

"I've lived longer than most who inhabit this realm. I've seen a good deal—though I wasn't around for the Rebellion. Still, I know secrets that would horrify people—some of which I'll never tell, not even with my dying breath. I'm not sure whether I know the truth you're keeping from me, but the fact is, almost nothing would surprise me anymore."

I nod. Something struck me when I looked into her eyes—some of her victims' clothing looked different than what I see people wearing these days. It looked a little old-fashioned, like some of the outfits I remember from films inside the Tower.

"I'm not popular among the Tethered of the Capitol, to put it mildly," Rivenna says. "I suppose that shouldn't come as a surprise. But I'm allowed to live because my weapon is of great use to the warring parties. I can use my skill at a distance to weaken enemies and bring them to their knees—and those who hire me know I have no real principles. I will work for anyone, so long as they promise to pay me, then leave me be."

"Why haven't they..." The question falters in my mouth. It's rude, at best—dangerous at worst.

Why haven't they killed you?

Maude's whisper snakes through my mind, invasive and biting. *~You don't need to say all your thoughts out loud, you know.*

"Why kill me when they can use me?" Rivenna replies, understanding the words beyond my eyes. "I suspect it's the same reason the Royals kept you around. I'm a pawn to be used by those who want the advantage."

"Are you going to bring me to the person who has Thorne?" I ask. "If I promise to tell you what I know?"

She snickers. "You don't seem to realize what you're walking into, Princess."

The royal title pisses me off more than I want to let on. The moment Rivenna revealed her true nature to me, it was like something shifted inside her—the friendliness that had begun to bond us turned cold.

This is a defense mechanism. You assume I see you as a monster, just because others do.

Instead of saying it out loud, I simply raise my chin and grind my jaw. "I don't care what I'm walking into."

"You should care. No one gets through the Capitol without an escort these days. It's a dangerous place, and you may be strong, but you won't be able to heal yourself quickly enough to contend with all the bloodthirsty Starless hunting you. If one of them was searching for you, you can bet there are a hundred more, all looking for the Shadow's daughter—though how they can possibly know about you is beyond me."

"How can I help you two lovely ladies?" the barkeep asks when she reaches the table.

"Two beers. Chicken, potatoes, and whatever desserts you have going," Rivenna commands.

The woman smiles, gives me a quick once-over, then turns and leaves. She reappears a moment later with two tall, cold-looking beers.

Grabbing hers, Rivenna holds it up.

"Cheers, you mysterious little package," she says. "I'm going to figure out your secrets if it's the last thing I do. And I'm not talking about the ones you learned from the Storian

—whether she's real or not. I'm talking about who you really are. Here's to your unhinged journey—and to the eventual rise of Magister Brant."

I clink my glass reluctantly against hers, then take a sip of beer before nearly choking on it.

"Wait—did you say *Brant*?"

"Why—do you know him?"

I cough into my arm just long enough to gather my thoughts, then say, "No. It's just, I've heard that name somewhere before."

~I know what you're thinking, Maude's voice chimes in, echoing in my mind. *But even if Brant is descended from the former president, that doesn't entitle him to lead.*

Maybe not. But it could energize his supporters if they knew the truth, and I could bring that truth to them. I could tell them all about President Brant, how Quinton overthrew her and positioned himself as a false king. How he killed anyone who challenged him. I could tell them everything.

I struggle to dig through the tomes of mental information that flooded my memory when the Storian gave me her so-called "gift"—but the task proves exhausting. The knowledge that drove its way into my brain was more than any human could possibly absorb or dissect in a single lifetime.

And the more I dig, the more my head begins to pound.

"It's a common enough name for Normals," Rivenna shrugs. "Or so I'm told."

She has a point. It's possible that it's pure coincidence.

I'm about to respond when I spot a figure moving toward us. At first, I assume it's the barkeep bringing our food.

But as it turns out...I couldn't be more wrong.

CHAPTER SEVEN

TIME SLOWS to a crawl as my gaze shifts to the figure sidling his way over to us. Out of the corner of my eye, I spy broad shoulders. Dark hair. A strong jaw and sculpted cheekbones.

In the split second before my eyes land on his face, my heart throbs in my chest, convinced it's Thorne who's somehow found his way to me.

I'm an instant away from leaping out of my seat to throw myself into his arms...

But then I take in his full face.

Whoever he is, he's handsome, his smile warm and friendly. He's dressed entirely in black. His trousers are leather, as are his boots, and he's wearing a tailored jacket of some luxurious-looking fabric with a partly unbuttoned shirt underneath.

His hair, too, is jet black, and his eyes are almost as dark as Rivenna's contact lenses, though when he comes close, I can see that they're twisting with color.

His eyes, dancing with reflected firelight from the nearby hearth, appear to be either sleepy or sly—or quietly alert.

I've heard the term *bedroom eyes* but never understood it until this very moment. He looks almost unnaturally relaxed, like he doesn't have a care in the universe.

His expression feels like a challenge to the world to try and shock him. He seems perfectly calm, as if he knows exactly how much power he exudes.

I don't need to study him to know he's a Tethered. It's written on every square inch of his muscular frame, every movement, every breath.

I'm not entirely sure I understand his gift, and on his approach, I recoil in my seat. Something about him feels threatening, as if, like Rivenna, he has the power to steal life from me, one moment at a time.

"Kith," Rivenna says, more than a hint of annoyance in her tone. "Are you here to take my bounty from me?"

"Hardly," he replies. "Tempting though she is."

With one foot, Rivenna pushes a chair out for him. In one quick motion, he grabs it, spins it around, and straddles it while tossing a leather pack to the ground from his shoulder.

"I'm only here to make sure the two of you survive long enough to make it to the Citadel."

His eyes lock on mine, and, like he's deliberately revealing himself to me, his power twists its way through my mind—and the second I understand it, I find myself impressed rather than terrified.

I've watched Thorne use silver wrist bracers in the past to take on new powers and defeat even the most daunting Tethered. This man, though—he can take on powers without the aid of bracers. I'm not sure how many Tethered he's robbed of their gifts, but inside him is a cocktail of impressive skills—and terrifying ones, as well.

The friendly tension between him and Rivenna is palpable on the air and I realize as I watch that it's entirely possible it's more than *just* friendly.

It reminds me of two people I once knew.

Two people who are now dead.

"You two aren't..." I say, pointing my finger between them. "Tell me you're not tethered mates."

"Fuck, no," Rivenna laughs. "He wishes."

"Just rivals," Kith replies with a chuckle. "Riv here tends to get the fun gigs, and sometimes, I like to show up and ruin her good time."

I sit back and breathe a long sigh of relief. The last thing I want is to bear witness to another doomed relationship when I have my own problems to deal with.

"You're trying to assess me, Hunter," the man called Kith says when my eyes move to his face again. "Aren't you?"

At the word Hunter, I push myself still farther back, seeking the protection of the shadows.

"It's all right," Rivenna tells me, reaching a hand down to stroke Berengar's head as the dog rests by her feet, indifferent to the stranger's arrival. "Kith is just...he's a little like you. He can read people better than most. He can see powers—though he's not *exactly* a Hunter."

"What the hell are you, then?" I ask him, and when his lips twitch into an amused grin, I add, "I mean—I'm sorry. That sounded rude. But...what's your gift called?"

He lets out what sounds like a genuine laugh and reaches for Rivenna's beer, taking a swig. "I'm what's known as a Blade. I can reach into someone and pull their power from them with surgical precision. Some call us 'power thieves'—but that's a little harsh, if you ask me."

“Oh, I’d say it’s pretty accurate,” Rivenna chuckles.

“We’re both thieves in our own right, aren’t we, Riv?” he asks before turning back to me. “Technically, I like to avail myself of people’s talents while neutralizing them. To be fair, I don’t always *keep* the powers. Sometimes, I give them back.”

“Kith can give powers to other people, too,” Rivenna says. “It’s pretty impressive, actually. If he wanted, he could swipe your healing power and hand it to me right now.”

The thought of having my gifts—the very thing that makes me a Tethered—snatched away from me feels like a hideous violation. I do my best to hide my horror when I say, “I see.”

“You’re here for the Shadow,” Kith murmurs, leaning forward, his eyes still fixed on me.

All of a sudden, I feel wretchedly self-conscious in my filthy dress and bare feet. Not to mention that I must smell like death.

~*You do smell ghastly,* Maude tells me. *Congratulations.*

Shut up.

“What makes you say that?” I ask Kith.

Instead of answering, he simply leans back and waits as the barkeep lays our food down before us. She stares at him with what looks like genuine longing before turning and walking slowly back to the bar.

When she’s gone, Kith grabs a piece of potato and scarfs it before saying, “I can always tell when someone is looking for the Shadow. Plus, I’m looking for *you.* And you, as well,” he adds, pulling his eyes to Rivenna.

“The Magister knows about her, then,” she says, nodding toward me. “We met a Starless in the tunnel who knew to look for her, too. The Lady must have been spying again."

"No doubt," Kith adds, leaning forward over the chair's back. "I'm not worried about the Lady. I promised the Shadow I'd guard you both with my life until we got to the Capitol, and I intend to."

"Does he know I'm his..." I begin, but Rivenna shakes her head, silently commanding me to shut my food hole. "I mean, do you work for the Magister, then?" I ask, eyeing him curiously.

"Sort of." He holds up a hand to reveal the same brand I saw emblazoned on Rivenna's flesh. "I'm Special Advisor to the Shadow, to be precise." He glances around before adding, "I would suggest we leave tonight to head to the Citadel, but you two must be exhausted. Best get a few hours' rest first, then we'll start off."

Reaching down, he opens the leather satchel he tossed to the floor earlier and pulls out a neatly folded pile of gray clothing, handing it to me.

"For you," he says. "Pants, a shirt, a sweater, socks, and I brought boots, as well. The Shadow wants you looking like one of us for the rest of the trek."

"He's really seen me, then? My—I mean, the Shadow?"

Kith lets out a low whistle, and points a finger into the air, twisting it around. "He has eyes on every mile of the tunnels. It's a necessity, given that people from the Isles have a bad habit of showing up with rage in their hearts—especially in recent days."

I lean forward a little too eagerly. "You've seen others from the Isles in the last few days?"

Kith narrows his eyes slightly, a dimple appearing in his

right cheek as he smirks. "I have, yes. A certain Royal Guard arrived in the Capitol two days ago, looking for the Shadow. A few Starless got to him first—but he's safe now and unharmed. He's being...detained in the Citadel."

Before Maude can shush me, questions tumble out of my mouth like a series of marbles scattering in every conceivable direction. "Do you know the guard's name? Is he all right? What's happened to him?"

"That's for you and the Magister to discuss. It's not really my business."

"Can you at least tell me what he looked like?"

He shrugs. "Tall. Handsome. Your usual hot guy with an attitude. To be fair, though, he did seem a little disoriented. They say he'd had his mind—"

"*Controlled,*" I interrupt. "Bent."

Kith doesn't look entirely surprised when I say the words. "Yes. A Bender had gotten to him. Sent him to the Capitol on behalf of the king. It's not the first time it's happened, but this Guard seemed more reluctant to obey than most, like he was fighting off the mind control with all his strength. I got the impression he wasn't particularly keen on serving the king."

"Fuck," I say under my breath. "We need to go. We have to get to the Citadel right now."

Rivenna reaches out and lays a hand on my arm. "You need your rest," she says. "The Guard will be fine." With an irritated look, she adds, "Won't he, Kith?"

His smile fades, and he looks genuinely aggrieved. "I'm sorry. Yes, of course he will. Look..." With a quick glance around, he speaks under his breath. "*Shara.*"

"You know my name."

"There's no need to play coy. I'm here because I know who the Shadow is to you—and you to him. And he knows about the Guard who showed up—Thorne, right? He's your... mate?"

My heart is pounding so hard now that I'm certain the tavern's entire population can hear it. I'm not sure whether to be relieved or terrified. If the Shadow knows Thorne is my mate, maybe he'll be kind to him. Maybe he'll convince the Magister to be merciful.

"Thorne is absolutely fine," Kith says. "He's in a cell for the time being, but trust me when I say he's being treated extremely well."

Tears well in my eyes, and I nod for lack of ability to do anything else.

"Thank you," I manage. I hate the idea of Thorne in a cell, but it's hardly the first time he's been locked up. If it's the worst thing that happens to either of us in the Capitol, we're already doing far better than we were in the Palatine Estates.

"Of course." Kith takes my hand, his touch sending a shockwave through my body. I don't know what power he possesses that's doing this to me—pouring endorphins into my system so that I feel instantly at peace, even happy.

Or maybe it's simple relief—an emotion I'm not even remotely accustomed to.

"Look," he says, "it's going to be all right. You're free now, Shara. You're safe."

He holds onto my hand for a beat too long, and, realizing how strange it is to be reveling in his touch, I finally draw back. Something crackles in the air between us—a nascent energy that frightens me.

Rivenna must feel it, too, because she clears her throat

and says, "Eat up, you two weirdos. I want Shara to get some sleep so we can get started sooner rather than later."

I have no idea what time it is at this point. All I know is that as hungry as I still am, I'm even more tired.

"Six hours," Kith says, watching me with those mysterious eyes of his as I scarf down a slice of chicken. "Then we leave."

I eat until I've had my fill, with Maude's voice reminding me that I'll need energy in the morning for our final push to the Capitol.

"I'm...going to go get changed," I say, taking hold of the pile of clothing Kith gave me. He reaches down and extracts a pair of gray ankle boots from his bag, handing them over, as well as a toothbrush and toothpaste.

I nod silent thanks when Rivenna points me toward a hallway where she tells me I'll find a bathroom.

Once inside the small room, I lock the door and, when I've pulled Mercutio's curled-up form carefully out of my pocket, tear off the once-blue gown that's barely holding together at the seams, then fill the dingy sink with warm water and do my best to wash myself, splashing water on my face and torso.

I change into the clothing Kith provided, which is at least comfortable, if not flattering. I yank on loose-fitting linen pants, a tank top, and a gray knitted sweater made of some sort of soft yarn. When I've tucked Mercutio into my pants pocket, I tie my hair into a knot at the back of my head, brush my teeth, then stare at myself in the mirror for a long moment.

I look tired to within an inch of my life—like someone who's been torn apart more times than any human should. I dream of the moment when I can find myself back in Thorne's arms.

I'm trying desperately to believe he's okay. If my father is on my side, and if he believes Thorne and I are truly meant to be together—I have little doubt he'll help me.

I just need to get to him.

For a moment, I consider storming out and insisting to Rivenna and Kith I need to leave right now, but Maude cautions me.

~You need sleep.

"I'm fine," I mutter.

~No, you're not. You'll be of no use to Thorne if you can't string a sentence or a thought together, let alone stay upright. You need to convince the Magister that Thorne is worthy of release. Save your strength. Your task can wait a few more hours.

As much as I hate to admit it, she's not wrong.

Without another word, I dump the crumpled gown into a garbage pail and leave the bathroom. I've just started heading down the narrow hallway when I spot a man moving toward me. He's tall and rail-thin, his shoulders slouching a little.

In the dark of the hall and with his chin down, I can't tell whether he's a Tethered or not. As I make my way by him, he grabs hold of my wrist, pulling himself close and hissing, "The Rebellion is a Lie."

I yank my arm away and he lets me go, staring me down for a moment.

His eyes are swirling with power.

He's a Porter, like my friend Nev—a Tethered who can teleport from one place to another. I glance down to see the Magister's mark branded into his wrist—the circle divided into segments by a series of curving lines. But a deep, red X crosses through it that looks as if it was deliberately carved into his flesh.

He looks desperate—wild, even.

"I know," I say softly, nodding in hopes of appeasing him. "I know about the lies. You don't need to tell me."

He shakes his head vigorously. "No. Not the most important of them. The truth needs to spread like wildfire."

"What truth? What are you talking about?"

A shout from within the tavern startles us both, and the man gives me one last, desperate look, then takes off down the hallway.

I twist around to ask him again what he means, but he's already vanished back to wherever he came from.

CHAPTER EIGHT

DAZED, I make my way back to the table, where Rivenna's black eyes veer to mine.

"What's wrong with you?" she asks, eyeing me like I'm covered in blood or worse—despite the fact that I'm significantly more presentable than I was a few minutes ago.

I throw myself down onto the empty chair and say, "Did either of you see a man heading down the hall toward the bathroom?"

Kith, on high alert, rises to his feet as though ready to go barreling after whoever I'm talking about.

"Don't bother. He's gone." I glance up at him. "He was a Porter—with an X cut through his brand."

"Fucking Starless," Rivenna sneers.

"Starless? He wasn't wearing a mask."

"He's still a Starless. They carve their brands up to let it be known they don't support the Magister. Did the bastard talk to you?"

I nod. "He said *the Rebellion is a lie.*"

"He didn't hurt you, did he?" Kith asks, sitting down

again and pulling his chair toward me. His protective gaze reminds me once again of Thorne, and I find myself warming to him, if only slightly.

I bow my head. "No, nothing like that. It was just... weird." I'm not sure how much more I can tell either of them without revealing too much of what I learned from the Storian about the Rebellion—that the event was properly referred to as "The Rise." The true name of the violent coup that put the man called Quinton on the first ever throne of Kravan.

I try my best to sound naive when I ask, "What did he mean, the Rebellion is a lie?"

"Those words are painted on every external wall in Kravan," Kith growls. "They're nothing new. What I don't get is why the hell a Porter would make his way to the Underbelly just to say them to you, of all people."

"Oh, come on," Rivenna replies. "You know why. They're all Ganders." Turning to me, she clarifies. "Propaganda spreaders. Liars. They sow chaos. Their job is to instill doubt in everyone so no one trusts anyone. It keeps us all on high alert and ensures no one can organize to fight against a common enemy."

"They won't turn me against anyone," I mutter. "I already know all about the lies."

~Careful, Shara, Maude says. *Kith doesn't know you've encountered the Storian.*

"What lies are you talking about, exactly?" Kith asks right on cue, intent as he leans toward me.

I glance at Rivenna, but she says nothing about the Storian or what I told her earlier. She gives me another surreptitious shake of her head as if to warn me against saying anything more.

I swallow. "Just...the lies everyone's been told about the Tethered through the years," I reply, pulling my eyes to Kith's. "That our kind is dangerous. That we caused the Rebellion. It's not true, is it? The Tethered didn't start it. We all know that—at least, we all *suspect* it."

I choose my words carefully, being sure to reveal nothing that's not common knowledge for every Tethered in Kravan.

"Oh—that old chestnut," Kith replies, looking satisfied. "Yeah, their propaganda is weak, at best. The Starless are little more than a chaotic bunch of assholes, but they're harmless, really."

"The Poisoner in the tunnel was far from harmless," Rivenna retorts. "If it weren't for Shara here, he would have killed me."

Kith doesn't look entirely surprised—nor does he look concerned. "I suspect he was just trying to scare you, Riv."

"He slashed my throat and poisoned my bloodstream."

At that, Kith looks mildly sheepish. "Shit. I'm sorry. Well, all the more reason for you two to rest easy tonight. I'll keep an eye out for any more of the bastards while you get some sleep. Come on, I'll show you to your room."

"You've already booked it?" Rivenna asks, then snickers. "What am I saying? Of course you have."

I rise to my feet and watch Berengar rouse himself from his rest to pad along next to Rivenna. She and Kith make their way to a door at the back of the tavern, glancing warily over their shoulders as they move.

We pass through the door, sealing it behind us, and head

down another long, narrow hallway. This one is carved of gray stone, and it's unsurprisingly cold and damp.

To each side is a series of doors, and when we reach the last one on our right, Kith pushes it open with the twist of a knob.

The lights flare on inside to reveal six narrow cots lined up against the walls, with striped mattresses. On each is a folded sheet, a wool blanket, and a thin pillow. Curtains on rods hang between the cots, offering minimal privacy.

"Riv—you may want to power down your hell-hound," Kith says. "Shara..." His voice softens when he addresses me. "Get some sleep. I'll wake you in a few hours."

"Where will you be?" I ask, hoping he's planning to stay close, despite the fact that I'm still not entirely sure I can trust him.

"Right here," he says, positioning himself by the door, arms crossed. "If any more Porters show up, I promise you, they'll be dead before they reach you."

I don't want to ask how he intends to kill them, so I simply turn away and set up the farthest cot from the door, draping the flat sheet over the mattress, then flopping down and yanking the blanket over myself.

My muscles and bones feel like they've been tenderized, and I admit silently that I'm grateful for the opportunity to be horizontal for a little.

I can hear Rivenna whispering to Berengar as she extracts this and that chip or memory card from a slot at the back of his neck, seeming to examine them for tampering.

After a few minutes, she says, "Fucking hell."

"What?" Kith asks.

"Someone bugged Beren with surveillance equipment.

They tapped into his ocular cameras. That must be how the Starless found us."

I twist around to watch as she throws what looks like a coin-disc to the floor and crushes it under her heel.

"I can't imagine how they got to him," she says. "He's been with me for days on end."

"Must've been a Courser," Kith says. When he sees my eyes land on him, he explains, "Tethered who can remotely disable electronics. One of their kind could have shut him down for a few minutes—long enough to implant a new chip that allows them to watch through his eyes. They probably did it while you were sleeping, Riv."

"I suppose," she says with a sneer. "If I ever find out who did it..."

"Yes, I know. You'll suck seven decades out through their left nostril."

"Something like that."

I don't tell them Thorne has a similar talent for manipulating electronics. In the Verdan residence, he shut down my Maude unit more than once so that we could have a little privacy while we talked.

I watch silently as Rivenna removes her dark contact lenses, inserting them into a white case. Her strange irises no longer frighten me. Instead, as I gaze at her through half-closed eyes, I simply marvel at how beautiful she is in her own quiet, elusive way.

I've seen many lovely women in my life—and just as many handsome men. But Rivenna almost seems like she comes from another world. In the room's faint light, her cheekbones look as if they're cut from stone, and her eyes shine even brighter than Berengar's. The scars on her cheek, trophies acquired during past triumphs, look like lines cutting through marble.

"Get some sleep," she says, slipping over and taking hold of the curtain next to my cot. "We have a long hike ahead of us—and I have little doubt the Magister will want to speak with you when you arrive. You'll need a clear head for what's coming."

Before she pulls the curtains shut, she whispers, "Remember what I told you about tethered mates and the Nether. See if you can speak to your man."

"How do I do it?"

"Close your eyes, empty your mind, and maybe you'll find out. Good night, Shara. Say hi to your special friend for me."

With that, she yanks the curtain closed, and I'm certain I hear her chuckling on the other side.

CHAPTER NINE

My eyes droop shut, and I half-expect to fall instantly into a deep sleep.

At first, my rest is troubled. My thoughts are a torrent of worries about Thorne and about Kravan's future. My mind veers to this and that worst-case scenario, fear gnawing at my gut.

But after a few moments, a vision forms, pushing all other thoughts away. I see a bright white space, its light so blinding that I feel like I've wandered into the outdoors at long last to walk directly under the blazing sun.

But instead of seeing trees, grass, or concrete, all I can make out is...

Absolutely nothing.

I'm no longer surrounded by walls, a floor, and a ceiling, but a void—as though I'm standing in an empty world.

A dream, I tell myself. *It's just a dream. It will pass.*

The absence of detail is disorienting, even frightening, and at first, all I want is to leave this place and ground myself in the Underbelly's back room once again.

But my desire to escape comes to a sudden halt when a figure steps out of the light toward me, dressed in dark trousers, leather boots, and a gray shirt unbuttoned at the collar.

His irises swirl with familiar powers—ones that I know as well as my own. Powers that he's shared with me on occasion, just as I've shared mine with him.

I feel his heart beating in my chest alongside my own as he rakes a hand through his thick hair, smiling when his lips form the words, "Hello, Beautiful."

I'm frozen in place, hardly daring to move a muscle. It feels like one step toward him could make him vanish like a twist of vapor, and the thought of losing him—whether he's an illusion or not—terrifies me.

"Is this a dream?" I whisper.

It has to be. Which means if my mind stirs to wakefulness, this ends.

I need to remain here as long as I can.

Stepping toward me, Thorne takes my hands in his, pulling one and then the other to his lips. His touch is so real, so utterly delicious, that I convince myself this is something entirely different from any dream I've ever had.

It's more like an out-of-body experience—except that I'm still very much *inside* my body. Every nerve is alive, every throb of my heart audible in duet with his.

This is as real as any moment I've ever experienced.

"It's no dream," he confirms, shifting his hands to my face. He pulls himself closer and kisses me deeply, as if to prove the truth in his words.

I push myself to my toes, absorbing the scent and taste of him, the feel of those perfect lips on my own.

"Thorne," I say again when he draws away. "Is...is this the *Nether*?"

"Yes, it is," he whispers, his breath stroking my skin. "I don't know how we came to be here, or how long we can stay together. I only know that I fucking need this. I need *you*."

I press my hands to his chest, still convinced my mind is playing tricks on me.

"Is it really you?" My eyes move down his body. "You feel so real, but..."

It's then that I see blood stains on his sleeve surrounding his right bicep. I reach for his arm, but he winces away. "It's fine," he tells me. "They do it to all the prisoners."

"The Magister's people, you mean?"

He nods. "It's a precaution—that's all. I'm all right, I promise."

"I don't understand..."

Slipping his fingers under my chin, he lifts my face to his own. "All you need to know is that in this place, right now, you and I are untouchable. Our souls are bonded. Our minds. Nothing matters but us. I feel no pain, I promise. Only pleasure."

"Good. I can't stand to think of you in pain. I've felt your heartbeat so many times since I left the palace," I tell him with a smile. "It's kept me going."

"As long as my heart still beats, I'm yours. Remember that—whatever may come. You and I will be together as long as we both live, I swear it. I can't wait to see you again in the flesh."

With tears burning my eyes, I nod. "Are you really okay? You're not in pain?"

He shakes his head. "No pain. I promise."

I move closer and press my lips to his neck, tongue tasting salt as a low moan escapes his lips, his hands gripping my waist.

"*How* are you so real right now? How can this be?" I breathe against his skin.

"We're bound to one another. Distance does nothing to disturb that. It only makes my desire for you grow and burn brighter." The rawness in his voice tells me he means the words with everything in his soul...as if I had any doubt. Our emotions mingle and twist together, becoming one. Yet I know in my heart how far he is from me. How unreachable.

"I would give anything to be with you right now," I whisper, dizzy with desire. "I want you so much that it hurts."

"Then take me. I'm yours."

I sweep my lips over his, undoing his shirt one button at a time, and pull myself backwards to watch as he reaches down and undoes his trousers. He drops them to the ground and steps forward, drawing a moan of pure want from my throat.

The boots he was wearing earlier have disappeared, as though they were never there. When he casts the shirt from his shoulders, he stands fully naked before me.

My eyes move to a series of angry-looking wounds on his right arm, but he shakes his head, telling me to ignore them.

"Now you," he says.

"I..." I'm suddenly self-conscious, as if the stark light in this place renders me too vulnerable to bare myself to him.

"Don't make me beg, Shara. Take off your clothes."

A smile slips over my lips. "What if I *want* you to beg?"

He takes a step toward me and, with a wicked smile, eases down onto his knees. "All right, then," he says, hands grasping my hips. "I beg you to take off your clothes. Please, Shara. I need to see all of you."

I ask myself again if this can possibly be happening—if his touch can possibly feel so real over so great a distance.

I peel my shirt over my head, revealing my bare torso, then slip out of my loose-fitting trousers, which drop easily to the ground.

My boots, like Thorne's, vanish away so that I'm fully naked now—fully vulnerable in this strange, perfect place.

Still on his knees, Thorne presses his face to the place at the apex of my thighs and inhales deeply.

"You've ruined me, you know," he says, slipping a hand onto the inside of my leg and easing it slowly upward. "You've ransacked everything inside me and taken every bit of my soul for your own. I only exist through your gaze—your desire. My blood pulses for you alone."

Gently, he bites down on my thigh, pushing my legs apart and sweeping his hand up until his little finger slides over the slickness that awaits his touch. After a torturous moment, he pulls his hand to his lips and licks at it with the tip of his tongue, his eyes locking on my own.

"Perfection," he mutters, easing forward and pulling at my folds, stroking his tongue over me as I rake my fingers through his hair.

If this is a dream, I never want to wake up. It's too good, too addictive. I want to trap myself in this place forever with him—a place where there's no hunger, no exhaustion. No need for anything but our two bodies and minds.

He rises to his feet and teases me with his fingers, easing two of them inside me just enough that I whisper, "Please..."

"Please what?" he breathes into my ear.

"Please, more..."

He pushes in deeper, then pulls out again, taking hold of his swollen length. Easing closer and brushing his lips over my collarbone, he presses himself against my clit until I'm silently begging him to destroy me.

"More?" he growls in a voice not entirely his—but I delight in how feral it is. He's as desperate as I am, as needful, and I want nothing but to absorb his desire.

"Yes," I moan, though I feel as if he's going to ruin me, break me...end me.

"Say it."

"I want every inch of you inside me," I tell him. "I want you to tear me to pieces. I want to feel *everything*."

Thorne draws back, a wicked smile setting fire to his eyes. "Then who am I to deny you everything?"

I've never felt so free, so alive as I do in this empty place... and yet, I know in my heart that we aren't truly together. This...isn't...real.

Yet it is. It has to be.

My fingertips dig into Thorne's shoulders, nails biting into his flesh just enough to leave red crescents in their wake. He lifts me, hands under my thighs, and I wrap my legs around him as he lowers me onto his steel-hard shaft. Inch by glorious inch, he splits me apart, reminding me what sweet, ecstatic agony it is to be with him.

Our tongues meet, desperate to entangle themselves. His tastes of sex, of lust, of everything I've been craving since the last time I saw him.

For a perfect moment, I forget the world is a terrifying place. All that matters is him and me—and what we are together.

“Shara,” he breathes into my ear, sheathing himself hard and drawing a cry from my lips. “There’s something I need to tell you...”

I’m just about to ask what it is when a hand takes hold of my shoulder, shaking me awake.

CHAPTER TEN

My eyes are still bleary when I glance up to see Kith leaning over my cot, his gaze locked on my face, a hint of a smile on his lips. The curtain behind him is open and the room's lights are on.

Shit. No, no, no.

I seal my eyes again, searching for Thorne—but he's nowhere to be seen.

It happened, didn't it? I felt him. I...

I want him back. Right now.

"Is something wrong?" I ask with a shaking voice. "I've only been asleep a few minutes."

"It's been six hours," Kith says, looking perplexed.

"Six...hours..." I stammer. Was my time with Thorne really drawn out for that long?

"I'm afraid so. We're about to take off for our trek to the Capitol. It's a long way yet, but hopefully your new boots will make the journey a little easier."

I scurry up to a sitting position. "Where's Rivenna?" I

ask, feeling suddenly vulnerable to the Blade. Something about Kith still feels too smooth...too good to be true.

Then again, there was once a time when I saw Thorne the same way. I didn't trust him, either—and learned the hard way that he was one of the few people in the world I could put my faith in.

"You're safe with me, Shara," Kith says, seeing the quiet panic in my eyes. "It's okay." He crouches down in front of me, reaching for my hand, but I draw away like a frightened kitten.

He lifts both hands as if he's letting me see he's unarmed.

It's not weapons I fear from you, Blade.

"Look," he says, "your father is eager to see you. It will be a little tricky to get you to him, what with the Magister overseeing who comes and goes from the Citadel. I may be your father's advisor, but I'm as much at Brant's mercy as anyone else is. Still, I have every faith that you'll be allowed inside."

"Brant," I repeat softly. It still feels like too great a coincidence that he shares a name with the former president—but I resolve not to reveal what I know. At least, not yet.

"Martin Brant. That's the Magister's name. Didn't you know?"

"I...suppose I'm still getting used to surnames," I confess. "Everyone in the Tower had one name only."

"Ah." Kith pulls himself to a standing position, stepping back, his eyes still piercing into me as if he can see right through my skin. His words, however, contradict the theory. "You're a walking mystery. You know that, right? A very *pretty* one...but a mystery, all the same."

I tear my eyes from his, my cheeks heating.

"I'm not good at taking compliments," I murmur.

Not from anyone who isn't Thorne, at least.

"I apologize. I didn't mean to overstep."

"Well, you did."

He goes silent, and I feel suddenly guilty. All he did was call me pretty, after all. It's not like he propositioned me.

I meet his eyes once again to see him looking remorseful. "I just woke up," I say, "and I'm disoriented. So let's just start over, okay?"

With a nod, he replies, "That sounds like an excellent plan. So—Rivenna and I will escort you to the Capitol. I'll secure entry into the Citadel, but I need you to keep your head down until then. It's one thing for Rivenna and me to know who you are, but it's best that we keep the secret to ourselves as long as possible."

"It sounds like I'm no secret anymore. The Poisoner and the Porter—they both knew I was here, like you said."

"Did they say your name? Did they say anything about why they were looking for you, specifically?"

I ponder that for a second, then shake my head. "I...no, not really. The Poisoner said something about the Lady, I think." When I try to recall his exact words, my mind draws a blank.

"Then I can't begin to guess whether they truly know who you are."

"I just..." I feel my lip threatening to quiver and command it to stop. "I really need to see Thorne, whatever it takes. I need to know he's all right." I don't tell him what I saw when I ventured into the Nether. The blood on Thorne's arm, the strained look in his eye that told me he was putting on a brave face so that we could revel in one another's company for a few perfect moments.

Kith nods his understanding, reaching again for my hand. This time, I let him take it, and he holds it gently in his own. His touch is warm and comforting, and once again, I feel a force coming from him that frightens me a little. It's like a spark of electricity coursing through my veins, working its way deep into my bloodstream.

No one but Thorne should make me feel like this.

"Shara—I vow, as your father's right-hand man, that you will spend your life by the side of your rightful mate. That is my promise to you."

Tears sting my eyes, and I thank him silently, forcing myself to look at him—to seek out something of his true nature.

I don't see cruelty in him as I did in Tallin or so many others. All I see is that he's served faithfully and willingly... and that he wishes to protect me. An almost feral benevolence spreads from him through my mind, like a beautiful contagion, filling me with a hope I've seldom dared to feel.

I'm about to speak when the door opens and Berengar comes trotting in, followed closely by Rivenna, who stops in her tracks and stares at us. My hand is still in Kith's, and I draw away quickly, tucking it to my side.

I stammer, "Kith was just..."

"Reassuring Shara," he says. "That we'll get her safely to the Capitol and her father."

"Mm-hmm," Rivenna replies. "Of course you were. I'm sure a lot of guys would like to *reassure* her."

"Don't be vile," he scolds, but he lets out a laugh that tells me there's no malice or hostility between them. "Fuck it. Let's get going. I want to get to the city before the next nightfall."

Silently, we gather our things. Once I've used the washroom to tidy myself up and brush my teeth, we leave the Underbelly and head toward the main tunnel.

"You're not worried after what happened yesterday?" I ask Rivenna as we begin to walk briskly through the chilly depths. "You don't think there's a chance we'll be attacked again?"

"Worried?" she says. "Never. On edge? Sure. But there are three of us now. Four, including Beren—and I've seen what you're capable of by now, Hunter. Stealing powers like a Blade is one thing, but everything else you can do? You're basically unstoppable."

"I can only steal powers temporarily," I remind her. "It's not exactly an infallible weapon."

"If you're anything like your father," Kith says, striding along at a rapid pace, "you're going to be an impressive presence in the Capitol. Your father is influential—more, even, than the Magister. Our people will embrace you with open arms, I'm sure."

"Tell me, how does the Magister feel about my father's influence?"

Kith chuckles. "I wouldn't know. No one is foolish enough to tell him the truth of it. As far as Magister Brant is concerned, he's top dog. Besides, we all know he will be the one officially in charge when the winds of Kravan shift. That's enough to satisfy him."

"Let's hope you're right," Rivenna tells him. "Because if you're not, we'll have a whole other war to contend with."

"The Shadow isn't one to enjoy the limelight. There's a reason for his title." He throws me a look and adds, "His daughter, on the other hand, should absolutely be center stage at all times."

"I'd rather die," I laugh.

We hike through the dark for hours on end. Kith entertains us by recounting stories about his youth, which he spent hiding in the Capitol's alleyways and corners, picking pockets and working odd jobs here and there before he came into his powers.

When I ask him at one point, "Do you interact much with Normals nowadays?" he shoots Rivenna a look of surprise. "You haven't told her, I guess?"

"Not yet," she says with a shrug. "I didn't think it was important."

"Believe me, it's important."

I'm baffled enough to ask, "Told me what?"

"We don't call them Normals—at least, not in the Magister's inner circle," Kith informs me. "It's considered derogatory."

"To them or us?" I ask with a laugh, but he doesn't seem particularly amused.

"To them, mostly. Look—the non-Tethered in the Capitol aren't our enemies, despite what we've all been trained to believe. It's not us against them. We're *all* at a disadvantage. We're in this together. Treating their kind as if they're interior—even if they are—is harmful."

"*Inferior*?" I choke out. "What's inferior-sounding about the word 'Normal'? Don't most people aspire to it? We're the ones they've always treated like freaks and blamed for the ills of the world, aren't we?"

Kith shrugs. "*Normal* implies dullness. Mediocrity. The Nobles in the Isles have managed to harness the notion that normality is to be desired, but we all know the truth. The Tethered are objectively superior in virtually every way. We're stronger, faster, more disciplined. But there's no need to rub their faces in it—not when we should ideally be equals."

This is not a debate I have any energy or desire to engage in further, so I simply reply, "Fine. If not Normals, then what do you call them?"

"Potentials," Rivenna says over her shoulder as she and Berengar stride ahead. "That's the supposedly inoffensive term for them. They're a delicate bunch of fucking flowers, if you ask me."

"We call them that," Kith adds, ignoring her last statement, "because they have the potential to become something greater."

"No offense to them," I mutter, "but I don't see how. It's not like they'll suddenly develop powers on their fortieth birthdays or something."

Kith throws me a knowing smile, his white teeth gleaming even in the shadows. "Won't they?"

"What aren't you telling me?" I ask, giving him a playful shove as we walk, which surprises me as much as it seems to surprise him.

Apparently, we're becoming friends.

He stumbles in an exaggerated way, then regains his footing and says, "A Blade like me can give the powers we acquire to a Potential. I can actually change them. So yes—

they can develop powers on their fortieth birthday or any other day."

Wait. What?

My jaw drops open. "You're telling me you can...*turn* someone into a Tethered?"

He nods.

"He's done it more than a few times," Rivenna tells me. "I'm just surprised the Magister hasn't demanded a gift for himself."

"He has," Kith replies with a chuckle. "But I'm waiting for just the right gift to bestow upon him."

He goes on to explain that he can only give a Normal—a Potential, rather—one power in their lifetime, and once it's theirs, it's locked in. "It's one thing to give a fifty-year-old the ability to teleport," he says. "But if it's not useful to them, what's the point? It's a wasted gift. The Magister has little interest in hand to hand combat—he has people to do that for him. So my goal is to find him a skill that will set him up for life, once he's assumed power in the realm."

"You really think that's going to happen, then," I say. "You truly believe a regime change is possible."

"I have every faith that the future leader of the Capitol is close at hand—and that it's not a member of King Tomas' family. I would stake my life on it."

"You'd better mean that," Rivenna snorts. "Because it'll probably come down to your life before this nonsense is over."

"Oh, I've *seen* it," Kith says. "I've seen a glorious future. I know what's coming."

I hesitate for a beat before asking, "How do you see the future, exactly?"

"I borrowed a power from a Seer a while back—with her blessing. An older woman, a Tethered living in the Capitol. She works as a fortune teller. Her clients tend to be a little hopeless. You know, people who need something to look forward to. They bring her food in exchange for predictions. And before you ask —yes, I gave the power back to her when I was done with it."

"Are a Seer's visions ever wrong?" I recall with horror what I've seen of Thorne's future and dare to hope my vision was nothing more than a manifestation of my deepest fears.

"You tell me, Shara." Kith stops walking long enough to take me by the arm and turn me toward him, forcing me to stare into his eyes. "Since you seem to be a blood mimic, let me show you what I've seen."

"Blood mimic?" My brows meet in confusion.

"Rivenna told me you can absorb powers through blood," he says. "You and I have thievery in common when it comes to taking gifts from people."

"When I take on someone's power, I don't deprive them of it," I protest. "I think we're a little different, you and I."

"I suppose that's true," he replies with a strange smile. "Your gift is far kinder than mine. But let me show you what the Seer gave me through the temporary loan of her powers."

His vision of the future comes to me, projecting itself into my mind. I see rolling green hills surrounded by perfect, beautiful homes. Then I'm in another place—one that feels familiar, though I'm not sure why. I'm standing under a large oak tree, and I see Kith smiling at me, dressed in a dark suit.

I see another man, too—a man I've only ever seen in the visions the Storian imparted to me.

My father. The Shadow.

He's striding toward me across a broad lawn of tidily mowed grass surrounded by beautifully tended gardens.

"Shara," he says when he reaches me. "Your Pairing has come at last."

I look down to see that I'm wearing a dress of deep gold, glistening in the sunlight.

I don't know where the location is, exactly, but it looks idyllic, and judging by the smile on his face, my father is genuinely happy. I, too, feel nothing but joy and excitement for the future.

In the distance, the outline of a large building begins to reveal itself, though it remains blurry and nondescript.

I turn around to see several happy-looking, well-dressed people moving about, and begin to wonder whether I'm bearing witness to some distant part of the Capitol that's been rejuvenated and rebuilt—whether the entire city could find its way to looking this lovely.

"Tell me," Kith says, dropping my arm. The vision evaporates, and I find myself releasing a stolen breath. "Does the future look real to you?"

"It does," I confess. "And it looks incredible. You've seen the same vision?"

"Only a little more than you've witnessed. But it was enough to wish to find you and meet you, Shara. I knew the moment I saw you that you were important—that the future of Kravan was tied inextricably to you." He lets out a satisfied breath. "When I tell you I've been looking forward to meeting you for a long time, I mean it. I couldn't wait to show you the happiest day of your life. I've been holding onto that vision for some time."

“My father is there,” I say. “He looks happy, too. He said something about a Pairing. What is that?”

“Ah. That’s a new law the Magister has set in place in the Capitol. It’s the equivalent of a wedding, where two of our kind pledge a vow in front of witnesses.”

I cock my head, confused. “Why would Tethered need to pledge any kind of vow?” I don’t say it out loud, but the bond Thorne and I share is stronger than any legally binding pledge.

“They don’t *need* to,” Kith says. “But it does allow two Tethered in the Capitol to marry, just as Potentials—*Normals*—do. It lets us share assets and more—so that if one dies, the other can inherit their possessions. It’s a protective measure, but more than that, it’s a symbolic one. If we’re to be considered equal under the law, then it seems only right that we should be allowed to declare ourselves before those we care about.”

What he’s saying makes sense—and more than that, it gives me hope. If what I saw really was the future, then there will come a day when Thorne and I can tell the entire world we love one another. The days of cowering and hiding our affection are ending.

A new era is beginning.

The thought of it seems so far off that I can barely imagine it. The luxury of being allowed to declare my love for Thorne in such a public place—it’s incredible. I can’t say I’ve ever given a moment’s consideration to a wedding, and I have no idea why we would bother. We’re already tethered mates, bound for life. We already love one another.

Then again...why *not* pledge ourselves? Why not declare our love freely in front of those we care about?

When Kith starts moving again, I follow along a little behind him, happy at first.

But after a few minutes spent dissecting what I saw in his vision, my blood runs suddenly cold in my veins.

Maude, I say silently, *you saw Kith's vision, right?*

~Yes. I saw you at your Pairing ceremony. She pauses, then adds, *But something was missing—something that disturbed me.*

I don't want to admit it, even to myself, but she's right.

The one thing missing from that future was Thorne.

CHAPTER ELEVEN

After several more hours of hiking with few stops to rest or consume the meager bits of food and water Kith and Rivenna have in their packs, we begin at last to climb steeply.

I'm hesitant to allow myself to hope we're nearing the end of our journey—but surely our ascension means exactly that.

In the distance, I finally spot a narrow shaft of light pouring in through a gap around what looks like a large set of doors.

After hiking for so many hours, I'm beginning to feel like someone outside myself is propelling me forward on legs that aren't entirely my own.

As much as I want to see my father in the flesh—as much as I want to see the Capitol from the inside—the only thing giving me strength is feeling the sensation of Thorne's heart beating out there somewhere, in synchronicity with my own.

We halt before the broad set of steel doors, and Rivenna turns my way.

“Do yourself a favor and keep your head down when we get out there.”

“Why? Is someone going to recognize me?”

I intend the words as a joke, but I realize there’s every possibility that if we’ve been watched this whole time, that means people know my face by now—it’s just a question of whether they’re allies or enemies.

“You don’t have a Magister’s mark,” Kith reminds me. “Which means no one will intuit which side you’re on. Don’t stray from Rivenna and Berengar, whatever happens.”

“I’m still surprised you haven’t killed me and taken credit for my little discovery, Kith,” Rivenna tells him with a smirk.

“I’m more than happy to give you all the credit in the world. I just want to make sure Shara gets to the Citadel safely—and you’re her best bet.”

“But my father is the Shadow,” I say. “Can’t we just—”

“Waltz in?” Rivenna asks.

“Well...yeah.”

I need to see Thorne. To talk to him. To touch him.

To prove to myself that last night was real.

“There are scanner drones all over the Citadel’s grounds and beyond,” she says. “If one of them mistakes you for a Starless, you’ll be killed before you get anywhere near your father or Thorne.”

I nod silently and watch as Rivenna pushes the doors open. Sunlight pours into the tunnel, blinding me for a few seconds as I trudge forward on numb legs.

I’ve lost all sense of time. I thought we’d be arriving in the middle of the night, but by the looks of it, it’s late afternoon now.

The first thing I’m aware of is a buzzing sound, like a

swarm of angry insects. As my eyes adjust to the brightness, I spot shapes flying in rapid zigzag movements through the air. They do look like insects, more or less—but as one halts to hover a few feet from me, I see that it's made of some sort of metal alloy, with tiny scales covering its body. Its wings flutter so quickly that I can't entirely see them.

"Dragonflyers," Rivenna tells me. "The Magister's little friends."

She raises her hand, revealing the brand to the minuscule drones, then nods toward Kith and me as if to say, "They're friends."

The Dragonflyers take off, disappearing over a tall stone wall to our right. In the distance beyond, I see smoke billowing into the sky, as if some building or other is burning.

"The flyers are part of the reason the Starless are usually masked," Kith explains of the drones. "Once their faces are in the Magister's system, they're targets."

"What happens if a Starless is spotted?"

"Sometimes nothing. Sometimes, they're tracked. If they seem like a threat, however..."

Kith doesn't need to finish the sentence. I can guess easily enough.

"It's just a little farther now," Rivenna assures me as we begin another trudge.

My throat is parched, my tongue dry, and I scarcely have enough energy to put one foot in front of the other.

When Kith reaches an arm out to wrap it around my waist, I don't even have the strength to push him away. I simply stumble along next to him, weary and desperate.

"Soon," he says softly. "The future you were always destined to live is so close."

I nod but say nothing. I want to be reassured by his words—there's nothing negative in them, after all.

But until I see Thorne and know he's safe, the notion of *any* future is something I don't want to contemplate.

I try to connect with Maude—to ask her if she's taking everything in—but she's gone eerily silent in my wrist and mind.

I tell myself she's dormant because she, too, is exhausted, and try not to worry.

Rivenna, Kith, and I walk for twenty or so minutes before we turn right and head down a narrow street flanked by structures that look like they may once have been row houses and businesses. Each of them is destroyed, their façades caved in, windows shattered.

Occasionally, a straggler wanders by us, head low, nodding reverently when they see Rivenna with her black eyes and daunting hound by her side.

When we arrive at a half-shattered stone archway to our right, Rivenna says, "This is the marketplace. We need to head through to get to the nearest entrance to the Citadel."

We pass under the arch to come to a large area, with stands set up here and there for vendors selling their wares, which seem to consist of anything from spare electronic parts to fresh-baked bread to cooked rodents—that I'll admit smell amazing—probably because I've barely eaten a thing in over twenty-four hours.

I reach inside my pants pocket and pull out Mercutio, laying him on my shoulder to partially conceal himself under my hair. He twitches slightly, his current charge just powerful enough to allow him to hook his tiny claws into my sweater and hang on tight.

"Soak up whatever sun you can, little guy," I whisper.

A surprising number of people mill about the marketplace. Some are dressed in what look like dark, informal uniforms, standing at attention as if expecting trouble. Each of them, I notice instantly, is a Tethered—an Elite of some sort—their uniforms emblazoned with the Magister's symbol.

Other people—"Potentials" and Tethered alike—stalk around the area, bartering with vendors or talking amongst themselves.

As we wander by a stand displaying bread and other goods, an argument breaks out between the baker and a customer who accuses him of overcharging. The customer leaps at the baker, throwing him to the ground, but a second later, the customer falls hard to his knees, letting out a cry of pain.

He crashes to his back, and it's only then that I spot the shard of glass digging deep into his neck. Blood pools around his head in a horrific halo, his eyes staring, panicked, at the sky.

Several feet away, a Netic Guard—a Tethered with the ability to hurl objects through space—stands watching the fracas, pulling at the collar of her uniform.

It was you, I think. *Why?*

"The man on the ground is still alive," I gasp, breaking rank with the others to scramble over to him. "I can heal him."

Rivenna looks like she's about to tell me not to when Kith

steps closer, holding out a hand, and says, "Go ahead, Shara. It's all right."

His voice is gentle and filled with empathy and admiration. He watches intently as I slip my hand onto the dying man's chest, feeling the dull thud of his heart strengthen under my touch. As I inhale a deep breath, the glass shard falls out of his neck, and the wound seals shut.

Glancing down, I see the Magister's mark on the man's arm, desecrated by the same *X* that I saw on the Porter in the Underbelly Tavern.

Oh, shit.

He's a Starless.

All of a sudden, I understand why the Guard unleashed her silent attack. And now, I've saved the life of a traitor to the Magister.

I pull back with a gasp when the man's eyes open, locking on mine, and he offers up a warm smile. There's no threat in his expression—only gratitude.

The Guard—the Netic who tried to kill him—storms toward us as if she intends to finish the job, and part of me wonders whether she's more motivated by the mark on his arm or the fact that he brawled with a vendor.

Either way, it seems a little extreme to want him dead.

I'm about to say something when Kith pushes himself in front of me, speaking a few words low into the guard's ear. Backing away and staring at him with what looks like genuine admiration, she nods once, then steps back to stand against the far wall.

"Are you all right?" I ask the man on the ground, who reaches for his neck and prods at it with his fingertips.

He sits up, glances at Mercutio, who's still clinging to my

shoulder, and says, "Yes. Thanks to you," then looks around quickly and leans closer. "The Rebellion is a lie," he whispers.

I manage to nod once before Rivenna grabs me and hoists me to my feet, dragging me away. "You do not want to be seen talking to a Starless," she mutters. "Come on."

"Fucking overzealous guards," Kith says in a growl as he joins us. He takes my face in hand and examines me. "Are you all right?"

"I'm fine."

"Good." He nods toward a tattered shopfront that lies beyond a few of the booths. "You two should head to the closest entrance. My contact will join you shortly. As for me, I have to go. I'm needed elsewhere."

"What?" Rivenna spits. "You're really leaving us right now? You're the one person who could get us inside easily."

"You'll be fine."

Rivenna lets out a groan of frustration. "I'd feel a hell of a lot more confident if you were coming with us. Can't your little side quest wait?"

"I'm afraid not. Seriously, Riv," Kith laughs. "You don't need my help. Besides, I promised you I wouldn't try to steal your bounty, didn't I?"

That seems to be enough to satisfy Rivenna into complacency. She crosses her arms, nods, and says, "Fine. I'll even admit I'm sort of impressed that you kept your word, Blade."

"As you should be," he replies, turning back to me and laying a warm hand on my shoulder. His voice softens almost to intimacy when he says, "I'll be coming around soon to check on you and make sure you're all right. Be careful—and don't say too much to the Magister's envoy. He can be a bit of a shitheel, but don't let him intimidate you. If he does or says anything dickish, you let me know, and I'll deal with him. All right?"

"Thank you, Kith," I reply with a nervous chuckle. "I appreciate you looking out for me—and everything else you've done. But could you do me one more favor?"

"Of course."

"Ask them to let me see Thorne."

His lips twitch a little, then he says, "Consider it done. I promise—you will see him."

I'll believe it when I have my hands on him and my lips on his.

With a nod and a wink, Kith leaves us, and I quietly admit to myself that I feel his absence instantly.

I don't know what it is about him, exactly, that makes him so addictive. I suppose it's the reassurance that comes with his extraordinary power—knowing he's probably close to invincible *and* he's looking out for Thorne and me. But when I delve just a little deeper into my mind, I realize that's not the only thing that makes me wish he hadn't left us.

I genuinely *like* him.

And for some reason, that feels incredibly dangerous.

CHAPTER TWELVE

"It's time," Rivenna says. "Let's get you to your man."

Excitement mingles with terror inside me, culminating in something that feels way too close to nausea for my liking.

I tell myself Kith is right—my father will surely be glad to know I'm alive. He'll help me free Thorne from his cell. He'll tell me about my mother, my sister—all the years that we've missed knowing one another.

I'll get to learn what sort of man he is after so many conflicting reports...and brace myself for the very real possibility that he might be terrible.

But even if he has no desire to play father to me, the fact is that I need his help.

And besides, Kith seems loyal to him...and Rivenna seems to respect him.

That has to count for something, at least.

We emerge onto a narrow street of ruined storefronts and façades of more abandoned buildings, their walls caving in on themselves, windows nothing but shards of jagged glass. Rivenna keeps her eyes alert, her head on a swivel even as Berengar peers around, on guard for threats.

Oddly, though, the streets seem emptier with each block that we pass by.

"Where is everyone?" I ask. "Surely there are still lots of people living in the Capitol."

"We're not too far from one of the Citadel's more discreet entrances," Rivenna tells me. "Which means most people stay far away. Normals know it's dangerous to be seen by the Dragonflyers—and the Tethered who don't want to be recruited into the Magister's fold hide from him. Not everyone wants to be branded like cattle."

"I can't imagine why anyone does, to be honest," I mutter.

"Watch yourself when you speak like that," Rivenna warns. "You can say it to me, but inside the Citadel, you'll want to be careful if you're offering up skepticism about the Magister. You need to learn to smile and nod, and keep your mouth shut."

"You're not the first person who's told me that."

"Well, whoever said it before me knew what they were talking about."

I'm pretty sure no one has advised me to nod and smile more during the course of my life than Maude.

Maude, who's always looked out for me, protected me, been my voice of reason...who has now pretty much vanished from my body and mind, leaving me feeling alone and vulnerable.

"As for why people want the mark," Rivenna says, "it's simpler than you realize. A lot of people gravitate toward power, whatever form it takes. A man who can instill fear—

like the Magister or your father—is considered stronger than one who's kind and just. Intimidation is the greatest weapon any human can wield. Trust me—a Reaper knows. If I take the black lenses out and walk down the street, every person we see will lower their head and cower before me, because they know what I'm capable of taking from them."

"Maybe *you* should lead Kravan, then."

At that, she lets out an explosive laugh that shocks both me and Berengar. "I'd rather live in a cave, thanks," Rivenna snorts. "Besides, most people don't want a Reaper leading them. Fear isn't a good long-term strategy. Hope, on the other hand, can win over the most cynical heart."

As we move along the street, I spot the Tower for the first time in what feels like years. A black behemoth looming up above the rooftops ahead, hovering over the city like a gruesome sentinel.

"Home, sweet home," I say under my breath.

"They say the upper levels are filled with Normals," Rivenna replies with a look of disgust. Clearly, she heard me. "*Potentials,* I mean. Whatever—they're not important or wealthy enough to be named Nobles, not pathetic enough to have to live in this hell-hole of a city. The irony is that they're prisoners just like the Tethered in there, and they don't even know it."

"Our warden was one. And our fight trainer. I heard them talking about the Capitol once in not-so-pleasant terms. I never understood what they meant until I saw this place with my own eyes."

"The bad news is that it will get way worse if we don't do something about it soon. The good news is, your father and the Magister have some kind of plan in place to take over the king's weapons." She nods up toward a flying object hovering a hundred feet or so above us. An autonomous mechanical flyer of some sort, scanning the Capitol for threats. "The Magister has taken down many of the king's drones over the years and reprogrammed them—at least, his *people* have. He has hundreds of them—possibly thousands. They want to take them all."

She nods toward the Tower, and for the first time, I notice what looks like a narrow horizontal window several stories from the top. As we speak, a few drones pour out of the opening, which then seals up and disappears.

"They're weaponized," Rivenna tells me. "With small bombs. Guns. You name it. They can pinpoint their targets and take them out. Mostly, though, they just run surveillance. Which means we should get through the entrance sooner rather than later—it's covered, and we don't want the Royals to see you and take you out before we can get you to your adorable little lover."

"He's not exactly little," I retort.

"I wasn't asking, but good to know."

As I stare up at the distant machines, I wonder who has an eye on them right now.

Can Tallin see me? Does he know I've made it this far?

I almost hope the answer is yes.

I want him to know he can't touch me—not anymore.

It's only a few minutes before we come to the front door of what looks like a run-down business.

Its large windows are boarded up, as is the glass section

of the door. Rivenna pulls it open and leads me inside, where we find two large men in black uniforms lounging in beaten-up old chairs whose upholstery is barely hanging on by a thread.

The men leap to their feet when we enter, eyeing Rivenna first with Berengar, then me. They look stunned to see anyone, particularly a stranger, venture into their haven.

"What the fuck are you doing here, Reaper?" one of them barks, though the moment he's done, he freezes, his eyes moving to the dog. Berengar gives him a growl of warning, baring gleaming steel teeth.

"We're meeting someone, Munce," Rivenna says. "Calm the fuck down."

The man—gray-eyed and menacing—steps over, grabs my left arm, and pushes my sleeve up as Berengar lets out another low growl.

"Call off your hound," the guard says, his eyes locked on the markings on my forearm. "She's a Tower Orphan?" he asks, like he's assuming I'm unable to speak.

"Excellent observational skills," Rivenna says.

"Why would you bring her here? She's a Green. The boss will have no use for her."

"He has a use for this one. If you're wise, you'll let us through."

A sneer from the man tells me he's far from wise. He reaches for a blade sheathed at his waist, his eyes swirling with color.

It doesn't take me long to see that he's what's known as a Rounder. He's strong and fast, and not much else. Under normal circumstances, I'd fear him—but something tells me the reason he hasn't drawn the dagger yet is a healthy fear of the Reaper and her hound.

"We've been ordered not to let anyone through," the other man says. He's a Velor, and when he makes his way to Rivenna from across the room in a split-second, showing off his talent, I gasp. I've seldom seen anyone move that fast.

Rivenna reaches out, and I half expect her to touch him. But instead, her hand just hovers in the air, and he freezes in place.

Without a word, I know she's using her power to draw the life from him and absorb it into her own body and mind. I can feel his horror on the air, intermingling with her bliss.

I watch her leech his existence one minute at a time.

"Stop," he croaks as the other guard pulls his blade. "Please..."

"I'll stop when you let us inside," Rivenna tells him, holding her other hand up toward the Rounder, who drops the blade to the floor with a clang.

Fighting simply to stay on their feet, the guards back away slowly, bowing their heads as the color drains from both their faces.

Finally, she releases them, and each man half-collapses against the wall, their hands reaching for their throats as if to ensure they're still breathing.

"That's a month each," Rivenna tells them, "because I'm going easy on you. A month you will never live to see. Now, open the fucking door, or I'll take another year. And if you call out for aid, I will take a goddamned decade."

The Rounder throws himself toward the back of the room, struggling for breath, and presses his palm to the wall next to an old metal shelf. The shelf slides to the right, and a doorway materializes where it stood. A dark corridor reveals itself beyond the door, lights flaring to life inside.

"Come on, Shara," Rivenna says. "The Citadel is through here."

I nod wordlessly, watching as a dull flush of color slowly makes its way back to the two men's cheeks.

When Rivenna and I have pushed our way through the door and it has sealed up behind us, I ask, "How did you and the Rounder know each other?"

"We were...an item. A while back."

My jaw drops open, and she snickers, glancing sideways at me. "Don't look so shocked," she says. "He's not my bound mate or anything. I was just looking for a bit of fun. I was going through a bit of a low point. Call it an experimental phase."

"And you had your fun, I guess?"

She shrugs. "Not as much of it as you might think." With that, she holds up her pinky finger. "Let's just say his proportions are a little...off."

"You took a month of his life," I reply without cracking a smile. "Sorry if I sound judgmental, but I can't imagine doing that to someone I've slept with." *Then again, the only person I've ever slept with is Thorne.*

"I may give it back sometime—if he does me a favor. But the truth is, he deserved it."

I go silent for a little, then say, "Could I ask you a question?"

"You're joking, right? You've asked me a thousand of them without getting permission first."

I chuckle. "When you use your power, is it always the same? Drawing time from a person's life?"

"Not always. I can pull most of their life away at once—or all of it. Or I can bring them to the brink of death without taking any actual time from them. I can choose how I commit my particular crime."

"Why would you ever want to bring someone to the brink, though? What would be the point?"

"To incapacitate. To torture. Or maybe just because they asked too many fucking questions."

"Oops."

"It's fine. I don't mind. Just be careful with the Magister. He's a man of few words, and he doesn't love being questioned. He takes it as a sign of disrespect."

"But—" I stop and glance around warily.

"Before you say it—no, it won't matter that you're the Shadow's damned daughter," Rivenna hisses. "The Magister will get pissed if you ply him with questions. The good news is that the guy makes himself scarce. I rarely see him—which means you probably won't be subjected to him much."

When we reach a door at the corridor's end, Rivenna inputs a four-digit code on the keypad embedded in the wall. By now, adrenaline and anxiety have granted me a second wind, and I'm restless, my desperation to see Thorne putting me on edge.

"Kith's guy will meet us here," Rivenna says, guiding me into what looks like a large waiting room. Fluorescent lights flicker in the ceiling and ratty-looking chairs line the walls.

"What the hell?" Rivenna asks, recoiling as we seat ourselves in two vinyl chairs, and she turns to look at me. She's staring at my face—only, she isn't. Her eyes seem to be fixed on my hair.

I'm confused until I reach for my shoulder, only to

remember Mercutio is still hanging on. I take hold of him gently and slip him into my pocket again.

"Surveillance," I tell her. "Thorne crafted him. He's been with me for what feels like a long time now. His name's Mercutio."

"Cute. But you're lucky Beren's not an actual dog, or he'd swallow the little guy whole."

"I suspect Mercutio would be hard to digest."

Rivenna smirks then pulls her gaze toward a door at the room's far end, as if she's expecting someone to come crashing through it.

"Do you know Kith's contact?" I ask.

"A little. His name is Terrence, and the guy's a total shit-goblin. But we need to play nice. He assesses anyone who's entering the Citadel for the first time. It's pretty well impossible to get in without his eyes on you first. Well, unless you're being brought in as a prisoner."

"Like Thorne."

"Uh, yeah. *He* was probably dragged in." Her tone is suddenly bitter. "I told you, Royal Guard aren't exactly well loved on the inside."

She looks like she's about to say more but is considerate enough to muzzle herself.

Unfortunately, I can read the thoughts on her face as clear as day.

We'll be lucky if Thorne is still alive by the time you get to him.

CHAPTER THIRTEEN

I'm about to ask more anxiety-riddled questions when a door opens at the far end of the room and a man strides in.

He's dressed in a dark suit with the Magister's round symbol pinned to its lapel. He's short, with thick, dark hair and eyebrows to match.

What stands out most about him is that he's a Normal. A *Potential,* I remind myself. A powerless man, unprotected and vulnerable. Yet he seems wholly confident that his life is in no danger.

"Rivenna," the man says with a nod, then turns to me. "My name is Terrence. I'm an envoy of the Magister's. Kith sent word that the Reaper had brought us a guest, and I'm here to make sure you are who you say."

He looks me up and down, assessing, then extracts a silver item from his pocket. It looks like a small box that tapers at one end to a point.

"Your hand," he says. "If you please."

When I hold out my right hand, he presses the box to my

palm, and I wince in pain before he pulls it back and flips it over.

I glance down to see a spot of blood on my hand.

"This is an Identifier," he says. "It tells me what I need to know by taking a sample of your blood."

"Couldn't you just have looked at my left forearm?" I ask with a scowl. "It's clear that I'm a...a *Tower Orphan*."

The words feel strange from my own lips, but they're enough to make Terrence take my arm, glance at it, and say, "So you are. That'll make this slightly easier."

His eyes turn back to the box, which is apparently offering up some vital information.

"Fine," he says. "You're his daughter."

Without mentioning my father, I know full well that he means the Shadow.

"I need to see a prisoner," I tell Terrence, attempting to take on the practiced tone of a commanding Noble. "A Royal Guard who was brought to the Citadel in the last few days. It's vital that I see him as soon as possible."

"You'll have to discuss that with the Magister," he replies, his tone devoid of emotion. "I do not have the authority to allow it."

"Can you at least tell me if he's alive?"

His jaw tightens, then he nods once. "I believe we have a newish Royal Guard among our number. There are at least a dozen of that sort in our cells, however. I have no way of knowing which one you might mean."

"They're alive? All of them?"

"As far as I know, yes."

Thorne is alive. I know he is. I haven't felt a shot of pain that tells me he's being tortured, or any wretched premonition since I left the palace. His heart still throbs in my chest alongside mine.

Still, something deep inside me is twisting with fear that I'll never see him again.

I push the emotion away, telling myself I'm being irrational.

I.

Need.

Him.

I want the happiness that has been denied us both for all our lives. I don't want to fight for this land—not if this land continues to refuse to allow me to be with the man I love.

I'm about to command Terrence to take me to the prison cells, but Rivenna grabs my arm, squeezing a quiet warning, and says, "Once you're inside, you're on your own."

"You're not coming with me?"

"I'll be around, but my home is outside this place. Make good on your promise. Help the Tethered to free Kravan, and I am your servant for life."

"I don't want servants," I tell her. "I don't want to lead. I just want my people to live the lives they deserve. I want the bombings to end. The senseless death. The conflict. I want the truth to come out."

"An idealist," Terrence snickers.

"A queen," Rivenna retorts. "A queen among a bunch of fucking insects."

"We'll see about that." He raises his chin and says, "It's time we left you, Rivenna."

"Fine. Just give me thirty more seconds."

With a terse nod, he says, "I'll be waiting in the corridor."

When he's marched off with a series of irritated-sounding footfalls, Rivenna takes my arm and pulls me close. "Good luck finding your man," she says softly. "Remember everything I've told you. And look—I have a friend inside the Citadel. Her name is Joy. She'll be on the lookout for you. She could help you on the inside."

"The inside," I chuckle. "You make it sound like a prison."

"It might be in the end if you're not careful. Kith will keep an eye on you, just like he promised. I can't stress this enough—keep your words to a minimum and don't trust anyone."

"I trust Thorne," I tell her.

"I'm glad. Just...be wary. Not all tethered mates are as locked in as they seem. There are rumors..."

"About what?"

"Are you coming?" Terrence calls out from the doorway, impatience raising the pitch of his voice.

"It doesn't matter," Rivenna says with a shake of her head. "Just go. Be with your guy—and enjoy every minute."

I nod once, then throw my arms around her neck and squeeze. Then, with one final pat to Berengar's head, I join Terrence in the passageway.

I'm alone now with this man, and for some reason, that makes me horribly uncomfortable.

Maude, I whisper in my mind. *Are you there?*

I can *feel* her inside me, trying to respond. But it's like she's struggling—scrambled and confused.

"Maude," I whisper out loud.

"Is everything all right?" Terrence asks.

"Fine," I reply, giving him a dubious side-eye.

I don't know what it is about him that I don't like,

exactly. I tell myself not to judge him for being a Normal. It's not his fault, after all.

But it's not just that. He feels...secretive. Arrogant. Something about him tells me he thinks he's superior to me.

I remind myself that Normals are raised to look down on our kind, just as we're raised to serve them. I can't blame him for being brainwashed any more than I can blame thousands of Tethered for eating up all the lies we're fed.

"If you're wondering why your Maude unit is scrambled," Terrence says, leading me through a door into yet another dark corridor, "it's that she probably is. They usually recalibrate when they're in the Capitol. There are a lot of remote signals being thrown around the city, and they tend to confuse the Maudes. Don't worry—she'll settle in soon enough."

I hope he's right, if only so that I feel the comfort of Maude's presence again. But of all the people I've encountered so far, this man seems the least like he gives a shit about my comfort.

"I should warn you," Terrence says, guiding me down the narrow passage lit only by torchlight, "No Royal Guard has ever been allowed to leave the Citadel once captured."

"So I've been told. But Thorne will."

"You say that with confidence."

"Because I am confident. I will fight for him."

He snickers, stops, and looks me up and down again. "Forgive me, but you don't look like much of a fighter. You're a marked Green—a Harmless."

"My father is the Shadow. He has influence. He'll help me."

Terrence raises his eyebrows then keeps walking, and I

match his pace. "If the Magister allows a Royal Guard to go free, he'll look weak."

I shrug. *Then I suppose it's time for the Magister to look weak.*

We haven't walked for more than two minutes before we come to another set of doors where a lone woman is standing guard. She's tall—probably close to six feet, with sandy-brown hair and green eyes, and she's wearing a khaki-colored tank top and trousers to match. Her arms are lean and muscled, and on her left shoulder is the Magister's brand, outlined starkly pink against olive skin.

"I'm bringing a Tethered through for the Magister and the Shadow," Terrence tells her, and the woman shakes her head.

"They're occupied at the moment," she says. "The Magister asked me to send you to see them in the council chamber, Terrence. I've been asked to take *her* to see the prisoner."

"Prisoner?" he asks, looking baffled. "That doesn't make any sense. My instructions were clear."

"Your instructions are outdated, I'm afraid. I'm to take her to see the Royal Guard. The one named Thorne. Now go —or I'll tell the Magister you defied his orders."

Terrence disappears with haste that would make a Velor proud, and I'm left with a thousand questions and a heart filled with hope.

CHAPTER FOURTEEN

My stomach twists with combined excitement and trepidation.

I'm going to see Thorne.

I may even be allowed to touch him.

Still, I shouldn't expect too much. He's a prisoner, locked away in a cell. It's not like I'll be able to tear his clothes off and continue what we started in the Nether.

"Well, then," the tall woman says. With Terrence gone, her tone has shifted to a friendlier, gentler one. "I'll take you to him now that we're free of that walking testicle. Don't worry—if you're lucky, you'll never have to see him again."

I muster a smile and thank her.

"My name is Joy," the woman tells me as we walk, but I interrupt when her eyes meet mine and her unusual power makes its way into my mind.

"Rivenna told me I might meet up with you. I didn't know you were a..."

"Morph," she replies. "They told me you shared your father's gift. Come on, let's get you to your mate."

I accompany her, almost too stunned to speak.

I heard of her kind in the Tower years ago—but Morphs, otherwise known as shape-shifters, were spoken about like something out of an ancient tale. Someone who can alter their appearance to look like any other person in the world. They're incredibly rare, and their gifts are considered extremely dangerous, given the Morph's ability to spy on unsuspecting people.

"I suppose you can guess how I escaped the Tower," Joy says. "And that I made sure to get out before they learned what I was."

"They would have killed you," I agree. "It's so rare for anyone to get out. How did you do it?"

"I figured out my gift before Placement Day. No one had assessed me yet, but I knew they'd label me a Crimson, or worse. I disguised myself as the warden during dinner one evening and walked straight out of that place, never to return."

When we reach a locked security door, she stops and turns my way, peering down at me. "I'm sure Rivenna's already told you that around here, Royal Guard aren't popular. But I have a soft spot for them. I know what it is to be indoctrinated in the Tower. I know they don't have agency—not even the ones who think they're *willingly* devoting themselves to the royal family. I will do whatever I can to help you and Thorne while you're here, so don't hesitate to ask."

"Thank you," I reply, more grateful than I can possibly say. I want to ask her everything. How long has Thorne been in his cell? How did he get here? Was he injured? What happened between the time he left the palace and the time he arrived here?

When we've made our way through a second door, the questions in my mind suddenly cease.

Ahead of us, at the far end of a large chamber, is a row of what look like Whiterooms—the cells where my cohort and I once lived inside the Tower. Only, the wall facing us is made of glass, so I can see inside each cell as if I'm staring at animals in a zoo.

Two are occupied by solitary women, slouching or lying on cots. In three others are men of various sizes.

On each prisoner's upper arm, I can see something metallic and vicious-looking, attached tightly around their sleeve.

"Those are called cilices," Joy tells me under her breath. "They slowly release a toxin into the bloodstream that cuts off a Tethered's ability to use their powers. They're considered necessary, given that each person in these cells is a Crimson Elite or higher. But if you ask me...well, they're not exactly humane."

When I spot Thorne in a cell at the end of the row, his name bursts from my throat.

He's lying on his cot, knees bent, a cilice tightly bound to his arm. His face is pale, hair drenched with sweat.

When he hears me, he turns his foggy eyes my way and grimaces, pulling himself up to his feet.

Without waiting, I leap over to the glass wall, pressing my palm to its surface. Thorne steps over and does the same from the other side.

His faint voice emerges through a series of small holes in the glass.

"I'm so fucking glad to see you," he says roughly. His eyes move to Joy, who has joined me. He winces, then shifts his gaze back to me. His body lists and leans against the glass like he's on the verge of collapse. "I'm not sure you should have come, though."

"I'm meant to be wherever you are, Thorne." My eyes search the glass for an entrance—a door or mechanism to let me inside.

"I want to see him," I tell Joy. "I need to."

"You're seeing him right now."

The words don't come from Joy.

The voice, deeply resonant, is one I don't know. And yet, it feels oddly familiar.

I twist around to see a man making his way toward us from the far door. He looks like he's forty-five or so years old. His hair is dark brown, with a few streaks of gray around his temples. His eyes are intense as they lock on mine, and I watch with a shock of familiarity as a smile slips over his lips.

The Shadow.

My father.

I first saw him in my mind's eye, in the vault where the Storian gifted me her memories.

I know in my heart that I should run to him and bury my face in his chest, just as any daughter would do when she hasn't seen her father in years.

Only—I've never *met* my father. I have no bond with him. And right now, he's keeping me from embracing the man I love.

"I need to go to him," I say. "He's not well. I can heal him."

"He's fine. It's the cilice that's weighing him down—

that's all. It strips his power and depletes his energy. It's the same for everyone who wears one."

"Why take away his power? He's not going to hurt anyone!"

The Shadow clicks his tongue against his teeth, shaking his head. "He's a Royal Guard. He works for the wrong side."

"You know as well as I do that Tethered have no choice."

A chuckle escapes from the corner of his mouth. "There is always a choice. Joy here made hers when she escaped the Tower—and so did I. Your Thorne willingly served the Verdans, and then the king. He is not to be trusted."

"You're wrong. He's the most honorable person I've ever met." I turn to Thorne again, both my palms pressed to the transparent wall between us. He slips downward until he hits the floor, his head leaning against the glass.

"Go, Shara," he mutters. "I'm fine. Go—do what you need to."

"No. I'm not leaving you."

Thorne's eyes open again and focus on mine for a moment. The swirl of color is gone, and all I see are two hazel irises, intense but devoid of their usual energy. It's the cilice—I know it. But from this side of the glass, I can do nothing to change his plight.

Turning back to the man called the Shadow—a man whose actual name I don't even know—I say, "What do you want from me? I'll do it if you let him out. If he hurts anyone, you can kill me. I promise you that."

He laughs. "Kith sent word that you're honorable, like your friend here. He said you helped Rivenna and killed a Poisoner in the process. You're a benevolent tornado, Daughter."

Daughter.

The word is jarring, coming from this stranger who seems so cold, so distant.

But the expression in his eyes warms as he looks at me. "Of course your Thorne is free to leave his cell," he says. "I'm not the monster others claim I am. I've already struck up a deal with the Magister. I want to make my way into your good books, after all. Thorne has a gift—and we hope he'll share it with us."

"Let him out, and I'm sure he will."

The Shadow nods toward Joy, who morphs into a balding man with brown eyes. Instantly, I recognize Terrence, and the sight disconcerts me more than I'd like to admit.

Joy steps to a transparent screen to the right of Thorne's cell, which scans her features before opening the wall wide enough for me to dart inside.

I leap in and crouch at Thorne's side, tearing at the cilice on his arm.

The Shadow says, "It won't open without the touch of a high-ranking member of the Magister's council." He steps over and reaches down to peel it from Thorne's arm.

I pass my hand over a series of deep, angry wounds, and feel the toxins leech from his bloodstream. Instantly, Thorne's eyes begin to twist with color again.

When he rises to his feet, he pulls me to him, holding me so tightly that I can feel the hard drumbeat of his heart through my chest.

"I wish you hadn't had to come the way you did," he whispers, "but I love you so much for it."

With my voice cracking at the edges, I say, "I would have

walked a thousand miles over broken glass in bare feet to get here. Oh, wait—that's basically what I did."

"Pfft. Easy to say when you're a Healer."

I pull back to see the light has returned to his eyes—as has the humor.

I take his face in my hands, his rough stubble the most beautiful thing I've ever touched.

"Now," the Shadow interrupts, clasping his hands together. "Let's head somewhere to chat, shall we?"

"Could we get cleaned up first? Maybe a change of clothes?"

He looks Thorne and me up and down. "Soon," he says. "I'd like to outline what I need from you both first—if you don't mind. You may be my kin, Shara, but I need you to agree to certain terms before I can set you both free."

Free.

The word feels like a spark igniting somewhere inside me. A profound jolt of the purest joy I've ever felt.

I'm not ready to trust this man—not yet. But he did release Thorne from the cilice and the cell. He's put his faith in us both.

I suppose I should return the favor.

Thorne wraps an arm around me. "It's all right," he says, reading my nervous energy. "Your father hasn't been cruel to me, Shara. I could have done without the cilice, I'll admit. That thing hurt like a bitch. Still—none of it is your father's fault."

I'm not sure whether he means it or is just saying it to get into the Shadow's good graces, but when I pull my eyes to Thorne's and see his expression, all I detect is kindness mixed with sincerity.

"You really mean it?" I ask my father, looking to Joy to see if she issues me any warning signs. "We're free?"

Without Maude's constant nagging, I feel like a fawn just learning to walk—as if my ability to make judgments or decisions for myself has been severely hobbled.

Which, I remind myself, is pretty pathetic.

"Free, yes," the Shadow replies, turning to lead us back down the corridor. "But free is a relative term around here. I will do my utmost to keep you both in or near the Citadel at all times—and when you venture out, I will insist that you remain close. Not out of a need for control," he adds, turning to smile at me over his shoulder. "Only out of a desire to protect you. I've lost one daughter to the cruel hand of fate. I have no intention of losing another."

So, it's true. My sister—the sibling I've never met—really is dead.

As if reading my mind, Thorne pulls me closer, pressing a kiss to my crown. My emotions are far too intense at the moment to bring myself to ask about Soleia, but I make a mental note to do so when I'm feeling less vulnerable.

When we reach the small prison's outer doors, my father turns to Joy. "Thank you for escorting my daughter," he says. "Please see to it that her suite is prepared, with fresh sheets, towels, and anything else they may need."

"Of course," Joy says, giving me a last, unreadable smile. "Enjoy your freedom."

In her eyes, I'm convinced I read the words, "While it lasts."

CHAPTER FIFTEEN

AFTER A FEW MINUTES, we find ourselves standing in a vast, circular chamber. Its ceiling is vaulted high overhead, and at its center is a large, round table surrounded by leather-upholstered chairs.

This, I know from the Storian's memories, is the council chamber where Kravan's last president used to meet with her administration. It's the very room where she stood when Quinton and his fighters stormed the Citadel and killed her before Quinton declared himself king.

The walls are littered with scorch marks and other signs of the battle that took President Brant down. Here and there, large, threatening cracks run from floor to ceiling as if some enormous fist once slammed itself into the walls.

I witnessed some of the combat in my mind's eye, and it was horrific. I saw the aftermath...and it was worse. No one has made any effort to hide the battle scars left behind. The council chamber seems to wear its wounds like trophies—a reminder of what the traitors of the past were capable of.

Thorne's arm is hooked around my waist, my body held

close to his, as if we both need our tether to strengthen itself once again. But he doesn't say a word as we take in the enormity of the room. His eyes simply bounce from the wall to the ceiling, then down to the floor.

"This room has seen a great deal of history," my father says solemnly. "But we don't speak of such things in Kravan...do we?"

My eyes narrow. I'm not going to dignify that question with a response. I'm not sure what my father knows about Kravan's last president or that she shared a name with the Magister.

All I want is to protect Thorne and me. To go unnoticed as long as possible.

Where are you, Maude? I ask silently. *I need you to keep me in check, or I'm bound to say something stupid.*

If that's not enough to get her to come back at me with an insult, nothing is.

But she remains silent.

"What do you want from us, exactly?" I ask the Shadow. "Because I suspect you're hoping for more than a sentimental father-daughter reunion."

"True." He eyes me with curiosity before adding, "My informant told me you had originally been assigned to work for Lady Verdan—but that you were eventually engaged to the prince. I'm assuming this is correct."

"I..."

My eyes flick to Thorne's, and I can see in his face the same thought I'm having right now.

"Who, exactly, is your informant?" Thorne asks. It's a bold question—but I'll admit I'm curious, too.

"That's no concern of yours," the Shadow retorts. "With

all the respect owed to you as my daughter's mate—you're on thin ice as it is. Do you have any idea how many Royal Guard are ever let out of their cells?"

When Thorne's jaw tightens, the Shadow answers for him.

"None. Zero. You are the first—and likely the last. And I am aware that I'm taking a risk by setting you loose on the world."

"Apologies," Thorne says with a quick, curt bow of his head. It's unlike him to be so reverent, but I know without asking that he's putting on a bit of a show for both our sakes.

I can see in the strain of his jaw that it pains him not to tell my father to go fuck himself right now.

"I didn't mean to offend," Thorne adds. "And you're right—you have no reason to trust us. Not yet, at least."

He's right. It's no wonder my father looks at us with skepticism—no wonder he locked Thorne away.

Everything I've done since leaving the Tower has been questionable, at best.

To my father, we must both look guilty as sin.

"I was never actually engaged to Tallin," I blurt out, my heart aching to leave this place so I can spend time alone with Thorne. I don't know what I need to say to earn that privilege, but whatever it takes, I'll do it. "I was only posing as Tallin's fiancée. They wanted me in the palace for my Hunter skills—the skills I inherited from you. I was to report to the prince and the king whenever I identified Tethered concealing themselves among the Nobility."

"Well," my father says with a sly smile. "It seems you left a trail of mayhem in your wake. I hear the palace has been in disarray these last few days."

"I..." My eyes shift to Thorne, then back again. "Yes. There was a fight. The prince was angry with the king. There were...other issues at play, too."

Like the fact that the king has two illegitimate sons who despise each other.

"I suppose you believe, like me, the realm would be better off if it weren't ruled by either King Tomas or his idiot son."

As I watch, his eyes begin swirling with color again, and I nod. "Of course I do," I say. "The realm should never have been ruled by any sovereign. It should be the people who select their leaders. Tethered and Normals—Potentials, I mean—but not Nobles. The hierarchy that exists now should never have been set in place."

"Or perhaps Kravan has simply been ruled by the wrong people." My father looks at Thorne. "On that topic, young man, I have a request to make of you."

"Whatever you need, I'll try my best to oblige." He takes my hand and adds, "As long as you let Shara and me be together."

"And if I should say no?"

Thorne's eyes darken when he says, "Then I'll have no choice but to kill you."

My father stares at him with the coldest expression I've ever seen...then lets out a deep laugh and claps Thorne on the shoulder.

"For that, you *definitely* have my respect, young man," he says. "You've uttered the words I never had the courage to speak when I fell for Shara's mother—when we were torn apart by an unforgiving, bigoted society. Well, then, I promise you this: if I ever take Shara from you, you have my permission to kill me on the spot."

"Good," Thorne says, his reverent tone entirely gone by now. "So, what is it that you want from me?"

"I've heard you're adept at crafting electronic devices that channel Tethered powers. Wrist bracers of some sort. Is it true?"

Again, I want to ask how he knows so much about us. But then, I suppose Thorne's talent is common knowledge. I became aware of his gifts long ago, on the day I watched him put my cohort through our paces in the Tower.

"Yes. It's true," Thorne replies with a hint of a smile.

"Then you will tell the Magister's people what materials you need in order to craft them. You will be given everything you require. But for now, I'd like to speak to my daughter alone."

When the Shadow sees the look on my face, he adds, "Yes, yes. I know how upsetting it is for you to be separated from him. But it's only for a little while. Thorne will go get settled in, and you and I can get to know one another a little."

He steps over to the wall and presses his hand to a rounded piece of stone that's darker than those around it.

After a matter of seconds, the door at the far end of the chamber opens, and Kith steps inside. For reasons I can't explain, I blush to see him, as if he is nothing more than a dream I once had.

His eyes meet mine, and he offers up a warm smile. "Hello, Shara," he says before stepping closer and nodding to Thorne. "Good to see you again."

"Again?" I stammer. "Wait—do you mean...you two have actually spoken? I thought—"

I was under the impression that Kith had only seen Thorne from a distance. But when I think back, he never said as much.

Thorne strides over to Kith, extending his hand. "And you," he says. "I can't thank you enough for what you did for me."

"Well, I'm just sorry you had to be incarcerated."

"It's nothing I'm not used to," Thorne says with a friendly grin.

"What the hell?" I ask, laughing. "What's going on here? Why are you two acting like old buddies?"

"When I first landed the Flyer in the Capitol," Thorne says, "I was still disoriented as I climbed out. I was ambushed—grabbed by some men in gray masks. I was still foggy-minded and hadn't regained my strength, and they dragged me somewhere and forced me to my knees."

My chest tightens as I realize how accurate my vision turned out to be. The Starless had taken Thorne, after all.

"What happened?" I shift my gaze from Thorne to Kith and back again.

"One of them held a knife to my throat and told me he would kill me unless I agreed to serve their leader." He nods to Kith and says, "Our friend here—he found me and got me out of there. Those men were going to kill me. I could *feel* their viciousness. I suspect they had no intention of bringing me to any leader."

His tale fills me with fear and gratitude at once. I turn to Kith with a relieved smile on my lips. If ever I had any doubt about his character, it melts away now.

"Why didn't you tell me about this?" I ask him.

Kith shrugs. "I only wanted you to know he was safe. That was all that mattered. It was never about me."

I step over and throw my arms around him, hugging him tight. "You don't understand. I had waking nightmares about that moment in time—I *saw* it. I was so afraid they would kill him—and *you* stopped it."

Kith hugs me back, laughing, and when I pull away, he bows his head. "I would do it all over again, just to see the smile on your face."

Thorne pulls me possessively close, and I slip my arm around him. "Thank you from both of us," he says, kissing the top of my head. "The cells here aren't exactly luxurious, but they're a hell of a lot better than death."

"On that note," my father says, clapping his hands together so the sound echoes off the chamber's rounded stone walls, "Kith—please escort Thorne to his destination. My daughter and I need to have a talk."

CHAPTER

SIXTEEN

"Shara." The Shadow says my name gently, and for the briefest moment, he *feels* like a parent.

This—here and now—is what I imagined it would be like to have a father. A warm, comforting blanket, protective and enveloping. His eyes are filled with an unmistakable affection, and for the first time in my life, I feel a freedom I've only ever imagined.

Whatever his past sins, I have a family now.

No one can take that from me.

"It's surreal to meet you after all this time," he says in that same smooth, soft voice. "And I'm so glad you're here at long last."

"Yes," I reply. "It's...wow. Strange."

Surreal doesn't begin to express what I'm feeling just now.

I've heard so many conflicting reports about this man—some frightening, others positive. I understand the fear people have of him now. There's no question that he exudes power as a lion might, quietly stalking through his territory with wary eyes.

But I am his to protect now. I'm under his roof—and whoever the Magister is, however powerful, something tells me there's a reason others think my father is the one in charge.

"I know you must be eager to spend time with Thorne," he says, smiling, "and you will, of course. I have no intention of keeping you apart more than is necessary—and I've already convinced the Magister of the same."

"Thank you. I appreciate it more than I can say."

My father seats himself in one of the leather chairs, steeples his fingers under his chin, and purses his lips. "Your Thorne has a rare gift," he says. "He's a Courser, as I'm sure you know."

"Courser," I repeat. "Yes. He can manipulate electronic impulses and that sort of thing."

He nods. "He's a Gilded Elite, as, apparently, are you. It's no wonder you two find one another irresistible."

At that, my cheeks flush with embarrassment, though I'm not sure why.

"But his gift...the ability to focus power as he does." He shakes his head and lets out a low whistle. "He's more than a mere Courser. Did you know that he has the power to control people, just as a Mind-bender would?"

I shake my head, stunned. "How would he do that?"

My father smiles, excitement chiseled into his expression. "Our brains convey messages to our bodies via a series of electrical impulses—like small bursts of lightning. We're wired, quite literally—and those impulses convey messages to our limbs, our organs—every inch of us. Given his power, your Thorne has the potential to take control of entire armies of Normals, as you call them—or Tethered alike. He's a marvel."

"He wouldn't do that," I say defensively. "He's not a threat—he's not like..."

Like Ellion Graystone.

"Oh—I wasn't implying that he would be reckless. Only that his strength is something I've seen in few Tethered. I knew the moment I laid eyes on him that he would prove an incredible asset."

I smile uncomfortably, trying to interpret my father's words in a positive light.

"But it's not Thorne's potential to bend minds that enticed the Magister. Over the next few weeks, Thorne will instruct our army and teach them to use the wrist pieces. We'll build them here, with materials sourced from the king's fallen drones and other metals. The fabrication isn't nearly so important as the power Thorne imbues them with."

"So, when you say Thorne and I will be apart at times..." I begin, bracing myself for bad news.

He drops his hands into his lap and grins. "I mean he'll teach classes, yes. Fight training. You won't be participating, naturally."

"Well, I'm not much of a fighter," I confess. "I never have been."

"Not to mention that you're far too important to risk. I won't let you on the front lines. Especially not after all you've been through."

My head cocks to the side, and I stare at him, trying to

discern his meaning. "How much do you really know about what I did in the Isles?"

"Enough," he says. "I know, for instance, that you met your mother."

My eyes widen. "How could you possibly have discovered all that?"

"Like I said, I have an informant—rather, a spy. A Tethered who is able to move in shadow. Really, they gave me the wrong moniker. He should have it. He's a Stealther who can render himself virtually invisible—and he's been back and forth to the palace more times than I can count."

"If you had a Stealther heading to and from the palace," I muse, "Why didn't he or she—"

"Kill the king?" My father rises from his seat and paces the chamber slowly.

"Well...yes."

"It's a fine question, and one I've asked myself often. The simple answer is that the Magister didn't want that to happen. He didn't want Kravan's new era to start with a murder. He felt the people would push back on it—as well they should. Better to try the king in a court of law and to determine whether he is guilty of the plethora of sins he's committed over time. So, in answer to your question—our spy was gathering evidence, and I can tell you, there was a great deal to be had."

"Like what?"

"Murder. Abuse of Tethered servants. Forcing Tethered to fight to the death for the amusement of Nobles—but you already knew about all that, didn't you?"

"You know I was at the Prince's Ball, then," I say.

"I know that's where you met Tallin. I'm sorry you were subjected to that feral jackass for so long."

Hearing the words feral jackass from his lips in reference to Tallin makes me like my father all the more, and I crack a smile.

"What is your name?" I ask, my voice tremulous. "I want to know."

"My name is Laurence," he replies. "No one calls me that, of course. I was the Hunter for so many years, and now... well."

Recalling what Rivenna told me, I add, "No surname?"

My father smiles. "I had one once, which means you did, too. But I've gone without for so long that I'm beginning to wonder if you and I should simply choose our own one day."

My mind flares to life. "Really?"

"I don't see why not. Whatever my old name was, I have no attachment to it. Perhaps we should simply get to know one another, then select a name that feels right to us both. In the meantime, tell me." His eyes brighten when he asks, "How is dear Evangeline?"

With a sigh, I say, "I'm afraid she's in danger. The Prefect's wife isn't fond of her, and she's not the sort of person who hesitates to kill Tethered if they displease her. I'm hoping she—my mother—has found a new position by now."

I don't tell him the position I'm—ironically—hoping for is in the Verdan household, alongside Lady Verdan's step-daughters, Devorah and Pippa. As much as I've always despised Devorah, she's not a monster—which means she'd be infinitely preferable to the Prefect's wife.

His expression and voice are unreadable when he says,

"Your mother is a kind woman. She doesn't deserve to be killed by Noble scum."

"Don't you have a way to bring her here? To help her escape?" I cast my gaze around, as if the answer is lurking in our immediate vicinity.

"Your mother had a chance years ago to get away, and she chose not to," he replies. "It's complicated between us, Shara. I don't know how much she told you about our relationship. We loved one another—we thought that was enough. But, as it turned out, I was meant to be with someone else entirely."

I balk at his words. "You cheated on her?"

My father looks taken aback. "No. We simply parted ways when I brought your sister to the Capitol years ago. I gave your mother the opportunity to come with us—to be with us. But she seemed to understand that we were not meant to be."

"My sister," I murmur, my worries about my mother overtaken by sadness.

The Shadow's expression turns cold as ice, a shield covering his emotions, before he looks away. "It seems you know already that I lost Soleia," he says quietly.

I swallow down a sound that wants to erupt from my chest, mourning the girl I never knew. "Rivenna told me there was an explosion. A bombing."

My father inhales deeply, then says, "The bomb hit the front of the house, where her bedroom was. We had an idyllic little cottage-style home on a residential street. They told me it was an old enemy of mine who ordered the strike—one you may know. A woman called Lady Graystone."

My jaw drops open.

If I didn't hate the Graystones enough already, my loathing has just increased a hundred times.

"I had tormented her a few years earlier," he continues. "She was no fan of mine. I've heard she lost an arm because of me, and I can only wish she'd lost far more."

He lets out a slow breath, then adds, "But Soleia did not die in the blast."

My eyes go wide, my heart pounding with a sudden ecstatic beat. "What?"

"What I'm about to tell you cannot leave this room. Do you understand me? Do not tell Thorne. Do not tell even your most trusted ally. All of Kravan believes my youngest died that night, because that's what I needed them to believe at the time. The lie lives on for reasons I can't explain now."

I nod, swallowing. "I promise, I'll keep it to myself."

He scrutinizes me for a moment, then says, "I sent her away, all those years ago. That very night, in fact, when we were expected to be sleeping in our beds. I had already planned it—it was mere luck, I suppose, that helped us along."

"Where is she?" I hate the question, because the only place she could be in Kravan that's not the Capitol is the Isles—which would mean she's living with some Noble family or other.

"I sent her away on a ship—one of the few that come to our shores these days. It was too late to save you from the Tower, but I knew, with Lady Graystone seeking revenge and with the state of Kravan as it was, that I could not raise a child safely. There were other factors at play—ones that I will explain someday. But not now."

"Do you know where she is? Does she stay in contact?"

He shakes his head. "I didn't want to know where the ship was headed. It would have put her in danger—put a target on her back. When people say I lost her, they aren't wrong. I really did break when she left. But not for the reasons everyone thinks."

"I understand," I tell him, my heart sinking. "Still, I wish I could have known her."

"She was a beautiful, sweet girl with the reddest hair you've ever seen," he replies with a wistful tilt of his head, as though he's straining to remember her. "She was bright, like the sun—and lovely, just like you. I called her Sol, for short. She was a wonder. I had managed to keep her hidden from our enemies for so long—or so I thought. But if you really wish to know who was at fault, look no further than the king and the prince. They're the ones who have been wreaking havoc on this city for years—and who ensure no one in the Capitol can live in peace. But my hope, Shara, is to change that."

I nod, forcing away the tears that want to fall for someone I've never met—someone I didn't even know existed until very recently. The faceless sister who's nothing more than a shadow in my mind—a specter who may never fully manifest.

I don't know yet whether I can trust this man. I don't know if he's an ally or something else entirely. But there's no question that our mutual pain brings us closer together. And there's no denying the bond between two people who have lost something they'll never get back.

I want more than ever to get to Thorne and bury myself in his chest, to feel his lips on mine again. I want to revel in our newfound freedom.

But I take in a deep breath and say, "You seem to know everything about me—but I'm not sure if you're aware I snuck into the vault at Lord Perrin's estate. I spoke to the Storian."

My father's expression shifts only slightly, then he nods. "The Storian. Really." He lets out a quiet chuckle, then adds, "You're full of surprises, my dear. Tell me everything."

I fill him in on what I saw in the vault. I tell him of the days when the streets were combat zones, when so many innocent civilians were killed. The days when broad channels were dug around the Capitol and the Isles created, then claimed by the Nobility.

I explain how Tethered and Normals alike were locked inside the Tower, isolated from one another and their children, then taught the rules that dictate that Nobles are in charge and Tethered serve them—and that emotional attachment is a crime for our kind.

"Kravan was not meant to have a king," I say at last. "Quinton—whoever he was—established the throne, set himself upon it, then stole away knowledge from generations. He robbed us of our past and replaced it with a fiction he had crafted."

"I see," my father replies after a long silence. "Kravan has long been on the wrong path. But you don't need to concern yourself with its future."

"Of course I do! The king—"

I force myself to stop talking. Maude would normally have shut me up half an hour ago, but she's still missing in action, and it's up to me to restrain myself.

"What about the king?" my father asks.

"He...he needs to be taken out. But even if he is, Tallin is a terrible man and would be a cruel leader."

"Worse than Tomas?"

"Not worse," I admit. "But they're both sadistic."

"We won't have to concern ourselves with the royal family much longer. I promise you that." My father rubs his palms together. "For now, though, perhaps you'd like to shower and eat something. You've had a harrowing experience, both you and Thorne. I want to see you well taken care of. After all, you're my heir, Shara."

I'm about to point out how strange his choice of words is when the door at the chamber's far end opens and Kith returns. My heart sinks a little when I see that he's alone.

He approaches, his eyes fixed on mine, and whispers something into my father's ear.

"Very good. Thank you, Kith," the Shadow says. Turning back to me, he presses his hand to something under his desk and adds, "It seems Kith and I need to meet with the Magister, who is currently speaking with Thorne."

"But I thought Thorne was in our suite?"

"He will be, soon enough. The Magister wants to ensure that he's amenable to our plans. I'll have him sent to you the moment we're finished. In the meantime, Joy will escort you to your suite, and you can get some rest and reunite with your...friend."

I get the distinct impression that it pains him to say *tethered mate.*

Kith throws me an enigmatic look when Joy slips into the room, smiles at me, and says, "Come on, Shara. I'll show you to your new home."

CHAPTER SEVENTEEN

"Don't worry," Joy says, noting my dour expression as we stride toward what I can only assume is the residential wing of the Citadel. "The Magister isn't much for talking, which means Thorne will be free soon."

Rivenna told me the same. Still, all I've wanted since the moment I fled the palace is to find myself in Thorne's arms again, and it seems that even now, when I'm so damned close, my hopes are being dashed at every turn.

"Tell me about your powers." Joy's voice is gentle as she touches my arm, guiding me into a right turn down a long, broad hallway. Flickering sconces line the walls, disorienting in their contrasting levels of brightness. The concrete ceiling drips here and there, and the floor is cracked in places, making for a slightly depressing walk. "I've heard you're a Gilded Elite. What can you do?"

I cast her a sidelong glance, wondering why she's so curious.

Rivenna did warn me to trust no one, I think. But Joy looks so enthusiastic and warm that I can't help but tell myself there's no harm in sharing.

I miss you, Maude, I think. *I've always relied on you to be my survival instinct and tell me who I should and shouldn't trust. Help me out here.*

Nothing. No response. Not even a quiver in my arm.

With a sigh, I say, "I'm a Healer and a Hunter. And I have this ability to absorb other people's powers temporarily."

"Like a Blade?"

I grimace. "Not exactly. I need their blood to do it."

"Oh. So you're a literal power vampire."

"Pretty much, yeah."

"There's an official term for it, you know," Joy tells me, stopping in front of a green door with the number twelve scrawled on its surface. "You're a Sapper."

"Sapper? I've never heard that word."

"That's because your power is rare. You sap gifts from others—share their strength instead of stealing it. From what I hear, it can develop into something extraordinary."

"It's really not that impressive. It's just a temporary thing. A little blood on my finger, and I can take on any power—but only briefly."

"Your skin is a barrier. If you want to absorb the powers for longer, there are other ways." She winks at me, as if she knows something I don't.

Involuntarily, I let out a long, frustrated breath. "Honestly, I would love never to have to use any powers again. I don't want to have to heal anyone, hurt anyone, take anyone's gifts. None of it. All I want is to live quietly, unnoticed by the world."

Joy lets out a laugh that proves contagious and brings an instant smile to my lips.

"What?" I ask with a chuckle.

"You—the daughter of the Shadow—hoping to go unnoticed. I'm afraid that's not going to be possible. That's not your fate."

"Why not? It's the Magister who will be in charge of Kravan, isn't it? There's no reason anyone ever needs to hear from me. Thorne and I can get a small house in the Capitol. We can live as the free people we've always wanted to be."

When she doesn't respond, I narrow my eyes at her. "Why do I feel like there's something you're not telling me?"

"My mother was a professional Seer once, long ago—a sort of fortune teller in the Capitol."

Her words bring a memory to the forefront of my mind. Kith, telling me it was a fortune teller who had shown him the future, too.

"There are quite a few Seers," Joy adds as if deliberately answering my tacit question. "Normals love to visit them in hopes of learning the world will change in their favor. My mother often lied to them. Told them whatever they wanted to hear, so long as they paid up. She knew they didn't want the truth. They didn't want to know their lives might not improve, let alone last more than a few years. But there are things she told me in confidence about this realm that stuck with me—things I've never told anyone. Some of them filled me with quiet hope—but I never dared let myself feel that hope fully until I laid eyes on you."

"Me?" I gawk at her, puzzled. "Are you telling me you've seen me in the future?"

There was something invasive about the vision Kith

showed me in the tunnel...but the thought that still more people have encountered me in their visions is even more disconcerting.

"I'm telling you that your fate is very much tied to all our futures," Joy says. "It was fate that brought you to the Capitol."

I shake my head, smiling through my unease. "No. It was Thorne who brought me here."

Joy lets out a sad-sounding breath, then says, "All things are bound together by one fate. It's up to us to choose what to do with it—but there is no escaping it once we're on the chosen path."

Her words are so final. So intense.

They almost frighten me—despite the fact that I don't believe them for a moment.

"You can tell me what the Fortune Teller predicted," I say. "I could use some good news."

"I can't." She shakes her head. "The knowledge a Seer imparts becomes a sworn secret—one that cannot be shared, as it could affect the choices you make going forward."

I wonder what she'd think if she knew Kith had shown me a Seer's vision of us standing in that beautiful green place together. Perhaps *he* broke some cardinal rule by revealing a future he'd seen with a borrowed power.

I only wish I'd seen Thorne's face somewhere in that vision.

I sigh. "At least tell me this: Will the Magister be successful in taking power?"

Joy raises her chin, looks me in the eye, and says, "The right person will be in charge one day soon. That's all I can say—that's all I *will* say, except that you, Shara, need to listen to your heart. It knows what's best for this realm—and I have faith in you."

She keys in a code on a panel next to the green door, and after the lock clicks, she pushes it open. "Four-Three-Four-Seven," she tells me as I follow her inside. "This is you."

The first of the suite's rooms is surprisingly large. A vast queen-sized bed with gray linens sits at its center, flanked by two small dressers. On the far wall is a door that apparently leads into a bathroom.

The room is dark but clean, and though I miss having a window that peers out onto the palace's exquisite gardens, I remind myself that the cost of such a view was the pretense of being engaged to a despicable man.

"At least I don't have to sell my soul to live here," I tell myself, wondering whether Thorne and I will ever be able to live together above ground.

"You'll find everything you need in various drawers and closets," Joy tells me. "There are fresh towels for you in the bathroom."

At that, my chest throbs. To think Thorne will be here soon, with me—and we'll live together in this place, without draconian rulers punishing us for loving each other.

Joy clasps her hands together and throws me a knowing look. "If there's anything else you need..."

I hesitate only for a second before replying, "There is one thing. Do you know what to do about a Maude unit that's gone unresponsive?"

"Hmm." She steps closer and glances down at my left forearm. "I suggest you get a reboot, if it's causing you problems."

The idea seems innocent enough—except for the way

she says it. There's a conspiratorial edge to her voice, as if she's suggesting I plant a bomb in the Magister's office or something equally nefarious.

"Is there someone around who can do that?"

She leans in and speaks in a whisper. "I hear your guy is a Courser. Don't let anyone touch your Maude but him."

Her demeanor has shifted entirely. She no longer seems warm or glowing, but is filled with dark suspicion and a tacit disdain for those in charge.

"I hear you," I whisper back. "Thank you."

Whether or not *she's* trustworthy, her advice is sound.

I trust Thorne, and literally no one else, though Rivenna and Kith have proven themselves reliable allies.

"I'm going to shower," I say, "and get ready to see Thorne."

"I'll bring you dinner in a little while. Remember—there are clean clothes in the dressers and closet that should fit both of you."

Part of me wants to ask her more questions, but I simply watch as she throws me a sly smile, then departs.

I lay Mercutio on a small charging pad on the nightstand, then shower. When I've changed into an outfit of gray trousers and a black shirt, I throw myself onto the bed and, against my will, fall into a deep sleep.

CHAPTER EIGHTEEN

I STIR awake to the sound of the door opening.

I turn onto my side and peer toward the door, assuming in my disoriented stupor that my eyes will land on Joy once again.

But instead, someone shoots toward me in a blur, the door slamming behind him as he moves. In an instant, he's on top of me, a shock of brown hair tumbling over his forehead, a knowing smile on his lips.

I'm convinced once again that I'm dreaming. I have to be —*this* is far too good to be true.

"Thorne?" I murmur, convinced he's nothing more than another vision implanted in my mind. "Are we in the Nether again?"

"Hello, Beautiful," he replies with a smile. "No. We're together this time. Though the Nether was pretty fun, as I recall."

I reach up and cup his cheek, then slip my hand onto his neck. My gaze moves over every part of him, relieved to take in the fact he's no longer wearing the cilice that the Magister's people forced on him.

Free. We're truly free.

"Are you really here?" I ask, tears stinging my eyes. "Can this possibly be happening?"

"It's happening," he whispers, leaning down and pressing the gentlest kiss to my lips. Somehow, the tease of sensation feels more real than something deeper would—a mere hint of reality. Just enough to remind me how fleeting it is.

He kisses my neck, his teeth scraping gently along my skin as if testing to make sure I'm real.

His heart beats so perfectly alongside my own that it feels like one organ has begun to exist inside the other. It's almost painful to love him this much—the sort of aching torment that's so close to pleasure that it's almost impossible to tell them apart.

"Promise me I'm awake," I breathe.

His hand ventures into my shirt, slipping upward so that his fingertips stroke my stomach.

"You're awake."

"Prove it."

"I'll do my best." He eases his hand farther up still, his eyes moving down to take in my chest. "You know, they say you can't tell if a person actually exists until you've experienced them with all your senses. Touch, sight, sound, scent...*taste*..."

He inhales deeply, then strokes his tongue up my stomach, drawing my shirt higher as he goes.

"So far, you seem real. But there's only one way to know for sure."

He pulls the shirt up until he's exposed me, his eyes glinting with pleasure as he takes in the sight of my breasts. My lips quirk and I look away, almost embarrassed by how aroused he is at the simple sight.

Yet to him, I know, it's everything. Everything he nearly lost when he arrived in the Capitol. Everything we are to one another. *Everything.*

He cups my breast, slipping a callused thumb over my nipple and drawing an arch from my back. His other hand goes to my trousers, pushing its way inside, and he moves it lower, lower, until he finds what he's looking for.

"I can *feel* you," he tells me when his fingers slip over me. With the tip of his tongue, he strokes my breast. "But I need to taste you to know for sure that you're real."

He moves down the bed, dragging my pants along with him, then buries his face between my legs, arms hooking around my thighs. I reach for him, trying to coax him back to me, to kiss him again.

More. I want more.

But instead, he resists and kisses the place between my legs, gently at first, then more insistent, burying his tongue deep inside me with an intense moan.

"Thorne," I whisper, my hips rising to meet his need. "Come back here."

Pulling away only long enough to tear his shirt off, he replaces his tongue with two fingers and I let out another moan as he moves up to kiss me, his mouth tasting of my own arousal. His tongue rakes across mine and I feel him dragging his trousers off and tossing them aside, then he takes my hips in his hands, sheathing himself deep inside me in one hard, delicious stroke.

He pulls out, backing away to look me in the eye.

"Please," I moan. "Again..."

"Greedy," he says, driving into me as I reach out and grip the sheets in tight fists, fighting back a need to cry out. "Greedy girl, always wanting my cock."

I tighten around him and he winces with the thrill of it, moaning unrepentantly. He pulls out and thrusts himself back in, kissing my neck, my collarbone, my shoulder.

My body writhes with the pleasure he feels—the connection between us offering up his bliss alongside my own. It's as if every sensation is amplified a hundred times, and each rock of his hips against me is a perfection almost too delectable to bear.

Reaching down, he works me with his finger, stroking the bundle of nerves between my legs—knowing exactly what's going to happen...because he can see it in his mind's eye. He anticipates my coming ecstasy, and exactly how to bring it about. How slowly, how gently...how to move his fingers against me and move inside me, filling me with everything I've craved since the last moment we saw one another.

I would die happy, I think, *if we could just live like this for a little—this free. This bonded. If I could know he would be mine each and every night and morning—mine to devour, to consume. To want.*

He pushes me toward the edge, easing in and out slowly now, watching my face as I fight back the craving to give myself over to my body's need. My eyes seal, taking in the sensation of his finger against me, his heart throbbing along with mine...his breath on my neck, eyes watching the place where he and I are joined.

"Too good," I say. "It feels too fucking good."

"There's no such thing."

"On your back," I whisper, and he grabs me by the waist, pulls me close, then flips onto his back in one fluid motion.

I rise up above him, taking him in as deep as he's ever been.

"The Nether robbed us," I tell him. "We never got to finish what we started."

"I intend to finish it at least four times tonight alone," he promises.

My hips move against him, my body throbbing with every perfect sensation of his thickness splitting me open.

"Do you feel it?" I ask, staring down at him as his hands come up to cup my breast or run a knuckle over my nipple. "Do you feel how close I am?"

He nods silently, sweat glistening on his brow. "I want you to come. I want to feel your pleasure, Shara—to remind myself what it's like to be inside your mind when it happens."

"If you insist," I tell him, slipping up, then letting myself take every glorious inch of him in again.

He slips a hand down between us, his thumb moving in the most delicate circles against me, and I seal my eyes shut against the sensation.

"It's too good," I say. "I won't last..."

"I know."

With those words, I explode against his touch, clenching around him as if claiming him for the hundredth time, my core taking possessive hold of his body.

Thorne drives himself hard now, fingers digging into my

thighs as he buries himself so deep inside me that I fear I'll explode with the perfection of it.

"Give yourself to me," I say, leaning down to kiss him, our tongues meeting, minds reeling. "Give me everything."

He quickens his pace, tearing into me with a wild force, his eyes locking on mine as I take his face in my hands. There was a time when I would have felt self-conscious, watching him approach his climax. A time when I would have sealed my eyes against the intensity of it.

But now, all I want is to devour every aspect of him—to feel everything.

When the burst of searing heat explodes inside me at last, I throw my head back, spine arching sharply, fingers raking over his chest, leaving a trail of red in their wake.

"Shara..." My name slips from his lips like a plea, and I collapse against him, enveloped in his arms. He's my prisoner now—yet it's me who's trapped, and I never want to be freed.

We belong to one another, yet to no one.

We are two free people of the realm of Kravan, and no one can take that from us now.

When we've rested in silence a little, I run my fingers over Thorne's arm, relieved to remember the cilice is long gone.

"I don't like how the Royal Guard are treated around here," I murmur. "I hated seeing you in pain."

"To be fair," he says, "the Magister has been decent to me. I didn't love having my powers temporarily taken from me, but I can understand it, given how dangerous the king has always been."

I slide my fingers down to take his hand in mine, and to my shock, he responds with a wince and a sharp gasp.

Horrified, I pull his hand closer and turn it over, only to see an angry red mark in his palm.

The Magister's brand.

How did I not feel his pain? How did I not know it was there?

"Thorne!" I breathe. "They made you do this?"

"No one forced me," he replies with a shake of his head. "It was my choice. I chose to vow my loyalty to the Magister—to your father. To you. It wasn't a tough call. I have offered myself fully to the Magister's cause, and the restoration of our land."

I'm torn between feeling proud of him and feeling utterly devastated. Proud that this brand means he will never return to the role of Royal Guard.

Devastated that the Magister left a permanent scar on his perfect body.

"Let me heal it," I tell him. "Please. It must hurt so much. I don't know why I haven't felt it, but..."

"It's not so bad," he insists, but I can tell it hurts far more than he's letting on. "I suppose I tried to hold the pain back—to keep it from you. I didn't want you to worry."

"I *am* worried. I want to make it feel better."

He looks hesitant. "If you heal it, it will still be visible... right?"

I smile and nod. "I'll make sure it is, if that's what you want."

"In that case," he says, and holds his hand out, palm up. "I'm yours."

I press my hand to his, knowing the initial shock of pain will be brutal. But he stares into my eyes and takes it, absorbing my power as I force away the rawness of the wound, turning it to scar tissue in a matter of seconds.

"You're a miracle," he says, pulling me close and kissing me. "My beautiful, perfect miracle. Now—" He glances over at the night stand and sees Mercutio lying there, his tiny eyes sealed. "Our little friend needs a proper charge, doesn't he?"

I nod. "When we head out above ground, I'll bring him. It was a long, dark hike to get here."

Thorne reaches over and touches his fingertips to the mouse, who instantly rises and scurries off the nightstand, disappearing under the door.

"Fully charged," he says.

"I guess we're both beautiful miracles, then," I laugh. Cupping his face in my hands, I smile again. "I just can't believe it. You're really here. You and I are so close to living a life I never thought possible."

He pulls himself off the bed, scans the room with his eyes, then says, "I want to think that's true. I want to believe your father wants us to be happy. But..."

He looks hesitant to speak.

"Whatever we have to say to each other, we can say," I tell him. "We're not in the palace anymore. There's no cruel king or prince around to throw us into the arena and make us fight to the death."

Thorne smirks. "Maybe not, but your father—he's a powerful man. In my experience, powerful men don't gain their strength through kindness and benevolence."

"What are you saying?"

Instead of answering me, he takes a step toward the bathroom.

"I need a shower, and you should join me," he announces.

My eyes widen with instant craving, my body tightening in anticipation. I slip out of bed and make my way hastily into the bathroom after him, where he's already turned on the shower.

Thorne, stepping around me, takes me by the waist and presses himself against my back, kissing my neck.

"There are rumors," he whispers into my ear as the shower sounds drown out his voice. "About the Magister."

"What sorts of rumors?" I ask, locking my arm around his neck as he presses closer, his swollen length betraying his renewed arousal and sending heat coursing through me.

"Some people are calling him a liberator—saying he'll free all Tethered—including the ones in the Tower."

I twist around and pull my chin up to look him in the eye. "That's a good thing," I tell him with a chuckle, then kiss him. "We can help him."

"Yes," he says. "We can—assuming he's as good a man as we hope."

I stare up into his eyes, seeking answers to questions I'm afraid to ask. Why does Thorne doubt the Magister, aside from the obvious fact that neither of us knows him well? He's a man who has allegedly devoted his entire existence to fighting the enemies that keep our people in shackles and force us to live lives devoid of love, of freedom, of humanity?

Whether he likes it or not, my father and the Magister are our best hope. The Magister has hundreds, if not thousands, of devoted followers. He kept Thorne alive—and he is allowing us to live here together, which is more than anyone else has ever offered.

"Shara," Thorne says, a hand combing its way into my thick, dark hair. "He's your father. I understand that you want to assume the best of him, but..."

At that, I pull back, my eyes narrowing.

I love Thorne. I would throw myself in front of a flying blade for him—and then some. He's everything to me.

But I have lived my entire life without a family. Without a father or a mother. And now, I've finally met my father, and he is powerful, respected, and the best hope this land has of healing.

"I'm not naive," I tell Thorne. "I know no leader is perfect—but neither am I. Neither are you. The Shadow—Laurence—my father—has given us hope, for the first time. Everyone I've talked to speaks highly of him. The king fears him. He is exactly what Kravan needs. Whatever sort of man the Magister is, I believe my father's goals align with ours."

Thorne bows his head and inhales a deep breath, then lets it pour out of his chest and brings his eyes to mine.

"I will follow you," he says. "To the ends of the earth, if there is such a place. I will support you—and any family you have. Because you're *my* family, Shara. You and I are bound by our souls—our hearts. Your hope is my hope. Your fears are mine. If I can help to make this world better, I'll do it. If you think this is the place we're meant to be—that this is the battle we're meant to fight—I will be there, every step of the way."

"Good," I tell him, only slightly grudgingly, then allow my lips the smile that's been waiting to form. "I won't let anything bad happen, Thorne. Maude and I—we'll keep an eye on things."

That is, if I can ever get Maude to wake up.

"I have no doubt of it," Thorne tells me.

"But you doubt my father. And the Magister."

"I doubt power-hungry people. I doubt the capacity of ambitious men to show empathy. But I will never, ever doubt you."

"Good."

We step under the water and, taking both my hands, Thorne presses me back up against the tile wall. He eyes me hungrily as a quiet gasp of pleasure escapes my lips.

There was a time not long ago when I wondered whether he and I would ever be in this position again—whether I'd ever feel his touch, taste his skin, devour the scent of him on my nose, my tongue.

"Tomorrow, you and I will roam parts of the Capitol," he says. "Together."

"I can't wait. I want to experience everything for the first time with you."

"Everything?" he asks, slipping a hand between my thighs.

"Some things won't be happening for the very first time..." I breathe.

"Let's see if I can make them feel brand new, all over again. And then, three more times before dawn."

He eases down onto his knees, pushing my thighs apart, his mouth on me as I let out a long, deep sigh of pleasure.

This is going to be a long night...and a glorious one.

CHAPTER NINETEEN

"I WANT TO KNOW EVERYTHING," Thorne tells me, winding a finger through a strand of my disheveled hair as I lie with my face against his bare chest.

"Everything?" I ask with a chuckle. "That'll take a while."

"I have a while. At least until I have to take on my first class of fighters."

I raise myself up enough to look into his eyes. "You're really going to train fighters? They'll be going up against Royal Guard, Thorne."

"Maybe, maybe not." He runs his fingertips along my forearm, pensive. "Maybe we can avoid an all-out war if we play our cards right."

"I don't see how," I moan. "But I guess we don't really have a choice."

"I'll do everything I can to avoid bloodshed—I promise. But for now, tell me—how did you get out of the palace?"

A sigh surges from my lungs as I lay my head down again. "Tallin. He went ballistic, literally. Valira and Archyr—they—"

Thorne presses his lips to my hair. "I felt it," he says quietly. "Your pain at the moment of their deaths."

"Really?"

The word slips its way past my lips, but the truth is, I'm not surprised. I've felt Thorne's pain acutely before. I've been through the trauma of knowing from a distance that he's hurting, aware that I can do nothing to help him.

I'm still a little stunned that I was unable to feel the agony of the Magister's mark on his skin.

"I felt part of you die inside me." There's a palpable tension in his voice now. "I was terrified—but I was under Ellion's control still, and there was nothing I could do except let my heart break for you."

"Fucking Ellion. He tore us apart to punish us for loving one another. He knew exactly what he was doing. I'm sure he and the king never expected you to bring my father back to the palace. They were setting you up to fail."

"Of course they were. The king has sent Tethered after Tethered to the Capitol, and most of them never return. Ellion *hoped* I would die, and he never expected you to escape. Which brings me back to my question. How the hell did you get out if Tallin was losing it?"

"Believe it or not, he commanded me to leave. He spared me, Thorne. I don't know why. Maybe he knew I loved Valira and Archyr, too."

"You think Tallin felt empathy—really?"

I roll onto my back, my eyes locked on the featureless concrete ceiling. "I do, yeah. I wasn't the object of his rage. I was a victim, like him. My tethered mate had been taken from me. My friends had died in front of me. Tallin was angry for *me*, as well as for himself."

"Well," Thorne says, climbing over me, his arms forming rigid columns to either side of my face, "will wonders never cease? By some miracle, I'm grateful to Prince Shithead."

"Meanwhile, I despise Ellion for what he did to us."

"Maybe Ellion did us a favor." Thorne leans down, his lips brushing mine.

When he pulls up, my eyes move to the swath of hair shadowing his face. "What do you mean, a favor? It seems to me we're both lucky to be alive."

"Not a deliberate one, of course. Ellion is a monster. But if he hadn't sent me to the Capitol, what are the chances that you and I would ever have found our way here together? We probably would have ended up suffering in the palace for years, serving against our will—or been killed. Now, we're free, Shara." He kisses me, teasing my tongue with his own before adding, "And for that very reason, I intend to take you on an old-fashioned date tomorrow."

"A date?" I laugh. "Wait—are you asking me out?"

He slides a hand between my legs, slipping his middle finger over me, coaxing a long, sweet sigh from my lips.

"I think I am," he breathes onto my skin. "Would you, Shara, consider going on a date with me?" He draws his finger to his lips and tastes it, then, taking hold of his swollen length, presses it to my opening, teasing me with the promise of things to come.

I let out a laugh. "I think the date usually comes before this part," I tell him, lifting my hips to invite him in, inch by magnificent inch.

"That's the old-fashioned way," he growls, then sheathes himself deep, drawing a hard cry from my lips. "What can I tell you? I'm a modern man."

An hour later, exhausted again with our breaths heavy in our chests, I ask Thorne a question that's been eating away at me.

"The vision I had of the men in masks. What exactly happened after you landed in the Capitol? I mean, before you encountered Kith."

He inhales, then closes his eyes as if searching for the memory.

"I had tried to shake off Ellion's powers since the moment I left the palace—tried to fight back against him when I was out over open water. But somehow, even from a distance, he had a hold on my mind that was unfathomable. Almost like..."

"Like what?"

"Like he'd renewed his grip, taking hold of my mind again, my extremities—all of me." He inhales deeply, then sets his breath free. "I felt almost weak, Shara. Depleted in a way I never have before and never want to again. I've never met anyone I couldn't fight off until that moment. I've never known a force that powerful."

"You're not weak. You could never be." I pull his hand to my lips and kiss the heel of his palm. "It's not easy to fight off someone bent on destroying you when all you're doing is trying to survive."

Thorne frowns. "I had landed on a decimated street. The buildings to either side were caved in, the road itself cracked and battered, like someone had taken an enormous mallet to its surface. I was still utterly disoriented when I climbed out of the Flyer. I knew I was in the Capitol to find the Shadow, but there was no part of me that cared whether or not I did. I just wanted to get back to you."

I wrap an arm around him and pull myself closer. "Tell me more."

"I fought hard against Ellion's power, and for a moment, I was certain I'd vanquished him. I tried to climb back into the Flyer, but someone grabbed me and pulled me backwards, then threw me to the ground. As it turned out, I was still disoriented and unable to fight back as I should have. When I looked up, I saw two men in masks, dressed mostly in gray. One of them had a device in his hand—some sort of stunner. He shocked me with it, and suddenly, I couldn't think or move.

"They dragged me some distance—I remember that I could still see the sky—then everything went blurry and gray. Next thing I remember, I was inside and on my knees in a dark, round room. I remember that its ceiling was arched, but other than that, there wasn't much interesting about it. There were no windows, just steel doors set in various parts of the wall, and detritus scattered everywhere." He goes silent for a moment, then adds, "When we were in the council chamber here in the Citadel, I was taken aback for a minute, because it reminded me a little of that other space."

Surprise lodges itself in my chest. "It wasn't...was it?"

"No. The other room was far smaller. Colder. Darker." Thorne tightens. "One of the men asked what I was doing in the Capitol, then struck me hard across the face when I didn't answer. I told him I wasn't sure why I was there—that someone had sent me, but I had no control over myself, let alone my own mind."

"Did they mention the Lady?" I ask. "The head of the Starless?"

Thorne shakes his head. "They said something about a leader, but I didn't know who they were, not until Kith told me later. I saw the Magister's mark on one of their arms. At the time, I didn't know what it meant, either."

I reply with a nod. "And Kith? How did he come into it?"

"There was a point when one of the masked men had a blade pressed to my throat. He growled out a threat, but the moment it met my ears, he went crashing to the ground, hard. I remember seeing blood staining his mask. Then another man fell, and another, one after the other like dominoes. My head was lolling around—I was dizzy, confused. Next thing I knew, Kith was untying me. He helped me up and got me to the Citadel. I can't recall how he did it—how he supported me for such a long way. I think the blow to my head messed me up."

"The Magister's people locked you in the cell after that?"

"After a doctor checked me out, yes. By then, Ellion's power had faded. I was livid—not because they'd locked me up, but because they were keeping me from getting back to you. Kith came to speak to me and talked me down from my rage. I remember telling him to look for you. Pleading with him. I knew you would come, I suppose—some part of me could feel it. He said to be patient—that he would hunt for you."

I nod. "He found me in the tunnels. He knew I was there, with Rivenna. I'm beginning to wonder whether one of his powers is psychic, because that guy always seems to know what's going to happen before it does."

"Wait," Thorne says. "Who's Rivenna?"

It hasn't even occurred to me that Thorne wouldn't know about her. She's been such a vital part of my life for the last two days.

"A Tethered who helped me and got me safely into the Citadel. She's the one who told me about the Nether, too. I'm sure you'll meet her soon. She does a lot of work for the Magister and my father. She's a mercenary. A Reaper."

"A Reaper? Really?" Thorne asks, seemingly shocked, though I can't see his face. "Wow. I didn't think they were real."

"You've heard of that power?"

"Oh, yeah—way back when I was locked inside the Tower. We all thought it was a made-up creature to scare us into eating our vegetables or behave ourselves. 'The Reaper will come for you if you're bad!'" His voice rises as he speaks the threat. "We all thought it was ridiculous. To be fair, we didn't know Reapers actually existed."

"She's very real. I've seen her eyes—her power. She's... well, she's beautiful, actually, considering she's death in human form."

"We all are, in our way," Thorne says, wrapping both arms around me and pulling me tight against him. "But right now, I have no desire to talk about death. I want to live life to its fullest fucking potential with you. I want to savor you. And even though that means I want to stay awake all night and make love to you until neither of us can walk, I think we're going to need to get a little sleep before morning." I feel his bliss as he speaks—a quiet joy moving through him as hope fills us both. "Tomorrow is the first day of our lives, Shara. Our first day of true freedom."

CHAPTER TWENTY

In the morning—I'm not sure what time it is, given the lack of windows in the Citadel—a gentle knock sounds at the suite's door, then it cracks open.

I've just scrambled my way into a white robe when Joy peeks her head inside the room and says, "I'm sorry to intrude, Shara."

"It's all right," I call out. *I'm just glad you didn't catch us ten minutes ago.*

She slips inside, carrying a silver tray covered in dishes of bacon, eggs, and fruit, and a carafe of coffee with two white cups. The smell of it brings me life, and a grateful grin tugs at my lips. "All of this is for us?"

Joy laughs. "It's nice to be treated like royalty, isn't it?"

"As long as we don't *act* like royalty, then yes," I snicker.

"Good point. Oh—I'm also supposed to tell you your father would like to see you and Thorne this morning. He's wondering whether you two might like to tour a neighbor-hood under renovation."

The bathroom door opens, and Thorne emerges with a

white towel around his waist, rubbing a hand through his wet hair. My breath hitches as I'm struck for the thousandth time by his glorious body—one I'd kill to drag back into bed with me.

"I've heard there are a few areas under the protection of the Magister," he says. "Some guards were talking about them when I was in the cell."

"Oh," I reply, turning back to Joy. "In that case...yes. We'd definitely like to go take a look."

The truth is, I'm downright giddy about the idea of leaving the Citadel's depths. I've been aching to experience the Capitol up close since I was a child—and the opportunity to peer into the lives of those who live here is something I've craved endlessly.

My brief stint in the city with Rivenna and Kith was fraught with anxiety and a burning desire to find Thorne—but the idea of exploring with him is a luxury I've hardly dared hope for.

Joy grins. "I'll tell your father, then. When you're ready, please come to the council chamber." She throws Thorne a quick up-and-down glance, then looks back at me, raising her eyebrows in silent approval.

When she's left and closed the door behind her, I call out to Maude.

"Are you there?"

After a moment of silence, she says, *~Yes. I am here, Shara.*

I should be reassured by her presence, but something in her voice is jarring. It's gone from familiar to a formal, almost robotic timbre.

I hate it.

"Are you all right?" I ask. "You don't seem like yourself."

This time, she projects her voice out loud so that Thorne can hear.

~I'm fine.

The reply is far from reassuring. It's almost like she's been drugged—though I'm not remotely sure you can drug an artificial intelligence unit.

My eyes meet Thorne's, and he looks almost as concerned as I feel.

I hiss, "What's wrong with you, Maude?"

~Nothing at all. I'm simply in the process of uploading new software.

"What?" I snap. "Who's installing it?"

~The technicians in the Citadel. It's standard protocol.

"Thorne," I breathe. "Do you know anything about this?"

I feel suddenly like someone is violating me, feeding my mind information that I don't want to receive.

Seeing the panic in my eyes, Thorne takes hold of my left wrist, and I feel Maude go dormant under his touch.

"I don't know who's reprogramming her," he tells me. "Or why. But remember—we always suspected your father might have been the one who rebooted her in the past. It's possible he's doing it again."

He's not wrong. Maude has told me before that someone had reset her system in order to protect me in the Tower. In fight class, Maude regularly shot a jolt of pain into my arm to weaken me and ensure that our trainer considered me a non-threat.

She was a little too good at that particular job.

"Well, it's freaking me out," I tell Thorne. "Can you, I don't know, change her back to her old self?"

He shakes his head. "I could reboot her, but maybe we

should ask your father first if this was his doing. It might be a bad idea to mess with her just now."

"You're not worried that someone is using her to watch us or listen in on our conversations?"

"Not particularly," he says, releasing my wrist. "I've been on high alert since I first entered the suite, and haven't actually detected evidence of surveillance. There was a moment last night when I felt a little paranoid—as if someone was in the room with us...but it's passed. Besides, we're here in *support* of your father and the Magister. There's no reason for them to spy on us—and if they did, they'd hear a lot of moaning, kissing, and me telling you how much I love having my head between your thighs."

I let out a snicker, but my mind instantly veers to a dark thought. "But...what if it's the Starless who did this? What if the man in the tunnel somehow got to Maude?"

Thorne leans down to talk into my forearm, smiling up at me, and says, "If you're listening, Starless Lady, you can fuck off. We want nothing to do with you or your crew of masked assholes."

That's enough to make me laugh again. "Maskholes?"

"Exactly," Thorne says, straightening up and planting a soft kiss on my lips. "Don't worry about it. Keep an eye and ear on Maude. If we need to, we'll shut her down for a while. Just...let me know if she starts doing anything totally unhinged, okay?"

"Unhinged, like shooting agonizing pain into my body repeatedly while I fight for my life? Oh, wait—she's already done that a thousand times."

"That's my point. She may be acting a bit off, but at least she's not being a sadistic shit anymore, right?"

"Fair point," I say with a sigh. "In the meantime, Maude, do you know the quickest way to the council chamber?"

~Yes. I'll guide you there.

Her voice is still expressionless and almost cold, like it belongs to someone I've never met before.

It pains me to listen as she dictates a route that takes us through what feels like a mile of winding corridors before we reach a large set of steel doors. They open on our approach, and we instantly spot two guards standing just inside. My father is seated at the large round table at the chamber's center, surrounded by tidy stacks of papers.

He rises to his feet, shuffling the papers into a single pile, then greets us with a smile.

"Thorne. Shara. I trust you both slept well?"

If he suspects that we did more than just sleep, he's not saying it.

"We did," I reply, glancing sideways at Thorne. I pause for a second, then blurt out, "I don't suppose you know why my Maude unit has been updated with new software, do you?"

My father chuckles, eyes Thorne for a moment, then says, "It's nothing to worry about, I assure you."

Relief scrambles its way through my entire body, though questions linger in my mind.

"It's hard not to," I tell him. "She's part of me. She's acting erratic."

My father's eyes soften, filling with sympathy. "I'm sorry—I should have warned you. She's been automatically updated by a remote programming unit here in the Citadel. The same happens to any ex-Tower dweller with a functional Maude unit. They're simply provided with the latest city maps, details about which zones in the Capitol are safe, and other information that could protect you. She's also received a map of the Citadel and the tunnels, as well as a little about local businesses. Since I want you to enjoy a certain amount of freedom, it seemed a logical precaution to provide you with any information that might prevent you from getting lost in the Capitol's more dangerous areas."

"That doesn't explain why Maude seems so...different," I say.

"Don't worry—she'll settle into her old self soon enough, I suspect. If she doesn't, let me know."

I nod, but Thorne reaches for my hand, taking hold of it tightly as if to say, "Let *me* know."

A silent tension between the two men feels like it's suddenly beginning to grow, so I cut into it with the sharp edge of my voice. "Joy mentioned something about us going to see a part of the Capitol today."

"Absolutely," my father says. "I want you both to enjoy yourselves before things begin to go sideways."

"Sideways? Why would they?"

"Let's just say there will soon be a battle for the survival of this realm. But the Magister himself will fill you in on the latest developments. Ah—there he is now."

On cue, the chamber's doors fly open and a man strides into the room. If there's anything remarkable about him, it's his *lack* of interesting features. He's of average height and average build. His hair is thinning, his eyes deep set and close together.

He's the most normal of Normals I've ever laid eyes on—including Terrence.

"Shara," my father says. "I'd like you to meet Magister Brant."

Despite his lack of imposing features, something about this man—a quiet, simple, focused dignity—daunts me. I bow my head, realizing I have no idea how to greet a person of his status.

It seems wildly ironic, given that I've eaten meals with the king and prince on too many occasions to count. I've lived in the palace, rubbed elbows with the Prefect.

Still, that was all play-acting on my part.

This is real.

"Nice to meet you, Magister," I say, eyeing him to determine whether I can uncover any similarities to the President Brant I saw in the memories the Storian gave me.

"And you," the Magister says with a nod and an attempt at a warm smile that falls flat. Something tells me he's neither friendly nor hostile—he's all business, his mind a tunnel-visioned machine with one goal in his sights: the presidency of Kravan.

"I come with good news," he adds, "which I conveyed to your father earlier this morning. It looks like we will have our work cut out for us over the next few weeks."

"Oh?" I ask, glancing at my father. "Why is that?"

"Because King Tomas is dead."

CHAPTER
TWENTY-ONE

"THE KING IS...DEAD?"

The shock is enough to bring me to my knees, but Thorne's arm locks tight around me, anticipating my collapse.

It's not like it should be any surprise. I know who did it. I know how it happened. I heard the explosions that shook the palace as I fled. Felt the walls tremble around me.

I only wonder if anyone else survived the altercation—including Tallin himself.

"How do you know?" I whisper in a rasp, my eyes on the Magister, an emotion clawing at my chest that's utterly new to me. Fear combined with hope—combined with...something entirely different.

I would be lying to myself if I didn't admit there's a little joy in my heart as well.

"I have allies everywhere," the Magister says, his spine straightening, body rigid. He looks suddenly as if he's in defense mode against an enemy who may or may not be in the room with us—I wonder if he thinks that enemy is me.

If I were a cruel person, I'd be bouncing off the walls right now. But the fact is, I'm not entirely vicious.

Against my will, I have empathy for the king.

I know how he died and how painful it must have been. Whether I liked him or not, he was a human being with nerve endings—and that's enough to evoke the barest kindness—if only for a second.

"Tell us what happened," Thorne says, his voice deep and filled with weight as his hand tightens around my waist. "Tell us everything you know—now."

I glance sideways at him, proud yet surprised that he would take this tone with the Magister and my father—men revered in the Capitol for their ambition and ability to recruit people to their side. Thorne sounds like a leader—or, at the very least, their equal.

A smile quirks my father's lips and he chuckles, amused by Thorne's aggression. But the Magister does not look entertained in the least.

"There was a battle in the palace. Fire and brimstone, all perpetuated by the prince himself." Turning to me, he adds, "Your father tells me you might know something of that, Shara."

"Yes. I..." I glance at my father, trying to recall whether I actually filled him in on what happened before I left. "The prince was enraged when I fled. I didn't see exactly what happened—I was running for my life, to be honest."

The Magister nods solemnly. "Three were left dead—aside from two members of the Royal Guard who had already perished. One person other than the prince escaped with minimal injuries."

"Three dead," I repeat, inhaling the words rather than expelling them. "Who, aside from the king?"

I don't know why I fear the truth. Of everyone in that arena—Tallin, King Tomas, Lady Verdan, Lady Graystone, and Ellion Graystone—there was not a soul I would ever mourn...but the outcome of that slaughter could well determine Kravan's future.

That's what frightens me.

"Prince Tallin lived, of course." The Magister's voice softens as though he senses my fear. "The king, as I said, was killed. It seems Lady Verdan was by his side when it happened—a fireball the likes of which few have ever seen took them both down at once. Lady Verdan survived with severe burns—but died shortly afterward."

"Daphne Verdan, dead," I say to no one in particular. "To think she's..."

"Gone," Thorne replies. I pull my chin up to look into his eyes and find I can't read his expression. Perhaps, like me, his emotions are a tangle. It was in the Verdan home that we got to know each other—and it's there that he went from being my nemesis to my lover.

But there's so much more to her story and ours.

Lady Verdan was the prince's mother, and though that information was kept a secret from the vast majority of the realm, I never doubted that she and Tallin cared for one another in their own, twisted way.

"Your...informant. He saw it happen? You're sure about all of this?"

The Magister nods but doesn't expand or explain.

Thorne pulls me closer still, sensing my horror.

There was someone else in the arena with us, then. Someone who saw all of it. The Stealther my father speaks of.

"Oh, God," I stammer. "I just remembered..."

"What is it?" Thorne asks.

"The last time I saw Devorah, I suggested..."

I glance over at my father, who's watching me intently. As always, it feels like he knows more than he's letting on.

With a swallow, I continue. "I told her I wanted Evangeline—my mother—out of the Prefect's home for her own safety and suggested the Verdans hire her as a Domestic. It's possible she's there now."

"I'll look into it," my father says, concern crumpling his brow. "I'll do my best to ensure she's safe."

"Ellion Graystone fled," the Magister says. "Some say he's taken shelter in his home and is avoiding the prince at all costs—and I can't say I blame him."

"Neither do I," I reply. "Tallin fought off his mind control once. I'm sure he could do it again."

"Speaking of Tallin," Thorne interjects. "Where is the prince now?"

"By all accounts," my father replies, "he's still in the palace. I can't imagine it's a pleasant place to be at the moment."

With a shake of my head, I say, "It must be absolute hell."

He stares me down for a few seconds, then asks, "Do you really think it's any more hellish than it's been for years?"

"Unfortunately, yes. The king was a nightmare. But he was a *controlled* nightmare. Tallin is like an uncontrolled hurricane. The only thing keeping his rage at bay is gone now. What he did to the king and the others? That's probably just the beginning—unless someone finds a way to get him under control. He'll suffer echoes of the pain he inflicted upon every person in that room, and it will be the worst torture he's ever endured. There's no way to relieve him of it. Which means he'll take it out on anyone who's near. He'll sow chaos on the entire realm if that's what makes him feel better. He's a bomb, waiting to detonate and take down every person in Kravan."

"We'll have to move soon, then," the Magister says, nodding to Thorne. "We have a couple of weeks, at the most, to get our recruits ready. Tallin cannot remain on the throne."

"You said Ellion fled," I reply. "If he's still alive—well, you probably already know he's also King Tomas' son. If Tallin is killed, Ellion will be eligible to sit on the throne. But you should be warned, in case you aren't aware—he's his own special brand of psychotic."

"Let me worry about Ellion," my father says, shifting his focus to a door at the far end of the council chamber. He turns back to us and grins, looking unperturbed by the grim topic of conversation. "Look—I realize our world is on the verge of implosion, but I'm not forgetting I promised you two a stroll outside the Citadel. You should do it today. Our smiths will spend the day crafting Thorne's bracers so the training sessions can begin first thing tomorrow."

Thorne nods his understanding. "Shara and I will strive to enjoy ourselves while we can, then."

I'm about to tell my father there's no way I can relax, knowing the palace is in a state of total upheaval. But the truth is, the king's death is probably the best news we could have received—and cause for celebration.

As volatile as Tallin is, he let me go, even when there was

rage literally burning inside him. He maintained some small modicum of rationality, despite the horrors tearing through his mind. That, at least, gives me a little hope.

Thorne and I will spend one day behaving like regular people. I want to know what it feels like to be truly free—and today will be the first time in my entire life when I have a chance to experience that sensation in all its glory.

My father signals with his left hand to some unseen entity, and the next thing I know, I hear a whirring sound, and a set of doors open at the far end of the chamber.

I reach into my pocket to check for Mercutio, and when I feel him stirring under my touch, I smile. Maude may not be her usual self right now, but it's comforting to know the little mouse is so close by.

A faint buzz meets my ears, and two Dragonflyers dart into the room, immediately taking position on either side of Thorne and me.

"These will be your guardians for the day," my father tells us. "They'll watch you and guide you, in case anything should go wrong."

"Thank you."

"Anything for my daughter," he replies with a warm smile, then gestures for us to follow the two small drones. "Go. Enjoy the calm before the storm."

CHAPTER TWENTY-TWO

Thorne takes hold of my hand as we make our way through the Citadel's maze of corridors and begin the climb toward the Dragonflyers' chosen exit. With my fingertips, I can feel the round outline of the brand on his palm as we move, and I cringe and pull away.

When he laughs at my unexpected withdrawal, I say, "I just wish they hadn't scarred you for life." My tone is more judgmental than I intend. I'm not sure why, but it bothers me that Thorne has been so quick to pledge loyalty to the Magister.

If we were truly free, we would never have to declare loyalty to *any* leader.

"It's a symbol of our desire to tear the Tower to the ground," Thorne says, "and free the Tethered of Kravan once and for all. The brand is a sign of strength, not weakness."

I'm about to respond when Maude speaks at last, her tone disturbingly robotic.

~We're about to reach the Citadel's southwest entrance. Doors opening.

While I would never have called Maude warm and cuddly before, she now feels like a stranger living inside my body.

I stop in my tracks and watch the doors open inward, but when I don't move, Thorne eyes me with concern.

"It's Maude, isn't it?"

"It's like she doesn't know me—and I sure as hell don't know her."

~*I know you,* Maude replies.

"Prove it."

~*You're not fond of cabbage. You enjoy flowers. You think mice are cute, but rats are vile. You are exceptionally fastidious with your chores—I trained you to be. I know everything about you.*

"Oh, really? Then tell me my most annoying quality. Say it out loud."

She ponders that for a moment, then, loudly enough for Thorne to hear, says, ~*I'm incapable of feeling annoyed, so that is an impossible request.*

There were so many damned ways she could have answered me: *You ask too many questions. You worry too much. You meddle, you have no idea how to keep your thoughts to yourself, and constantly put yourself in danger.*

The Maude I know would have had a thousand retorts—and none of them would have been *I'm incapable of feeling annoyed.*

Thorne doesn't look nearly as concerned as I feel, but he seems to sense my sadness. "She's probably still recalibrating and re-uploading all her data. It will take some time."

"Is that normal?"

"Not normal—but not necessarily that unusual, either. I can't compare her to my own Maude, given that she and I aren't exactly on speaking terms."

It's true. Thorne's ability to manipulate and control electronics means he's better off without a Maude unit inside him. The fact is, most Tethered prefer to go through life without one.

Then again, most Maudes don't have much of a personality. For some reason, I'm addicted to mine—even though she's a total pain in my ass.

When we step outside, I should revel in the feel of the sun against my skin. But at the moment, I'm incapable of taking in our surroundings. All I can do is look at Thorne, questioning.

"Here." He takes me by the left wrist and says, "Let me try something."

I nod silently, and he closes his eyes. As we stand there, the Dragonflyers flitting this way and that, I feel a sensation of warmth build between his palm and my forearm—a warmth that eventually turns to heat, and just as it's growing too hot to bear, he lets me go, pulling back as though my flesh has seared him.

"What is it?" I ask when I see a look of quiet concern in his eyes.

"The reason she's acting so erratic isn't that she's changed. It's that her data is being withdrawn," he says. "*Downloaded.*"

Shit.

"Maude has access to every memory I've ever had, including the *Storian's* memories..."

The realization strikes Thorne just as it hits me.

"Can you make it stop?"

He nods, taking my wrist again, and almost instantly I feel something inside me grind to a halt, a sharp breath leaping into my lungs.

"Give it a few seconds, then call to her again."

I do as he says. "Maude?"

She's silent for a moment, then I feel her voice.

~Yes, Shara?

"Are you there? Are you all right?"

~Of course I am. I just replied to you, didn't I?

"You haven't been yourself lately. I thought—"

~Of course I'm myself. Who else would I be, you noodle loaf?

"Oh, thank God." I've never been so happy to take an insult from my internal nemesis. "What happened there? Who was downloading my memories? Was it my father?"

~No, Maude replies. *Though I'm not entirely sure who is responsible.*

"Then how can you know it wasn't my father?"

~Because they were being downloaded to a server in the Isles. A Noble's residence. It could be the palace, but there's no way for me to tell.

At that, I look into Thorne's eyes, and he nods with immediate understanding.

"You heard her," I say. "Do you think it's Tallin? He's no tech genius—but maybe he's terrified because he's realized I have a hell of a lot of information inside my mind that could turn Kravan on its head."

"I suppose it could be him," Thorne says. "But if Maude can't tell, neither can I—not without more information."

"Maude—did they actually gain access to the Storian's memories before Thorne stopped the download?"

Maude seems to rifle through her memory banks, then says, *~They accessed a little—only enough to know there was a coup and the president was killed—but nothing after that. They know Quinton's name and that he was the first king.*

"You're sure? Nothing else?"

~Not that I can tell.

"Well, I don't see what harm that would really do," I reply with a sigh of quasi-relief.

"You're probably right," Thorne replies, taking my hand and pulling me close. "It's done now, and hopefully they won't go digging into your mind again."

By now, the Citadel's doors have closed behind us, and we're standing at the center of a narrow alleyway flanked by tall, gray concrete walls.

The Dragonflyers are still hovering close by like watchful sentinels. Had they come from anyone but the Magister and my father, I'd find them slightly terrifying. But there's something reassuring about the strange little metal companions.

I turn to Thorne, pulling myself close and finally allowing a rush of joy to flood through my body and mind—one I've been holding behind a cruel dam for so long that I'd almost forgotten what bliss feels like.

"Freedom," I say softly, brushing my lips against his. "I never thought we'd see this day. When Rivenna told me what happens to Royal Guard in the Capitol, I thought..."

And just like that, joy is replaced by anxiety.

"Don't," Thorne says, his hand slipping to my cheek. "This realm has been in conflict since long before you and I were born. As much as I hate to say it, the members of the Royal Guard in the prison aren't on our side, Shara. They would kill the Magister and your father if they had half a chance. It's what they were trained to do. And as much as I'd like to free them from their indoctrination, you and I both know it's almost impossible. I've worked with the Royal Guard, and most of them refuse to see the light."

"I want to think you're right," I tell him. "I really do. Still, I wish they were given a chance at a fair trial. They all looked exhausted when I saw them. Depleted of life."

"It's the cilice. It saps their energy. But trust me, they have no intention of going quietly back to the palace. And once they learn of the king's death, their rage will only increase."

"Without a king to serve, they should revel in their freedom."

"They'll still be willing to die for Tallin. Their loyalty is to the crown—not to the individual royals themselves. But when we free Kravan and abolish the monarchy once and for all, things will change. I promise you that."

I take hold of his waist and savor the sensation when he pulls me to his chest. "I know. And I love you for it. If anyone can bring about change and mobilize an army, it's you."

"Speaking of change..." Thorne cranes his neck to stare up over the buildings in the distance.

I follow his gaze until I see the structure casting a shadow over half the Capitol. My heart sinks when my eyes land on the Tower looming over us in all its horrific glory.

For a few minutes, I'd banished its existence from my mind.

I narrow my eyes, taking it in, reminding myself that on many of the lower levels are hundreds of Tethered children and teenagers, trapped between its walls and forced to sleep each night in cells. Each day, they're reminded by those in charge that touching one another—even innocently—will land them in solitary confinement.

Standing on the outside now with the man I love, the structure seems more terrible and inhumane than it ever did before.

My eyes well with tears when I murmur, “I hope the Magister really is powerful enough to bring it down.”

“If he isn’t,” Thorne says, “then we will do it ourselves.”

At that, Mercutio slips out of my pocket and leaps to the ground, pushing himself onto his hind legs and focusing his small eyes on us. When we’ve acknowledged him, he begins to scamper away, turning back to ensure that we follow.

“He’s sick of waiting for us to live our lives,” I say. “And he’s right. Let’s get on with it.”

CHAPTER
TWENTY-THREE

The only sound meeting our ears is the Dragonflyers' perpetual buzz alongside our steps, which echo off the surrounding walls like a slow series of ricocheting bullets. For a few minutes, it seems like we're making our way through a deserted world.

Still, nothing can dampen my lightened mood as I stroll along with Thorne's arm around my waist and mine around his, my mind reeling with hopes and plans for a future together.

Our strange, sparkling bodyguards hum along above us, and Mercutio bounds ahead, turning occasionally to make sure we're still close.

When the walled corridor comes to an end, I'm pleasantly surprised to spot a tree-lined avenue stretching out before us with a series of wooden houses to either side.

Tidily mowed, lush green lawns greet our eyes, as well as pretty flowers planted carefully in well-watered garden beds.

"Wow," Thorne breathes. "I genuinely didn't know the Capitol could look like this. All I've ever seen of it is ruin."

A shock of joy wraps itself around my heart, and it takes only a moment to realize it's Thorne's bliss that I'm feeling—*his* hope shared with me, the most exquisite gift imaginable.

"I feel like we've just walked into a dream," I say softly, watching Mercutio scurry along ahead of us, soaking up the sunlight pouring down from the cloudless sky. "This is how I always imagined a town should look—how I imagined life should feel."

We stroll along for a few blocks, our eyes taking in every pretty home with their window boxes and immaculately painted façades. Here and there, wooden rocking chairs perch on pleasant porches, awaiting their owners.

Toward the middle of the fourth block, Thorne's hope begins to turn to rage, and I feel it heating inside me—a growing conflagration.

His jaw tightens, the muscles of his neck tensing with emotion.

"What is it?" I ask. "What's wrong?'

He nods toward the distance, and my eyes follow his gaze.

I've been so consumed by the perfect homes surrounding us that I hadn't even noticed that the idyllic avenue seems to come to an abrupt end about ten houses down, where it meets an intersection that looks like it's part of another world entirely.

Some of the houses are flattened to nothing but shards of their former selves, while others have gaping holes in their roofs or walls, scorch marks scarring their exteriors.

A few old oak trees, refusing to succumb to the mayhem unleashed on their home, still stand guard over the houses. But they're all that's survived the onslaught.

"A few blocks of beauty," Thorne says. "A little taste of perfection. That's it. Then we get to see just how horrific the king's slaughter was. The people who resided here—they were families who wanted to live their lives in peace."

"Why would Tomas do this?" I ask, my voice strained. I'm not sure who I'm addressing. Thorne, Maude, or me. "What purpose would it even serve?"

"It kept people desperate—preoccupied with survival. Every day they spent trying to simply exist was a day they wouldn't rise up against him. It was a clever plan—and a cruel one."

Thorne's ire is intense, and I love him for it. His heart rages on behalf of people he's never even met. He is their champion and will fight for them until his dying breath—simply because it's the right thing to do.

"Who the hell would want to rule ash and rubble?" I ask. "King Tomas is—*was*—a dick, no question about it. But this seems extreme, even for him."

"Do you think it might have been someone else who did this?"

"I really don't know. I've heard all these conflicting stories—that rebels in the Capitol sow chaos to create confusion. The Starless could have been behind it, I suppose. They're not exactly pleasant."

"True...but I'm not about to absolve the king. He's the one who equipped the Tower with hundreds of unmanned bombers."

I can't argue with that.

We begin to walk again, our hands clasped in desperate solidarity, and when we reach the destroyed end of the street, it feels like we've strolled out of a full-color world into a black-and-white one. Almost every surface is coated in countless layers of ash. Makeshift barriers made of wooden boards have been erected here and there to keep people from stepping into deep trenches carved by bombs.

On the boards' surfaces are posters and stenciled, spray-painted messages.

I instantly recognize the saying I've heard from more than one Starless.

The Rebellion is a Lie.

But it's another message that draws my eye—one I haven't seen before.

"Thorne, look," I say, pointing to an ominous series of words scrawled in dripping red paint.

"*The heir will bring ruin on us all,*" he says slowly, and as the words meet my ears, my eyes move from one temporary wall to the next, only to see the phrase written over and over again. Here and there, someone has drawn arrows pointing toward the devastated end of the street with its derelict or flattened houses, as if blaming the "heir" for the destruction of the neighborhood.

"The heir?" I whisper. "Do you suppose they mean Tallin? But that would mean they know the king is dead—and you and I just learned that, ourselves."

Thorne shrugs. "Let's keep moving. Maybe we can work it out as we go."

He holds my hand tighter, more out of protection than affection, wary as his eyes dart here and there in search of threats. Mercutio, too, looks like he's on high alert, stopping every few feet to perch on his hind legs and peer around.

The Dragonflyers shoot back and forth through the air at chest height, giving the distinct impression that they don't want us going much farther down the street.

"Thorne?" I ask softly, pulling myself closer to him. A sudden, deep apprehension has begun to radiate from his mind and heart, and I know from experience that he's seeing more than just what lies before us.

He lets my hand go, yanking himself away as if my touch has just caused him pain.

I'm almost afraid to ask the question on my lips.

What...just...happened?

He stares at me for a long moment, sadness sketching its way over his features. When I try to tap into his emotions, all I can feel is a frightening emptiness.

He shakes his head. "It's nothing. Really. Nothing..."

A loud buzz interrupts us, and I pull my eyes up to see a large drone flying high above. Thorne and Mercutio seem unbothered by it, despite the fact that on its bottom, I spot what looks like a royal crest.

~The Citadel has control over that drone, Maude announces out loud. *There's no need to fear it.*

"It's true," Thorne concurs. "It's ours."

"In that case, let's walk just a little more. I'm not ready to go back just yet."

After about half a block, we come to a paved pathway leading up to a damaged yet charming house. Its front lawn is surrounded by what was once a white wooden fence with a little gate. It's sullied with soot now, and here and there, its slats are broken—but it still evokes a sense of home like none I've ever known.

A large wraparound porch adorns the house's façade. The

roof is partly caved in, the front door ajar. The place doesn't look inhabited—or inhabitable. Come to think of it, I'm not sure any of the houses are—not even the perfect ones closer to the Citadel.

I take Thorne by the arm and say, "Let's go inside."

He looks like he's about to protest, but when he sees my expression, he laughs, seeming to forget the worry that attacked his mind a minute ago, and kisses me. "Okay, you adventurous little minx. Anything for you."

His sadness seems to have passed like an errant cloud, and I'm grateful for his sake.

We make our way up the walkway and scale the precarious stairs to the house's porch, pushing the door in and stepping inside.

The floor is covered in dust and chipped bits of plaster. The ceiling is full of holes, and below one section where the roof has fallen in—just above the kitchen at the back of the house—the floor is damp and rotting away in spots.

The living room, with its couch and two armchairs, is remarkably intact. A large bay window at the front of the room is boarded up, but another series of windows to one side allow light to flood in.

Mercutio scurries around the place, sniffing at every corner. Maude cautions me that the house's structural integrity isn't entirely sound, but I ignore her and make my way toward a shattered window where a branch covered in green leaves is intruding upon the house's interior. Along the branch's surface here and there are roses of deep red, blooming exquisitely despite the messy chaos that surrounds us.

"Look, Thorne," I half whisper, gingerly taking hold of

one of the flowers. Its petals are delicate and soft as silk. "The roses don't care that the world is a disaster. They just want to live their lives."

At the Verdans' home, one of my jobs was to tend the gardens. But never have any flowers seemed so lovely and strong as these roses, persisting in the face of so much hopelessness.

A lump forms in my throat as my eyes take in every corner of the space around us.

I barely whisper the words, "This house is magical."

Thorne wraps his powerful arms around me from behind, resting his chin on my head. "Maybe one day, we can live somewhere like this."

"A dream," I say with a nod.

On the walls are a series of faded rectangles—places where pictures once hung. I imagine smiling children. A dog in the park. Generations of family gathered to celebrate various milestones.

When you spend your entire life in a prison, the simplest things become a dream, and freedom becomes the most valuable currency imaginable. Though it's on the verge of collapse, this house is the embodiment of every small, trivial fantasy I've ever had of a life devoid of oppression.

As small as it is, as decrepit—I would rather have a home like this than all the palaces in the world.

"I wonder how long its previous owners managed to live in peace," Thorne muses. "How long this house existed before it was destroyed."

"I don't know. But one day, I hope you and I have one just like it. Roses in the garden. A dog in the yard. Now that the king is gone, maybe the dream can become a reality."

Thorne's reply bites at the air. "Tallin would burn the world to the ground before allowing the Capitol to enjoy a state of peace. You and I both know it."

He's right.

Tallin thrives on destruction. There's no telling what he might do to prove his might as Kravan's new leader.

"I wish I could argue with you, but I can't," I sigh. "He's the poster boy for the saying *Misery loves company.*"

~He's the poster boy for Asshat of the Year, too, Maude replies as if to remind us she's still here and very much back to herself. *Chode of the Century. Fuckface of the Decade. Garbage Fire of the Millen—*

"Enough, Maude!" I say out loud, laughing. "Don't get me wrong—it's impressive that you rose from the dead only to develop the mouth of a sailor. But maybe you should take it down a notch."

Thorne doesn't look quite so amused when he says, "We will take the prince down. I promise you that."

"Maybe I should be the one to do it," I reply. When Thorne looks like he's going to protest, I add, "Don't forget that just before he went on his rampage and killed his parents, he told me to run. He trusts me. Maybe I can get close to him."

"Get close to him, and you will die." He slips his fingers around my neck as if to remind me of my vulnerability. He moves his hand down to rest on my collarbone but doesn't squeeze—he wouldn't, not unless I begged him to. Still, it's enough to refresh my memory. I haven't forgotten what the prince has done to me in the past—how he tortured me emotionally, threatened me, and frightened me, every chance he got.

And that was when he actually *needed* me.

He no longer needs a Hunter; what he needs are sycophants and yes-men who will do his bidding and help him hold onto the power his father left in his hands.

Thorne is right. I can't take the prince on myself. Tallin let me go once, but that doesn't mean he won't murder me the next time he sees me.

I raise my chin to Thorne and smile. For now, we're safely tucked inside this little dream house, broken and battered as it is.

"You know what?" I say. "I don't want to think about Tallin. Only you and me."

Pulling free of his grip, I slip toward the wall, turning to summon him with my eyes.

"War is coming," I breathe. "Maybe we should make the most of the time we have."

CHAPTER TWENTY-FOUR

In two strides, Thorne has his hands on my waist, lifting me onto a broad windowsill. A cool breeze wafts in from the back of the house, caressing my neck as I lift my chin, inviting him closer.

He intakes a violent breath then slips a hand under my top, his fingers stopping, delighted, when they reach the curve of my breast.

"Fuck," he murmurs, pressing his face to my neck. "No bra."

I opted this morning for a tank top and sweater again, knowing—or at least *hoping*—this moment might come.

The delight in his voice is enough to tell me I made the right call.

"No bra," I repeat as he curves a finger, slipping the knuckle over the hard peak of my nipple.

"How do you walk through life with such perfect breasts?" he whispers, the ripples of his delighted laugh brushing against my skin.

He lifts my top, exposing my torso to the cool air, and stares.

"Hold your shirt up for me," he commands, landing on his knees before me, a small cloud of dust exploding from below.

I obey as he bites gently at one nipple while slipping calloused fingers over the other, drawing a moan from my lips and a tight clench from my core.

"Your body..." he whispers. "Always calling my name."

"Always."

He reaches down, slipping a hand slowly inside my loose-fitting trousers, and growls with delight when he discovers how wet I am for him. I shove my hips forward, demanding more, and he succumbs, stroking his fingertip over me as his lips close around my nipple, tongue teasing.

"The Dragonflyers might come in," I laugh. "I want you inside me before they catch us."

"I know," he says, his words foggy against my flesh. "But I want to feel you come for me, first."

"Thorne..."

"I'll stop if you want me to," he promises, his eyes flicking up to mine. "But only if you demand it."

I shake my head. "I'll never ask you to stop. Not in a million years."

"Good. Because I sure as hell don't want to."

Taking the waistband of my pants in his hands, he drags them down and buries his face between my thighs, lifting my knees over his shoulders.

I move into his mouth, my hips taking on a mind of their own, brazen and shameless in their desire. Thorne responds with a low groan of pleasure, his tongue working me in long, drawn-out laps, pausing only to tend to the bundle of nerves he loves so well. He sucks at me, forcing pulses of pleasure to vibrate and throb through my entire body.

I'm already so close to the brink; a wave, about to crest then crash into a glorious shore...when an angry, wild buzz meets my ears. Thorne leaps up and I jump off the windowsill, yanking my pants back up. I'm convinced at first that someone has slipped into the house with us.

It takes a few seconds to realize the sound is coming from outside—somewhere in front of the boarded-up bay window.

"What's happening?" I whisper.

Thorne leaps forward, peeking through an opening between the wooden slats as I scramble to join him. I watch through another narrow gap as the Dragonflyers flit around in front of the house, their wings creating a loud, angry thrum the likes of which I've only ever associated with power tools.

It's then that I see four figures, each dressed like the Poisoner that Rivenna and I encountered in the tunnels. Each of them is wearing a stiff, gray mask, their clothing dull-colored and dirty.

"Starless," I breathe.

Thorne nods almost imperceptibly.

"They know we're here," he says. "They must."

He's barely uttered the words when a large drone bursts into the sky overhead like a shot, coming to a sudden stop twenty or so feet above the strangers' heads.

Shouts erupt among the Starless, with one of them pointing up at the sky...

But the warning comes far too late.

A projectile hurtles through the air, a precisely aimed weapon that explodes in an angry, violent blast at chest height between the four figures. The Starless fly backwards in a horrific burst of crimson, and I leap away from the window, nausea assaulting my insides.

There's no question in my mind that all four are dead. I'm not even sure their bodies still look human.

A whimper escapes my lips and Thorne turns and reaches for me, pulling me close, my head against his chest.

"Your father was protecting you," he whispers into my hair. "He—or the Magister—did that to ensure you made it back to the Citadel alive. Those people might have killed you otherwise, Shara."

"I could have talked to them. I could have—" I begin, but Thorne holds me tighter, silencing me.

"With the masks on, it's impossible to know their powers until it's far too late. You don't know what they might have been capable of. Chances are, they didn't come here to talk."

"You're right," I reply, pulling away and wiping at my eyes. "But the drone was protecting us *both*. You're the Magister's most important asset. My father said as much. You're their greatest hope for winning the coming war. Maybe, if we can do that, no one else needs to..." My eyes move to the window, and I'm suddenly grateful that it's boarded up.

At that, Thorne grimaces. There's no doubt in my mind that he's thinking what I am. *We just watched four people die without a trial. Without having committed any crime other than walking down a street.*

If this is how the Magister doles out justice, is his rule going to be any better than King Tomas's?

"Let's get back to the Citadel," Thorne says gently. "Let's get you safe and figure out our next steps. The sooner we can get rid of the prince, the sooner we can work on restoring peace."

As my heart rate slows, I take his hand in mine, my fingers interlocking with his. I stare up into his exquisite eyes, taking in their potent blend of emotions.

"It's really happening," I say. "Isn't it? The world is about to change at last." I glance toward the window, then back at him. "You and I will help make sure that never happens again. Whoever those people were, they didn't deserve to be killed like that."

"Maybe not. But this is war, and the regime you and I have known since we were born is about to be brought down. You..." He combs a hand through my hair, pressing his forehead to mine, "and I...*we*...will be a part of it. The next time history is recorded, you and I will be remembered for our part in the liberation of Kravan. We will do whatever it takes—kill whoever we need—to achieve our goal."

Something in his voice jars me—a cold ambition I've never once heard from Thorne.

I jerk myself backward, searching his eyes once again for his meaning. He sounds almost bitter—as if he's actually looking *forward* to the mayhem to come.

When I first met Thorne, he seemed mischievous—almost malicious at times, like he was looking to hurt me for pleasure. It took me some time to realize it was all a tactic on his part. He wanted me to fear—even loathe him—so that no one would question his recommendation to have me work in the Verdan home with him.

But this, right now, is no act. This is real.

And it frightens me.

"I don't care about being remembered as a liberator," I snap. "I'm not after glory. I care about our people. I care about all the innocents who have been murdered and starved, and pitted against each other, all so the rich could get richer. If my name disappears forever, it doesn't matter, so long as I do everything I can to help in the meantime." My voice almost breaks when I ask, "Since when are *you* looking for fame?"

"Not fame," he protests, a shield mounting around his heart so that I can no longer feel his emotions. "All I want is to be remembered one day as someone who helped make things right. We should all aspire to that, don't you think?"

The reply appeases me slightly, and I nod, though I'm still shaken by what we both witnessed.

Everything in this place feels a little off right now. The Dragonflyers should be reassuring, yet they feel more like spies than protectors. The shocking contrast of new homes and ruins feels manufactured by design, rather than hopeful.

But Thorne is the one I'm most concerned about. It's like a switch inside him has been flicked and his priorities have shifted along with it. His thoughts are concealed behind a thick curtain, and he's suddenly harboring fantasies of being revered as a war hero.

Maybe my father and the Magister are getting to him—giving him too much power by naming him a military leader. I don't know.

All I know is that I don't want to be here anymore.

~He's showing his confidence, Maude says. *He needs to, Shara. You can't win a war if you don't believe victory is possible. He needs to feel protective of you for now—needs to feel in control.*

Had those Starless gotten any closer, things might have ended very badly.

I suppose you're right, I reply silently.

Thorne is riled up, just as I am. Angry. Defensive.

I remind myself he's simply coming into his own at long last. This has always been his fate—to lead, to train, to help. He's always been powerful, and he knows how to charm people and how to take charge—important characteristics of an effective leader.

Perhaps he is entitled to a little fame, after all.

"Come on," Thorne says, taking my hand. "Let's get back to the Citadel before your father sends men hunting for us."

"I have to find Mercutio," I say, clicking my tongue against my teeth and waiting until I hear the scurrying of tiny feet as the little mouse darts toward me from a far corner. I scoop him up in my hand and let him fall into a pocket to curl up and go dormant.

Thorne manages to guide me out the house's back door, which is splintered as though someone has kicked it in. We skirt around the side of the house to avoid having to see the worst of the carnage, but for some reason I can't explain, I turn briefly to glance back at the bodies, instantly regretting it when I see that one of the dead is a young woman. Her chest is torn open, her jacket soaked with blood.

In her hand is something that glistens in the sunlight. At first, I assume it's a weapon, and a sense of relief overtakes me to think the drone operator might have picked up on a genuine threat from these strangers.

"Hang on a second," I say, pulling away from Thorne to step over to her—only to see that it's not a weapon, but a silver chain and pendant held firmly in her hand.

The object looks at first glance like the Magister's symbol—the circle with lines inside its perimeter—only, when I look more closely, I see that instead of curved lines, the circle contains what looks like an abstract outline of a sword or a dagger.

I pull it from her fingers and hold it up to study it.

"What's that?" Thorne asks.

"I'm not sure," I tell him, examining the object. "A variation of the Magister's symbol, I guess. Maybe it's some special Starless pendant."

"Or a trophy," he says as I slip the pendant into my pocket. "Taken from a previous kill."

"Why would she have it in her hand like that if she was coming to kill us, though?"

Thorne shrugs. "Some of these people aren't exactly rational. If they were, they wouldn't be looking to take down the Magister's allies. We're here to help them—not to fight."

I want to believe him. I want to think he's absolutely right—that we're on the right side.

But I can't get the image of the explosion out of my mind. The unceremonious slaughter of four people who had no weapons in their possession.

Then again, they were probably Tethered. Which means they *were* weapons in their own right.

"Shara," Thorne says softly, a hand on my back as my eyes move over the remains of the four victims.

"Hmm?" I reply, half frozen in place.

"Let's go back to our suite. I want to hold you every second that I possibly can."

With a grateful nod, I turn away from death and begin to walk.

CHAPTER TWENTY-FIVE

THE DRAGONFLYERS GUIDE us back to the Citadel, then hover overhead to ensure we enter the structure safely via the doors we came through earlier. Thorne and I stride inside, relieved when they seal up behind us.

A few minutes later, we're safely in our suite, lying together on the bed. My head is on Thorne's chest, his arms around me. His shield has receded a little, and inside him, I can feel a shifting jumble of conflicting emotions.

He's gone unusually silent since the incident with the four Starless, and it takes me a little to find the courage to ask what's wrong.

His chest rises as he takes in a deep breath. "Before the drone attack...something happened to me out there."

I push myself up to a sitting position and look at him. His eyes are locked on something—or possibly nothing—on the other side of the room.

He looks as troubled as he ever has, and it unsettles me, threatening to tear apart the small shreds of hope I've managed to hold onto.

"If this is about the attack," I tell him, "you were right—the Starless are dangerous, whether I like it or not. They could have killed us. As much as it pains me to say it, their deaths were probably inevitable."

"No—it's nothing to do with that." His eyes swim with power, a multicolored ebb and flow that reminds me that his gifts, like mine, are strengthening with our growing bond. "I—saw something out there, and I wasn't sure whether I should tell you about it."

"Something to do with the Starless, you mean?"

He shakes his head. "Something to do with the future. *Our* future."

Almost against my will, I try to feel his thoughts, his emotions—to gauge what he's talking about before he has a chance to tell me.

I'm almost afraid to learn what he saw. I recall the look in his eye when he spoke of being remembered—when his cold desire to kill was on full display. A chill creeps over my skin to think of him being so candid about this new, raw ambition.

"You're freaking me out," I murmur. "What, exactly, did you see?"

"I saw *you*," he replies, stroking a hand over my arm, his tone dead serious. "Beautiful you, standing in a field of grass. You looked different. But it was still you. Still incredible."

"What's sad about that?" I ask, calming a little. "I mean, I'm not fishing for compliments, but..."

"You were smiling," he says. "Your father was there. Other people, too. Everything was perfect."

"I still don't see how this is bad news."

"The thing is..." His lips tighten into a stark line, and he blows out a breath. "I wasn't there. It was like I was seeing a future where I didn't belong—one that I had no part in."

"Well, that doesn't make any sense, does it?" But the truth is, a quiet foreboding has begun creeping through my mind. In the tunnels, Kith showed me a similar scene. What my father referred to as my "Pairing."

And Thorne wasn't there, either.

"Are you trying to tell me something?" I ask him, my voice thinning through a smile, a taut, silken thread threatening to snap. "Are you having second thoughts about us?"

At that, his eyes widen. He grabs me by the shirt, pulls me to him, and kisses me hard enough to draw any doubt from my mind. "God, no. Of course not. You're fucking amazing, and I love you more than anything in the world, Shara. I'm just trying to figure out how I fit into your future—into the world you and I want to build."

"You fit in very, very well," I say, chuckling as my hand reaches for the swollen bulge pushing against the front of his pants. "I mean, I'll admit that sometimes, it's a tight fit. But..."

Thorne laughs and throws me onto my back, pressing his lips to my neck. "You always know what to say, don't you? You take my troubled mind and tenderize it with your perfection."

At that, I let out a proper laugh. "Now, *that* is poetry."

I'm about to suggest we rid ourselves of the inconvenience of clothing when Maude buzzes a sharp warning into my arm.

~Someone's coming this way, Shara. I'm afraid you two tedious lovebirds are about to be interrupted.

"Damn it," I curse under my breath. "Why do people always have to ruin everything?"

When the knock sounds at the door a few seconds later, I open it to discover Joy looking sheepish on the other side, as if she knows exactly what Thorne and I were about to do.

"I'm so sorry," she says. "Your father wishes to see you in his private office, Shara." She peers over at Thorne and adds, "Alone."

"Why alone?" I've kept my promise to my father—I haven't told Thorne or anyone else about my sister Soleia's disappearance. But other than that topic, I can't think of a reason he would exclude Thorne from this meeting.

"I'm not exactly sure. But don't worry—I'll be bringing you two some food later, and you can eat here, in the privacy of your suite. I'm sure you're both still exhausted after everything you've been through."

Something in Joy's eyes tells me she's aware of far more about both of us than she lets on—but if so, she doesn't say a thing about it.

"Thanks, Joy," Thorne tells her with a nod of his head. He steps over, kisses me once, and adds, "I'm going to take a shower and head down to the smithy to check out the progress on the bracers. We'll meet back here?"

With a nod, I tell him I'll be back shortly, then accompany Joy to a distant wing of the Citadel.

My father's office is tucked away down a quiet hallway. It's a dark chamber, long and high-ceilinged, an entire wall lined with shelves covered in leather-bound books and ornate wooden boxes of various sizes.

Joy gestures for me to enter, nods silently, then immediately leaves.

On my father's broad desk is a series of what look like discolored old papers, and as I take a step forward, he grabs hold of them, stacking them neatly into a pile.

"What are those?" I ask, though I know perfectly well it's no business of mine.

"A little bit of history," he says. "Nothing to concern yourself with just now."

He tucks the papers into a drawer, then gestures to me to take a seat in one of two leather chairs facing the desk. When I've obliged, he smiles, then lets out a sigh. "My dear daughter, I hear my drones encountered a hunting party out there, and wanted to make sure you were all right."

I nod, my mind just barely absorbing the fact that he said *my* drones—not the *Magister's* drones. Not *our* drones.

Mine.

"Four Starless," I tell him. "They were killed instantly."

"I'm sorry you had to bear witness to that," he says, his head tipping to the side in sympathy. "Truly. I fully expected you'd be alone out there—you and Thorne. I wanted you to have a pleasant stroll and get a taste of Kravan's future."

"It was beautiful while it lasted," I tell him. "The houses, the landscaping—the Magister's people have put in a great deal of work."

"Yes. The reconstruction is moving along well and will only accelerate in the coming days."

"Do the Starless often come so close to the Citadel?" I ask, trying my best not to show vulnerability. The truth is, I want to scream every time I think about how much death I've witnessed over the past few months—how much needless destruction and cruelty. Today sent shockwaves through my soul.

"Not often. But chances are, word has gotten out that my daughter is here. They know hurting you would hurt me—and our cause. I suppose I was foolish to let you and Thorne out without a proper guide."

Let us out.

The words stick somewhere in my gut, with their insinuation of possession and imprisonment.

All my life, I've craved a father, a mother. Siblings. I wanted to belong to someone—and yet, now that I do, the idea of ownership grates at my mind.

I fled the palace seeking freedom, not to be controlled by yet another person.

I've found my mother and father—each mysterious in their way. I discovered I had a sister, even. But all I can think of now is that small house that Thorne and I visited briefly, with its potential for a little garden. A space of our very own where we could live a quiet life, free of control. *Free of shackles.*

"Please," I plead, "don't keep us locked up in here. I've spent my whole life under lock and key—I need a little taste of life on the outside of prisons."

It used to be that when I used the p-word, Maude would buzz an angry warning. But no more. Now, she's silent, as if in solidarity with me.

My father stares at me with what appears to be a combination of affection and concern, then finally lets out a sigh.

"I will need your Thorne to remain here in the Citadel for

the next while. With the news of the king's death, we have only a small window in which to act, and every moment he can spare for the cause is crucial. Meanwhile, I will let *you* out—but only on two conditions."

"Name them."

"One, you will have a chaperone—a guardian. One of my best—someone who will take great care of you."

I nod. "Fair enough."

"Two, you will only head out to areas our drones have already scanned. I want you to see everything, Daughter. I want you to take in what you may one day oversee from the seat of a leader. But I want you safe, as well."

"Wait—*leader?*" I laugh. "Hardly. I realize you're more or less at the top of the food chain in the Capitol—but *I'll* never oversee anything. I'm here to help in any way I can, but I'm not looking for some kind of misplaced glory. All I want is a simple existence and a quiet life."

He laughs then—something low and warm—and leaps out of his chair to stride over to me, taking hold of my shoulders. "Your sister Soleia would have liked you so very much. She was so like you, Shara—at least, for the short while that I had the pleasure of her company. She lived for simple pleasures as all children do. She was blue sky peeking through dark cloud—a newly blossomed tree. Quiet, beautiful, sweet—perfect. She was never going to aspire to leadership—I could tell from the time she could walk. You're so similar, and I admire your lack of ambition, truly. I *respect* it."

The words feel like the most backhanded of compliments, but I choose to take them in the most positive light possible. After all, in my experience, ambition is a trait reserved for cruel men and women. I have no desire to count myself among them.

"*But* you're wrong," my father adds. "You will likely be expected to take on a certain amount of power one day, whether you like it or not, my dear. Even if you never serve in any official capacity, you've already made quite a name for yourself in these parts. It may interest you to know there may be another reason entirely that the Starless came looking for you. Word has it they're already calling you the *Regent Killer*."

"What?" I nearly choke on nothing but air. "Why?"

He lowers his chin and gives me a knowing look that tells me I'm far too intelligent to ask questions like that.

"News spreads quickly. The Capitol has already begun to whisper that the king is dead—and they are also aware that a certain young woman fled the palace shortly after his death."

"But the king was still very much alive when I left!" I nearly shout, drawing back in horror. "I didn't know he was dead until I got here!"

"You're forgetting that you arrived many hours after he died," my father says with a doleful *tsk*. "Which means many will logically assume you killed him. It's not your fault—word from my informant has it the prince himself is the one who started spreading the rumor."

A surge of fear overtakes me, and it's all I can do not to double over with nausea. I want to flee this chamber and sprint back to Thorne's waiting arms, to hide in his grip until the world has come to its senses.

"They *can't* think I killed King Tomas," I croak. "That's ridiculous. I'll spend my life with a target on my back!"

With a frown, the Shadow says, "Let me ask you: what would *you* think if you heard about a Tethered infiltrating the palace, disguised as a Noble woman—one who flees for her life the moment the king is dead? Come, now, Shara." With another laugh, he seats himself in the other leather chair. "What conclusion would you draw—that a beloved prince killed his own father, or that it was a Tethered infiltrator who did it? Not to mention that your lover had already fled to the Capitol, presumably hoping to meet you here. It's all very incriminating—which means we'll need to do some damage control in the coming days, and you will certainly need protection at all times."

I ask Maude whether she knows anything about this—if she thinks it's really possible that the Capitol's citizens think I'm so awful.

~I'm afraid it's entirely possible. You have a target on your back now. You'll be seen by some as a villain, Shara. But by many as a hero. The king isn't exactly popular with everyone in the Capitol, remember. You could work this to your advantage.

Her gravity makes me wince. I've never particularly enjoyed sincere Maude. I want her to crack stupid jokes and make jabs about how bad I smell.

Anything but this level of earnestness.

I liked you better when you were robotic and weird, I tell her.

~I liked you better when you weren't nauseated with fear or horny all the time, but here we are.

"I'll be with you every step of the way, Shara," my father vows, apparently oblivious to the fact that I'm having a silent spat with my inner demon. "Don't you worry for a moment. Now—on the topic of seeing the Capitol—Kith will take you to see the sights while Thorne is in his training sessions with our men."

"Kith?" I ask, the heaviness inside me lifting just a little. "Really?"

If I'm to be heading back out there with anyone other than Thorne, I suppose he's the best possible choice.

"Of course. He's a fine young man. Without him, I don't know where the Magister and I would be. I've relied on his help and intellect for years. There's no one I trust more in this world to keep my daughter safe."

"He is impressive," I concede. "I'd be happy to have him as a guardian. But now, if you don't mind, I'd like to head back to spend some time with Thorne before I lose him to the training sessions. Joy said we're to have dinner in our suite tonight."

"Actually," my father says with a mischievous glint in his eye, "I wanted to invite you and him to dinner in the Magister's dining room this evening. I thought I'd invite your friend Rivenna as well. She's another reliable fighter—and I feel that I owe her a good deal after she looked after you in the tunnels."

Something inside me curdles a little at the mention of Rivenna, but I can't say why. After all, I like her—not to mention that she saved my ass more than once in the tunnels.

So why am I feeling a shock of dread right now?

Maude's voice slips into my mind again. *~Oh, I don't know. Could it be because Rivenna is beautiful, and your tethered mate has eyes?*

Of course not. Why would you even say a thing like that?

I can almost hear the shrug in her voice. *Because I enjoy messing with you.*

"Joy will knock on your door when the time comes," my father says, rising to his feet, once again oblivious to my internal conversation. "You're free as a bird to do as you please....for now."

I leave his office, half-jogging back to the suite with two words twisting through my mind and clawing at my thoughts.

For now.

CHAPTER TWENTY-SIX

BACK IN OUR SUITE, I've barely had time to kiss Thorne, shower, and change into khaki pants and a white blouse when a gentle knock sounds.

Thorne and I exchange a frustrated look as he strides over to the door.

His tone is surly when he pulls it open and issues an aggressive, "Yes?"

"Rivenna!" I cry when I see the figure standing in the doorway, dressed entirely in form-fitting black clothing.

She's rid herself of the dark contact lenses for now, and her eyes sparkle and twist with color in the hallway's dim light.

"Where's Berengar?" I ask, looking around.

"He's with a friend in the city. They don't love having murder hounds in the Citadel, so I thought I'd let him hang out in a nicer environment."

"Rivenna," Thorne murmurs, his voice shifting instantly. "I'm sorry—I didn't realize—"

He gawks at her, stepping back as if taking her in from so

close up is proving impossible. Something in his body language sets my nerves on edge, but I tell myself not to overanalyze it.

We've had a weird day. We're both a little off at the moment.

"Come in," I tell Rivenna, glancing at the bed only to realize it has the disheveled look of one that's been recently used for a *lot* of sex.

Quickly, I throw the covers over it and turn back to face our guest.

With a knowing chuckle, she says, "Don't worry—I'm not here for a visit. The Magister asked me to grab you both and bring you to dinner in his private dining room."

"My father mentioned something about that. I'm glad you'll be joining us. I'm sure Thorne is, too."

My eyes land on him, only to see he's still staring at her a little too intently.

I can't read his expression—whether it's one of admiration, curiosity, or something else, I can't tell. But a quiet fear begins to grow inside me despite all attempts to quell it.

He's speechless in the face of a beautiful woman. That's not like Thorne.

~I did warn you, Maude says, her tone irritatingly smug.

He isn't ogling her. He's just...

~Captivated? Intrigued? Smitten? Aroused?

Don't make me electrocute you.

~You'd electrocute yourself in the process.

It would be worth it.

"I'm glad, too," Rivenna replies, staring back at him with an intensity that almost matches his own. "I...I mean, if it's all right with you both that I'm dining with you."

With some effort, she drags her eyes back to me.

"Of course," I say, taking Thorne a little too possessively by the arm. "Isn't it?"

~Thorne's heart rate is elevated. His pupils are dilated. Clear signs of attraction.

You're not helping even a little, Maude. I thought you were supposed to protect me.

~I am. But let's face it. She is objectively beautiful. It wouldn't surprise me if she and Thorne—

Enough. Shut it.

"We should probably go," I stammer, and after a prolonged silence, Thorne finally speaks again.

"Yes, we should."

After slipping on his boots, he gestures to Rivenna to lead the way, and we follow her out of the suite and toward the executive wing, which, according to her, houses my father and the Magister, as well as Kith and a few other high-ranking members of the Magister's inner circle.

"I hear you're quite a fighter, Thorne," she says over her shoulder as he and I walk hand in hand behind her.

I'm not entirely sure who initiated the handholding, but I have a bad feeling it was me. *It's ridiculous to feel threatened,* I tell myself. *He's my tethered mate. We love each other.*

Then again, given that we've both had recent visions of the future where we're not together, it's not so easy to feel confident right now.

"I dabble in combat," Thorne says.

"You must do more than dabble if the Magister agreed to let you out of your cage. No Royal Guard ever gets released. *Ever.*"

Thorne's grip on my hand tightens when he says, "He

released me to be with Shara. I'm sure the Magister didn't want to tear the Shadow's daughter from her bound mate. It would have broken us both."

My confidence grows again, at least a little.

"Yes," Rivenna says, turning her face away so that I can no longer see her expression. "It *would* tear you apart."

When we get to the Magister's quarters, he and my father are already seated in his dining room along with Kith, who rises to his feet as we enter, his eyes landing on me. He focuses on my face, ignoring the others entirely, and smiles.

"Welcome," the Magister says without cracking so much as a smirk. "Come, sit."

Thorne and I seat ourselves on one side of the table opposite Kith and Rivenna. My father sits at one end, the Magister at the other.

The serving staff brings out large dishes of chicken, beef, rice, vegetables, and bread—enough food for a small army. I should be starving by now, but every time I consider taking a bite, I notice Rivenna and Thorne watching one another over the table and my stomach does a lurch.

"You'll be pleased to hear that Rivenna will be attending your fight training sessions," the Magister tells Thorne after shoving a large forkful of food into his mouth. "She's one of our best. You'll have a lot to talk about."

"Ah," Thorne replies. "I...look forward to seeing her there in the morning."

Another twist of my stomach is enough to make Maude ask if I'm all right.

Fine, I mutter internally. *Just...fine.*

~I was joking earlier, you know. I genuinely didn't expect

sparks to fly, or I would never have been so insensitive. But now that I see the way they're staring at each other—

That will do for now.

"I've heard about your impressive wrist bracers," Kith says, eyeing Thorne. "Word has it they enhance Tethered powers."

"They can enhance, to be sure," Thorne replies. "They can also grant a Tethered *new* powers temporarily. Sort of like what you do—only it doesn't involve taking gifts from someone else."

I'm not sure if I'm imagining the slight hint of hostility in Thorne's tone, as if he's accusing Kith of stealing souls.

The last time I saw the two talking, they seemed like the best of friends. I can't imagine what's changed, if anything.

"So, not at *all* like what I do," Kith says, and there's a little sass in his tone, too. *Okay. I'm definitely not imagining things.* "I rid problematic Tethered of their powers and in doing so, I neutralize threats. I give those gifts to people who are, shall we say, more deserving."

"The difference is that Thorne's bracers can offer a Tethered a selection of *multiple* powers," my father says. "He has agreed to configure them to suit each fighter's abilities. He'll train our recruits to use them effectively—which means we'll soon have an army that's virtually invincible."

"Good," Kith replies with a raised eyebrow. "We'll need that army when the time comes."

"I'm not sure why Rivenna would need to attend training sessions," I interject, my voice more desperate-sounding than I would like. "I mean, given what she can already do."

I feel like a paragraph is written across my face: *I don't want her going to fight classes. I don't want her and Thorne to spend all day every day staring into one another's eyes. I don't want to think of them together.*

No.

Stop it, Shara.

This is just my past insecurity talking—feelings from a time when I didn't yet know Thorne with my whole heart and soul. Those were the days when I discovered a diary and wrongly assumed it was Devorah's—then convinced myself that she and Thorne were in love.

I was wrong. I was foolish.

And I'm certain I'm wrong now, as well. I'm imagining a deep, heavy tension between them that doesn't exist.

"I still want to learn," Rivenna tells me, her bright eyes locking on mine. "I need to. And besides, I'd like to get to know your Thorne."

~That's exactly what you're afraid of, Maude's irritating voice echoes in my mind.

No, I'm not.

~Could've fooled me.

You know, I think I'll have you rebooted again. You're being way too attentive tonight.

~You would never do that. You love me. She practically sings the words.

"She's got a point," the Magister says. "Rivenna is acquainted with some of our fighters—mercenaries recruited from the Capitol. Kith has already trained many over the years, but the ones Thorne is about to deal with are new and undisciplined. She can help steer them in the right direction."

Great. So she's going to be his *assistant.*

"Shara," Kith says, leaning forward. "Are you all right?"

Great. It seems my mood is written all over my damned face.

"Hmm?" I ask, glancing sideways when Thorne looks at me. "I'm fine. Why?"

"You look a little ill."

"Nope," I tell him, stuffing a piece of chicken into my mouth. "I'm fine, like I said."

Dinner drags on far too long, and I only feel worse as it goes. There's far too much conversation over the table between Thorne and Rivenna while the rest of us look on, watching their friendship blossom and grow. They speak of fighting styles, past altercations, and the benefits of large training facilities. They even go so far as to show one another various scars.

At one point, Rivenna rises to her feet and lifts her shirt, revealing a set of formidable abdominal muscles and a long pink scar slicing its way up a beautifully curved waist.

All the while, I remain silent, wishing myself a million miles away.

"I called you all to dinner because I have news," the Magister finally announces as our plates are being gathered. Relief assaults me, and my attention shifts instantly. Something in his tone sounds almost giddy, though his face certainly doesn't betray any emotion.

My eyes veer temporarily to my father, who looks staid and composed as if he already knows what the Magister is about to say.

"In three weeks' time, there will be a public hanging of a number of convicted criminals held in our prison cells. A final show of strength—justice doled out for the people of

Kravan to witness. After that, we will announce the coming election. I will run, naturally—and I fully expect to win."

"The prince is still alive. So how, exactly, do you intend to take power?" I venture to ask.

The arrogance on the Magister's face is irritating, to say the least—and I get the distinct impression that he thinks he's owed the rule of Kravan.

"You should know the answer to that, Shara dear," my father says, his tone a little condescending. "You're the one who told me about Kravan's past. About President Brant."

"*President* Brant?" Rivenna gasps, her eyes flicking from one face to the other as if she's just now realized why I reacted so strangely when I first heard the Magister's name.

"As luck would have it," my father says, "the last president of Kravan—back in the days when our people were allowed a vote—was an ancestor of the Magister's. She had children and a husband—all of whom were spared and all of whom lived on—though they were imprisoned in the Tower. For a long time, their descendants lost track of their history. But as it turns out, the Citadel contains enough information that we've been able to piece together the Magister's ancestry. Testing has proven that in fact, he is a descendant of our last president."

"It doesn't matter. The presidency isn't inherited," I protest, my tone more hostile than I'd like. I'm supposed to support his cause, but still, I don't want him or anyone else assuming they're entitled to lead. "The people must have a vote. That's the important thing."

"And they will, naturally," the Magister says. "When the time comes, Shara, ballots will be cast. Each vote will be equal, whether it comes from a Tethered or a Potential. Once we have liberated Kravan from the tyrannical dynasty that has ruled it for far too long, our land will become free, just as it was so long ago."

I breathe a quiet exhalation of relief, and under the table, Thorne takes my hand and squeezes. I glance sideways to see him smiling at me as if to say, "It's really happening."

My heart warms with his expression, all my nagging fears laid to rest.

I was being ridiculous, I tell myself. *He loves me.*

"Tell me, Magister," Thorne says with a reverent bow of his chin, "will you be releasing the imprisoned members of the Royal Guard when the prince is unseated?"

The Magister levels him with his dead-eyed look. "I'll deal with them on an individual basis. I'll assess each case with care before making a final decision. You have my word."

Thorne's voice tightens when he says, "Thank you."

"Well," my father says with a clap of his hands, "I say we all go enjoy a pleasant, relaxing evening. Tomorrow, training will begin, and we will prepare for the next phase."

I blow out a breath, more than a little eager to get back to our suite. When we've risen to our feet, I take Thorne by the hand and guide him toward the door, but Rivenna stops us.

"Thorne," she says softly.

I twist around, frustrated, and glare at her.

"Yes?" he replies.

"I'll see you in the morning." She steps toward us and lays a hand gently on his arm, her voice smoother and softer than I've ever heard from her lips. "I'm really looking forward to getting to know you."

Her words are so brazenly flirtatious that all I can do is stand frozen for a moment and stare, slack-jawed, at her as she leaves the room, her exquisite, powerful body on full display.

~There's nothing inherently wrong with what she said, Maude whispers. *Perhaps she was simply being polite.*

It's the way she said it. Like she wanted to hug him to her perfect breasts and stroke his hair.

~You raise a good point. I hadn't thought about her breasts before, but they are objectively—

Stop.

Without another word, I lock my arm into Thorne's and wait until Rivenna is out of sight before leaving the Magister's quarters.

CHAPTER TWENTY-SEVEN

THE MOMENT we're free of Rivenna, I assure myself I'm only feeling paranoid because I'm not accustomed to being around Thorne in a social setting.

I'm not used to him staring at beautiful women, nor them at him—but if I'm going to spend my life by his side, I need to get over the feelings that gnawed at me through dinner.

The thing is, I'm not even remotely convinced *that's* what's bothering me. I have no problem with Thorne and Rivenna getting along. I don't even have a problem with the fact that he might find her attractive.

He'd be a fool not to.

What's eating away at me is that there seemed to be something far deeper between them—an unspoken, instant bond that I couldn't read. An immediate affection. Secrecy, even. A private joke that had never been spoken, but was nevertheless born between their minds.

I don't fear that Thorne will stop loving me...But I do fear a powerful bond is growing with someone else entirely.

"Are you all right?" Thorne asks when we're back in our suite. "You've been awfully quiet tonight."

"I'm..." I consider telling him the truth but veer away from it at the last second. "I think I was exhausted after today."

He pulls me close, and, relieved to feel the comfort of his touch, I bury myself in his chest. "I know," he says softly, pressing a kiss to my head. "I'm sorry. I wish I could have kept you to myself tonight."

I don't want to admit how reassuring those words are.

"Really?"

"You're all I think about, Shara. Every second I get to spend with you is a gift, and I don't take it for granted."

I pull away, peering up into his eyes to gauge whether he means it.

I see nothing but sincerity and absolute truth.

"You and Rivenna seemed to hit it off." I try to brush the hint of envy-laced suspicion away from my voice.

"There is something about her." When he sees the look in my eye, he chuckles and hastens to add, "I don't mean it like that. It's just—I feel like I've seen her somewhere before. But I'm sure we've never met. Maybe it's just that you told me about her. I don't know."

"You worked for the Prefect. You came to the Tower to test my cohort. Maybe you ran into her in the city back then."

"I don't think so. It's more like...I've dreamed of her."

Wow. This is doing nothing whatsoever for my confidence.

"Anyhow," he says, "she's got fighting experience. She'll be a help in the arena, I'm sure."

"I'm sure," I echo, though I wish I could beg him to send her away tomorrow morning, and tell her never to return.

She did nothing wrong, I remind myself. *And Thorne loves me. There's nothing to worry about.*

~She did stroke her hand seductively along his arm, a voice whispers inside me.

Oh—I just remembered something, Maude.

~What?

I hate you.

When we make love that night, Thorne gives himself wholly to me, telling me over and over again that he loves me, that I am everything to him. He's gentle, affectionate, sweet—almost as if he's doing everything in his power to prove that I'm the only woman who will ever have his heart.

When we've exhausted ourselves completely, I manage to fall into a deep sleep, despite the growing dread that he'll be seeing Rivenna again in the morning.

I dream of her face, tears streaking down her scarred cheek. She's staring at someone, heartbroken, and it takes me a moment to realize Thorne is lying on a bed nearby.

Rivenna moves toward him and falls to her knees, taking his hand in hers, and kissing it. Thorne stirs, smiling when his eyes meet hers.

"I love you," he says. "So much that it hurts. I'll never stop—never. I promise."

I wake with a start to realize that Thorne is sitting next to me, watching me sleep. His hand reaches for me and he strokes my hair.

"You were having a bad dream," he says. "That's all. Whatever you saw, Shara...it wasn't real."

I peer into his eyes, hiding my fear as best I can while my breath slows.

If it wasn't real, then why could I feel it so acutely when he touched her? Why did it feel so like the moments Thorne and I spent together in the Nether?

"Come here," he whispers, lying down next to me. I turn my back to him, and he wraps an arm around me, drawing closer. "I'll never love anyone but you," he whispers. "*I promise.*"

After the dream, I barely sleep. My mind reels with nighttime paranoia—dark thoughts that I know will dissipate when dawn comes.

Sure enough, my mood brightens when Joy brings us breakfast. But it falters instantly when she tells us we have a half hour before Thorne's first day of training begins.

I thank Joy and shut the door, a flock of overactive butterflies fluttering their way around my belly. *It was just a dream,* I repeat to myself. *Nothing more. Your brain sucks.*

~*It does,* Maude points out.

Fuck off.

"Do you think they've already made enough wrist bracers?" I ask as Thorne and I dig into our bacon, eggs, and toast.

"Probably not yet," he tells me. "But it's possible that not all the trainees will need them. Some of them, I hear, are what are called *Newborns.*"

"Wait—you're going to be training actual babies?" I can't help but laugh at the image of a herd of infants lying around the arena as Thorne tries to explain the intricacies of hand-to-hand combat.

Shaking his head, he lets out a chuckle. "Fully-grown adults who have recently come into their powers. It seems Kith has been busy converting Normals into Tethered. I have to admit, the Magister has done an impressive job of bringing our two kinds together to fight as one. It was a brilliant plan to get Kith's skills involved."

"I'm not sure how to feel about that," I tell him. "For every newly-gifted Tethered, there's another one who's had their powers stolen. Much as I like Kith, it feels a little cruel."

Thorne shrugs. "It's entirely possible that some Tethered see their power as a curse. I'm sure there are some who would prefer to live a life without the title of 'outcast' hovering over their heads. Not everyone wants to be a Velor or a Poisoner. Think of all the times you and I have simply wanted to live our lives in peace."

"I suppose you're right." I think of Tallin then—of the curse his powers have inflicted on him all his life. Feeling a constant cycle of pain echoing through your mind and body is a cruel fate—one I wouldn't wish on anyone.

"Anyhow, Kith seems like a decent man," Thorne says with a grin. "And he definitely has good taste, given that he obviously has a thing for you."

"For me?" I nearly choke on the eggs I'm currently shoveling into my mouth. "What are you talking about?"

"I saw how he looked at you last night over dinner. He may not have said much, but the guy is smitten. Respectfully quiet about it—but definitely attracted to you."

I'm stunned.

I spent the entire evening watching Thorne and Rivenna. Not once was I aware of Kith's eyes on me.

"You're wrong," I tell Thorne. "I would have been aware of it. Anyhow, it's not like he looks at me like Rivenna looks at—" I stop myself. It feels like a bad idea to put notions into his mind. "I mean, I've seen her look at a few guys with admiration. But Kith, looking at me? You're wrong about that."

"You underestimate your beauty. You always have," Thorne says, taking my hand across the small dresser that doubles as a dining table and pulling it to his lips. "You're the most beautiful woman in Kravan, Shara. I can't exactly blame Kith for wishing you were his."

"Hardly," I tell him, but the blood rushes to my cheeks, and I thank him silently for his words. I don't care if no one else ever finds me even a little bit pretty, so long as Thorne desires me.

"Now..." With one final kiss to my palm, he rises to his feet. "I've got to get my day started. Why don't you come with me to the arena? Kith can find you there for your little walk."

Shit.

I'd completely forgotten I'm supposed to head into the Capitol today—*with a man Thorne insists is attracted to me.*

It's fine. It doesn't matter. Thorne is wrong. He's just... projecting.

Or something.

Dressing hastily, I agree to accompany him, curious to see some of the men and women the Magister has amassed to take back Kravan at long last.

CHAPTER TWENTY-EIGHT

When we step into the arena, forty or so students are already gathered on its vast dirt floor, awaiting their instructor. Rivenna is there as well, with Berengar by her side, tongue drooping out of his mouth, as usual.

The space is large and drafty, with wood beams lining the ceiling far overhead. It looks far too much like the arena in the palace for my liking—but I remind myself with a wince that at least I won't have to watch my friends die in this place.

There is hope here, and quiet strength.

I give Berengar a pat and greet Rivenna even as her eyes move to Thorne's face. This time, he doesn't so much as glance back at her. Instead, he strides to the arena's center and calls out to the trainees to assemble around him.

"He's a handsome guy," Rivenna says in a sultry voice, nodding toward Thorne. "You have good taste, Healer."

"Thanks," I reply, an instant chill clinging to my voice.

"Do yourself a favor, Shara." She sidles in a little closer, and I shift uncomfortably. "Enjoy him while you can."

There's menace in her tone—something I can't quite place—and I balk at the warning in her words.

"I intend to enjoy him for the rest of my life," I snap. "Thanks very much."

"Good. Because you never know how long a life will last around here."

My neck twists and I stare at her. She's wearing the black contact lenses again, and maybe that's why it feels like she's hiding something from me. Some dark secret that will destroy my life.

Is she planning to *kill* me? Is that what this is about?

I step away to position myself in a broad seating area to one side of the arena, and watch the training session begin.

Thorne calls out to the gathered students to assemble into tidy rows, and instantly, they obey.

Around the arena's edge in a long line is an assortment of target dummies. When the trainees have gathered around him, Thorne gestures to the dummies and says, "When war comes, you won't be fighting stationary objects like these. But for now, this is your enemy. In real life, your opponents will be members of the Royal Guard. They're elite fighters who have trained half their lives, at least. The king has traditionally selected the best, strongest Tethered to serve him—so trust me when I tell you that you will be fighting people stronger than any you have ever encountered."

"Who cares? The king is dead!" one man cries out. His words are followed by a roar of laughter. A few of the trainees exchange whispers and point toward me, bringing a flush of self-consciousness to my cheeks.

"*Regent Killer*," I hear someone mutter.

Thorne storms over to a young Netic, grabbing him by

the front of his shirt and yanking him close. The man's eyes go white with terror as Thorne snarls, "What the fuck did you just say?"

"I..." The man's eyes move to me. "They say she killed the king. I just—"

Thorne strikes the trainee's chest hard with his flat palm, sending the soldier flying backwards to smash hard against the arena's far wall.

The Netic slumps down to lie helpless on the ground, his head lolling.

"One of the Citadel's Healers will deal with you later," Thorne tells him. "You are not welcome in this arena again. And if I hear another one of you spreading unfounded rumors, I will not be so gentle."

My heart swells with pride as I watch Thorne straighten his collar and take up position before the assembled trainees again.

"The prince is still alive," he calls out. "*You* may not have encountered him, but I have. Prince Tallin is cruel. He thrives on watching people suffer—and if you think he would spare you in a fight, you're wrong. He's a Cendiary. A flame summoner."

The words are met by murmurs of shock. Clearly, word hasn't yet spread through the Capitol that the prince is a Tethered.

"He would burn you all as soon as he got a look at you. That's why I'm here. Listen to me, and you might just live to see the end of the coming battle."

As Thorne continues to warn the gathered crowd about the perils of confronting the prince and his minions, someone taps me on the shoulder.

I twist around to see Kith leaning in close. He whispers, "Hey—do you want to get out of here?"

Not really, I think as Rivenna and Berengar stride over to stand next to Thorne, as if that's their rightful place in this world.

But the truth is, I don't particularly want to stay here and watch whatever is about to unfold. It's all a grim reminder that death is coming in greater numbers than Kravan has seen since the Rebellion.

"You know what?" I whisper back to Kith. "Yeah. I could use some fresh air."

I follow him out of the arena and down a few twisting hallways until we climb steeply to the nearest of the Citadel's exits.

"I trust you're settling in all right?" Kith asks when we reach the fortified steel doors. "I was disappointed not to get to speak to you more last night, after what happened to you with the Starless. That must have been terrifying."

"It was," I admit. "But Thorne was there to protect me." With a sigh, I add, "It's been a little challenging to be here, to be honest."

"Oh? Any reason in particular?"

I choose my words carefully, deftly avoiding any mention of Rivenna's admiration for Thorne—or his keen interest in her. "I thought I'd feel free once I was in the Capitol. At least, I hoped so. But it seems it's just more of the same. Fighting between factions. Lust for power. Rules, danger, death. Is there any part of this realm that's not constantly going to set me on edge?"

"I'll tell you what," Kith says, laying a soothing hand on my shoulder and nodding toward the doors. "I'm going to take you out there today, and I promise you, there will be very little risk of Starless showing up. We're going to go shopping, you and I. We'll eat lunch in a restaurant. You'll get to see what the Capitol used to look like—and what it will look like again, sooner than you think. Today is about hope, not despair."

"How can you guarantee there won't be any Starless? Thorne and I had Dragonflyers with us yesterday, and they still came."

"Because I requested that an army of drones surveil the area this morning," Kith says, pushing the doors open and jutting his chin upward. "Trust me."

When my eyes have adjusted to the blinding brightness of the sun, my gaze follows his to the sky, where I spot small specks that almost look like hovering birds, darting left to right, up and down. Drones. Thirty of them, at least.

But then, my gaze shifts back to ground level and my breath catches in my throat.

"Holy shit," I say. "What is this place?"

Before us lies an entire street of shops, cafés, and restaurants—but not just the run-down businesses I've seen before. They're in pristine condition, as if freshly painted just for this outing of ours. The street itself is covered in new-looking cobblestones, like someone laid it just this morning.

A few people wander up and down white sidewalks wearing the type of clothing I've always pictured on civilians. Skirts and blouses, comfortable pants, light sweaters.

I've never seen anyone look so at peace as they do.

"*This* is Magister's Row," Kith says as two Dragonflyers buzz down to scan our faces, then fly off. "Newly built and unmarred. This area, right here, is the most protected part of the Capitol—and everyone you see is in the Magister's employ. Most of them work in the Citadel from day to day, but have been given time off to enjoy the fruits of their labor. This is their reward for loyalty and hard work—at my suggestion."

"That was good of you," I tell him, offering up a look of admiration. "I'm sure they're grateful."

"People need to know their leaders appreciate them. It helps with morale."

It's strange to hear him call himself a leader, but I suppose that's exactly what he is. I've watched as people bowed their heads before him. Stared at him with an awe that few can inspire.

After the Magister and my father, Kith is third in command—at least, on our side of the political spectrum.

"Well, this place is...wow." I can't quite find the words to describe the feeling of quiet euphoria settling inside me. "I've been to shops in the Isles—the ones the Nobles frequent. But I've never actually seen where average people shop, and for some reason, it's hard to take in how wonderful it is."

A lump forms in my throat, as strange as it seems to be moved by something so simple as a few storefronts.

It's not so much that I have an urge to spend money. I don't have any, after all. It's simply the normality of it all—the exquisite banality. There is no evidence of war as far as the eye can see. This is simply a slice of life in a part of the city that doesn't currently face the dread of attack.

"Why didn't my father send Thorne and me here yesterday? Why did he tell us to go to the ruined sector?"

"He was probably waiting to surprise you. Magister's

Row was still receiving its final touches yesterday," Kith says. "Also, your father is a realist. He wanted you to bear witness to both the potential of the Capitol and the trauma it's endured. He doesn't want you seeing it through rose-colored glasses. But today, I felt you needed this. I could sense your stress in there," he adds, nodding toward the thick steel door leading back into the Citadel.

Tears sting my eyes as I look into his, watching the swirling power within him, the history of every talent he's swiped away from a Tethered. He's so strong—so deadly. But right now, he reminds me of a sweet, kind dog who wants nothing more than to please me, and I almost want to hug him for it.

Except for one small problem.

Is he really attracted to me, or was Thorne imagining it?

~Elevated heart rate, dilated pupils, Maude says. *Like I've told you, those are clear signs of attraction. Also, I've noted a rush of blood to his—*

Okay. Enough.

~I'm just saying, evidence points to arousal of a sexual nature.

Well, I'm in love with someone else, so it's irrelevant.

I can almost feel Maude shrugging inside me as if to say, "Just enjoy having a man wanting you, for fuck's sake."

"Come on," Kith says, taking me gently by the arm. "Let's go shopping."

I freeze and shake my head. "You do know I don't have money, right? In fact, I'm not sure I've ever even held money in my hand. In the Isles, I just showed the Verdans' crest to pay for things."

"No need for money. I've got this. Besides, you'll have wealth of your own soon enough."

I let out a laugh. "Do you know something I don't? Has my father been saving up for me all my life or something?"

"Something like that," he snickers. "Just relax and come with me, Shara. I want to treat you like a princess today—which means no worrying about trivial things like money. You deserve a little pleasure after everything you've been through."

Normally, the idea of being called a princess would make me cringe. The only royalty I've ever known has been horrible at the very best of times.

But the way Kith says it is surprisingly charming—enough, at least, for me to allow myself a smile.

That's right. I'm a damned princess—if only for one day.

CHAPTER TWENTY-NINE

THE FIRST SHOP Kith and I venture into sells everything from coffee mugs to hand-knit scarves and hats.

"Autumn is coming before long," he tells me. "It will be your first outside the Tower, I assume."

Strange though it is to admit, he's right. The crisp bite of morning air on one's skin is a concept I've only ever read about. The tumble of colorful leaves to the ground is a sight I'm looking forward to more than I can say.

"My first ever autumn, at the ripe age of nineteen," I laugh. "It feels sort of magical."

Every single item in the shop is colorful and warm. The mugs are hand-made pottery, decorated with brightly painted images of birds and flowers. The mittens look as though someone's grandmother knitted them herself, and their subtle flaws make me want to run my fingertips over every inch of them.

Joy permeates my every cell as I move around, my eyes roaming from one display case to another, taking in toys, playing cards, and electronic devices for controlling small animals not too different from Mercutio.

I only wish I could have brought Thorne with me. The one thing I'm missing is the feeling of his arms holding me from behind as we both marvel at the treasures surrounding us—and the fact that, for the first time in our lives, we could even purchase one or two of them—that is, if we had any money.

The idea of having a coffee cup of my very own is enough to make my eyes well with new tears.

"This is incredible," I breathe, my fingers stroking their way along every surface as if to prove to myself that this place is real.

Watching me, Kith lets out a gentle laugh.

"What's so funny?" I ask with a chuckle. "Are you teasing me just because I look like a small child who's seen a mountain for the first time? Speaking of which, I've never seen one of those, either."

"Not teasing. But I do forget sometimes that you spent your entire life locked in the Tower. It's quite something, seeing the world through your eyes. As volatile as our existence has been on the outside, no one who was raised on the Capitol's streets would lose their mind over a little shop. But here you are, and it's beautiful to see."

I lock eyes with him, wondering if he *is* mocking me after all. But from the look in his eye, I'd guess he's entirely sincere.

"It's just..." I sigh and pick up a pretty notebook with a drawing of an ethereal-looking tree on its cover. "Okay, this is going to sound ridiculous."

"Try me."

"Fine." Gesturing to the shop around us, I say, "I've never considered what I wanted to do with my life. When I was in the Tower, I was always told I'd end up a Domestic in the home of some Noble or other. I was good at it, but it wasn't exactly a passion, you know? But this—*this* is a dream."

"Wait—you're saying you want to own a shop?"

"I mean, maybe?" I sigh again. "To be honest, I've never given it a moment's thought before today. But yes, it appeals to me. To have my own space and be able to fill it with things I love—that would be incredible. I've never dreamed of anything even close to that. I was never even *allowed* to dream."

He steps closer, and when I look up into his eyes, I feel like he's staring right into the depths of my soul.

"What is it?" I ask, this time with a nervous laugh.

"You're really beautiful, Shara," he says, then quickly adds, "Your mind, I mean—since you don't seem to like compliments about your physical appearance. The simple joy you derive from small things is refreshing. It cuts through my lifelong cynicism like a knife. Most people around here are obsessed with being fearful or enraged. But you—you genuinely want peace and quiet."

"I thought *everyone* wanted peace."

"Some people definitely don't. I don't think I ever did either. Not until I met you."

My cheeks heat and I look away, unable to meet his gaze. "We should pop into some more shops," I blurt out, fingering the fringe on a leather jacket. "Don't you think?"

"Shara..." His voice is so gentle when he steps toward me and takes my hand in his.

My eyes lock on the floor. "I love Thorne," I whisper.

"I know you do. I can see it in you. I can feel it. But..."

But is a terrible word, and enough to grant me the strength and irritation to look at him.

"But what?" Nothing good could possibly come out of his mouth at this point.

"You saw how Thorne and Rivenna looked at each other last night."

At that, I turn to walk away, but he takes hold of my arm, pulling himself close.

"Everyone did," he whispers. "It wasn't just your imagination. Those two clearly had an instant connection—something profound."

"They have a lot in common," I reply, yanking myself away. "It's fine."

"I don't want to see you hurt—but I feel it right now. Your sense of betrayal."

"Thorne would never hurt me," I protest, but right now, I'm not sure I believe my own words. If Kith was aware of the bond between those two, then he's right—I wasn't imagining it. It was real.

"He's my tethered mate," I say, trying too hard to convince myself of the fact. "He and I are bound to one another."

"Tethered can have more than one mate. Things happen —I've seen it. Your father once believed he was tethered to your mother. But he was wrong, and they chose to live apart. Others *grow* apart. Sometimes, a tether weakens and breaks, believe it or not. What feels like fate right now may prove nothing more than a fleeting affair. You and Thorne fell in love while you were both servants to the Nobility. But now that you're free, things will evolve. Perhaps, after all, you're not meant for one another."

"I'm not forcing him to be with me," I growl. "If he stops loving me, I'll be the first to leave him and wish him well." The lie burns my chest as it escapes my mouth, a jagged knife scraping along the inside of my heart.

"I just...I want you to know I'm here for you," Kith whispers, "whatever happens. If you ever need someone to talk to, a shoulder to cry on. Anything. I'm not asking for anything from you. I just want you to know you can rely on me."

"They won't, Kith," I tell him, swallowing hard. "But... thank you all the same."

"Good." He nods, then says, "Then let's forget this entire conversation and keep on shopping. There are a few more stores I'd love to show you."

When I look dejected, he adds, "Look—I'm sorry. It's not my place to poke my nose into your relationship."

"I know you're looking out for me. But...I wish you wouldn't."

With a shake of his head, he says, "I made you feel bad. That was poorly done on my part. Truly."

When I see the remorse in his eyes, I can't help letting my heart melt a little. "It's all right," I tell him with a smile. "Really. I know you well enough to know you'd never hurt me."

"I'm glad to hear it."

There's part of me that feels remorse of my own for my reaction. Kith is so kind. So good. Handsome, too—*more* than handsome. If it weren't for my mind being entirely focused on Thorne, I'd admit to myself that he's downright gorgeous.

His eyes are somehow intent and the essence of calm, all at once. His lips have a way of twitching into a smile almost of their own volition, as if there's always a slightly mischievous thought steering its way into his mind.

There's definitely something compelling about the Blade—but I remind myself I'm too loyal to Thorne ever to be lured by his charm.

Besides, Thorne's heart is mine and mine is his, in more than just a poetic sense. We're linked, body and mind.

We may not own one another—but we still *belong* to each other.

And no amount of self-inflicted doubt will ever change that.

KITH and I visit several more shops, and we both make an effort to shy away from talk of emotions. Instead, we banter about the Capitol, his friendship with my father, and life in the Citadel.

He's proving to be a good friend. That's exactly what I need right now—and it's all I want.

At the last shop we visit before lunch, I find a display of floor-length gowns of thin, flowing silk. I'm not entirely sure why anyone would ever want one around here; all the Nobles live on the Isles, after all.

"Are there a lot of formal balls in the Capitol?" I ask with a snicker.

"Hopefully there will be soon," Kith replies. "A celebration of our victory would be an excellent excuse for a ball."

I crane my head and shrug. "Cheers to that."

"You know," he says, taking a red gown in hand and eyeing it, "back in the day, it's said that there was an opera house in the Capitol, a symphony orchestra, and all sorts of plays and musicals. If our plans come to fruition, that will be our reality again soon."

"Well then," I tell him, "I suppose I'd better look for a dress, just in case."

When I rifle through the rack and come to a beautiful, floor-length gold dress with a corset bodice, I let out a quiet gasp. In the vision Kith showed me—my supposed wedding day—I was wearing a dress exactly this color.

A smile curls my lips to think it could be the very thing I wear the day Thorne and I marry.

Not that we're engaged. Still, there's no reason we couldn't have a Pairing ceremony and declare our love in front of a few honored guests...

Kith seems to confirm what I'm thinking, because he nods and says, "I know. I've seen it too, remember. Go ahead—try it on."

The shopkeeper—a woman in her fifties—smiles at me from behind the counter and calls out, "It really would be lovely on you."

"Really?" I glance first at Kith, then over at the shopkeeper, who nods enthusiastically.

"I'll get a dressing room ready for you."

"Fine," I say with an exaggerated roll of my eyes, like this is some great inconvenience. Pulling the dress off the rack, I stride to the back of the shop, where I find a series of curtained dressing rooms.

"I'll wait out here," Kith tells me. "Shout if you need anything."

When I'm tucked behind the small cubicle's thick curtain, it takes me a few minutes to peel off my clothes and slip into the gown. It's only after I've pulled the narrow straps over my shoulders that I realize I need help tightening the corset bodice.

I stick my head out through the curtain, looking for the shopkeeper.

"I think she's with a customer," Kith says. "Can I help?"

"I..."

Maude takes it upon herself to reassure me.

~You're entirely covered, Shara, except for your back. He won't see anything.

I'm not wearing a bra, I remind her. *I had to take it off.*

~You're fine. He's a gentleman, isn't he?

Fine.

"Actually," I tell Kith, opening the curtain. "I need a set of hands to tighten the laces."

His eyes slip down my body, then back to my face, and he lets out a low whistle.

"Amazing," he says. "I knew it. It'll be even better when it's laced up."

He slides into the dressing room with me, closing the curtain behind him, and I turn around, pulling my long hair away from my back. Kith pulls gently at the laces, tightening the dress around me, then ties it up.

I watch myself in the full-length mirror as he looms over me, eyeing my body, made more shapely thanks to the beautifully constructed garment.

"What do you think?" Kith asks.

"I love it," I tell him with a sigh. "The color—it reminds me of the sun—which always reminds me of freedom. It's a perfect dress." I don't mention that the sun now reminds me of the sister I've never met.

Soleia. *Sol*, my father called her.

"Yes, it is perfect."

I spin around, looking at it from all angles, then say, "Ah, well. It will find a good home with some lucky woman."

"Yes," he says. "*You*."

An explosive laugh leaps out of my chest, and I turn to face him. "I told you, I have no money."

"Well, I have lots—and we both know you're destined to wear this gown, Shara. Let me buy it for you. Please."

"Kith..."

He lowers his chin. "*Shara*. Your father gave me explicit instructions to look after you. That's exactly what I'm doing."

"Fine." I reach for the price tag and glance at the number. "I can't tell—is this expensive?"

Kith looks down, his eyes going mock-wide. "Holy shit, I take it back. No dress for you."

When I look like I'm about to rip the garment off, he says, "I'm joking. Besides, I tied you in tightly, so there's no escape. Here...let me help you so you can change again."

Almost reluctantly, I turn my back to him. He undoes the ties, loosening them all the way down my back. I'm not sure whether I only imagine the feel of his fingertips brushing against my skin as he goes.

But when my eyes meet his in our reflection, he seems to confirm the theory when he stares at me for a second longer than he should.

He senses my discomfort, lowering his eyes, and

breathes, "I'm going to wait out there. You should be able to manage on your own now."

He escapes the room and leaves me to slip out of the dress as quickly as I can, trying to convince myself I don't feel the echoes of his touch—a silent residue of something sparking between us that shouldn't exist.

You're imagining things, I tell myself. *It was nothing.*

When Maude doesn't come back at me with a snide comment, I let out a quiet laugh and slip out of the dress, standing only in my underwear as I stare blankly at my reflection.

"Get a grip, girl," I scold under my breath, reaching for my clothes, which are lying on the bench next to the mirror.

When I straighten up to pull my bra on, I let out a gasp.

Kith is standing just outside the dressing room, and to my horror, the curtain is slightly open.

He's staring at me, his eyes darkening with an expression that I've only seen on Thorne's face when he's about to claim me as his own.

Almost instantly, Kith vanishes, and I scramble to pull my clothes on. I storm out of the dressing room, my cheeks searing.

Kith follows me as I half-sprint out of the shop, the door closing behind us.

"Shara—the dress," he calls after me.

"Fuck the dress," I snarl, spinning around on the sidewalk to face him. "What the hell was that?"

He raises his chin, eyeing me carefully. "Does it really bother you that I look at you with desire?"

"Of *course* it does."

"Why?"

My brows meet in an angry scowl. "Because I'm in love with someone else—and you know it."

"Well, I'm *not* in love with anyone else. You have a beautiful fucking body, and I'm not going to apologize for wishing you and I could—"

"Kith!" I snap.

He grabs my wrist and holds on, drawing my angry eyes to his. Instantly, my rage quells, and the purest, sweetest calm floods me. I want to fight it—to rage against it. But it's potent. It's addictive.

"I'm sorry," he says, his voice softening. "I glanced in, but only for a second. I didn't realize I would see so much of you. But my God—what I saw. The things I would do to you if I had the privilege, Shara."

I know how wrong it is, but all I feel is...*flattered. Excited.*

No...

I fight off the sensation, yanking my arm away. "Stop it," I growl.

A smile works its way into his eyes before moving to his lips. "Stop what?"

"Your magical touch, or look, or whatever the hell it is you do to me. I will not have you manipulate me. Stop that shit right now, or I swear, I will slap the grin clean off your face."

"I'm done. Promise." He combs a hand through his hair. "In my defense, it's nothing I haven't seen before, Shara. I'm not entirely inexperienced. I've trained with women for years. I've seen *Rivenna* naked, for fuck's sake."

"Wait," I gasp. "Rivenna?"

I don't know why it bothers me to know this. It shouldn't.

But it does.

"Of course. She and I have known each other for a long time. We've hunted traitors together. More than once, we've had to shower in the same place at the same time. My point is, I looked at you, yes. I admired you. But there was no nefarious intent. I just...enjoyed the sight of you for a second. I apologize for the rudeness of it. It won't happen again."

A curse bubbles up inside me, but I force it back before it reaches my throat.

God, I'm overreacting to literally everything, aren't I?

"It's...fine," I say. "I'm having a lot of trouble trusting people right now."

"You forgive me, then?"

I look into his eyes, narrowing my own. It's not like he was watching me the whole time. I only saw him for a second, and the moment my eyes met his, he looked away. So what if he saw a bit of skin? There was nothing inherently intimate about the moment.

It was just...awkward.

"Yeah, fine. I forgive you."

"Then let's go get you something to eat. What's your favorite food?"

"I'm not sure I have a favorite food. But..." I force a smile and say, "There is one thing I've always wanted."

"And what would that be?"

"A hamburger. The thing is—"

Kith lets out a laugh. "Very sophisticated choice. Your wish is my command, my Lady. I know just the place. It's not quite as new and fancy as some, but they do make the most delicious burger you'll ever taste."

When I don't move, he cocks his head to the side, his

brow lined with confusion. "Hard to get our meal if we're standing in the middle of the sidewalk."

"I just...Could we do it another time? I'm a little tired. I think I'd like to go back to the Citadel and rest."

Kith looks pained when he nods and says, "Sure. Of course."

"We'll do burgers tomorrow," I promise. "Or some other time."

"You're upset with me."

With a shake of my head and a genuine smile, I say, "No, I'm not."

The truth is, I can deal with the way Kith looked at me. I've been honest with him about my commitment to Thorne.

But what upset me the most is that when I saw his eyes filled with quiet desire...I realized it was exactly how Thorne looked at Rivenna last night.

CHAPTER THIRTY

I SPEND the rest of the day in our suite, either pacing impatiently as I await Thorne's return or trying in vain to sleep.

By the time seven o'clock rolls around, Thorne still isn't back, and the food Joy brought us for dinner is getting cold. Anxiety has begun gnawing away at my mind, so I decide to head to the training wing to see if he's still there.

When I arrive, I pause for a moment at the arena's doors, taking in a deep breath and summoning enough courage to push my way inside.

~*Are you sure this is a good idea?* Maude asks as I step into the large chamber, my eyes taking a moment to adjust to the shadowy depths.

No, I tell her. *Not in the least. But I'm no good at waiting around. Besides, it's not like I'm going to accidentally stumble upon...*

~*...that?* Maude asks when my eyes land on two figures silhouetted at the dirt floor's far end.

I don't have to move any closer to know what I'm seeing.

Thorne and Rivenna are alone, standing mere inches apart and speaking quietly.

I can't hear what they're saying, but at one point, she takes his face in her hands. I'm almost convinced they're going to kiss—but what happens instead is almost worse.

Thorne stares into her eyes for a moment, then presses his forehead to hers, saying something softly, shaking his head as he speaks.

That intimate gesture—one I know all too well—has always been his and mine alone. Thorne presses his forehead to mine when we're having a heavy talk, or when he wants to remind me of our bond, of his love. It's his way of conveying how tightly bound we are to one another.

So why the fuck would he do it to someone else?

I'm about to flee the space when I hear his voice barreling through the air toward me.

"Shara?"

I turn back then, wishing I had the power of a Stealther. Now would be a perfect time to turn invisible.

Rivenna raises a hand to greet me, and like a fool, I mirror the movement as she and Berengar turn to leave the arena.

Thorne, on the other hand, runs toward me.

As I step onto the dirt floor, mustering the fortitude to chastise him, he grabs me and spins me around in the air, kissing me deeply.

Which only serves to confuse me further.

"I missed you so fucking much today," he murmurs into my hair. "I can't tell you how much I wanted you—needed you. All I could think about was the time I was losing by being in this damned place. I'm sorry it took so long to finish up—the last of the trainees just left."

Is he protesting too much, or does he really mean all of this?

I pull back, narrowing my eyes at him.

He *looks* sincere...but maybe he's faking it in an attempt to compensate for what I just witnessed.

Don't forget, I warn myself, *you've doubted him before. Tread carefully, now—and don't accuse him of things he hasn't done.*

"Did I walk in on something?" I ask, choosing my words with caution. "You and Rivenna...you looked..."

"Oh," he says, glancing back toward the place he was standing a minute ago. "Rivenna was just...she was warning me. Telling me to enjoy my time with you. We've been strategizing, and I think she's a little worried that something will go awry when the time comes for the big battle. She's kind of intense, in case you hadn't noticed."

Taking my bound mate's face in her hands? I wouldn't call that intense.

I'd call it overstepping.

"That's all?"

Thorne looks bemused when he nods. "Of course. You didn't think—Oh. Shit."

He lets out a laugh, then strokes a hand over my cheek. He *seems* like himself. Only...an exaggerated version of himself. As if his happiness at seeing me is amplified more than it should be.

I tell myself I'm only imagining it. After all, I can feel his genuine joy right now. There's no sense of panic or guilt—only a quiet, pulsing gratitude that we're together again.

~Kith did ogle your bare breasts today, Maude reminds me. *Perhaps you should cut Thorne some slack.*

You raise a good point.

"Hey," Thorne says, taking me by the hand and nodding back toward the training area. "There's something I'd like to show you." Holding up a finger, he adds, "Wait here a moment."

He moves to the floor's center and lifts a hand into the air. A whirring sound meets my ears, and at first, I'm convinced we're about to be assaulted by an army of drones.

But when I look up, I see a series of thick, knotted ropes descending from the ceiling.

"Climbing ropes," Thorne says. "Want to try one?"

I laugh. "We had these in the training room in the Tower. When I was little, I could make it all the way to the top of one. Now, I'm not so sure. But go ahead and show me your prowess."

Like me, Thorne is dressed in loose-fitting clothing. Linen trousers, a t-shirt, and leather boots. He climbs a few feet up one of the ropes then twists it around one leg in a spiral. Once he's secured, he lets himself fall backwards to look into my eyes, his shirt riding up.

"You're upside down," I laugh.

"By design," he tells me, raising his eyebrows suggestively. "Come closer and kiss me. That's an order." It may well be an order, but there's a plea in his voice that fills me with desire. I step forward and take his face in my hands.

When I kiss him, the sensation is completely, enticingly new. Meeting his bottom lip with my top lip feels...different. But incredible, as though I'm no longer sure which one of us is upside down or upside right. Gravity deserts me, my head swimming with renewed desire.

Our tongues mingle, exploring the novelty of the sensation as my hands move their way over his bare torso.

Thorne lets himself down a little farther, the rope shifting around his leg, adapting to his position. He's holding on with only one hand, and with the other, he reaches for my shirt and pulls it upward.

"Thorne—someone could walk in," I laugh, eyeing the ridges of his abdominal muscles.

"They won't," he insists. "I locked the doors the second we were alone—and it would take someone with powers stronger than mine to get in."

"Sneaky," I tell him, pressing my lips to his stomach, my tongue sliding over his salty flesh. All doubt has left me now, all images of Rivenna banished. There are only two people in the world once again, and one of them is hanging several feet in the air.

I need to remember this feeling next time I let negativity needle at my mind.

I reach for the tie at the waist of his pants and loosen it, pushing the waistband toward his thighs. In the same few seconds, Thorne mirrors the movement, pushing my pants to the ground, and I step easily out of them.

When I take hold of his swollen length and guide it to my lips, he pulls my thighs apart, burying his face between my legs.

With a moan, he inhales and says, "Defiance of gravity is about to become my new favorite pastime."

I take him in my mouth, my tongue exploring his veined shaft, fingers curled around him and stroking slowly as I marvel at the feeling of our bond—of once again finding my way into his mind and body, adopting his sensations as my own. Every flick of my tongue, every small movement of my hand is a shot of pure pleasure...and knowing that he feels what I feel only enhances the bliss of this moment.

His tongue works my swollen clit in small circles even as his fingers dip inside me and split me apart.

"You taste like a miracle," he groans against me as I take the perfect, thick column deep, my lips trapping him, laying claim to him as he throbs under my touch.

I feel him getting close then pulling back, prolonging the pleasure of this moment, the faint chill of the arena's air stroking at bare skin.

The last thing I want is for anyone to interrupt us, but I want to laugh at the wildness of this scene—of us, silhouetted against a row of training dummies, clothing rumpled, bodies taut with need.

Thorne's hand slips up my shirt, his fingers gently pulling my bra aside, stroking their way over the hard tips of my nipples, drawing a quiet purr of pleasure from my lips.

"Fuck, Shara," he groans. "Your mouth is velvet."

"And you feel like iron," I whisper over his flesh, drawing my tongue over him. "Iron and fire and flesh, all in one."

"With enough heat, iron will surrender," he says. "Bend me. Break me. Forge me into anything you like. I'm yours, now and always."

An image forms in my mind of the gown I tried on today —of how beautiful it was. How much Thorne would love it. I think of the vision Kith showed me—and how I would love to declare our bond in front of others.

I'm yours, now and always.

He tenses under my touch, his muscles stone-hard, his mouth working me as his mind moves cautiously toward the cliff's edge, ready—yet reluctant—to fall...as if we'll both shatter the moment we give in to the crackling flames that flare between us.

You are mine.

When he thrusts two fingers inside me, I pull my chin down and watch him, his eyes on his movements as he dips deep inside me then retreats, drawing his fingers to his lips to taste them before sheathing them once again.

"I love fucking you more than anything in the world," he murmurs, brushing his lips over my clit. "I do. But eating you upside down is one of the greatest things I've ever gotten to experience."

I laugh, and he wraps his lips around the bundle of nerves, sucking, pushing me closer and closer to bliss. My legs want to give out under me, my head is spinning, my chest erupting in flame.

When I take Thorne between my lips again, hands working him in rhythm with his movements, a pulse thrums through his body, and another.

Then, with a loud, wild moan, a throbbing wave of liquid heat pours into my throat, driving its way into my every vein and nerve.

Feeling his ecstasy, my back arches and I explode, barely able to remain on my feet. He roars against me, his mouth engulfing me now as if to capture the shards of my bliss on his tongue.

When the climax has died away, leaving a perfect wake of rippling pleasure behind, I let out a laugh and press my face to his abdomen.

"We must look so ridiculous right now."

I feel Thorne's stomach clench with his laughter.

"We look incredible," he protests, untwisting himself in one elegant motion and landing next to me. With another quick gesture of his hand, the ropes retreat into the ceiling.

"Sometimes, I forget you have the power to do that," I say. "Your mind is incredible."

He yanks his pants back up and ties them, and I do the same before he takes me by the waist and pulls me close.

"My mind is yours," he says, kissing my forehead, then my lips. "My heart, too. You know that, right? No matter what?"

I nod. In this moment, there's absolutely no question. Several minutes ago, I'll admit, was another matter. But I'm not about to revisit those emotions. Thorne has more than made up for any doubts that were eating away at me.

"Of course," I reply, hesitating a moment before adding, "I think...it's hard for me to believe sometimes that someone like you could love me. I never expected love to be a part of my life. But you? You're a dream. You always have been. You're what I would have designed, if I'd been asked to craft my perfect man—my perfect mate."

"What does that even mean?" he laughs. "I'm no dream. I'm as real as this place and everything around it—and I have loved you in a very real way from the second I first saw you."

"Like I said," I whisper, kissing him. "A dream."

An hour later, we're lying on our bed together, finishing off our now-cold dinner when Thorne thrusts himself to his feet and begins to pace the room.

I ask what's troubling him.

"The damned training," he growls. "Every day, they want me in that place—away from you. It feels like such a waste of time."

I let out a confused chuckle. "You have a battle to win, and we have all our lives to spend together. A little time spent in the arena here and there isn't the end of the world."

The reassurance in my own words surprises me. A few hours ago, I hated the idea of him being in the arena all day—and now, I feel perfectly confident that it's the right thing.

Thorne doesn't smile when he slips back onto the bed toward me. He looks deep into my eyes, a frown on his lips, and says, "Being apart from you sure as hell felt like the end of the world today."

"What do you mean?"

His jaw tenses, but he shakes his head and snickers. "I... just missed you. That's all."

"I missed you too," I tell him. "I felt so at peace today, but I wanted you there. I wished..."

My voice halts as I recall the moment when Kith's eyes landed on me, his hungry stare boring into mine.

And then, there was the moment when Rivenna took Thorne's face in her hands.

"You wished?" Thorne murmurs.

"I wished for you," I say, shaking the thoughts away.

He kisses me, and the moment our tongues meet, I feel every ounce of my foolish doubt washing away. My head clears, our connection re-intensifies, and I tell myself I've been an absolute idiot.

And not for the first time.

"So, the training wasn't all you'd hoped for?" I ask. "All that sparring and—whatever else you did?"

"All I'd hoped for?" He combs a frazzled hand through his hair. He seems energized in a way I've rarely seen him—almost as though he's swallowed a barrel of coffee and been hit by some powerful realization. "*This* is all that matters. You and me—and the time we have, before..."

"The battle?"

He nods. "I know the soldiers need their training. They're an undisciplined bunch, honestly. But every minute I was in that arena, my mind was on you."

I can feel his heart in his chest as though it were my own, thudding violently, the blood storming its way through his veins.

"I'm so sorry," he says. "I never even asked—what happened with Kith today? What did you see and do, exactly?"

I suck in my lips, contemplating how best to answer the question. "We went window shopping in a new area called Magister's Row. I...got to try on a beautiful dress."

"Really?" He slips a hand under my bathrobe to land on my waist and I inhale a sharp breath, a smile yanking my lips into a wicked crescent. "Well, that's it," he adds, kissing my neck. "I'm officially envious of Kith. I'll never tire of seeing your perfect body in a gown. It's hardly fair that another man should get to lay his eyes on you."

I steer my mind away from the rapid-fire memory of Kith's gaze on my mostly naked body and say, "I couldn't buy it, of course. I have no money. Still, I felt...I don't know. Like I had the right to be there. For once, I didn't feel like a fish out of water."

"I'll have to thank Kith for taking you, then," Thorne says, his hand easing its way upward. "Though I do wonder why he's not involved in the training sessions with Rivenna and me. Seems a bit weird, don't you think—when Kith is allegedly such an incredible warrior. Someone like Joy could as easily accompany you into the Capitol."

"Joy is a Morph," I point out. "Kith is like a one-man army. He's basically my bodyguard."

"And what a body to guard," Thorne replies, yanking my robe open and nipping at my breast.

I let out a quiet, joyful cry. "Just think—someday soon, we'll be able to do this in our dream house. Every morning. Every night. Just you and me—together in a space we'll call our own."

Thorne pulls his head up and grins. "It really is a dream, isn't it?"

"More than you know. I never wanted to live in a mansion or palace. I just want a small piece of the world to call our own. It would mean everything."

He cups a hand under my breast, stroking the pad of his thumb over my nipple. My breath hitches as he stares at me. I watch and absorb the raw desire in him—the need churning behind his eyes.

"What are you thinking?" he asks, pushing my hair back to kiss my neck. My core throbs with renewed want for him with each brush of his lips, and I drag my fingers across the broad muscles of his back, absorbing him with every one of my senses.

"I'm thinking how glad I am to have you in my life," I whisper. "How grateful. How I'm the luckiest person in the world."

"Luck has nothing to do with it," he says, slipping down to take my nipple gently between his teeth. His lips twist into a smile, his tongue stroking its way over the peak, before he adds, "But even if it did, who needs luck when you have breasts as beautiful as these?"

A laugh explodes from my chest.

"Enough of this," he mutters, grabbing me by the waist and twisting me around so that I land on my hands and knees. Lifting the robe, he slips his fingers between my legs, gasping at how wet I am once again.

"Tell me if you don't want me," he whispers, pinching me gently between thumb and forefinger. "Tell me to stop, and I will. I promise."

"I always want you," I murmur over my shoulder. "Always."

"Good. Because...well..." He teases my opening with his swollen head, enough so that a deep throb shoots through me, the pain of desire engulfing my entire body.

"I feel it," he whispers. "Your need. And I'm going to take it away."

"Good."

When he sheathes himself deep, my core clenches around him, taking relentless hold.

"Hard," I command. "Don't be merciful with me."

He obeys, driving himself into me with a force I've seldom encountered from him, his face buried in the back of my neck. He tears me apart, fingertips digging deep into my hips. My body is a mass of pulsing nerves, trembling with the depths of my craving.

He wraps an arm around me, fingers working me in rhythm with his thrusts, and it's not long before I feel myself on the verge of explosion again.

"Give in," he whispers. "I want you to come for me—then, I'll give you all of myself."

He drives into me with wild abandon, his fingers never letting up until he feels me tumble and careen over the edge, shuddering violently as the explosion rolls over my mind and body in equal measure.

"Oh...God...fuck, that feels so good, Shara..." he moans, his hips moving harder, faster, until I feel a burst of heat inside me spreading in a fast-moving flame. His pleasure is my own once again, but this time alongside it comes a shot of heartache—almost as if he fears this perfect life of ours will shatter like we just did.

He collapses against my back, arms around my waist, a surge of liquid heat streaming down the insides of my thighs.

"I'm sorry," he laughs against me. "I hope I didn't hurt you."

"It's quite all right, I assure you," I reply, my head spinning, my every extremity tingling with the pleasure of a thousand aftershocks. "That was...everything."

When he pulls away to grab a warm washcloth and clean me up, his lips caressing my thighs, I watch him with so much affection that I can hardly bear it.

"Promise me you'll let me know if you ever get tired of this," I say. "If this ever ends for you, promise you'll tell me, instead of protecting me."

Tossing the cloth to the stone floor, he slides over me, cups my chin in his hand, kisses me deeply, then says, "I don't need to promise any such thing. My last breath in this world will come long before I grow tired of this...or you."

CHAPTER THIRTY-ONE

"Do you think they watch us?" I whisper to Thorne as I lie with my cheek pressed to his chest. "The Magister or my father, I mean?"

"In bed?" He snickers. "God, I hope not. Your father would probably have an aneurysm if he saw what I do to you."

"That's terrible!" I laugh, smacking him on the arm. "No —I mean, do you think they have some way of watching our suite? I feel like they keep their distance, but I don't know. It's like their eyes are always on us. On everything, for that matter. My father basically told me there was an invisible Tethered lurking around the palace the whole time we were there. God knows what he—or she—saw."

"I'm sure there are eyes and ears on us every second of every day." Thorne kisses my neck, pulling me closer. "But I can tell you with absolute certainty there's no electronic surveillance in this suite except for Mercutio. Speaking of which..." He looks around. "Where is the little guy?"

I shrug. "He's been going off on solo adventures. I suppose he gets bored in here all alone."

Thorne laughs. "He's incapable of boredom. I made sure of that when I programmed him. Anyhow, whether we're being watched or not, the fact is, this is a new life, Shara. You and I are working for the best cause in the realm. We're going to be part of the force that finally liberates Kravan. The true Rebellion is about to take place—the one against the monarchy. The people will reclaim their power—all because of what we're doing."

"What *you're* doing," I correct. "I went dress shopping today, while you changed the world."

"That may be, but something tells me you'll have a part to play before all this is over."

"What, exactly, is telling you that? My father has me wandering the city with a chaperone. I'm not exactly breaking glass ceilings here—or mustering an army. I'm just existing while everyone else does the important work."

Thorne goes silent for a few seconds. "Do you believe in fate?"

"No," I hasten to reply. But when I've thought about it, I semi-retract my answer. "I mean, not really. I believe we make choices that lead us to specific results. I believe things happen because of those choices—not because of some external force."

"What about visions of the future?" he asks. "The one you had of the Starless holding me in that chamber—it came to pass, despite the fact that neither of us wanted it to."

"Predicting the future isn't the same thing as believing in fate."

"What if I tell you that once someone has seen the future, there's little they can do to stop it?"

"I would tell you I disagree," I chuckle. "There's always a way to change things."

"I hope you're right," he says mysteriously.

I lift my chin to look at him. "What have you seen? Where is this coming from?"

Thorne's jaw clenches, and for a moment I'm convinced he's going to tell me something momentous. But instead, he shakes his head, kisses me, and says, "I'm just pondering the great questions of the universe."

I nod silently, recalling with a shiver the graffiti we've seen around the Capitol.

The Rebellion is a Lie.

The heir will bring ruin on us all.

Are they predictions, or simple attempts at manipulation, as Kith and Rivenna insist?

"Is there a plan?" I ask, ushering the disturbing words from my mind. "I mean, other than just storming the palace and hoping to catch Tallin off guard?"

"There's a plan brewing. It's the whole reason I'm training this army. According to the Magister, we'll be heading to the palace soon to take on the prince's forces. Whether we'll catch him off guard is another matter entirely."

"So, you're going to kill Tethered."

Thorne tenses under me. "Not necessarily. Every Royal Guard will have the chance to come over to our side. They will have a shot at their own liberation. I've insisted on it."

"They won't be liberated if they're dead." I roll onto my stomach, propping my chin on my folded arms. "Will they?"

"What would you have us do instead?" he replies, exasperated. "Leave Tallin in power?"

"I don't know, honestly. But Thorne—you were one of those Guards until very recently. Wouldn't you have wanted someone to warn you—to give you the chance to turn *before* the attack?"

"Of course. But..." He ponders what I said for a moment. "Maybe there's a way..."

He goes quiet, and I can tell he's working his way through a plan.

"You're on to something, aren't you?"

He nods, smiling. "I'll let you know when I've worked it out."

"Good," I reply, leaning over and kissing him on the cheek. "I don't want to spend the rest of our lives regretting what we do in the next few weeks. I want as clean a conscience as either of us can possibly have, when we start our new lives."

"Speaking of new lives, I heard something today," Thorne adds. "Something that might throw a pretty ugly wrench in the works."

"Oh, shit." I look him in the eye, wincing in tense anticipation. "What was it?"

"They say Ellion Graystone is challenging Tallin for the throne. He wants to be named king."

"What?" My eyes widen. "How can he? Tallin is the heir. He's the oldest. He may not be the king's legitimate son, but still, he's the prince. He always has been."

"Ellion was there when the prince killed his father—which means he's claiming Tallin has lost his mind and is unfit to reign."

"I suppose that's good news for me," I say bitterly. "I'm not exactly fond of being called *Regent Killer*. By the way, I never thanked you for kicking that Netic's ass this morning. Did he ever get medical treatment?"

"He'll be fine," Thorne chuckles. "He was carted off to the Citadel's medical wing." With a yawn, he adds, "On the other front, if we're lucky, the brotherly conflict will keep both Tallin and Ellion distracted for a little."

"I hope Tallin doesn't underestimate that psycho," I say pensively.

"They're *both* psycho," Thorne mutters.

"Maybe they'll kill each other, and neither will be named king of Kravan."

Thorne lets out a grunt. "It's too late for that. Tallin is the king already."

"What?"

"You didn't know?"

I shake my head.

"The Prefect made the announcement earlier today. Tallin has officially been crowned."

My heart sinks. "It's still a meaningless title—one that should never have existed. Soon, we'll have a president, and Tallin can disappear into the murky shadows where he belongs."

Thorne combs a hand through my long hair. "I do love your idealism."

"It's not idealism," I snicker. "I've *seen* it. I mean, I've seen what Kravan looked like in the days before the Rise—before Quinton's ascension to the throne. It was beautiful. It was whole. People were happy. Kravan even had ties to other lands—we had the means to travel and communicate with them. The world is so much bigger than this realm, and one day, it will open up again."

"What I want to know is, why was this land cut off from everyone else?"

I shrug. "I suppose it was a matter of control. Quinton wanted to keep the new generations from learning the truth, and it would have been impossible to hide it if the lines of communication had remained open. Quinton knew the only way to control Kravan was to limit its resources in every conceivable way."

"What a piece of shit that man was," Thorne growls.

"Was," I repeat. "He's long gone, and we never have to worry about him again."

"True." Thorne pulls himself closer and kisses my forehead. "The Magister has given me three weeks to get the army trained up and ready for infiltration. After that, this realm will get to start over."

I stroke my fingers over the ebbing muscles of his forearm, contemplating his words. "Three weeks...and then freedom for Kravan's people."

Thorne nods, then goes quiet again.

"What are you thinking?" I ask.

"I'm not sure you'll like it."

"Go ahead. Try me."

"Fine. Rivenna told me something that set my nerves on edge. Something I didn't tell you earlier—but I feel like you should know."

At the mention of her name, I stiffen, but try to mask my feelings by looking Thorne in the eye. "What was it?"

"She said our bond will be threatened in the coming days. She said she's seen it in her heart and mind."

My brows meet, quiet ire heating my blood so that my heart seems to churn back into motion. "What does that mean? She's not a Seer."

"I don't know. Rivenna can be a little intense, so I just assumed she meant the attack on the palace will be dangerous."

"I hope that's *all* she meant," I murmur.

I don't say it out loud, but it sounds like Rivenna is intending to come between us.

Reading my emotions, Thorne grabs hold of me, and in a blur of rapid-fire movements, throws me down onto my back and positions himself above me, his hands pressed to the mattress on either side of my face.

"You're letting the dark thoughts in," he chastises, then kisses me. "Which is exactly why I didn't want to tell you. You don't believe in fate—which means you believe we can control this, Shara. We control our future."

"I know. But I would never ask you not to fall for someone else," I say quietly. "If that's what's going to threaten our bond."

"What?" He seems confused—baffled, even.

"Rivenna," I reply. "Kith mentioned today that he'd noticed the way you look at each other. I saw it last night, then again today. There's something there—between you two. It's obvious."

Thorne looks genuinely stunned. "I'm in love with you."

"I know, but..."

He holds up a hand, stopping me.

"No buts." He's kind yet forceful with the words. "What you don't seem to understand is that love isn't the *end* of my feelings for you—it's just the beginning. I've barely begun to scratch the surface of what you are to me—how deep you live in my blood, in my mind—my heart. I live and breathe to protect you and everything you and I hold dear in this world —and if I can help to make the world a better place, it's for you, and you alone. Without you, our dream house is just an empty shell—and so am I."

"Thorne..." I begin, but the truth is, I don't know what to say.

He has just taken every doubt I've ever had and quashed it. He's fed my soul and healed me, all at once.

He presses down and brushes his lips over my neck.

"Never forget it," he whispers. "Never doubt it. I love you, Shara, Daughter of the Shadow."

"All right," I reply, tears running down my temples. "And I love you, too."

He sighs into my hair. "Good. I see that you and I understand one another. Now...enough with the talking. There's only one way I want to exhaust my tongue."

For the next two hours, all thoughts of Rivenna and her strange, terrible predictions vanish from my mind.

CHAPTER
THIRTY-TWO

In the morning, after too few hours of sleep, Thorne kisses me and takes off to the arena.

I allow myself the luxury of sleeping a few hours more, then head to the executive wing to meet up with Kith for our daily outing.

I haven't forgotten about the burger he promised me—though I promise *myself* I will not be trying on any more dresses in front of him.

Kith greets me with a friendly grin and to my relief, no awkwardness whatsoever. Within fifteen minutes, we're out of the Citadel and wandering along a boulevard lined with businesses that fill me with renewed hope.

We pass by a series of establishments, some of which are under construction. Others look newly finished, their signs shiny as if freshly painted just this morning.

"How the hell are they rebuilding so quickly?" I ask, my jaw dropping in wonder. "I mean, don't get me wrong—I love it. But *how*?"

"Velors and Brutes," Kith says with a shrug. "Speed and

strength. It's amazing what you can do when Tethered are on your side—and motivated. And it helps that the king is no longer bombing the shit out of the city."

"I guess I've never quite realized how many Tethered were in the Capitol. I always figured there were secret ones born here—the lucky ones who weren't forced to live their days in the Tower."

"There *are* some of those," Kith says. "The policy was always to force any Tethered woman to give birth in the Tower, but they couldn't force Normals—Potentials—inside. They simply never anticipated so many births of Tethered children from parents who didn't possess gifts themselves. That was one reason your father was known as the Hunter. He tracked down many secret Tethered who were threats to Kravan."

"He didn't report them to the Prefect, though," I say, swallowing down a wretched thought. "Did he?"

"God, no. He was never on their side. Your father's enemies were people like Lady Graystone—the ones hiding among the Capitol's citizens solely to protect themselves while actively conspiring against our people." Kith looks at me with all the sincerity in the world when he adds, "Your father is a good man—regardless of what anyone says. He has always wished for Kravan's renewal and for Tethered to be freed from their shackles. I aim to help in that fight when the time comes."

I want to ask Kith how, exactly, he plans to help when it's Thorne who's in charge of training the army, but the thought gets disrupted when we arrive at our destination.

The restaurant appears to be behind the others in its schedule and in dire need of a makeover. The façade is dominated by two large, foggy windows and a sign swinging lazily from one hook that reads, "Chelsea's Roadhouse."

Kith gestures toward it and says, "Best burgers in town." A small, charming bell chimes as he pushes the door open. "As far as we're concerned, that means they're the best in the world."

The floor is covered in dust and piles of swept-up plaster. Remnants of the king's last bombing, no doubt.

A woman behind a cracked wooden bar eyes me suspiciously, but smiles sweetly when her eyes land on Kith, and tells us to take a seat.

There are only a few patrons inside, scarfing down what look like massive slabs of meat shoved between two equally enormous buns.

My mouth waters at the sight.

When we've seated ourselves at a table by the back wall, the woman behind the counter strides over with creased paper menus in hand.

"You here to eat?" she asks in a gruff tone, but her sour expression softens again as she eyes Kith.

I glance at him, noting a subtle shift in his features. I'm not sure whether it's real or imagined, but I'm convinced he's...*charming* her. Whether by using some stolen power or his own charisma, I can't say.

He's always been painfully handsome. But in this moment, it's as if his face has altered slightly to be even *more* pleasant, more inviting.

"Two cheeseburgers with the works, and two chocolate shakes," Kith says with a smile, and the woman lays a hand on his shoulder and says, "Anything more, Gorgeous?"

Her voice has transformed into something light and airy, in stark contrast to her hard features.

"Two sparkling waters," he adds. "That will be all. Thank you."

"Anytime, darling." She's about to turn away when she adds, "And may I just say you're the most handsome man I've ever seen?"

"That can't possibly be true," he replies with a gleaming smile. "But thank you all the same."

"What just happened?" I ask under my breath, snickering as she walks away.

"Nothing at all," Kith replies. "Just using a borrowed skill. She seemed a little grumpy, and I wanted to get on her good side."

"Borrowed. You mean you stole it from someone."

"I did."

I lean in and whisper, "How many powers have you collected over the years?"

At that, he looks a little remorseful, as if I've just asked how many bodies he's left in his wake. I suppose that might be *exactly* what I'm asking.

"A few," he replies cryptically. "As you know, a Blade can keep a power or pass it on to someone else. He can also choose to give it back to the person he took it from, depending on his benevolence. Even if I wanted to, I couldn't keep all of the gifts. It would prove overwhelming to anyone's mind—even my own."

"You keep saying *he*. Are you telling me Blades are always men?"

He nods. "With rare exceptions, yes. I suppose it's one of the world's great injustices. *Your* ability to sap powers from others, on the other hand, is unusual for anyone, regardless of gender."

"Speaking of power..." I begin, interrupted by the server stumbling her way back to us with a tray of drinks. I wait as she sets them down, her eyes locked on Kith the entire time.

There's a moment when I'm almost convinced she's contemplating leaning over and kissing him.

"Speaking of power...?" he repeats when she's gone. "You were going to say?"

"Who do you suppose will run against the Magister if there's an election?"

"Oh," he chuckles, "there's never a shortage of ambitious assholes around."

"Would you ever do it?"

With his chin down, he narrows his eyes at me, teasing. "Are you calling me an ambitious asshole?"

I laugh. "No! I just mean—you're a good man, Kith. You want what's best for Kravan. You're unattached and young. You're powerful as all hell. I think you'd make a good leader—and Kravan could use a Tethered in that position, don't you think?"

Kith's features darken, and he lays a hand on my arm, a warning in his eyes.

"The Magister wouldn't like hearing you say that," he cautions.

"I'm speaking in hypotheticals, I promise. Still—I'm curious. Would you ever want to lead?"

Kith pulls away and sits back, contemplating the question. "I have other things on my mind than the presidency. But...we'll see."

"I wonder how it works in the other realms," I reply with a long sigh.

"Other realms?" Kith asks, and my eyes widen with horror at what I may have just exposed.

"I...thought everyone just assumed the world was bigger than Kravan," I tell him. "Rivenna seemed to think so. I just..."

The fact is, I can't take the words back.

"I'm kidding," he laughs. "We do assume—of course we do. Some of us even *know*. I've seen maps, heard some things. I know there are Tethered out there in the other lands, just like we have in Kravan. They say there were once ships that moved about the ocean, bringing goods from one land to the other regularly. I've heard there was an experiment long ago—a sort of bet between leaders of various realms to see who could create the most effective hierarchy and maintain control the longest. I'm not sure whether it's true or not—but it would be fascinating to learn how the other realms are run."

"If every realm has a different hierarchy," I say slowly, "then there has to be one out there that favors the Tethered. One where our people are truly free."

"Maybe. Maybe not. It's probably more nuanced than that."

My brows raise and I cross my arms, sitting back. "Tell me more," I say with a smirk.

Kith chuckles. "Each time we strive for freedom, we give something up in order to obtain it. If we wish to lead, it means we must take accountability when we fail—or when we do harm. We must suffer the consequences of our sacrifice. So, if the Tethered were in charge, they would have to surrender a little of themselves to accommodate the needs of others. Tethered are powerful, and we like to throw our weight around. It's why we were imprisoned in the first place. We got greedy, and tried to take over. We abused our power—and paid for it. If we ever get the chance to lead, we must be more disciplined than in past."

I want to tell him that's a lie he's been fed all his life. The Tethered never rose up. It was Quinton who spread the myth. Quinton, who used that lie to brainwash generations into accepting their fates.

But that would mean revealing a secret I've only ever divulged to my father and Thorne. So instead, I simply say, "I'd rather suffer the consequences of my failures than not be allowed to try. Wouldn't you?"

Kith is about to reply when a blur of movement catches my eye and his. A large, gray form shoots toward me, grabs my arm, and tugs me violently to my feet. Only when I'm a few inches from him do I see the dark gray mask covering his face. Against my will, I inhale the scent of sweat and alcohol swirling in a mist around him.

His voice is a hiss when he breathes, "The heir will—"

But before he can finish the sentence, Kith is on him, hurling him to the floor and stepping hard on his throat. Instantly, his fist is at the man's chest, a dark red stain spreading under his touch.

Kith draws back, wiping his palm on his trousers. I have no idea what he just did or how—only that the man is dead, a deep, blackened wound penetrating his chest.

CHAPTER THIRTY-THREE

"A Velor," I breathe. "He moved so fast. I—"

Nodding, Kith crouches down and pulls the mask up, then takes hold of the man's throat. At first, I think he's checking for a pulse. But with a jolt of horror, I realize that's not what he's doing.

I watch him draw something indescribable from the lifeless body, as if pulling the man's soul out through his flesh.

My voice is a monotone—a stranger's drawl—when I say, "You took his power."

"It's standard practice when I defeat an enemy. I'll hold onto it until I find someone worthy, then pass it along. I've snatched gifts from many a Velor over the years—they're as common as pigeons."

The way he speaks of a dead man sends a shudder through me. I suppose when you've killed as often as Kith has, taking a life ceases to mean much. But I don't think I could ever get used to being surrounded by death.

Our server leans over the counter and gripes, "I assume you're cleaning that up, Blade." Her former look of admiration has left her expression entirely. Apparently, murdering someone in her establishment outweighs handsomeness.

"Of course," Kith calls over his shoulder, but his eyes are locked on mine.

"You're disgusted with me," he says softly as he dumps a few coins onto the table to pay for our meals. "For what I just did. I only did it to defend you."

"I know. But...he *was* a Velor. If he'd wanted to hurt me, he could have done it, and quickly. In an instant, he could have cut my throat. He didn't."

"He might have wanted to spew his nonsense before killing you. You never know what motivates a Starless. Thorne told you himself that one had a knife at his throat when I found him. They are not known for mercy."

With a wince, the memory stirs in my mind of the Poisoner—of the oozing wound he cut into Rivenna's throat.

Kith is right. Mercy was not on that man's mind.

"Of course," I reply, expelling a hard breath. "I'm so grateful to you. My point was that I think this man was only trying to tell me something."

Kith lowers his head, shaking it, and lets out a laugh. "Yeah. The same thing every Starless will tell you—the words you'll see painted on the Capitol's walls over and over again. It's fucking lunacy. Propaganda, spread by people like him to push doubt into the minds of anyone weak enough to believe them. He was trying to indoctrinate you, just like they brainwashed you in the Tower."

I want to tell him I wasn't entirely brainwashed—that I always suspected something was amiss in our realm. But instead, I say, "Tell me, then. What does the saying mean? *The heir will bring ruin on us all.* Who are they talking about?"

"It's another of their mantras, like *the Rebellion is a Lie.* It's meaningless. He didn't know what he was talking about."

"Are you sure about that? Maybe he was referring to Tallin. Maybe the prince plans to attack us, and we don't know it yet."

"I highly doubt that. But even if he is, we'll be ready—thanks to Thorne." With a shrug, Kith reaches down to grab the man's feet and begins dragging him toward the restaurant's door, leaving a trail of deep red behind him. When we reach the exit, Kith holds a hand out, and the stains we left behind immediately vanish.

I'm beginning to wonder just how many Tethered gifts he's stolen over the years.

Hoisting the man over his shoulder, he opens the door, gesturing to me to hold it. "The words mean whatever they want them to mean," he grunts. "Maybe they're talking about Tallin—I don't know. It doesn't matter. The Starless are nothing but confused miscreants who want the ongoing chaos to continue. They've fought the Magister at every turn, and clearly don't want him to succeed. They want our population fearful. It's the whole reason our people are working so hard to restore this city. We want to show the Magister's strength—to convince them we're on the side of good."

His words jar something in me, and I swallow, then follow him out to the street.

"But how did the Velor know to come talk to me? Did he know I was the Shadow's daughter?"

Kith's eyes focus on mine once again, and I watch as a multitude of colors swirl in his irises—the amalgamation of every power inside him. "They speak to everyone and anyone who looks like they might be willing to listen, Shara. As much as I admire you, he probably thought you were just another commoner with fear in her eyes." He nudges the body with his fingertips. "Come on—we've got to take this bastard down to the catacombs so a Bonesmith can deal with him."

"Catacombs? Like—underground burial grounds?"

Kith nods. "There's no room in the Capitol for graveyards, so we preserve the bones of the dead in underground chambers. There are hundreds down there—thousands, even. Tethered and Potentials alike."

"Who put them there?"

"If you mean *who killed them,* the answer is enemies. Those who bomb us relentlessly. The former king. As for who carries them? I do—and so do many others. The Bonesmiths do the rest."

Silently, I accompany Kith for several blocks, watching as others—Normals and Tethered alike—stop in their tracks and bow their heads, either out of respect or fear. A powerful man is walking among them with a masked Starless over his shoulder, dead.

I can only imagine what they're thinking right now.

When we arrive at a tall stone wall, Kith passes a hand over its surface. A door appears, unlatching and opening inward, and he nods to me to enter.

"I still don't understand why anyone would side against the Magister or my father," I say, stepping into the darkness of a narrow tunnel only to have a series of lights flare to life. I can see now that it leads steeply downwards, and I begin to walk. "I don't see why the Starless risk their lives like that, just to speak to strangers."

"You were raised in the Tower," Kith says. "With respect, you've seldom gotten to bear witness to the complexities of humanity. Most people want to be left alone—but there are many in the world who live to cause strife. The Starless are that breed."

"*That's* why they say the Rebellion is a lie? Come on—I may be a naive Tower Orphan, but that's a little hard to swallow."

"Conspiracy theories amuse them. They're an easy way to stir up trouble. That's all."

Kith strides quickly down the steep ramp and along a dark, curved tunnel of roughly carved stone and earth. We haven't walked more than a minute or so when we pass under a sign that says,

Here Lies the Empire of the Dead

The surface of the walls alters the moment we're past. No longer are we seeing stone and dirt, but what look at first like rounded rocks and jagged tree branches.

It takes me stopping and examining them to realize I'm staring at a vast array of human skulls. Hundreds of them, piled atop one another like bricks in rows.

Under those rows are layers of what look like femurs, arranged like firewood, chopped and stacked tidily.

Some of the skulls are fractured, probably from blows from some weapon or flying piece of an exploding building, and my heart hurts for every soul I see represented before me.

"Come," Kith says gently. "We're almost there."

We walk a few more minutes until we reach a broad door to our right.

"The first Bonesmith chamber is through here." Kith knocks three times, then drops the Velor's body to the ground unceremoniously.

I wince when I look down at him, recalling the touch of madness in his voice when he tried to speak to me—and the horrific nature of his wound.

But something else is sitting heavy inside me, and when a man opens the door to speak to Kith, I step back to gather my thoughts, pushing myself against the opposite wall of the corridor before remembering my back is touching bone.

"The Bonesmith is going to look after the Starless," Kith tells me over his shoulder. "Come—you should see the chamber."

"I'd rather not."

With a laugh that only slightly reassures me, Kith steps over, takes me by the hand, and looks into my eyes. Calm moves through me, slithering and slipping along every inch of my body and mind. Kindness. Warmth. A protectiveness I've only ever known from Thorne.

~I sense nothing but honor and loyalty in him, Maude tells me as if picking up on the same thing. *As you've said, he's a good man.*

The thought weaves its way through my mind even as I remind myself that I just watched him kill a man who had committed no crime other than touching me.

"Trust me," Kith says softly. "I would never hurt you, Shara."

"Okay," I sigh. "I'll do it."

But I can't promise I'll like what I see.

CHAPTER
THIRTY-FOUR

I'M NOT sure what I'm expecting to see when I step into the Bonesmith's chamber.

I've witnessed horrors. Deaths, and horrible injuries, including many of my own through the years.

But this place feels like it shouldn't exist.

The chamber is constructed of stacked, uneven stone, which would already give it a cold air, even if it weren't for the countless red-stained shelves covered in human remains.

Six or seven shelves stretch the length of the far wall, and the top three are nothing but skulls, bleached and cleaned, presumably ready for placement in the catacombs.

But it's the rest of the room that sets my stomach churning.

In one corner lie the rejected limbs, which haven't been cleaned by human hands. Instead, they're being gnawed on by insects, maggots, and vermin of various kinds—rats, and other creatures I don't even want to look at.

I reach inside my pocket to realize Mercutio is peering out, no doubt taking in the sight. Unlike him, those small creatures are flesh and blood. This is their sanctuary. Their home. They feed on human death.

A man stands at the room's center in a blood-stained apron, a wheeled metal table to his right. On it lies a woman's corpse.

She's naked, her arms and legs roughly hewn from her body. The smith hasn't yet gotten to her head, which I suppose is a blessing.

Her limbs lie by the table's side, gray and awful. On one arm, I spot the Magister's brand.

"Parker," Kith says, nodding to the man, who bows his head with reverence.

"Blade," the Bonesmith replies, then pulls his eyes up to glance at me. "Forgive me, but who is she?"

"She is none other than the Shadow's daughter," Kith says, and the man's simpering reverence only seems to increase.

"You are most welcome here," he says, lowering his chin again. "It's an honor."

"I...thank you," I reply, then force myself to raise my chin in an attempt at worthiness. This man obviously worships my father and Kith as others do—and me by extension. "Who is that woman?" I ask, gesturing toward the partial corpse.

The smith frowns. "A traitor," he says.

"If she's a traitor, why is she wearing the brand? It's not crossed out—so she's not a Starless, is she?"

~*Watch out, Shara,* Maude warns. *I'm not sure you want to question a man who hacks off limbs for fun.*

Kith moves to reply, but I hold up a hand, addressing the silent smith again. "Tell me."

"It's not the Magister's mark," he says. "Look more closely, if you would."

I do as he says and see that he's right. The brand is a circle cut through with twisting lines, but at its center is a blade—a knife or a sword. Just like the pendant I took from the hand of a dead Starless.

"What is its meaning?" I ask, my voice softening.

"It is a mockery. A twist on the Magister's symbol. It's a threat."

"Seems a little weird, don't you think? To bother branding your skin as a jab at the Magister?"

"The Starless want plausible deniability," Kith interrupts. "They want to be able to claim devotion. The slight variation is a code—that's all. Anyone who glances at it quickly will assume loyalty to the Magister. It takes close inspection to see the dagger at the circle's center."

"What was this woman's crime?" I ask. "Other than a brand that doesn't match the Magister's, I mean."

The smith narrows his eyes, looking quietly irritated, but Kith growls, "Just tell her."

"She tried to steal food from one of the Magister's warehouses."

I glance over at the body again, realizing now how prominent her ribs are.

She was probably starving.

"Why didn't she have food?"

"Everyone in the Capitol is given what they need, so long as they're loyal to the cause," Kith insists. "She has the mark of a Starless. The mark of a traitor. If she was turned away, it was only because she was considered dangerous to our kind."

"Our kind," I repeat, rounding on him. My nausea has abated and now, I'm just angry. "We are Tethered. Is *that* what you mean?"

"I mean those who wish for a better world," he says, his voice even, calm, smooth as always. He reaches a hand out and lays it on my shoulder, and instantly, a wave of warmth works its way along my extremities to settle somewhere at my center, as if he's just injected me with whatever sort of powerful drug he stores within his touch.

I want to scream—to slap his arm away. But I can't bring myself to do it.

"Shara—things are ugly here. Surely you knew that before you came to the Capitol from the Isles."

"I didn't know we were killing our own," I remind him. "Tell me...do we have any Starless prisoners in the Citadel? I've only seen Royal Guard."

Kith and Parker exchange a look, and Kith nods.

"A few," he says. "They're kept in cells on the lower levels."

"I'd like to speak to one."

"Why?"

"I have my reasons."

"You really shouldn't," Kith replies with a shake of his head. "They're dangerous. Your father wouldn't allow it, besides."

"I don't particularly care what my father would and wouldn't allow. I want to speak to a member of the Starless. A so-called traitor. Every single one I've tried to talk to has ended up dead or vanished. I'd like to hear more from them than mere catch phrases and propaganda. I want to know how they *think*."

"Fine," Kith says, dropping his hand. "I'll see to it that it happens."

"Today."

Kith nods, and I turn away. "I'll wait in the hallway," I tell him, and stride toward the door.

Once I'm outside the smith's chamber, my eyes move to a place on the wall above the skulls where it looks like some text was once painted but has faded almost to nothing. I can just make out the faint outline of letters:

The queen will save us.

I stare at the words, convinced I'm only imagining them.

Kravan has no queen. The last one was Tomas' late wife, but she's long dead. And I can't imagine anyone marrying Tallin—or Ellion—anytime soon.

When Kith leaves the Bonesmith's chamber, I reach for him to point out the writing. The second my fingers brush his hand, my mind flashes with a rapid-fire series of faces.

Some look calm and at peace.

Others scream.

I draw back, shock temporarily paralyzing me.

Without asking, I know what I was just looking at were the faces of those Kith has killed over the years.

The only question is, why haven't I seen them before now?

Kith has touched me a dozen times over the days we've known one another, yet my power has never activated in that way around him. It's almost as if he's blocked me from seeing the full extent of his might—and the terror he's unleashed.

"Are you all right?" he asks, reaching for me again.

This time, when he touches me, I see nothing of his history.

All I feel is that warm, comforting sense of calm that falls over my mind when he lays his hands on me.

I chew on my lip for a moment, then nod toward the message on the wall. "Do you know anything about that?"

His lips quirk into a smirk and he chuckles. "The queen? That's an old one. An attempted bit of propaganda that never took hold. The queen died years ago, so no one thought much of it. The Ganders—the propaganda spreaders, I mean—gave up on that message when they realized it wasn't going to take hold."

My face crumples. "Who, exactly, comes up with these sayings? *The Rebellion is a lie, the heir will bring ruin on us all?*"

With a shrug, Kith says, "They probably come from the Lady herself. She's convinced the world she's some sort of powerful Seer—that she has witnessed the future and knows all. But the truth is, her followers are fanatical, and they'll believe literally anything she says. Honestly, I wouldn't be surprised if she spread that queen rumor, too, to elevate herself in their estimation. She's probably referring to herself in some metaphorical way."

With his right hand, Kith reaches toward the wall. A twisting shadow spreads from his fingers, covering the words permanently with a layer of onyx darkness.

I've never seen a power like the one he's using now, and it unsettles me more than I'd like to admit.

"There. All gone," he says. "Now—you wanted to speak to a prisoner, so I'll bring you back to the Citadel. But I'm telling you—you don't want to commune with the Starless. They're psychotic—every last one of them."

"I don't care. I'm willing to take the risk."

For a moment, I'm convinced he's going to deny me the request. But finally, with a sharp breath, he says, "Fine. Maybe if you meet one face to face, you'll come to understand."

When we reach the Citadel, Kith takes me to the cells, as promised.

They're situated in the structure's depths, a level down from the council chamber. The prison wing is filled with inhospitable, small cells, creeping moss coating the walls as thick, glossy liquid drips from the ceiling.

I can see into each cell via a small, barred window in the door. Each contains a single prisoner, most of whom are pacing or lying in fetal position on small cots.

"Will they ever be freed?" I ask quietly.

Kith's face is emotionless. "Not likely. They'll probably be hanged for the crime of committing themselves to the Lady for life."

"But they could live in the Capitol. They could start over. She's manipulated them, just like I was manipulated in the Tower. They shouldn't be punished for loyalty."

He looks like he's about to say something more, but instead, he stops, reaches out, and unlocks one of the cell doors.

"This woman is a Starless," he says, nodding to me to enter. "Ask about her *loyalty*. Go ahead."

I step inside the cell. A young woman is seated on her cot, looking emaciated, as if she hasn't consumed a meal in weeks. A cilice is firmly strapped to her right arm, digging into her flesh, and I have to fight to resist the urge to leap over and heal her.

"You're a Starless," I say, my voice quivering slightly to see a Tethered in this state. "Correct?"

She nods weakly, but I can still sense strength in her. Her powers are subdued by the cilice, but I feel them trying to surge through her veins—trying desperately to make themselves known.

She glances up at Kith, eyeing him nervously. The moment she registers who he is, she shrinks down inside herself.

I almost wonder whether she's encountered him before.

"Would you leave us for a moment?" I ask him, and he nods, then steps out of the cell, sealing the door behind him.

"You are loyal to the Lady of the Starless—right?"

The young woman snickers, snorts, then slaps herself on the forehead. I realize for the first time just how thin her arm is—little more than sinew and bone. It's a wonder the cilice even manages to hold on.

"Yes," she says. "Free! I was free for a time. The Lady—she showed me the truth." Her head seems to swim as she speaks the words.

Maude...

My internal voice rouses her from her dormant state.

~Yes?

Is this woman drugged?

She's silent for a moment. *~I'm not sure. But she certainly seems unstable.*

"Would you like to be free again?" I ask the prisoner.

The woman shakes her head rapidly, then looks toward

the wall. "No. Out there? That isn't freedom. I'd rather be in here. I'd rather die. Bones on the walls. Bones..."

"You wouldn't have to live in the Catacombs," I tell her, assuming that's what she means. "You would live above ground, where it's sunny. You might patrol or protect the Citadel. You would have a status—a life. You could find someone to be with. A tethered mate. Someone to love."

She glares up at me, then, baring her teeth like a wild animal, leaps at me, hands outstretched, and slashes at my throat. I jump out of her reach just in time for a length of chain to snap her backwards—attached to one of her ankles.

I don't know whether this rage is drug-induced or not, but whoever she is—whatever her state of mind—this woman would rather be chained to the wall in this cell than outside, living life in the Capitol.

Why?

She tumbles onto the cot, chest heaving. As if in answer to my internal question, she holds up her hand to reveal a brand in her palm.

Only, it's not like the other brands I've seen. It's not the Magister's mark.

This one reveals the image of a crown. It's an angry red color, and oozing liquid as if it's infected. It looks new, as though it had only been inflicted on her in the last few days.

"Who did that to you?" I gasp.

With tears in her eyes, she hisses, "*He did.*"

She's staring at her hand, offering me no clues. *He* could mean anyone, from the king to Tallin. Perhaps the king's spies patrolled the Capitol in search of people to mark. Perhaps it was his way of claiming this woman as his property.

"Who is *he*?"

I step carefully toward her, passing a hand through the air between us to heal her skin. Instantly, she takes in a deep breath, then our eyes meet.

Hers are suddenly clear.

"It was that man," she whispers under her breath. "The *Hunter*."

"The Hunter? You mean...the Shadow did this to you?" I whisper. "They don't call him Hunter, not anymore. You're saying he branded a crown into your flesh? Why would he..."

She stares at me, looking disoriented once again. I can see her mind pulling itself beyond her reach, as if someone else is controlling it.

"The Rebellion is a lie," she rasps. "The heir will bring ruin on us all!"

"I know about the lies," I whisper back, glancing over my shoulder to ensure Kith hasn't stepped into the cell. I move closer to the prisoner, then crouch down before her, only mildly confident that she won't try to attack me again. "I know the past isn't what we think it is."

"The past?" she hisses. "No—not the past. I'm talking about the future. It's coming. It's almost here."

"What do you mean—"

"Shara!"

Kith's voice snaps out at me like the end of a whip. He flies toward me from the doorway, grabbing my arm. "We need to go. Now."

I twist around to see his eyes bright with intensity as he stares at the prisoner. There's a warning in his gaze, and the moment he pulls me toward the door, the prisoner lunges at me again. But she stops before reaching me, as if she has no intention of wounding me. Her only desire, it seems, is to convey some mysterious message.

"What did you mean, the future?" I ask her.

She scuttles back onto the cot, pressing herself to the wall and tucking her knees under her chin, burying her face in her arms. A long, brutal whimper escapes her lips.

"She's not going to answer you," Kith says. "She's lost it."

"Lost it, or been forced to lose it? Is she drugged?"

"If she is, it's just painkillers. That's all."

Kith looks like he's planning to take my arm again. But when I shoot him a look of warning, he stops himself.

"Your father will want to check in with you," he says softly. "Please. Leave her. She's of no use to you. She's too far gone. I'm sorry."

I nod once and turn to leave the cell.

As out of it as the woman seems, and as delusional, there was truth in her wild eyes when she spoke of the future.

And I intend to get to the bottom of it...even if it kills me.

CHAPTER

THIRTY-FIVE

"How are you today, Shara?" my father asks when Kith and I enter his office a few minutes later. His voice is gentle, his eyes filled with compassion.

My gaze locks on his, trying to take in his true nature.

Could it really be that the prisoner was talking about him when she said the Hunter branded a crown into her skin?

Why would he do such a thing?

"I'm all right," I insist, though the truth is, I'm a confused jumble of nerves. I'm sad. Angry. Exhausted.

During my brief time with the prisoner, I forgot what had happened in the city earlier. The trauma of it—the wretchedness of seeing the Starless die and the Bonesmith's gruesome domain.

It storms back into my mind like a dark cloud, and I blurt out, "Have you ever branded a prisoner, Father?"

I try to keep my voice steady as I utter the question—try to remain calm. I don't want to think him capable of such a thing. I don't want to accuse my own flesh and blood of that kind of cruelty.

But I don't know what else I'm supposed to think.

"I have branded prisoners, yes," he admits. "With the Magister's mark. But something tells me you're asking about another mark entirely."

I nod. "It was a crown. The prisoner said the Hunter did it."

My father and Kith exchange a look that I can't quite read, then my father lets out a long sigh. "She was lying. I've never branded a crown onto anyone's flesh. What reason could I possibly have for doing such a thing?"

"I don't know," I admit. "But I felt the need to ask."

"You do realize," he says, turning his attention to Kith, "that you had no business bringing my daughter to see a Starless prisoner. I don't know what was going through your mind, given that she had been attacked by one earlier in the day."

"You know about that?" I ask.

"I see a good deal of what happens in this city," he replies. "I've told you—I have my spies."

"I did warn Shara about seeing the prisoner," Kith says. "But I take full responsibility for my actions. I put her in danger, and for that, I apologize."

"It was my fault," I assure my father. "I wanted to speak to her...to see if I could figure out what motivates the Starless."

"I can only assume you were unsuccessful."

"To be fair, she didn't seem entirely coherent."

My father looks irritated when he turns back to Kith. "And the Starless in the restaurant—did he threaten my daughter's life? Is that why you killed him?"

"He was a threat," Kith says, without *actually* answering

the question. "He grabbed Shara violently. I had little choice but to act quickly."

"You could have taken his powers from him and rendered him defenseless. You are a Blade, after all."

Kith shakes his head. "There wasn't time for that. He had his hands on her already when I grabbed him."

"Only one hand," I say. "And he wasn't hurting me. He was just speaking."

"Spreading propaganda, yes," Kith says. "He was a danger. We can't know his intentions."

"True," my father snarls. "Well, I suppose I owe you my thanks, Kith. Whatever his intentions, the man is gone now—and we must move on. We have plans to discuss, after all—a new king to overthrow, and an army to muster."

"Let's not forget," I interject, "We also have the small matter of Ellion to contend with. If we overthrow Tallin, Ellion will just move into his place. It seems to me that's what people are talking about when they say *the heir will bring ruin on us all.* It probably has nothing to do with Tallin—maybe they know something we don't."

"Ellion Graystone won't be a problem," my father chuckles as if Ellion is little more than a gnat to swat away. "It's Tallin we need to focus on just now. Word has it he's shut himself in his father's old chambers and is only willing to speak to his most trusted servants." His brows rise when he adds, "You know, Shara, I've actually heard from a source that he's been asking after you."

My eyes meet Kith's briefly, then my father's. "Me? Why?"

"He wants you to return to his side. It seems you calm his nerves."

"I definitely don't," I half-laugh. "It was Valira who—"

The mere act of saying her name brings a lump to my throat.

Valira, who was literally Tallin's medicine in human form. Valira, who sacrificed everything to keep the realm from falling to Tallin's madness.

"The prince—or king—or whatever he is now—may well hate me by now," I finally say. "He must know I fled to the Capitol. If I wasn't his sworn enemy before, I suppose I am now."

"I believe he has a soft spot for you, Daughter. Tallin let you go, didn't he?"

I draw in a breath and nod. "He did," I confess. "Why, I don't know. But I still wouldn't want to be alone in a dark room with him."

Not only did Tallin let me go—he *demanded* it.

Just before murdering his parents.

"It's not surprising at all," Kith interjects, running a hand through his hair, "that the new king would be fond of such a beautiful woman."

My eyes widen with shock that he would say such a thing in front of my father. Yet the Shadow looks utterly unfazed, as though he expects this sort of talk from his closest advisor.

"Don't worry, Shara," my father says. "The plan is not to send you back to the palace. I would never risk your safety so recklessly."

"Then what *is* the plan?"

"Each of us will play our part," Kith says. "Thorne has already done incredible work, equipping our fighters with bracers. With his help, we have the power to overthrow the entire Royal Guard with ease—or any other force we come up against."

"At this point," I say, "it seems like it would be easier just to bomb the palace. It would also keep us from putting our fighters at risk."

"There will be no bombing of the palace," my father snaps. I expect him to tell me it would be cruel to kill so many members of the Royal Guard, or some equally humane-sounding excuse. But instead, he adds, "The palace is an exquisite structure that deserves to be preserved."

With a snicker, I ask why. "It represents everything we abhor. Wealth, opulence, the bullshit gap between rich and poor, powerful and weak. It represents the oppression laid at the feet of the Tethered for generations, starting with that asshole Quinton."

The Shadow's eyes narrow. He looks at Kith, then back to me.

With a jolt of horror, I realize Kith still may not know the name of Kravan's first king.

As usual, though, Kith looks calm and collected.

My father, on the other hand, looks infuriated.

"Do not speak that name again," he warns. "Not until our mission is complete. Do you hear me?"

A stabbing pain assaults my left arm and I cry out, clutching at it as my father grinds his jaw.

Kith steps over and takes me by the shoulders, turning me toward him.

"Are you okay?" he asks.

I nod. "It felt like..."

I stop myself.

It felt like the pain Maude inflicted on me so often when I

lived inside the Tower. The pain she regularly used as punishment for saying the wrong thing at the wrong time.

A warning.

But why would she be punishing me now? We're no longer under the jurisdiction of the Tower, the Warden...or the Prefect.

I'm *supposed* to be free.

~That was just a warning not to overstep again.

It was a bit violent, don't you think?

~If it helps keep your mouth shut, then I'd say no.

"What the hell just happened?" Kith asks, turning toward my father, rage scrawled across his face. "Did you hurt her?"

"How would I do that, Kith?" the Shadow says. "I'm not equipped with your multitude of powers."

"Bullshit," Kith scowls. "I *saw* her pain. It was like someone took an excavator to her arm."

"Kith," I say under my breath. "It's okay. It was just Maude—she was warning me not to speak out of place. She's right. I shouldn't have mentioned the first king's name—it was reckless. I apologize, Father."

"It's all right," the Shadow says gently. "Just remember, my dear, that knowledge is not always a blessing. It can also be a curse. Our history may seem simple to you, but it's layered—complicated. It's easy to unearth secrets in front of the wrong person."

"I assume you're not referring to me," Kith says, wrapping an arm protectively around me. "I already know about Quinton. I'm well aware of the history that brought the Citadel to its knees so long ago."

I stare at him, shocked. I didn't think anyone knew the

first king's name. I'd come to understand it was a deep, dark secret, known only by the Storian and a few others.

"Yes," my father tells Kith. "I know you do. But my daughter must learn to contain herself, or she will find herself in a tight spot one of these days."

I pull away from Kith, eyeing him. "You really know about Quinton?"

"I do. I have for a long time. A few years back, I discovered a treasure trove of historical writing hidden here in the Citadel. I passed it on to your father at that time—but not before reading enough to learn the name of the man who killed the last president."

"He didn't just do that," I sneer. "He also imprisoned our kind and divided Kravan into rich and poor. The Tethered were turned into a class of servants, robbed of all rights—even the right to feel. He was a monster."

"Were we really robbed of feeling?" my father interrupts. "Are you telling me you have no emotions?"

"We were never allowed to act on them. Never allowed the freedom to love anyone."

"Ah, but it's possible that long ago, when Quinton seized power, our emotions were too violent and unpredictable. Has it ever occurred to you that maybe the Tethered have *benefited* from our incarceration?"

"Benefited!" I scowl, and not for the first time, I wonder if I've misread my father. "You, of all people, must know that's not true. You're the one who wants to overthrow the king so the Tethered can be free again."

"True. But one day soon, fate will deal us all a difficult blow—and you will understand then that laws need to be laid down on occasion—for the good of Kravan."

His words *should* feel like an encouragement—a step in the right direction.

But instead, they feel almost like a warning.

"I hope, when the time comes, that the people of Kravan can elect their new leader," I say. "I will be glad when that day arrives—and proud to be a part of bringing it about. So will Thorne, I'm sure. We'll do anything we can to help."

"You've already helped," Kith says. "Both of you. More than you can possibly know."

"Well, then," my father says. "I believe we all want the same thing. We wish, more than anything, to help our realm heal from its many deep wounds."

"Good thing we have a Healer in our midst, then." A warm grin slips over Kith's lips, and in his eyes, I see something I haven't felt in what seems like far too long.

Hope.

CHAPTER THIRTY-SIX

THAT EVENING AT DINNER, I fill Thorne in on everything from the supposed "attack" by the Starless Velor to the Bonesmith —to the prisoner and my father's strange reaction.

"I don't know what to think anymore," I confess. "I don't feel entirely safe here in the Citadel, but the city feels even more dangerous. I don't know whether to believe the Starless who claimed my father had branded her with a crown. I mean, why would he do that?"

"Did she actually say it was your father, specifically?" Thorne asks. His hand is holding my own, a much-needed anchor after this wild and terrible day.

"She said *the Hunter*. Which in itself is weird, don't you think? He hasn't really been called that for years."

"Yeah, it is," Thorne says, pushing aside his plate and moving over to crouch next to my chair. He lays a gentle hand on my cheek, looks into my eyes, and says, "I'm so sorry. I should have been with you through all of it—not Kith."

"It's all right," I say, taking his powerful hand in mine

and bringing it to my lips. "Tell me, though...how was your training session?"

Ever since he walked in the door at the end of the day, there's been a grimness in his expression I don't quite recognize. A deep concern lines his features, as if something grave has happened.

I want to think the expression was born out of empathy for me—but something tells me it was there long before he walked in the door.

"The Magister is talking about changing the timeline," he says. "He wants the public hangings to take place somewhat earlier than he'd planned—mere days from now. Which would mean...well, it would mean a lot of things."

His words jar me. "Is it because of the king's death and Tallin being crowned? Are you worried the fighters aren't ready?"

He shakes his head. "The fighters are fine. They'll be able to do what's asked of them with flying colors. But that's not what's worrying me."

Pushing himself upright, he guides me over to the bed. We lie down, my head against his chest, his arms around me.

"I hope you're not worried about our future," I say, "because I'm not. I think about our little house every single day—I daydream about it. It will happen for us, I swear to you."

"I want it to," he tells me. "You don't know how much."

I draw myself up to look at him. I've never heard such sadness in his voice. Never seen such pain in his face. Yet...I can't *feel* it anymore. It's like there's a wall between us, something invisible yet impenetrable.

Behind his eyes lies a deep concern that troubles me. A "but" that he refuses to utter.

"Thorne...you can tell me anything. You know that, right?"

His smile straightens into a narrow line as his jaw clenches. "Someone told me something today that troubled me. I suppose you might say it was a prediction of sorts."

"Why would you worry about predictions? You can see into the future for yourself. You know what's going to happen before it does. You always have."

"I have," he says. "But my vision only extends so far into the future. And lately, those visions have become more and more vague. Hazy, as though there's a veil over my mind. It's like...like my other powers are growing, but that one is waning."

I swallow hard, realizing I've felt the same thing. Ever since the vision about Thorne being captured by the Starless and the one Kith showed me in the tunnels, I've seen nothing of the future whatsoever—no flashes of it. No hints, even.

I stroke a hand through Thorne's hair. "What did this person tell you?"

"They told me Kravan can be the land it was always meant to be," he says, lifting his eyes to mine. "One where the *people* hold the power, instead of a select few. But that you and I would be tested first in ways that are unimaginable."

"Okay, well..." I let out a relieved laugh. "That's sort of vague, don't you think?"

He nods. "Very."

"So, why is it troubling you? It sounds like a positive thing for Kravan. We've always known it wouldn't be easy to bring about change. You and I are hardly new to being tested."

"It's just...I never wanted your life to be anything less than what you see in your dreams. I want you to have your happily ever after, Shara. You don't know how much I crave that for you."

"Then we'll make it happen," I say with a smile. "We'll craft our own future. But first, we'll help Kravan thrive. We'll make sure the right person is in power—you and I will ensure it, together."

"Together," he says sadly, tucking a strand of my hair behind my ear. "Just remember when the time comes that I love you more than anything in this world. That everything that I do is for you—and for Kravan."

Fear whirls inside me, a twisting pool of dread. Something in his voice is so unlike Thorne—so distant, so defeated.

"We make our own destinies," he says, almost absently. "That's what you believe...isn't it?"

"Of course. You know that."

"Then I have to believe we're choosing the right path."

I tuck myself into his chest, pressing my cheek to his heart, and sigh. "We've always had one goal—and that was to learn the truth. We've already helped the realm by revealing lies told by fraudsters and cheats. Taking Tallin down will be the icing on the cake."

Thorne's chest rises, then hollows out with a sigh.

I slip over him, my hair cascading down in brown curtains framing his face. "Are you happy? Right now?"

"I have the most beautiful woman in the world on top of me. How the hell could I be anything but happy?"

A relieved smile steals my lips from my worries. "Then that's all that matters. We'll deal with the rest as it comes, Thorne."

He goes silent for a few seconds, looks away, then says, "What would happen if we couldn't be together?"

I tighten in spite of myself and climb off him to sit on the bed's edge, facing the other way. "Why wouldn't we be together?"

The last thing I want is for doubt to infiltrate my mind again—for my former insecurity to rear its hideous head.

"I suppose I'm telling you that I have faith in you, Shara. That no matter what happens between us, *you* will fight for this land. It's who you were before I met you, and it's who you'll always be."

"Of course. But what do you think is going to happen between us?" I venture a glance over my shoulder. "What aren't you telling me?"

He moves over to me, kissing my neck, and says, "Sometimes, I worry I'm not worthy of you. That's all."

"Not worthy?" I laugh. "Unless you've done something terrible, you're definitely more than worthy. I love you. And it's not like I'm some..."

"Queen?" he asks with a chuckle.

"Well, yeah. I'm just me."

"Just perfect Shara," he replies, holding me close. "I don't want you to worry about anything. Not now, not ever. Remember our little dream house—always. If ever you feel sad, worried, or anything else—remember the dream we will always share."

CHAPTER THIRTY-SEVEN

THORNE SLIPS out in the morning to leave for his training session before I'm awake—and it's a knock at the door that finally drags me out of bed.

I throw on a white bathrobe before calling out, "Who is it?"

"It's Kith."

When I open the door, he grins, his eyes moving down my body, then back to my face.

"Thorne is a lucky guy, isn't he?" he asks.

I've gotten used to his compliments by now, insisting internally that they're innocent enough. But there's something behind his eyes with this one—an almost aggressive hunger—that's both flattering and terrifying.

I take a step back. "I'm sorry I'm not dressed yet," I say, pulling my hair back and twisting it into a knot.

"I assure you, I don't mind at all. And speaking of dressing—I brought you a little something."

He hands me a soft package, wrapped in brown paper and tied up with string.

"I've got business of my own to attend to, so I won't be able to escort you to the city. But I brought you this to make up for my absence."

"What is it?"

Instead of answering, he thrusts it toward me. "Something I've been holding onto. You should have it."

My eyes widen when I take it from him, opening it gently.

When I see a flash of fabric, I let out a gasp.

"Kith!" I say, tearing the paper apart and extracting the sun-colored gown, holding it up before me. "I can't believe you bought it."

"I couldn't resist. Besides, there will come a time when you need a beautiful dress like this one."

"I don't know about that. We haven't taken Kravan back just yet."

He chuckles. "Trust me—the day will come when you feel a need to celebrate."

This is the gown I saw in the vision Kith showed me—I'm sure of it. The gown I will wear to my Pairing ceremony, when I am bonded with Thorne in the presence of those we love. I have every faith that Thorne will love it as much as I do—and for the same reasons.

Still, as I conceal the dress behind the other clothing in the closet, I'm silently, painfully aware of how hesitant I am to reveal it just yet.

When Thorne and I are alone together that evening, his mood seems to have brightened, and he's all warmth and smiles. We talk again about our dream house, enumerating the features we both hope for in our future home. A little white fence. A dog. A fireplace. A small rose garden.

But as we lie together in bed after we've made love, his joy seems to disintegrate. There's a sudden, silent fear in him —an apprehension I can't quite put my finger on. Like a storm is looming on the horizon that neither of us will be able to hold back.

I tell myself he's focused on the coming conflict—that he knows how hard it will be to go up against the prince's Royal Guard and any other Crimson Elites who support them.

Only, it's not like Thorne to fear a battle. He thrives on fighting for the right side. It pained him in the palace that he never got the opportunity to take Tallin down himself. I know how much he hated the prince, how hard it was to hold back.

He wanted Tallin dead for what he'd done to me.

But I'm not sure that's what's eating away at him now.

"What's going on with you?" I ask, running my fingers through Thorne's hair.

He doesn't turn to look at me. "What do you mean?"

"I mean, you're a thousand miles away tonight. Is it just me? Is it..."

He rolls onto his side and cups my cheek in his hand—a gesture that should feel like the most comforting sensation in the universe.

"It's not you," he half-whispers. "You're a bright light in the darkness."

"Since when are we in the darkness? A few minutes ago, you were talking about our future home. Now, you're all gloom and doom."

He looks like he's going to offer up an explanation, but instead, he smiles. "Maybe I'm just in a mood. It'll pass. I suppose I need a little of the sunshine that is Shara."

I pull away and smirk, which inspires a laugh from him. "What's that look?"

"Well...you said sunshine—and I've been wanting to show you something. It's from a shop in the city."

"Oh?" Thorne sits up, grinning. "Show me."

I slip out of bed and rush over to the closet, extracting the gold gown from its hiding spot. I hold it up in front of me, the silken fabric flowing to the floor. "What do you think?"

When I pull my eyes to Thorne's, the color has drained from his face, his smile twisting into a grimace.

His voice goes cold. "Where the hell did that come from?"

"I—Kith got it for me after our shopping excursion. I loved it so much that he..."

"Put it away."

"Thorne!" I say with a shocked laugh. "You don't like it? I thought it was beautiful."

"Please...put it away, now." I can see the tension in his shoulders, a pain tearing through him whose cause I can't possibly guess. "I can't look at it. I won't."

Quiet irritation begins to roil inside me. He's being irrational. Ridiculous. "It's a beautiful dress. What's wrong with you?"

"Nothing. And everything. Just—tell me you won't wear it."

"You hate the color that much?"

"I hate everything about it."

He's never behaved like this—so negative and hurtful about something I love. It's baffling.

~*Maybe he has an irrational fear of silk,* Maude speculates, and I can't tell if she's sincerely trying to help, or just being a smartass.

"Fine," I tell him, shoving it back into the closet and slamming the door with a force that seems to shake the room. "It's gone. Happy now?"

"Happier, yes."

I want to tell him he's being absurd and that a fucking dress shouldn't drive a wedge between us. Is he pissed off because another man bought it for me? Is this how Thorne manifests jealousy?

"I didn't ask Kith to buy it, you know," I say, my voice breaking. "It wasn't like that."

"I know."

"Then what?" A tear streaks its way down my cheek, and I wipe it away, angry at myself for letting it fall.

"Shara," he says. "Beautiful Shara. Come here."

No way, I think, crossing my arms tight across my chest like a stubborn child. "Not until you tell me what the hell your problem is with that dress. Is this about Kith and me spending time together? Because—"

"Kith?" he replies. "No, it has nothing to do with that. It was kind of him to buy it."

"Then what?"

"I wish I could explain it," he sighs, rubbing his eyes as if he's exhausted. "Look—I know you think I'm just being a dick."

"That's because you are."

"Then I'm being a dick." A smile slips over his lips at long last. "But you'll forgive me, because you're kind and patient and beautiful...and perfect."

"You're getting there," I mutter. "Slowly. Say more things about how great I am. Right now."

"You're also sexy as hell when you're angry."

I take a step toward him. "Better. But I'm still mad. You know this is the first time in my life I've ever owned something that beautiful, right? The first time I've had a dress that was just...mine?"

"I know. I'm sorry. It's a lovely dress. It just...reminds me of something I don't want to think about."

My heart sinks.

"Does your hatred of it have something to do with the fact that you've seen me wearing it...in the future?"

He looks like he's about to deny it, but he relents. "I saw it on you, yes. In the vision of a Pairing ceremony—a wedding—where you stood alone."

"Well, *that* makes no sense. Like I told you—I wouldn't marry myself, Thorne. Besides, I've seen that same future, and in it, I was happy. I was euphoric, even. If you weren't there, I would have been miserable. Inconsolable. There's no way I'm marrying anyone else."

"Or...maybe you *had* fallen in love with someone else."

At that, I can't help myself. A laugh launches itself out of my chest and into the room with us. "Sorry—I don't think you realize how ridiculous you sound right now."

"No—I get it, trust me. Saying the words out loud makes me realize they're ridiculous. Just...do me a favor and leave the gold dress in the closet for a little. Someday soon, I'll explain everything, and hopefully then, you'll forgive my dickishness."

"I believe the proper term is dickitude."

"My mistake."

"I suppose," I say, kissing him, "I'm just a little surprised that you hate golden dresses so much."

He smirks. "Well, we still have a lot to learn about each other. I'm sure there are things *you* hate, too. Tell me one."

~*Me*, Maude says.

I don't hate you. Except when you butt into a conversation I'm having with Thorne.

~Argument.

Respectful disagreement.

I ponder Thorne's request for a moment, then say, "Mushrooms. I absolutely fucking despise mushrooms."

"Fine. I promise never to wear a suit made of mushrooms if you promise we don't have to speak of the gold gown again tonight."

"Good. Because that mushroom suit would be weird as hell."

CHAPTER
THIRTY-EIGHT

Our disagreement seems to fuel our love for one another, and for the next two days, things feel back to normal between Thorne and me.

The incident with the gown was strange, even unfortunate. But ultimately, it means nothing.

Each morning, we eat breakfast together. Thorne heads to the arena, while I head out with Kith into the Capitol to wander and take in the new builds, offer food and drink to the workers, or simply bask in the glow of Kravan's budding renaissance.

Our lives have quickly settled into the simple, quiet existence I've always dreamed of. A daily routine for each of us, followed by nights spent wrapped in one another's arms.

I know in my heart that free people take this sort of life for granted. They may even find it painfully dull. But for us, it means never again being locked in a cell or controlled by forces outside of ourselves.

It means we alone control our own destinies.

We are free—even underground. Even in a windowless suite.

We. Are. Free.

But as the days pass, a worry begins to fester inside me like a disease—one that I've been afraid to name, for fear that expressing it will provoke it into metastasizing.

One evening, the invisible wall between us returns with a vengeance, and our tether—the tie that binds us—falls under threat. I can no longer feel Thorne's joy. I no longer sense the sharp bite of pain when he hurts himself, or the profound hope he had not too many days ago.

All I feel when I seek him out is a sort of detachment, as if he's given up on us and pulled himself away.

I ask him repeatedly to tell me what's troubling him, but he gives me nothing. In his eyes, I see sadness, fear—pain. I reach out with my mind and heart, trying to absorb it into myself, to feel it alongside him. But somehow, our tether is slowly fraying and breaking down—and I can no longer share in his sorrow.

He makes love to me each night as if our world is about to end, instead of about to begin. In the mornings, he heads off to train Tethered to kill, and I venture into the city with Kith to try and keep myself from going mad.

It's three days before the public hanging that an incident nearly breaks us both.

Near the Citadel on Magister's Row is a large, warmly decorated pub called The Tabby Cat. Once or twice, Kith and

I have ventured in to order take-away coffee for the Tethered working on rebuilding the local businesses.

But today, after wandering for several hours to check in on a few new builds, we head to the pub for a treat of our own.

"The best beer you've ever tasted," he tells me. "I promise."

"I've only had a few in my life," I confess as I push the door open and step inside. "So I'm no judge."

I seat myself at a high table by the window as Kith heads to the bar to get us two pints. At first, my eyes are fixed on the buildings outside, my mind reeling at how quickly the landscape of Magister's Row has changed. It's a beautiful street filled with hope, and my heart swells with pride for the Tethered who built it.

It's only when I turn to look toward the bar that my heart stops.

Across the pub, sitting in a dark corner...are Thorne and Rivenna.

Their faces are close, Rivenna's hand stroking Thorne's on the table. She's speaking low, and Thorne's eyes are locked onto hers with a depth of emotion I haven't seen in him in days.

Maude...can you tell me what they're saying?

She hesitates for a moment, then amplifies their conversation for me. It's Thorne's voice that comes to me first, clear as day.

"We're just putting off the inevitable, Riv. It's going to break her heart if we tell her."

They both fall silent, and for a terrifying second, I'm convinced they've seen me.

"We know our fate," Rivenna finally says. "It's always led us here. I never wanted to hurt Shara. But..."

"But..." he repeats. "But you're right. Just—let me do it when the time is right, okay?"

"We don't *have* much time. It's only a matter of days before—"

"I know."

Rivenna nods solemnly. "It's going to destroy her either way, you realize."

Thorne takes hold of her hand again, clenching it tight. "I—"

The next word never comes.

Instead, I'm flung from my seat by a blast so powerful that the window next to me explodes into a thousand fragments, the force of it hurling me across the space to crash into a table twenty feet from where I was just sitting.

"Kith..." I breathe, but the air has been stolen from my lungs.

Debris falls from the ceiling, and the floor is littered with shards of wood, glass, and plaster.

A pair of hands reaches for me, then a low voice says, "Heal yourself. You're badly wounded."

I look down to see a deep cut in my leg and another in my side. Blood stains my clothing. I glance around—but don't see anyone else who's injured.

Small mercy.

Outside, I hear screams. Drones flying overhead. More explosions.

Stunned, I pass a hand over my wounds and say, "What is happening..."

"An attack."

It's Kith's voice. His hands are on my shoulders, calming me. I watch figures fleeing the scene outside as smoke and ash fill the sky. Cries of anguish assault the smoke-filled air, but Kith's touch keeps me from joining in the gruesome chorus.

A memory crowds my mind, and I turn to where Thorne and Rivenna were sitting a moment ago. They're still there, eyes locked at first on the shattered window. Debris is scattered around their table, their eyes wide with the same shock I was feeling when I first spotted them.

Then, Thorne's gaze moves to me.

Horror slams its way into his features and he rises to his feet, leaping over to where I'm still sitting on the floor.

"Shara..." he gasps.

I hold up a hand, shaking my head. "No," I say. "No. Go back to Rivenna. I don't want to talk to you."

When I lift my eyes to Kith's, I can tell he's fully aware of what I saw. His stare is locked on the same far table, where Rivenna looks horrified. His hand is still on me and I'm grateful for the anchor he's providing during a tumultuous storm.

I turn to him, push myself to my feet, and say, "Do you think the attack has ended? I can't stay here."

He nods silently, slipping an arm around me, and together we head out of the pub.

An eerie feeling of calm falls over my mind. All I can think is that Thorne has betrayed me. That Rivenna is a devious, cruel woman. For a moment, I forget that Magister's Row is in shambles.

We've walked less than a half block toward the Citadel when I hear Thorne's voice behind me.

"Shara!"

I wipe away a tear and stop in my tracks, but refuse to turn around.

He grabs at my arm, but Kith shoves him away—hard. It's then that I turn to look, only to see deep-set rage on Thorne's features.

"This has nothing to do with you, Blade," he snarls. Behind him, plumes of smoke rise into the air as if an apocalypse has been unleashed on the Capitol.

"It has everything to do with me. I'm in the business of protecting Shara. That's literally my job."

"You don't need to protect her from me."

"Don't I?" Kith gestures back to the pub. "Do you want to tell me what I just saw, then? What *we* just saw? Do you have some kind of bullshit excuse to throw my way about how you were holding Rivenna's hand and looking like two people very much in love?"

"Kith," I say, trying and failing to step between them. "Don't."

"He's not good enough for you, Shara," he snarls. "He never has been. He's a liar. He's betraying you—tearing at the tether between you. Don't tell me he isn't. I know you've felt it. I know you doubt him."

A pain assaults my chest so brutally that it's all I can do not to double over. "Thorne is an adult," I say. "So am I. If I'm not what he wants, then I'm not going to force him to be with me. I'm not going to chain him to myself."

"A real man wouldn't need to be chained," Kith growls. "He would give himself to you more than willingly."

"You think I feel shackled?" Thorne asks, reaching again for me. But this time, I pull away, my eyes narrowing. His gaze locks on Kith's hand, which is gripping my waist tightly.

"Apparently not," I tell him. "It seems our tether is made of the weakest thread."

"Shara..." he says, shaking his head. His eyes veer to Kith when he says, "What you heard back there—what you saw. Fuck, it's not—"

"It's not what I think?" I laugh. "It doesn't matter, Thorne." I gesture to the devastated street behind him. "Magister's Row is in ruins. That's what matters. We're fighting a war. So go do your job, and fight. This...thing between you and me does not matter. Now, if you don't mind, I'm going to see if anyone needs the services of a Healer."

"We'll help these people. But right now, let's talk. You and me. I'll tell you everything I can."

I chew on my bottom lip, fighting back tears. "I don't want to talk. I made my way through miles of dark tunnels—I risked my life to find you. Instead, I found *her*. I suppose I shouldn't be surprised a Reaper stole my life away."

There's sudden movement behind Thorne, and I look over to see Rivenna staring at me. Her black eyes are expressionless, neither triumphant nor sad. Somehow, that makes it worse.

"You win," I tell her. "He's all yours."

"You would really give him up that easily?" she asks.

I shake my head. "I will always love him, until the day I die. But I'm tired of being kept in the dark. I'm tired of guessing—of being shut out. At least if I walk away, I'll be in control of one small thing."

"Don't walk away," Thorne pleads. "Go—do whatever

you need. I'll help here. I'll find the wounded and make sure they're tended to. But meet me in the suite later. We'll talk."

I want to say no. I need to.

But instead, I nod once. "Fine. We'll talk."

Rivenna takes Thorne by the arm, whispers something, and they turn and walk back toward the devastation.

Tears streak my filthy cheeks, and I wipe them away, searching for wounded people.

I see a few stumbling here and there, and silently make my way over to heal them.

"You're shaking," Kith says, taking my hands in his when I'm finished.

His touch calms me instantly, as always, slowing my heart and quelling the anxiety that's tearing at my insides.

"Who did it, Kith?" I ask. "The bombing...who would do such a thing?"

"The king has done worse to the city for years," he says bitterly.

"The king is dead."

"There's a new king. You've said yourself that Tallin thrives on the suffering of other people."

I nod, but my brows meet as I try to understand. "He's calculated, though. I can't imagine him bombing the Capitol a few days after being crowned. He's terrible, but he doesn't want to be hated—not deep down. It makes no sense."

"It does if he's trying to show his might. Rulers do that—they often try to prove their strength early in their reign so that no one challenges them in the future."

What Kith is saying makes logical sense.

But I know Tallin.

This doesn't feel like his style.

Then again, who else could it have been? The Magister's people have been working day and night to rebuild the Capitol. I've seen their progress each day when I'm out with Kith. The Lady has no access to drones—at least, not as far as I know.

Kith lays a hand on my shoulder. "Your nerves are shot," he says softly. "Let me get you back."

"I don't want to go back to the suite. Is there somewhere else we could go? I'd just pace the suite until Thorne returns—or I'd throw up. Or both."

Kith nods. "I know just the place. Come on."

He guides me along a few streets until we're free of the destruction wrought by the bombing. When we come to a tall hedge and an iron fence, he unlatches a gate and pushes it open, escorting me into what looks like a private garden.

At any other moment in my life, I would find it charming—beautiful. But right now, it feels like somewhere I've come to mourn.

We take a seat on a stone bench under a large elm tree.

"I'm so sorry," he says softly. "What you saw—I know it was painful."

"I just..." I swallow. "I don't understand it. I know he loves me, Kith."

His jaw tightens when he nods. "Love is complicated. And you don't deserve to be treated like an outsider in your own relationship."

New tears form in my eyes and I nod. "I wouldn't have believed it if I hadn't seen and heard it myself. I told myself you were exaggerating when you spoke of their bond—trying to convince me...I thought maybe you just wanted me to..."

"That I wanted you," he repeats. "The truth is, I do. But not like this. Not hurt. I want you to know I'll be here for you whenever you need me, Shara. Always. But I'm not here to take advantage of you."

I lay my head on his shoulder, giving in. I'm spent emotionally. Physically. Humanity let me down today in every conceivable way. The only person who *hasn't* disappointed me is sitting next to me.

"Thorne wants to talk. I don't know what he can say to make this better."

"He should tell you the truth, regardless. He owes it to you."

"I know." I pull my head up and bite my lip, fighting against my tears. "But the truth is what I'm afraid of."

CHAPTER THIRTY-NINE

I've been lying in our suite for hours now. The tears are dry, and my skin is parched with dehydration. My heart has already begun its recovery, mending itself with each breath, each thought.

Today on the street, when I looked into Thorne's eyes, I felt his emotions again for the first time in days. What he was feeling wasn't love for someone else. It wasn't deceit. All I felt from him was a sense of helplessness.

And it took me hours of digging through my mind and heart to realize it. It took being apart from Kith—away from the influence of his touch.

Ellion couldn't control my mind...but sometimes, I fear that Kith can.

When he touches me, my mood alters instantly. Usually, he calms and comforts me, stealing away my worries—and I welcome the sensation.

But today, as his arm wrapped itself around my waist, I felt a bitterness penetrating my cells. A growing, festering mistrust unlike anything I've ever felt toward Thorne. I forgot for a little that above all, he loves me. That we're bound to one another. It was like a spike-covered shield had been erected around my heart, rejecting faith in everyone but Kith.

I tell myself I'm imagining things when the door opens and Thorne walks in, his chin low.

"Hey," he says.

"Hey," I reply, sitting up. "I—"

He holds up a hand, stopping me. "Don't you dare say anything. I've been an ass. You feel betrayed—lied to. And the truth is, I *did* lie to you, Beautiful. But not for the reasons you think. I would never, ever—" He lets out a breath. "I wish you would have faith in my feelings for you. I wish I could show you—"

This time, I'm the one who holds up a hand. The truth is, even as I watched him with Rivenna—even as doubt nagged at me—I *knew* he loved me. I had faith in our bond, despite its tenuous nature.

That faith only deserted me when Kith laid his hand on me.

"I doubted you long ago," I tell him. "Back at the Verdans' home. And I was wrong then. I know how you feel about me —but that's why I'm so confused. So sick with worry. If you love me as much as I think you do, then why..." My fingers toy with the hem of the bedding, and I bite my lip just long enough to construct the question in my mind. "Can't you just tell me what's going on? It's one thing for you to be secretive. But I heard what you and Rivenna said to one another. You said my heart would break, Thorne. There's only one thing in this world that could break my heart...and that's losing you."

His eyes move to the floor, the muscles in his jaw pulsing as if unspeakable words want to burst out of him.

"I'm so sorry." I can hear the emotion in his voice. "Fuck, Shara."

He sits down and reaches out to cup my cheek in his palm. The heat of him works its way through me like a panacea.

"I can't explain everything," he whispers. "But soon, you'll come to understand. For now, though—you need to know—to *feel*—how much I love you. That will never change, whatever happens. But *you* need to fight. You have to do whatever it takes to help make our dream come true."

"We both will," I reply, puzzled. "Unless you tell me you don't want that life anymore."

"I'll never, ever want anything else." There's so much sadness in his eyes. "If you knew how much joy it would bring me to live with you in a home that was just ours—a place where we could one day raise a family, if you wanted to." He lets out a bitter chuckle and says, "We've never even spoken about children."

"We're too young for that, Thorne," I say, wiping away a bittersweet tear. "We have lots of time."

"Time," he repeats. "*Rivenna* has time. A Reaper has all the time they want. We may not be so fortunate."

I tighten, and Thorne's eyes meet mine. "She cares about you, you know. A lot."

"I care about her, too—even though I want to hate her sometimes for being so...I don't know. Shady, I suppose. I may not understand your relationship, but that doesn't mean I despise her."

"Good. I don't want you hating her. She hasn't done anything wrong."

"Except fall for you." I offer up a forced smile. "I mean, who wouldn't?"

Thorne laughs. "You underestimate her. And you *over*estimate my allure. Rivenna isn't in love with me. I've never met a person who enjoys solitude more than she does. But even if she loved me more than life itself, I would never look at her with the love I have for you."

I want to argue—to challenge him. I still feel a sharp sting when I think back to her hand on his, stroking his skin so gently. He didn't pull back or resist. If anything, he looked enthralled by her. There was an intimacy to that gesture that was enough to slice deep into my heart and tear a part of me away, leaving my emotions raw.

"Come here," Thorne says, and against my better judgment, I force myself to take a step closer. He envelops me in his arms, kisses my hair, and says, "You're going to be okay, Shara. You're a fighter, whether you know it or not."

"I'm beginning to realize that," I tell him. "The problem is, I hate fighting. Maybe I'm too weak for it."

"No. You're not." He draws back, stepping away from me, his eyes locked on my own. "You're going to need your strength for what's coming, and it's in you—it always has been. Please don't give up—no matter what happens. Promise me you'll fight."

"I would never give up. I have too much to live for."

He smiles, but there's no joy behind his eyes, and I wonder with a tacit sob if he'll ever seem happy again.

"I need to leave early tomorrow morning," he says. "It's our last day of training."

"And after tomorrow, what then? Will things ever go back to something like normal?"

Thorne's jaw twitches, and he shakes his head. "I don't know. I only know that I love you more with each day that passes. That I wish I could explain to you that the world is about to go through a momentous change—and that I would give anything never to have to hurt you."

"Then don't. Just...tell me the truth."

"The truth," he repeats. "The truth is, I don't deserve you."

His words are a dagger. "Don't say that. It sounds like an excuse for deceit—for cruelty. Like you're setting me up for something brutal."

With a shake of his head, he says, "Fine, then. I deserve you. For now."

CHAPTER
FORTY

I SPEND the next morning alternating between pacing the room and resting, emotion eating away at me.

The last few days have been so intense, so painful that I just want the simplicity to return to our lives—for all our worries to vanish.

It's Maude who finally snaps me out of my despair.

~Perhaps you should distract yourself today. Given that it's unlikely you'll be allowed to venture into the city after yesterday's attack, you might want to amuse yourself with a visit to the Citadel's newest prisoner.

"What prisoner?"

~One that you'll find interesting.

"Who, Maude?" I huff impatiently. "Stop teasing."

I swear she knows exactly what she's doing when she pauses, then says, *~Prince Tallin.*

"What?"

The word darts from my mouth, a projectile exploding against the opposite wall of the room.

~Go ask your father, if you like. Tallin is being held in a cell, here in the Citadel.

It's eleven a.m. by now. Thorne isn't due back at the suite for hours yet, so without thinking twice, I throw on a change of clothes and storm to my father's office to pound on the door.

"Ah, Shara," he says when he opens it. "I've been expecting you."

"Is it true?"

"I assume you're asking about the former prince's arrival."

"Yes."

"Then yes, it's true."

"How? How did you manage to get that man all the way here and imprison him? Even Ellion couldn't control him."

My father takes a deep breath, then invites me to sit down in one of his leather chairs.

I oblige reluctantly. I'm not sure what I'd rather do. Bounce off the walls? Scream? Run to the arena and tell Thorne?

When my father has seated himself, he says, "It may surprise you to learn Ellion helped us. He offered his half-brother in exchange for a peaceful transition—and you might be shocked to discover how easy it was."

My mouth hangs open, and I am numb.

Tallin's reign died a swift death. But the thought of Ellion on the throne is disgusting. Horrifying. For all I know, he's the one who sent those drones to attack the city yesterday—which, when I think about it, would not surprise me in the least.

"Ellion is despicable," I say, throwing myself into one of the leather chairs.

"Yes, I know. An atrocious human being. Even if I wasn't aware of how awful he is, the fact that he facilitated his half-brother's capture would be proof enough. He offered to mind-control every Royal Guard in the palace. But, as it turned out, it was wholly unnecessary. Tallin came willingly, believe it or not."

"Willingly," I breathe. "Why?"

"Your guess is as good as mine, my dear. But I'm glad you came to see me, because as it turns out, the former prince—then temporary king—would very much like to speak to you. He's being kept in a cell on the third sub-level. You are permitted to see him, if you wish."

"Good," I say, pushing myself to my feet. "And whether he helped our side or not, you need to understand how dangerous Ellion is, Father. You don't know him like I do."

"Then perhaps you should figure out a way to end him."

The way the Shadow says the words is ominous and strange—like he's *hoping* I'll slay the new king. *Craving* it.

It almost feels diabolical.

I would love little more than to see Ellion dead. He's unpredictable, sadistic. The sort of person who would take control of the world just to watch it destroy itself.

"You have an entire army set to do battle," I say. "I don't think I'm the one who's meant to end Ellion, or anyone else."

"The army will play its part. But that part does not involve slaying our mind-bending ally. Now, go see the prince. I'm sure he has a good deal to say to you."

CHAPTER FORTY-ONE

I SPRINT along what feels like a thousand corridors until I reach a door to the stairwell that will lead me to the high-security prison wing.

A facial scanner awaits me, and I test my father's words by standing before it as it assesses my features, then the lock clicks open. Without hesitating for a second, I leap through and toward the stairs. But just as I reach the first step, an arm grabs me and twists me back toward the door.

"Where are you going?" Kith growls with a feral aggression that's almost frightening.

"To see Tallin. I want to speak to him."

His eyes soften alongside a chuckle of disbelief. "You can't possibly mean that." I can feel his power working through his touch—a calming, soothing sensation streaming through my veins. "Tallin is a maniac."

I jerk my arm away, refusing to fall for his charm. "I *do* mean it, actually. Please—don't try to stop me."

Kith looks at a loss for words as he drags a hand through his dark hair, pushing it back off his face. "I wish you wouldn't. I really do, for your sake. There's a lot you don't know, Shara. Your father has plans—and he needs you to stay alive."

"The prince wants to see me. He won't kill me."

"No, you're wrong." A derisive huff echoes against the stairwell's walls. "I barely even know the man, and I know he would take your life in a second if he could. That guy is deranged."

"I don't care. If I can get any information from him about what Tallin knows—what the Royal Guard are planning—it will be worth it. Thorne is leading the army. He could be killed. I need to know what he's up against."

"Don't worry about Thorne. He won't be fighting."

There's a quiet cunning lurking behind Kith's tone with those four last words—something I've never heard from him before—and it unsettles me and gives me hope, all at once.

"What do you mean, won't be fighting? He's one of the strongest Tethered around."

He takes a step back, seeming to contemplate his next words more carefully. "Your father has a plan," he says again. "The Shadow is wise. He knows what needs to be done. Now, please—go back to your quarters. For Thorne, if not for yourself."

With a long, exasperated sigh, I say, "I appreciate you looking out for me. And if you're right—if Thorne isn't going to fight—then you have my thanks, Kith. But I still wish to speak to the prince. So please, let me go."

He looks like he's going to grab me again, but in the end, he raises both hands in surrender, smiles, and says, "Good luck then, Shara. Be safe. But just remember—there are people in the world who love you—and you're taking a huge risk, doing this."

"I know I'm taking a risk," I say, ignoring what he said about people loving me. I can only assume he's talking about Thorne, and possibly my father. But my reasons for wanting to speak to Tallin involve helping them—and all of Kravan.

When I reach the bottom of the stairs, I encounter two guards, each dressed in charcoal gray uniforms.

"My father—the Shadow—told me you would allow me to see the prince," I announce, chin high, forcing the same authority into my voice I occasionally took on as a fake Noble, back in the days when I was posing as the prince's fiancée.

The guards move out of the way wordlessly, and for once in my life, I feel genuinely powerful. I proceed toward a door that swings open on my approach, and find myself standing in a large, mostly empty chamber.

Tallin is seated on a cot at the far end, but rises to his feet as the door seals behind me.

I nearly spin around to leave when I see that there's no cilice around his upper arm, but he holds up a hand and says, "It's all right, Shara. There's nothing to fear from me. My fire has been extinguished."

I half expect him to make his way over to me, but when I see a shackle around his left ankle, I understand. He's chained to the wall.

As he should be.

"Come over here," he says. "Let's have a talk. I've missed you."

I let out a tense laugh, but move closer, inspecting him to make sure he was telling the truth about his fire.

His eyes, which used to whirl with color, have gone dark and still. There's no sign of his power. No sign of danger of any kind.

"How did it happen?" I move close enough to see him clearly—but not enough for him to reach out and touch me.

"Friend of yours," he says. "Kith, I believe he's called." He hisses the name through his teeth, like it disgusts him.

A surprising explosion of pride surges through my chest. *Well done, Blade.*

"I take it you tried to fight him off?" I ask.

Tallin laughs. "Fight him—while Ellion was mind-controlling every one of my guards? No. I did not. I *asked* him to do it, the moment I realized what he was."

I narrow my eyes, untrusting. "Why would you do something like that?"

A slow shrug drags his shoulders skyward. "What can I tell you? I like to keep people guessing."

He looks...amused. No. More than that, he looks giddy. Content. Almost happy, even.

I have never seen Tallin happy. I didn't believe he was capable of it.

"I'm free," he says softly when he sees me studying him. "That's it. I'm free of pain. Free of the constant, churning memories of others' suffering. Free of trauma. For the first time in my life, I'm able to forget—and what I can't forget, I compartmentalize. I have never known, since childhood, what it was not to feel like a million knives were jabbing me in the brain all at once. The only relief I ever had was Valira—and I realize, now that I'm free of pain, just how much I inflicted on her."

"I'm glad," I say. "Truly. For your sake. Valira would be happy, too."

He shakes his head, his joy depleted instantly. "I used her so cruelly. I did love her, you know. Not as a bound mate does, but I loved her—and it was more than just the service she provided me. I cared deeply for her. I was a selfish prick."

"Yes. You were." I pause for a few seconds, then summon the courage I need to speak again. "I have some questions for you."

Tallin seats himself on his cot and pats the mattress next to him. I throw him a dubious look and say, "No, thanks. I'm good here."

"Go ahead, then."

"Ellion is on the throne now—yes?"

"In a manner of speaking. The thing is, most of Kravan doesn't yet know Ellion was my father's son. As lacking in tact as that little shithead is, he is calculating his next move carefully. It will take time for the official announcement."

"I've seen graffiti on the Capitol's walls. It says, *The heir will bring ruin on us all.* Do you suppose there's a chance it's about Ellion? Maybe someone knows more than they're letting on."

Tallin ponders that, then shakes his head. "It's possible, I suppose," he says. "But few people could have seen my abdication coming. I didn't know until yesterday that I would even consider it—not until I knew a Blade was heading to the Palatine Estates."

"You knew Kith was going to be there?"

"I had been warned, yes. I have my spies, just as your side has theirs. I've known about the Blade for some time. Handsome fellow, isn't he? A little...mysterious?"

I don't dignify that with a response. "If you have spies," I half-whisper, "then do you know what the Magister's plan of attack is?"

Tallin grins, his eyes sparkling in the dim light. "You're worried about your mate," he says. "How sweet. I hear he's been training soldiers to fight."

"Yes, he has."

"I wish him luck with that. But I have my doubts as to whether that particular battle will ever occur. Like I told you, I have spies of my own."

So, it seems Tallin and Kith agree on one point. Thorne won't need to fight.

"Are you saying Ellion wouldn't fight back?" I ask.

"Oh, he'd fight. He's a twat. He'll do everything he can to stay on the throne—and if you send fighters, he will break them. The only way to get to Ellion is to send a beautiful woman his way."

"Excuse me?" I nearly choke on the words.

Tallin's lips twitch into a cunning grin. "The guy is a horny little shit. He's had sex once—maybe twice—in his life. He's itching for it. For reasons I don't care to divulge at the moment, he's looking for his queen. Whoever she is, I pity her. Point is, any half-pretty human with breasts can manipulate that little scrotum with a bat of her eyelashes. The trouble is, he can read minds—which means he'd see right through the act."

He can't read my mind.

I don't believe a thing Tallin is saying, but I humor him. "If Thorne's fighters aren't intending to do battle, then what's the purpose of all this?"

Tallin lets out a deep, mournful sigh. "Your guess is as

good as mine. I only know what I've heard—and what I've heard is that the Magister is in no state to send troops to the Isles. Which means you're all going to need to get on your knees and beg your new dickhead of a king to treat you kindly—or get rid of him."

I don't know what he means by that, but I'm not particularly keen on where this conversation is going. For all I know, Tallin and Ellion are working together—hoping to lure me back to the palace to end me once and for all.

"Well, then," I say, turning to leave. "I think we're done here."

"Shara...wait."

I turn back and focus on his eyes, trying to tell whether he's about to say something kind or awful.

"What is it?" I snap.

Tallin rises to his feet. "I need to speak—so bear with me for a moment of earnestness. It's not exactly my forte, so I'll just have to do my best."

Crossing my arms, I say, "Fine."

Tallin's voice is low and steady. "I never pretended to be a good man. But over the years, my father cultivated me into something so much worse than I should have been. He twisted a blade that he could so easily have extracted instead. He crafted a cruel beast instead of a prince." His eyes, which I had only ever seen as vicious, dampen with tears when he adds, "I became a sadist's favorite toy. And while that will never excuse my behavior, I hope one day, you can find it within yourself to forgive me for how I treated you—and how I treated Valira."

I want to snarl my reply at him, but I don't have it in me. Not when Tallin, of all people, looks genuinely aggrieved. So instead, my voice softens. "Why would you care what I think of you?"

"Because," he murmurs, "I have always seen goodness in you. On the first night we met, I knew instantly that you were a person of honor. I suppose I resented you for that—but the truth is, I also admired you. So often, you could have tried to hurt me—*really* hurt me. Yet you never went for the jugular. You abided my cruelty to protect Thorne, Valira, and everyone else. You are a good person, and your opinion matters to me."

"I can't forgive you—not yet. But I'll consider it in future."

"Thank you. And Shara..."

I raise my eyebrows.

"Don't trust anyone here. Not even those closest to you."

"Why do you say that? Is it something your spies told you?"

With a shake of his head, he says, "Call it newfound intuition. But if you want more—if you want information that will help you get through the next few tumultuous days—there's someone in the Capitol you should seek out."

"Who?"

"The Lady of the Starless. Find her. Ask her to tell you the truth. She will not lie to you as everyone else has. Go—now."

CHAPTER
FORTY-TWO

My hands are shaking.

There was a strange, desperate quality in Tallin's voice when he instructed me to go find the Lady.

Something deep, meaningful. Sincere, even. Completely out of character for the prince—and for that reason alone, I'm convinced I need to take him at his word.

Maude, am I insane for thinking I should follow his advice?

~Insane? No. Foolish? Probably.

How would I even go about finding the Lady? Wouldn't she kill me, besides?

~I'm not sure, but again...probably.

I return to the suite and pace, chewing on my nails, grateful that today, of all days, I don't need to spend time with Kith. If anyone is likely to talk me out of venturing out to see an enemy who apparently wants me dead, it's him.

I'm not sure just how long I've been striding back and forth across the floor when a knock sounds at the door.

I dart over to open it, hoping it's Thorne. Maybe he's finished early—after all, according to the prince, all his training sessions are a pointless waste of time. Maybe he, too, has realized it.

When I open the door and see Joy's face, I freeze.

"Hi," I say. "I..."

I'm not sure what I'm about to say. *I'm busy? I'm having an existential crisis? I'm about to do something incredibly stupid, so if you don't mind...*

"My mother wishes to meet you," she says, interrupting me before I've sorted myself out.

"What?" The word leaves my mouth before I can consider my rudeness. "Why does your mother even know who I am?"

"I told you once that she used to be a Fortune Teller. She's a Seer, and a talented one. She has something to tell you."

I struggle to keep my tone polite when I reply, "Joy...I can't. There's someone else I need to find. I'm just trying to figure out how. I'm sorry, but—"

She steps inside the room, closes the door, and moves closer to me. "Do you trust me?" she whispers.

"I'm not sure I do, to be honest." I trusted Rivenna once, and she and Joy *are* friends. But Rivenna isn't exactly my favorite person at the moment.

"Let me rephrase that. Do you think I want you dead?"

"No, of course not."

"Then trust me on this—you want to meet my mother. I can get you safely to her, Shara. She'll answer some of the questions that are troubling you right now. But you're going to have to borrow my power to leave here. You need to morph into someone else. There's no way your father will let you out of the Citadel after yesterday's bombing."

"Fine," I sigh. "I'm making all sorts of terrible choices. What's another one?"

Joy digs into her pocket and extracts a small folded blade, pulling it open. She jabs herself in the fingertip until a spot of blood appears. "Go ahead," she says. "Take on my power—and disguise yourself as one of the guards you saw earlier by Tallin's cell."

"How did you know I saw..." I shake my head. "You know what? Never mind. I've given up trying to understand how everyone in the Capitol is all-seeing."

When I do as Joy instructed, feeling the throb of her power swelling inside me, I seal my eyes and envision one of the two men who were guarding Tallin's prison.

Almost instantly, my body jerks and pulls this way and that, bones lengthening, muscles expanding, and when I open my eyes again, I'm...a man, complete with charcoal gray uniform.

"What the fuck," I murmur in a stranger's deep voice, half amused and half horrified. "This is wild. I'm tempted to take a peek inside my pants. But I won't."

"Probably for the best," Joy laughs. She takes in a breath, and a moment later, she's standing before me in the guise of the second guard.

"Come on—we need to go."

Familiarizing myself as quickly as possible with someone else's body, I scramble after her until we reach a door concealed at the end of a dark hallway. She keys in a code then pulls it open, summoning me to follow. A pair of Dragonflyers outside the Citadel barely seem to take note of our existence.

We walk for an hour or so through broken, twisting

streets, mostly in taut silence. In the distance, smoke billows into the air from the explosions that shook the Capitol so recently—and I work to push the wretched memory from my consciousness.

Joy offers little explanation as to where we're going, or why, but she finally tells me, "If you see Starless when we arrive, don't panic. They're not what you think."

I stop in my tracks. By now, Joy's power has waned. I'm back to looking like myself, and so has she—but the transition happened so easily this time that I wasn't even aware of it. "Starless have tried to kill me!" I say in my own voice. "Why wouldn't I panic?"

"*Who*, exactly, tried to kill you?"

"A Poisoner in the tunnels, for one. I mean, technically, he tried to kill Rivenna. But still..."

"Did you see his mark?"

"The brand? Yes. I mean, I think so."

"Was there an X through it?"

I strain my mind, trying to think back to the encounter in the tunnel. Did the Poisoner have a brand? I'm almost certain he did. The X, I'm not so sure about.

"I don't recall," I say.

"Has any other Starless tried to hurt you—*really* tried?"

"No. But one had a knife to Thorne's throat the day he arrived in the Capitol."

"Again—are you certain it was a Starless?"

"I...no. I suppose I can't be certain."

"Then trust me just a little longer, Shara. Okay?"

I shake my head. "I'll trust you when you tell me why you're taking me to your mother. What is this, really?"

She glances around like she's debating whether or not to

grab me and drag me with her, then whispers, "My mother... is the Lady."

"The—"

"Yes. *That* Lady. The leader of the Starless. The much hated, much maligned evildoer. Only, she's not evil, and neither are they. It's just that certain people want you thinking they are."

I'm about to argue when I recall the eyes of the man in the Underbelly—the Porter who told me the Rebellion is a lie, the man I healed in the marketplace who did the same, and the Velor in the city—the one Kith killed. None of them *actually* tried to hurt me.

The Poisoner was truly cruel, but I'm not even sure he was in his right mind when he attacked us.

"Why does your mother want to see me, of all people?"

"She knows things about the future—she wants to prepare you for a fate you aren't going to like. She needs to warn you."

"Why can't *you* warn me? Just tell me what she's seen. It's simple."

"Because, as I've said before—it's a terrible idea to share a Seer's vision. It can fuck with the world in ways I can't begin to express. My mother is wise. She's smart. She'll only tell you what you need to hear. No more, no less. Besides, I'm a Morph—I'm not equipped to advise you."

I'm still skeptical, but I continue to trudge along with Joy.

Maude hasn't yelled at me or told me I'm a fool lately, and I'm taking that as a sign that I'm doing the right thing.

When we finally reach a set of engraved steel doors set in the façade of what looks like a rusted warehouse, Joy knocks in a beat pattern that seems to be some sort of code, and the doors open to reveal two masked women standing just inside.

On seeing us, one removes her mask and embraces Joy. On her forearm, I note the Magister's mark, crossed out with a violent X like the ones on other Starless I've seen.

Joy brings me through to another room—one that looks like my father's office. Books line shelves from floor to ceiling on two walls. A large wooden desk sits to one side, with a simple folding chair.

As we enter from one end of the room, a door at the other end opens, and a woman with graying hair cropped into a tidy bob walks in. She's a few inches shorter than me, with a pair of glasses that seem to reflect the light in a slightly violet tint, which prevents me from seeing her eyes clearly.

Joy strides over and embraces her, kissing her cheek, and the woman beams.

"Shara," Joy says, turning back to me, "This is Lady Allegra."

The Lady moves toward me, seeming to glide along the floor. She's dressed simply, in linen pants and a knitted sweater, as well as what look like sensible flat shoes.

"You never know when you'll have to make a quick escape," she says when she sees me eyeing her clothing. "Well...*I* do. But most don't." Her voice is smooth, calm—soothing. "Come, sit."

She pulls the folding chair around the desk for me and seats herself casually on the desk itself.

"You're wondering why you're in the lion's den," the Lady says, raising the sleeve on her right arm. The Magister's mark is indelibly branded into her skin, along with the X I've come to expect from the Starless.

"I am," I confess, looking from her to Joy and back again.

"I'm sure my daughter has told you I'm a Seer. There are few who know me as anything other than a myth. I'm a bit of an enigma in the Capitol, which is how I like it. Still, I feel I should tell you that the Starless are not your enemy."

"They sure feel like it," I retort. "With respect, I'm sure you're a nice person. But..."

"But you've had encounters that lead you to believe we mean to harm you. One in the tunnel. One that ended in four of my people dying at the hands of a drone."

"Yes," I say.

"The Poisoner was not one of us," she replies.

"But you know about him."

She laughs, but there's nothing menacing in it. "There's very little that happens in our land that I can't envision in my mind's eye. If it's important, I know about it. The Poisoner was intended to look like a Starless, yes. But I don't hire killers to do my bidding. We aren't an army. We're survivors. We hide because if we don't, they'll kill us."

"Why would the Poisoner dress like one of you? He told me you wanted to see me."

"Did he? But I thought he wanted you dead."

"He—" I'm about to deny it when I realize she's right. He wasn't exactly coaxing me gently to accompany him.

I turn to Joy, gesturing to her mother. "Does the Magister know about you?"

Joy chuckles. "Do you think the Magister would allow me anywhere near the Citadel if he knew? Hell, even Rivenna doesn't know yet, and I count her among my friends. Only a select few are aware of our connection."

"So, you're a spy."

"In a way, yes."

"Yet you told *me*."

"Like I said when we first met—I've been awaiting you for a long time, Shara."

I turn back to the Lady. "Okay. I'm thoroughly confused now."

"Confused by design," the Lady sighs. "Someone else sent that Poisoner for you, and there's no question that whoever it was, they wanted to turn you against me. Probably in hopes that we would never speak as we're doing now. It's the same reason they killed my envoys when I sent them looking for you. Speaking of which, I believe you took an object from one of those four."

I'd nearly forgotten the symbol I extracted from the hand of the dead Starless—the circle with a small dagger outlined within its perimeter.

"I did," I say. "I didn't mean any disrespect. I was just trying to figure out its meaning."

"Her name was Liana. She wanted to show you the pendant."

"Why would she do that?"

"Because you are going to need to use your powers in the coming days, and that pendant is a symbol of your strength. Shara..." She seems to gather herself, then pushes her glasses on top of her head so that I can see her eyes. They spin with her power, color pulsing almost as intensely as Rivenna's. She is strong, I can tell, and holds almost as much knowledge in her mind as the Storian.

Except, instead of memories, her mind contains visions of things to come.

"In the next few days," she says, "you will come to understand the meaning of the word strength—and pain, as well. I take no delight in saying this to you, Shara, but it's inevitable at this point. You will feel betrayed—and crushed under the weight of grief. You have already had a taste of it, but there will be so much more, and it will be terrible."

I clench my jaw, debating whether or not to believe her. Is she playing mind games? Trying to force me into panicking?

"What's going to happen?" I ask, my voice quivering in spite of myself.

Instead of answering, she pulls up her sleeve and shows me her brand again. "Do you know why we carve an X through the Magister's mark?"

"I assume it's because you hate him. But I'll admit, it does seem extreme to slice into your own flesh."

"As much hatred as we have for the Magister...what we hate more is that he implants us. Tracks us. Claims us as his own. And so, we carve up our arms to extract the implant, which latches onto our tendons. It's almost impossible to remove, but over the years, we've developed a technique to get it without losing our limbs."

She shakes her head, then continues.

"The Magister is no better than the bastards who run the Tower and imprison our kind. Then again, it *was* your father who started the practice here in the city. There was a time when the man known as the Hunter would force an implant on any Tethered who was in hiding, marking their powers for others to detect more easily."

"I was aware he did it," I say, recalling what Lady Graystone told me. "But *all* Tethered?"

"All the ones he deemed useful allies—or dangerous enemies. At first, at least. It was meant as a means to keep traitors from moving too easily through the Capitol, and for a while, it was effective. He stopped doing it years ago, when he realized how easily the system could be abused." She sighs. "By then, it was too late. The Magister had begun tracking and branding everyone in the city, Normals and Tethered alike."

"Okay," I say.

This isn't great news, but it's not the grand betrayal she seems to assume.

"I'm sorry," I add. "I'll speak to the Magister—ask him to stop. Maybe our people can find common ground, after all is said and done."

"There will be no common ground," the Lady snaps. But I get the impression it's not me who makes her angry. She slips off the desk and moves closer. "I brought you here not to ask you to negotiate on my behalf, but to tell you I have seen the days ahead."

The foreboding in her voice sets my bones trembling, but I raise my chin and meet her gaze, convinced that she's trying to manipulate me.

She takes my hand gently in hers and crouches in front of me, sorrow behind her eyes. "Someone has made a choice on your behalf, Shara—and I want you to know it was done out of love, because it will not feel to you like an act of kindness."

A shock of fear fists around my heart. "What are you talking about? What choice?"

"One that will ultimately save this realm. But first will come a sacrifice."

Dropping my hand, she steps away, pacing the room as if she's grown restless.

"When I look to the future, I am always presented with many possible scenarios at first. They come at me quickly, painfully, but eventually, are reduced to two possible paths. In the case of Kravan, there is only one path that can lead to freedom—and you are at the center of it, walking unsteadily along. It is a cruel fate that is being thrust on you, my dear. But I'm afraid you alone are in control."

I stare at her, knowing that asking questions is pointless. She will only tell me the bare minimum—enough to confuse me, to make me question myself.

"Tell me what I need to do, then. Because I'm lost."

"When the time comes for you to make a choice of your own, I am pleading with you now—say yes. Even if it hurts your heart. Say yes. Give yourself over to the feeling of calm that comes with that word. It's the only course of action that will liberate this land."

Anger swells inside me in a growing tide, threatening to crash against my mind. "None of this is making sense. You're talking in riddles, and expecting me to go along with something, yet you refuse to tell me what it is."

"I know—and I'm sorry." The Lady looks at Joy, then back at me. "Tonight is going to be...difficult. Seek out your allies. Look for support. Embrace it. Revel in it. Recognize that the future is on your shoulders. You are so much stronger than you know."

Joy looks as serious and sad as her mother, and a cold

sweat begins to dampen my brow. Is this about my father? About Thorne? "You're scaring me now."

I stare into her eyes, searching for the truth. But the more I focus, the more the color wanes and fades until they go completely white, staring blankly back at me.

"He has already chosen," she says cryptically. "He knows his fate, and you will learn it soon enough."

Her grip on my hand tightens so that it's almost painful, and I leap out of the chair, pulling back.

"*Who* has chosen?" I cry, twisting my head around to find Joy. "What is she talking about?"

But Joy shakes her head. "I can't say. I'm sorry."

"Go back to the Citadel," the Lady says, rising to her full height. "Prepare yourself, Shara. And when the time comes... say yes."

Without another word, she strides out through the door where she came in.

"Joy," I breathe, fear trembling its way through my insides. "Is there a Porter here among the Starless? I need to get back to the Citadel—now."

CHAPTER

FORTY-THREE

Joy finds a Porter called Linn, who immediately agrees to help. When she's pierced her finger to draw a drop of blood, I snatch up her power, shooting myself back to my quarters in the Citadel and leaving Joy behind to walk back.

When I find the suite empty, I ask Maude what time it is.

~Seven p.m.

Seven, and Thorne is nowhere to be seen. There's no sign that he's been here at all.

Relief overtakes me a few seconds later when I hear the lock clicking and the door opens.

But it's not Thorne who's standing in the doorway.

It's Kith.

He looks grim, his chin low, his eyes barely willing to meet my own.

"What is it?" I ask, praying internally that he doesn't know about my visit to the Lady. I don't know what my father or the Magister would do if they found out, but I can't imagine it would be pretty. The things she hinted at...

"It's Thorne," Kith says, his tone solemn.

Oh, God.

"Has he been hurt?" Instantly, I'm frantic, my chest heaving. "Did something happen during the training session?"

"He's been arrested. Taken by the Magister's guards. He's in a cell, Shara."

"A cell? Why?"

"They believe he was responsible for the bombing of Magister's Row yesterday—that he took control of the drones and attacked civilians. They think that's why he was in the bar at the time it happened, instead of in the arena where he was supposed to be."

"Bombings?" A laugh bursts out of my throat. "That's insane. He would never do that!"

Kith looks sympathetic, at least, when he says, "You and I both know Thorne is the only person around with the capacity to take control of drones. Most Coursers possess only a fraction of his power—enough to illuminate a lightbulb, to start up a watch battery. But Thorne is different. I'm afraid he hasn't expressed to you quite how powerful he's become."

I think of the ropes in the arena, retreating into the ceiling. The doors locking, even from a great distance. He's right—I have no idea how powerful Thorne is.

"He may be strong," I snarl. "But that doesn't mean he would bomb innocent people and destroy everything the Magister's crews have worked on for weeks."

Kith shakes his head. "I don't think he's capable of it, either, but we both need to admit it doesn't look great for him."

I'm not doing this. I'm not debating Thorne's innocence. Yes, he's been acting strange and secretive lately—but this?

Never.

Still...

He did ask what I would do if we weren't together—he wanted me to promise I'd pursue our dream, no matter what.

Did he know this was going to happen? Is it possible...

~Don't jump to conclusions, Maude whispers into my mind.

It's a little hard not to...but you're right. There has to be a better explanation.

I try to push past Kith into the hallway, and it's only then that I see my father standing behind him, a grim shadow lurking in the darkness.

"I have to see him!" I cry. "Where is he?"

"I don't think it's a good idea," my father says.

"Please, let me talk to him. Please...why is this happening?" My voice is desperate, almost childlike.

"You've known from the beginning, Shara." He levels me with a cold look. "No Royal Guard ever leaves here alive. Thorne received far more freedom or respect than most. The Magister is not kind to those who have served the king, I'm afraid. He has no tolerance for those who allow their minds to be taken by the enemy."

"But you said—"

"What I say doesn't matter. The Magister is in charge. I am his second, and I can't override his decisions. I can't let Thorne go, Shara—I'm sorry."

"But you know he didn't do it! He would never do such a thing!" I shout the words, but they flatten in the air and vanish, meaningless.

With a sigh, he replies, "Thorne confessed to the crimes."

I want to laugh hysterically. To cry. To scream at both the men standing in the hallway, staring at me as if I'm the one who's lost my mind.

Nothing either of them is saying makes sense. I'm the only person who's being remotely rational.

You will feel betrayed—and crushed under the weight of grief," the Lady told me. *"But first will come a sacrifice....*

Is this what she meant? Could Thorne really have done these things? Is that what he was discussing with Rivenna—the thing that would break my heart?

"Let me talk to him, Father," I say, my voice a monotone. "Or I swear, I'll never speak to you again."

He and Kith exchange a quiet look, and finally, my father nods once. "Fine. I'll bring you to him myself."

"No," Kith says. "Let me. Please."

"Fine. Take good care of her."

Kith escorts me to a wing I haven't seen before—a guarded area with only a few small cells, all of which lie empty but one.

When we reach Thorne's cell and I see him sitting on his cot, his face in his hands, my shoulders begin to shake with silent sobs.

"I don't understand what's happening," I whisper through the tears. "Why would he confess to something he didn't do?"

Kith touches my arm, drawing my eyes to his. My tears subside, a sense of quiet comfort filling me—healing me. "I don't know. But I promise you, I'll talk to the Magister and see what I can do. You know how persuasive I can be. I will convince him to let Thorne go. For you."

"If he thinks Thorne is guilty of an atrocity, there's no way he'll let him go."

"The evidence may be circumstantial. It's hard to prove a Courser's interference—there are no fingerprints or anything else left behind. I can argue that Thorne was coerced into a confession. It happens. Magister Brant would do well to stay on your good side—if only because your father is an important ally. I'm confident he'll listen to me."

I nod. "Thank you. Please—do everything in your power. Charm him, if you have to."

"I'll go see him now," Kith says, wiping a tear from my cheek.

He's about to leave when I say, "Kith…I just realized…"

"Yes?"

My voice trembles. "The public hangings are tomorrow morning. You don't think…"

He shakes his head. "No way. Even if Thorne is guilty as sin, the Magister wouldn't execute him so soon—and certainly not in public. Brant may seem like a cold fish, but he always gives his prisoners a chance to tell their side of the story. I promise—he'll come around."

I thank him again, then turn to the guard outside Thorne's cell, who presses a number into a keypad next to the door. I leap inside, taking Thorne in my arms the second he rises to his feet.

"How did this happen?" I sob as he cradles my head against his chest.

"They came for me at the training session. They claimed I was in the city to initiate the bombing—that I needed to be above ground to control the drones. They think it was an act of revenge for the years I spent in the Tower."

"But it's all lies," I say. "Thorne—tell them they're liars."

He draws away, pushing my hair from my damp cheeks. "It doesn't matter," he tells me. "I'm sure they've already told you I confessed."

"Why?"

I stare into his eyes, searching for the truth. But I don't need to find it. I know in my heart that he didn't do this thing. Thorne would sooner die than hurt innocent people.

"I had my reasons," he murmurs. "I'm sorry."

I shake my head, wiping at my eyes. "Kith is fighting for you. The Magister will come around."

"You don't understand, Shara. It won't matter."

"Of course it will!" I stare at him, baffled by the sense of defeat swirling through the air between us. "Why wouldn't it?"

He seals his lips and shakes his head.

"I love you so much," he says. "I told you so many times that I would love you until my last day in this world, but the truth is, I will love you beyond. You'll find me one day, waiting for you. Never straying, never thinking of anything but your voice, your scent. The touch of your skin, your perfect lips—and your goodness. Because Shara—you *are* good. You are hope. You are what the realm needs most of all. I'm nothing more than an appendage. A distraction. I always have been. The world is far bigger than just me, and you'll learn that soon enough." With a final sigh, he says, "But you and I—we were nothing more than a dream."

My head is shaking against my will. "What are you saying?" I sob. "Why are you acting like this?"

He stares back at me, the swirl of power in his eyes gone,

thanks to the cilice around his arm. Now, he simply looks eerily calm. Cold, even.

"Maude will look after you," he says. "So will Rivenna. You need to follow the path, Shara. When the time comes, say yes. No matter what. *Say yes.*"

The Lady said the same thing. What the hell does it mean?

"What?" I choke. "Say yes to what? Tell me!" I thrust my palms into his chest, attempting to shove him, rage tearing through me. But he's far too strong, even without his powers.

He takes my wrists in his hands. "Say yes to strength and power. Yes to calm and comfort."

Two guards sweep into the room—a Velor and a Rounder —and the Velor hits him across the face with such speed and brutality that Thorne's head slumps to the side and he falls back against the wall. The guards take hold of my arms and drag me toward the door.

"You can't do this!" I scream. "Please!"

I want to stab one of them—to steal their powers and flee with Thorne.

"Why didn't you fight?" I cry when his eyes land on mine.

There's so much pain in my heart. Deep, despairing sadness...but I'm not sure anymore whether it belongs to him or to me.

"Fighting would have prolonged the agony," he says softly. "There was no point."

"Let go of me!" I growl, but the guards drag me toward the door. "Thorne!"

"I love you," he says, watching me go. "I promise—I will love you until my last day. It's you alone who will win this fight, Shara. Take back the world for those who deserve to live in it."

"How?"

"When the time comes, you'll know what to do." He presses a fist to his chest, and under his breath, he adds, "The queen will save us all."

CHAPTER FORTY-FOUR

I DON'T SLEEP that night.

I can't imagine I'll ever sleep again.

When morning comes, Joy knocks at my door then lets herself in, but I don't turn to her. I'm staring, my mind reeling and empty, at the wall.

"Shara," Joy says, "you're to attend the hanging this morning."

"The hanging," I repeat mindlessly. "Thorne...he..."

Joy hesitates, then says, "Kith tells me he spoke to the Magister last night. He said everything is looked after."

For the first time since I saw Thorne, I dare to feel hope, if only the smallest, weakest scrap of the emotion.

I don't want to attend the hideous event. I don't want any part of the Magister's so-called "justice." But I *will* attend, because this moment represents a new dawn. Today is the day that is supposed to set in motion Kravan's rebirth.

I'm just not sure what that means. Will Ellion turn himself in, as Tallin did? Will an election finally be announced?

"Do you know if Tallin will be there?" I ask.

"I believe so. I expect part of the spectacle will be killing the prince turned king. It would be seen as a show of strength."

"Yes, I suppose it would." Fire and ice meet in my veins. I don't know how to feel about Tallin dying, to be honest. I've always thought I hated him—and yet, there's some twisted part of me that actually...*enjoys* him. He's the most honest person I've ever met. The most transparent.

With Tallin, I never doubted where he stood. He simply... was.

As backwards as it sounds, I wish the world had more Tallins in it so that I would know whether or not they were to be trusted.

"Do I have to wear anything in particular?" I ask.

"Anything will do. It's a public affair, so best not to stand out too much. You probably want to blend in with the crowd, in case things go awry and there's a riot or something. In other words, don't wear your best gown."

I turn to narrow my eyes at her, wondering if there's any way she could possibly know about the golden gown.

Not that it matters anymore. There will be no happy wedding day in my future—not unless Kith really did manage to convince the Magister to free Thorne.

With a nod, I thank Joy. "Do you think I could see Thorne if I stayed here? Kith and my father will be at the hanging with the Magister, right?"

"I've been told the Magister isn't feeling well," she replies with an apologetic shrug. "He'll remain in the Citadel, as I understand it. As for seeing Thorne, I wouldn't push your luck. There will be guards on high alert today, preventing anyone from interacting with prisoners. Go to the hanging. Afterward, maybe you can visit him."

"Joy," I utter one last time.

"Yes, Shara?"

"Do you know what's going to happen? Everything your mother talked about when I met her—have you seen it?"

"Yes, I have."

"Is the future going to destroy me?"

She bites her lip, nods once, and leaves the room.

THE WALLS that used to surround the Tower at the Capitol's center are gone. Whether bombed or torn away, I can't say. The large park of green grass is open to the public now, with shady trees and benches laid here and there.

The city's entire population seems to have congregated en masse at the Tower's base, chattering among themselves, their voices rising with palpable excitement. Perhaps it gives them a sense of power to watch a hanging.

Maybe they're all psychopaths.

I don't know, and I don't much care anymore.

I spot my father and Kith standing with a group of guards by a horrifying wooden gallows with three nooses drooping like lifeless bodies from a thick wooden support.

Part of me wants to head over to the Shadow and ask whether he knows about Thorne's likelihood of being freed, but another part is terrified to even contemplate it.

I'm about to muster the courage when a voice speaks my name.

"Shara...I'm so sorry."

I twist around to see Rivenna and Berengar. Rivenna's black eyes are locked on the gallows, and Berengar seems to be picking up a scent on the air.

"Sorry for what?" I ask, my tone chilly but not hostile. "Is it that you knew Thorne would be arrested, and you did nothing to stop it?"

"I wasn't in the arena when it happened. But there's nothing I could have done."

"You were with him in the city. You could have told them he wasn't killing people with fucking drones. You were having some deep, emotional conversation with him when the first explosion happened."

"He could have defended himself by telling the truth. But he confessed, from what I heard."

"Yes. Why is that, exactly? Was he protecting you? Was the bombing your doing?"

Rivenna turns her black eyes to me. "He was protecting *you*," she says. "Everything he does is to protect you."

"Yes—confessing to a horrific crime definitely seems like a protective measure." Sarcasm drips from my voice. "I'm just grateful Kith spoke to the Magister. He says Thorne will be all right."

Rivenna says nothing at first, then, "The festivities will start soon, at least. They don't like to drag these things out. Word has it Tallin's here somewhere, but it's hard to know. They usually hide the prisoners, then bring them out with hoods on."

"You've been to hangings before, then."

"Unfortunately, yes. I'm hoping this will be my last."

I scoff at that. "If this is the Magister's justice, I doubt it will be the last. Sounds like he's likely to win the presidency when the time comes."

"Magister Brant is..." she begins, but she cuts off when she sees my father step up onto the gallows to address the crowd.

His voice booms and echoes against the Tower, amplified by the enormity of the cruel prison.

"Today," he shouts, "several prisoners will pay for their crimes against Magister Brant and the realm of Kravan." The crowd's murmurs subside. "What you will witness will be difficult to watch—so I am warning you now, go home if you must, but understand that this day represents a new dawn for our land. A new beginning. Soon, the power structure in this realm will shift. No more will Tethered be treated like lesser beings. No more will Potentials—Normals, as you know them—have to fear our kind. Our people will be united and equal, just as the Magister wishes."

Cheers rise up, and I wince. *God, I hope you're right, Father.*

"We will now begin." Without further ceremony, he steps down to make room for the prisoners to be ushered onto the gallows.

First comes a giant of a man in an opaque black mask and matching uniform. The executioner, I assume.

He waits as three hooded prisoners climb up to stand on the gallows. Two guards accompany them and quietly remove their hoods to reveal two men and the emaciated woman I spoke to in the cells. Each of the men bears the mark of the Starless—the red X through the Magister's brand.

Each is given the chance to speak their final words.

The men refuse.

The woman, on the other hand, turns to the crowd and shouts, "The heir is coming, and with him, ruin!"

The executioner grabs her and shoves her head through a noose, then does the same to each of the men. Within a matter of seconds, he's pulled a lever and each of them has fallen, their bodies breaking or juddering with what will be their final breaths.

I turn my face to Rivenna's shoulder, too angry with her to touch her, but too afraid to witness three simultaneous deaths.

"Come with me," she says over the crowd's cheers. "We need to move closer."

"Why?"

"I want to see their faces before they die. You can look away all you like, but I need to see their eyes."

We push our way through the crowd until we're twenty feet or so from the gallows. We watch as six more prisoners die the same way—all of them former Royal Guard, as far as I can tell. I can see now that each of them still has a cilice tightly wrapped around their arm, digging into their flesh to rob them of their powers.

None of them chooses to speak. A few look terrified, but take the punishment with quiet dignity. My heart breaks for them, nausea rising up inside me and threatening to double me over.

When nine prisoners have been killed, another is brought out and dragged up the gallows stairs, hood covering his head.

Even so, I recognize him instantly—though I am probably the only person in the crowd who would know his stride so well.

Tallin.

I swallow, reaching for Rivenna's arm and holding it tight. Emotions rage inside me, a fight to the death between sadness and reluctant relief.

Tallin killed his father. His mother. Lady Graystone.

I suppose I knew his end would come one day—but I never wished this for him.

When the executioner removes the former prince's hood and asks him to speak his final words, Tallin searches for me in the crowd. His eyes find mine after a few seconds, and he smiles.

"Be strong!" he shouts. "Be good. You're a better person than I ever was—and you'll do the right thing."

With that, the executioner slips the noose over his head and yanks the lever.

Tallin's eyes slam shut in anticipation of his death.

But the trap door under his feet doesn't open, and he does not fall.

The crowd gasps, then I hear a laugh rising up in someone's throat.

Tallin is cackling, almost choking himself, doubling over at the waist as he howls.

"The Magister has decided to keep you around a little longer," the executioner tells him in a rumbling voice, clapping him on the back. "That's good news for you."

"What the fuck?" Rivenna mutters, and other murmurs rise up in the crowd. Some sound amused, others enraged.

"I suspect they want information," I reply, secretly

pleased. "He knows things that could benefit the Magister's forces if they attack the palace. He's useful."

I never want to see Tallin back on the throne, but he did let me go. He let me run to Thorne and to freedom.

For that, I'm grateful enough to be happy for him.

"Well, I guess that's that," someone says, and the crowd begins to disperse, turning to head back to their homes.

"Wait!" a man shouts. "There's another one!"

He's right.

One last prisoner is being marched to the gallows just as Tallin is taken back toward the Citadel.

"Rivenna," I breathe.

"I see him."

Though the prisoner is hooded, I can tell exactly who he is—and so can she.

CHAPTER

FORTY-FIVE

WHEN THE EXECUTIONER pulls the hood off Thorne's head to reveal his perfect face, I struggle to keep my legs from giving out under me.

A scream cuts through the air—a long, jagged cry—and it takes me a moment to realize it's escaped my own throat. I leap forward, trying to push myself to the gallows.

I'll jump up there. I'll fight the executioner myself, if I must. I'll fucking take his powers—whatever they are—and kill him.

But two guards rush over and take hold of me, shoving me backward.

Somewhere to my left, I see that my father, too, is shouting at the Magister's guards, and so is Kith. The guards press their hands to the men's chests, forcing them back.

Someone shouts, "Magister's orders! He's dying today. Nothing anyone can do."

My chest caves in on itself as though my heart has been torn out.

I look up at Thorne, whose eyes are directed straight ahead.

A fight has broken out around me—absolute, chaotic mayhem unleashed by the crowd. Most don't know what they're fighting for. They don't know who Thorne is, or why he's up there.

They don't care.

They're only here for the blood they're owed.

"Let him go!" I scream, my voice lost among the chorus of cries from the crowd. "He's innocent!"

"It's okay," Rivenna's voice says softly, her arm wrapping itself around my waist. Berengar presses himself against my leg. "It's okay."

"It's not!" I cry. "They can't do this!"

I'm living a cold, vivid nightmare. This can't possibly be reality.

Thorne and I have a future together. A life. A house. A fucking garden, with roses.

This—whatever it is—is not the future we were meant to have.

Just as the thought circles my mind, the Lady's words come to me:

You will feel betrayed—and crushed under the weight of grief. You have already had a taste of it, but there will be so much more...

And it will be terrible.

The executioner lays a hand on Thorne's shoulder, and I see it now—the cilice cutting into the arm I love so much, blood trickling down. Thorne's hazel eyes are clear when the executioner asks whether he has any final words.

It's then that his eyes finally find mine. Tears brighten

them so that their color is unbearably beautiful, and a sob bursts from my chest.

"I will love you until my last day in this world," he calls out. "And beyond."

When the executioner pulls the lever, the tiniest hope ignites inside me that this whole thing is some cruel joke. That, like Tallin, he will simply stand there and laugh at the absurdity of it—and I will laugh, too.

But the floor crashes out from under his feet, and he falls, the noose tightening around his throat.

Some of the prisoners thrashed and struggled against the rope's vicious force when they fell.

But Thorne merely falls, then...slows. He hangs quietly, his body instantly limp, as if all the fight left him long before the noose was ever slipped over his head.

I'm barely aware of Rivenna next to me, her arm around me, her lips muttering some unintelligible curse, or of Berengar licking my hand in sympathy.

I seal my eyes against the sight of Thorne's body, desperately reaching for him in the Nether. Surely he's there, waiting for me. Surely...

I find myself in the white space for the second time, my eyes hunting for a shadow, a hint of movement, anything.

For a fleeting moment, I see it—a shape, moving toward me. *His* shape, broad-shouldered and powerful. I can't make out his face, but I know it's him. Our tether is still intact.

A whisper flits through the air.

The queen will save us.

And then, he vanishes.

I fall to my knees and weep, and Rivenna crouches next to

me, her eyes still locked on Thorne, as if she's hoping for some sign of life. She holds me as I sob, Berengar standing guard over us both while the crowd is forced back by the Magister's soldiers.

"You're okay," Rivenna whispers. "You're going to be okay."

I don't know how long we've been here. How long I've been frozen, hopeless, my eyes sealed against the image of Thorne's body suspended in the air.

"How?" I whimper back.

It's only then that I realize we're alone. The sky has darkened with clouds, giving the illusion that night is approaching.

The crowd has grown weary and retreated back to their homes. My father and Kith, too, are gone.

The only people left are the executioner and a few guards, who are carefully pulling Thorne down and laying him on a cart to take him to some horrible place. I try to rise, to run at them, to see him one last time. But Rivenna holds me back.

"They won't let you near him," she says softly. "They'll kill you before they'll allow it."

I watch as they pull the rope away from Thorne's neck and steal his body from me. It's only then that Rivenna allows me to dart up to the gallows and take the rope in hand.

It's not like other rope I've seen—brown-gray and coarse. This noose is made of silver threads and gleams in the sunlight.

"What is this?" I ask in a juddering voice.

"Silver cord," she replies. "Less likely to fray and break

than regular rope. Can't be eaten by rodents. It's strong, so they like to use it for Tethered."

I drop it like it's just burned me, and turn away.

"Where will they take him?" I whisper.

"They'll likely bury him in an undisclosed location," she says. "One day, we'll find out where, and you'll be able to visit."

I nod once. This is all so surreal that my emotions ricochet violently between disbelief and excruciating sorrow, and I can't begin to tell which is worse. It doesn't feel real. Yet I just watched it. I felt the rope. I saw...

"Rivenna?"

"Yes, Shara."

"Did he do it? Did he bomb the city?"

She goes silent. "We've all done things we regret. Thorne was imperfect, just like the rest of us. But he loved you. That's the only thing that matters."

"I know."

Inside, I'm numb, but I'm also on fire. Burning with rage, with torment, with love. I seal my eyes, trying again to find him in the Nether—looking, hoping.

But there's not so much as a hint of him there now. With a pang of pain so profound that it feels like every nerve is being twisted and stabbed at once, I feel the last of our tether fray and threaten to give way.

One final thread holds fast, and I hang onto it for dear life.

For the rest of the evening, I refuse visitors, other than Rivenna and Berengar. I don't want to see my father or Kith —don't want to hear their excuses or explanations.

Rivenna stays with me that night, in our suite. She sleeps next to me, with Berengar lying at our feet. When I weep, she holds me until I push her away. When I cry out, she takes me in her arms and cradles my head to her chest.

"You knew, didn't you?" I ask her in the darkness. "That's why...it's why..."

I can't finish the sentence. My voice is a quivering mess.

"I knew," she nods. "Yes, I knew this day would come."

"Why didn't you tell me they were going to hang him? He and I could have hidden ourselves somewhere. We could have gotten away. There are other realms—other places than just the Capitol. We could have lived in one of the tunnels for years before anyone found us."

Rivenna lets out a deep breath, and says, "You'll never believe me, but the alternative would have been worse than what happened."

"Worse." I let out a bitter laugh and wipe away a tear. I cannot comprehend how my body is capable of producing so many fucking tears. "Worse than losing Thorne. Worse than the world thinking he's a murderer. As if there's anything that comes close."

"Yes." Her voice is cold. "Worse. And not just for you. For this whole damned realm. Thorne did the most selfless thing imaginable. He knew it would destroy you, yet he did it. For you. For all of us. It was an act of love."

"Love!" I pull away from her, irate. "What aren't you telling me?" I snarl. "What did Thorne know? Why did he have to...to..."

No. I will not say the word *die.* I will not.

"I don't know, exactly. All I know is that the coming days are going to be difficult." Rivenna lays a hand on my arm. "You'll feel empty—exhausted—as if you'll never regain the energy you once had. You'll wonder if this pain is ever going to pass, to get easier—and I'm here to tell you that it will spread itself thinner over time. It will...hurt in a different way. But no, it will never go away entirely."

I swallow down a sob, flick on the light on the nightstand, and turn to her, not caring in the least that I'm a disheveled, rancid mess.

"It happened to you...didn't it? You lost your tethered mate."

She nods. "Yes. I lost her years ago."

"Her," I repeat.

Rivenna snickers. "You really didn't know, huh?" she says with a crooked grin. "I enjoy ladies. And here I thought I was hitting on you in the tunnels."

"But that guard—the one you told me you'd slept with—he was no lady."

She shrugs. "I enjoy the company of both—but I've only ever loved one person, and she was a woman. Sue me."

"I'm not good at picking up on signals, I guess," I say, wiping at my eyes. I wish I had enough emotional strength left to laugh.

"The only person I ever truly loved was my tethered mate," Rivenna says. "That was a long time ago—long enough for me to be able to tell you the pain evolves. You learn to harness it—to remind yourself that you were given life when they were denied it. I try every day to live up to what she wanted me to be. I try to be a decent person, believe it or not. To help others. She was so much better than I am. And before she died, she asked me to do something."

"What was that?"

"To pay attention to my dreams. I didn't know what she meant—not until very recently."

"Thorne wanted me to live my dreams," I reply. "But I..."

The grief is too raw. I can't say it.

"I doubted him for a minute there, Rivenna," I lament. "I shouldn't have. I'm so fucking obtuse, aren't I?"

"You're also fucking human. Our minds play tricks on us all the time. It's what makes us interesting, and what makes us ridiculous."

"Does it still hurt—the broken tether?"

She pulls her face away to look at the far wall. "It's more an ache than a sting nowadays. But it won't be the same for you. It's different for everyone."

Slipping off the bed, she paces for a minute, then turns back to me.

"Look—I know nothing will dull your pain right now, and I'm not here to try and convince you it's not the greatest agony you'll ever endure. But I have something for you—from Thorne." She reaches into a pocket and pulls out a small white envelope, sealed with a red stain of hard wax. "He wrote this before they took him. He gave it to me in the bar—a few minutes before you saw us together. Before the bombing."

I take the letter from her and hold it in my shaking hand, staring at it. I want desperately to read it, but I'm terrified, too.

The brutal truth is that when my eyes meet the last word, that will mean the end of everything.

"I'm going to leave you alone to read it," Rivenna says, whistling for Berengar to jump off the bed and come with her. "I'll stay close by in the coming days—keep an eye on you. In the meantime, take care of yourself, Shara. What's that saying—the world is always darkest before the dawn, or something?"

Shaking my head, I say, "I don't know. I don't really care."

"Well...this is the darkest your world will ever be. I promise you that with my entire heart. Stay strong—but let yourself be weak, too."

I watch her and Berengar leave, then pull open the letter.

CHAPTER FORTY-SIX

Dearest Shara,

No.

That's not right. "Dearest" sounds so inadequate to describe the woman who has changed my life, my soul, my very blood. It sounds almost generic when the truth is, you are the most important, exquisite person in the world.

But I'm not sure how else to start. How does one write one's last words without getting at least a few of them wrong?

Still, I suppose I'll have to try my best.

There's no need for euphemism or sugarcoating. By now, you know I'm gone.

There's no shame in death. It's just an absence of life, after all—and eventually, the reaper comes for us all. No one is immortal. No one is invincible.

I've known my fate for some time. I've told you that more than once, I've seen a future devoid of my existence—one where you are destined to begin your happily ever after without me.

I made a discovery several days ago. My damned powers were strengthening, all because of my bond with you. While you were afraid to look into the future, I reveled in it. It was all I wanted—to see you live out your dream, and to see myself standing alongside you.

My only dreams were to share in your happiness, to help this realm—and to make love to you every day and night. To thrive on the mundane, the simple. I wanted our dream house as much as you did.

And I hope that one day, you find yourself in it.

The time we've spent together in relative freedom has been such a gift, Shara—and I hope you remember those days with the same love in your heart that I have felt for you since the moment I first laid eyes on you in the Tower.

You're probably wondering what I learned about the future. I want to reveal it to you...but I know you'll be angry with me, because I'm not going to.

At least, not exactly.

I believe Rivenna once told you she suffered from recurring nightmares. She saw people being killed.

Hanged, to be specific.

But what she didn't tell you—because she didn't know it herself at the time—was that your tethered mate was one of those people. So, when she met me face to face in the Citadel, she was shocked, and so was I.

Because I had seen her in a vision long ago, as well. One where she helped you to become something far greater than either of us had ever imagined. A vision so extraordinary that my mind took it for a dream.

She didn't tell me about her nightmares right away, and when she finally did, I didn't want to believe her.

I was tormented by the possibility that she was right—that I was going to be hanged. The day came when I snuck into the city to speak to a Seer—one I suspect you've encountered by now. I've met the Lady of the Starless, Shara—and she's not the evil creature we've been led to believe.

She told me everything that would unfold if I didn't meet my fate at the end of a noose. She told me there were two possible futures. In one, you learned my death was coming, and you persuaded me to flee with you. In that future, the drones came for us—and you died in my arms.

I railed against her words—told her we could change our fates. But she showed me the truth, and I felt it deep in my bones. I knew she was right, and that there was no way to escape.

I had to make a choice…so I chose your life. But not only out of love. There was duty to consider, as well. Duty to you and to the realm of Kravan.

You thought I had fallen for Rivenna—that I was attracted to her. It always seemed so ironic to me because I wanted to stay a million miles from her. She reminded me each day what was coming.

Keeping the truth from you has been the hardest thing I've ever done. I wanted to spill it all—to tell you everything. But I know you.

I know how much you love me.

You would never have sat back and waited for my death to come. You would have put your own head in that noose if it was enough to save me…and that's only one of a million reasons I love you.

You will face a choice, Shara—very soon. And when the

consequences play out at last, you'll understand all of this—all the pain, the anguish, the sadness.

Please trust me one last time when I tell you that you must say yes when the time comes—as hard as it will be. Say yes, and the world you and I have dreamed of may just come to pass.

I've been told a tether never dies, never breaks fully. I want to think it's true. I want to believe that wherever I am now, I am still bound to you eternally.

I'm yours, whatever happens. I always have been. And you've always been mine.

You're fucking mine, Shara. Whether you know it or not.

Remember, I will love you until my last day in this world. That is a promise I intend to keep.

Love,

Thorne

p.s. I've left something for you in the top drawer of your dresser. Wear it in good health, and use it wisely.

CHAPTER FORTY-SEVEN

With tears fogging my vision, I dig through the top drawer of the dresser until I find Thorne's gift—a delicate silver bracelet, as light as air.

I stare at it, confused, then slip it onto my wrist. When my vision begins to clear, I see symbols etched into the silver: a wolf. A heart. An arrow.

"What do these mean?" I murmur.

~I suspect it's a bracer like the ones Thorne made for the trainees, Maude tells me. *Only, this one is customized for you. The wolf is likely the symbol for a Morph. There are ancient legends about humans who can shape-shift into wolves. The arrow might signal a Porter's skill. As for the heart, I'm not sure. Perhaps it simply speaks of love.*

"Perhaps," I reply.

I sit down to read and reread Thorne's letter a hundred times, new tears staining its words until they begin to blur and fade away.

This lone piece of paper is the last of him.

A piece of the man I knew and loved—and still love. I still

feel our tether, our bond. Still feel a pull toward him, wherever he is.

He explained so much with his words...yet so little. Rivenna's nightmares were about him—and he had seen her before ever meeting her, as he suspected. That explains why they were drawn together. But why did he speak to the Lady? Why was he so certain we couldn't alter our fates?

Why did he allow a Seer to convince him he needed to die for me?

"We could have found a way," I say under my breath. "We could have survived. Both of us."

But maybe I'm wrong. Maybe fate is more powerful than I've ever thought.

Why, though? Why couldn't he have told me he was going to give himself to them?

~He knew you would have tried to stop him from confessing, Maude says. *He knows you almost as well as I do. You would never have accepted Thorne's confession. You would have done everything in your power to get him to run—and if what he said was true, you would have died.*

Maybe I was meant to die. Thorne shouldn't have sacrificed himself for me.

~I suspect he sacrificed himself for more than you, Shara. Maybe there was a greater reason—something he understood. It seems he felt you needed to live to see the next days and weeks.

What do you mean?

~Truthfully, I don't know. I wish I did. I have never felt sorrow like this inside you—and I am sorry.

I've never lost someone I loved as much as I love him. I just...I wish he could have told me in person.

~Brace yourself, Shara. Wait for the days to come. Perhaps your questions will be answered.

When morning comes after various failed attempts at sleep, Joy brings me breakfast, but I refuse to eat it. Sadness fills her eyes when she leaves me, as if she wishes she could help—but knows she can't.

An hour or so later, when I've been staring numbly at the wall, my father comes to the suite, knocks, then pushes the door open when I mumble to him to stay away.

"If everyone knows the entry code to this suite, I'm not sure what the point is in having one," I snarl when he steps inside.

"You're upset with me," he says, standing rigid in the doorway.

"You could have stopped it. You must have known he was going to be there."

"I tried to stop it."

"Did you?" My brows meet as my eyes hurl daggers at him. "Did you *really* try?"

"Are you implying that I wanted to see my daughter heartbroken?"

"I'm implying that you waltz around here like you're this powerful figure, when the truth is, you're as much a prisoner as I ever was in the Tower. Tell me—where is the Magister? Is he feeling better? Was he too much of a coward to show his face yesterday, knowing what was about to happen to the man I loved?"

His jaw sets tightly when he says, "The Magister is

unwell. As for cowardice, there aren't many options for sentencing, when a man confesses to a crime as egregious as Thorne's. You must know that."

I rise to my feet and step closer to him, livid. "He confessed to protect me."

"If he was innocent, he would have done better to defend himself and come home to you."

I'm about to speak again when I realize there's no arguing with my father. To him, Thorne must seem like a criminal—one who not only destroyed parts of the city, but crushed the soul of his daughter. He probably despises Thorne right now as much as I despise the Magister.

"Leave me alone," I finally mutter. "Please."

"Can I do anything for you?"

"No."

"Shara."

My tears are flowing now, my shoulders shaking, and my father steps over and wraps his arms around me, holding me tightly to his chest. "I'm sorry, my girl," he says. "I'm so sorry you have to endure this."

"It's not fair," I breathe between sobs. "Not right."

"I know."

He's smart enough not to try and explain it away—not to try and tell me I'll get over it. I don't want to stop feeling—to stop loving.

I'll love you until my last day in this world.

"Listen," my father finally says, pulling back and taking my shoulders in hand. "Kith wants to talk to you. He feels terrible about what's happened. Is it all right if he comes to see you?"

I'm about to say no—that I don't want to see anyone. But

I nod miserably. If Kith really does feel awful, he may as well share my grief.

Misery loves company, after all.

"Yes. He can come."

My father nods and turns away, but I stop him. "Father... is there going to be an election, after all?"

Please, say yes. Tell me something good will happen in this bleak fucking world.

His jaw tightens when he twists back to me. "Until the Magister is well, no. But I do foresee a change of leadership in the near future, if all goes according to plan."

I take in a deep breath and watch him leave, sealing the door behind him.

Well...at least Kravan is on the right path, even if nothing else is.

It's not long before another knock sounds at the door. This time, I open it myself, knowing it will bc Kith.

He looks down at me with kindness in his mysterious eyes, and when I break down, he takes hold of me and pulls me close.

I weep into his chest, reveling in the calm that glides through me with his touch, craving more respite from my grief.

"I'm so sorry," he whispers. "God, I'm sorry."

I don't say anything. There's nothing *to* say, anyhow. I can't tell him it's okay, because it's not. I can't tell him I'll survive, because I'm not entirely sure I will.

Kith lays a hand on my cheek and draws my eyes up to

his. "I'm here," he says. "Every day and night. Anytime you need me to take away the pain, you call on me, okay?"

I nod. "I'll be calling on you a lot in the next few months."

"That's all right. It's what I'm here for. I should use my powers for good every now and then, don't you think?"

At that, I let out a quiet snicker and wipe my eyes. "I'm a mess. I don't know if I'll ever not be a mess again."

"You will. You'll be all right. You're strong, Shara."

He pulls me to his chest again, and I can feel it—the gentle tide of peace that he's sending my way even as he draws my pain from my mind and body.

With a quiet shock, I realize he's doing for me what Valira did for Tallin. He's steering my emotions away from torment and pain, and easing my sorrow.

I wonder if that means...

"Kith," I say softly.

"Mmm?" he asks, chin resting on top of my head.

"Do you feel my pain when you do this? When you... make me feel calm?"

He draws back to look me in the eye. "Do you really want to know?"

I nod.

"Yes. I do. Does that bother you?"

I think about it for a second, then say, "No. I'm glad you understand. I'm glad to know there's someone in the world who knows my grief—even though that's a selfish thing to say."

"Not selfish," he replies. "Empathy is never selfish, whatever way it moves."

He holds me for a few silent minutes, then says, "Look—I'm going to leave you in peace. I only wanted to make sure you were all right. But I will come every day and see you. Every day, I'll help you to heal. I never want to take from you what he was. I only want to make you feel like you can navigate your way through the pain. Does that make sense?"

I nod, wiping a tear away. "Thank you," I say, and I mean it. "If it's ever too much..."

"It will never be too much," he tells me, kissing my cheek. "Now, you call on me whenever you need me. But I promise you—every day I'll come see you. If you ever feel up to it, we'll start our walks in the city again. Okay?"

Again, I nod.

When he leaves me, I lie down on the bed, the smallest flicker of hope in my chest.

I will get through this. I will survive.

And maybe one day, I'll understand why fate did this to us.

CHAPTER
FORTY-EIGHT

THE WEEKS after Thorne's hanging pass in a wretched haze.

I seldom leave my quarters. I eat my meals on the bed—that is, when I can find the strength to consume anything.

Morning, afternoon, and night, I seek the Nether, trying to find a piece of Thorne. Some small remnant of him, to prove to me that our tether is still intact. Occasionally, I'm certain I see a silhouette in the distance, coming toward me. I convince myself that I feel the faint pulse of his heartbeat next to mine.

But each time I call to him, he vanishes as if he was nothing more than a teasing figment of my imagination.

I read Thorne's letter daily, always searching for deeper meaning behind his words. I torture myself, trying to guess at the choice he mentioned—the *yes* I must ultimately say.

But as the days pass, the question never comes. I'm left in the dark once again—and this time, without the support of the man I love.

Each day, I contemplate asking Joy to bring me to see her mother. I try to summon the courage to demand that the

Lady tell me the whole truth—to explain why this fate was forced on us, and how I'm supposed to find the will to exist in a world where my tethered mate does not.

But I know better than to waste my meager energy on futile pursuits. The Lady didn't answer my questions before Thorne left me.

She won't answer them now.

Let him go, Shara, I tell myself over and over again, trying desperately to abide by Thorne's wishes. *Let him go. Live your life. It's what he wanted. Honor his memory by finding a purpose in this awful world.*

Rivenna checks in on me frequently. Every time I see her, she says, "If there's anything I can do, let me know."

I always respond, "Bring him back."

Kith comes to see me daily, just as he promised. He asks how I am, strokes my cheek, and steals away a little of my sadness.

Sometimes, I cry into his shoulder.

Sometimes, I manage not to shed a tear until after he's left.

When I finally find the strength to venture out into the Citadel's hallways, I walk around like a husk—soulless, lifeless.

Pathetic.

I keep expecting Maude to kick my ass and tell me to lighten up, but she never does. She's turned *kind*, and it's beginning to frustrate me. Occasionally, I needle her, trying to get a rise out of her. A snide retort. Anything.

But she refuses to succumb.

Maybe she knows all it would take to shatter me once and for all is the lightest breeze.

Two Months Later

During the weeks I've been inside, Magister's Row has been rebuilt—again.

And one day, when I'm feeling strong enough to bear it, Kith takes me to see the progress.

He keeps an arm around me, which I take more as a sign of support than affection. I stare out at the new builds—wishing so badly that I could bring myself to marvel at their beauty.

Instead, I eye them distantly, my emotions stagnant. Beauty means little to me now.

Maybe one day, that will change.

"I haven't seen the Magister in ages," I observe as we walk. "Did he ever recover from his illness?"

"He's weak," Kith tells me. "Unfortunate that he's not a Tethered. We tend to do far better with illness than Potentials."

"I'd offer to heal him. But...I won't." My tone is bitter, and Kith lets out a laugh.

"I can't say I blame you, after what that bastard did to you."

We walk a little more until we come to a small park, and Kith guides me to a bench, where he sits me down.

He looks frazzled as he begins to pace up and down the walkway in front of me, jamming a hand into his hair.

Finally, he comes to a stop, his eyes focusing on mine.

"It's been two months," he says. "Since the hanging. Kravan is on the verge of change, and I'm hoping you're still willing to play a part."

"But...you said the Magister is weak. Is he really well enough to run in an election?"

"No, he's not." Kith's jaw tightens, then he blows out a puff of air before succumbing. "I'm telling you I want to throw my hat into the ring. I want to seek leadership of this land."

For the first time in weeks, I feel something. I'm not sure what it is, exactly. Surprise, I suppose.

"You?" I stammer. "Really?"

He paces for a minute more, scratching at the thick, dark stubble on his jaw.

"You've told me I'm a good man, Shara—and I have tried to live up to your expectations of me."

"You have," I tell him. "You've been a good friend, Kith. You kept your promise and came to see me every day, when even my own father avoided me. You've helped me through the worst time of my life, and I'll always be grateful to you for that."

He steps over and crouches before me, taking my hands in his.

"I'm so glad you say that." He draws in a hard breath, then says, "The thing is, I believe the realm would be quicker to accept me as their leader...if I had a wife."

"A...*wife*." The word trembles its way up my throat. "Kith, I...I..."

Shock tears into me like a wild animal. Is this the question I've been waiting for? The choice I'm supposed to make?

No. It can't possibly be.

Why would Thorne ever want me to say yes to another man's proposal?

But...

Oh...*God.*

In the vision Kith showed me so long ago of the day of my Pairing, there was no Thorne. I had always told myself he simply hadn't arrived yet—that I was a happy bride, awaiting her groom.

Never did I imagine I could find that happiness pledging myself to someone else. It's simply not possible.

"I never pictured myself marrying anyone other than Thorne," I say slowly—evenly. "And even then, I felt we were too young. I..."

He places his hand on top of mine, calming my frayed nerves as always.

"I know. You need time to consider it. I realize you and I aren't tethered mates. As much as I care about you—as much as I have always felt a powerful bond with you—I know your heart lies elsewhere. Thorne will live on in your memory, and I would never try to replace him. But please, consider it for the sake of Kravan. You know you and I would be a good team. We would be just rulers...and kind. Think about it, and then say yes, Shara."

Calm eases its way through my veins like a cool breeze sweeping over my tortured soul. I look down at his hand, knowing full well he's working this magic on me.

But I don't want him to stop.

Say yes, and the world you and I have dreamed of
may just come to pass.

Those were Thorne's words. But if *this* is the question—if *yes* means accepting another man's proposal...how could I possibly go through with it?

I chew on my lip, overcome with confusion and sadness.

Why would anyone want me to marry Kith, other than Kith himself? What could pairing with him possibly do to help our land?

"Shara..." he whispers. "I'm sorry if it's too soon. I had simply hoped you would consider it. I believe you and I are good for one another—and that I have helped you to heal, as you have so often helped others."

"You *have* helped me," I tell him, and with that, my voice shatters.

My mind is addled with a twisting, nauseating sea of emotions.

There's no question that I'm fond of Kith. He's flawed, like any man, but he's kind, strong, and generous. He's made an effort to protect me since the very first day we met.

"Please, Kith," I add, "just...give me a little time to take it in. It's a lot to think about."

"Of course."

A touch of his hand to my cheek brings another dose of warmth and comfort, and the sensation of relief is so great that I'm tempted to say yes immediately—to give myself to him, and ask him each day to draw the pain from my body and mind, as Valira did for Tallin.

I smile, thankful for the kindness. "You've helped me through the hardest days of my life. Please know how grateful I am for it—no matter what happens. I don't want you thinking I don't care about you."

"I know you do," he says, moving closer.

I've never kissed Kith. Never betrayed Thorne's memory, or even come close. But right now, it feels like he's on the verge of pushing the boundaries.

"When you touch me," I say, trying to keep his lips from brushing against mine, "you calm me. You soothe the anger inside me, and the sadness."

"Yes," he says. "It's a power I took from someone long ago."

I look up at him with a questioning expression, certain I already know what he's about to say. "The way you can alter someone's mood—did it come from a Netic?"

He nods. "You've encountered the skill in past, then."

"Prince Tallin had someone—a friend of mine—who would draw out his pain. It was a gift and a curse. She unburdened him of his agony, but it meant she took it on for a time."

Kith nods, a sad breath pushing its way out of his lungs. "I feel your sadness, it's true," he says. "When I touch you. I have always sought to improve your mood—to remove the anxiety that weighs you down so often. I feel your fear, Shara, and I want to help you through it. I want you happy, more than anything. After Thorne died..."

He looks away then, wincing.

"You felt my heartbreak," I say.

He nods. "With everything inside me, I felt it. I grieved with you. *For* you. I wept when I was alone, because I knew how broken you were inside. I want to spend my entire life taking away that pain and mending you as best I can. Look—I don't want you to forget him. I only want you to be able to live as he would have wished for you."

I allow myself a brief smile when I say, "He always did want me to have my happily ever after."

Kith's grin is bittersweet. "Then what better way to live it than with someone who loves you deeply?"

I slip my hand onto his cheek.

I don't love him—not exactly. I'll never love anyone like I love Thorne. But I like him.

The truth is, I would rather be alone. I would rather find a way to obtain my small house, to tend its garden and live a quiet life, all in Thorne's memory.

But the Lady's voice in my mind tells me that's not what I'm meant to do.

"Give me a day to think," I tell Kith. "Tomorrow, I promise—I'll give you my answer."

I already know what it will be—but not because of any love I may hold in my heart for Kith.

If I say yes, it will be out of love for Thorne. This was what he wanted. I'm certain of it.

I only wish I knew why.

I LEAVE Kith when we reach the Citadel's entrance, too dazed to even ponder what's just happened. I head to my father's office, my head low, energy depleted.

~*Shara,* Maude says. *Maybe you should rest a little.*

"I need my family," I tell her, my voice flat. "I want to see my father."

I knock on his door, and when he tells me to enter, I push my way inside.

The smile that lands on the Shadow's lips seems almost as forced as the ones I carve onto my own features almost daily.

"Ah," he says. "The day has come at last."

"You know, then. You know Kith proposed." I hasten to add, "I haven't accepted."

He steps over and takes me by the shoulders, his chin raised as he appraises me. "I know it's hard for you to imagine moving on, especially so soon. But you must do this, Shara. Say yes to him."

"Why would he even *want* to marry me—pair with me—whatever we Tethered call it? And why does this matter to anyone but Kith?"

"It matters, because he intends to lead this realm in the Magister's stead. He knows it would be a wise strategic move to take a wife. Marriage tends to give the perception of a stable leader. Besides, he loves you. He told me so, shortly after meeting you. It pained him to watch you with Thorne, you know—but he held back each day that he spent by your side. Did he not protect you and look after you, even in those days?"

"Yes...But if I wanted protection, I'd ask Rivenna to lend me Berengar. I don't need a husband."

My father frowns slightly. "You may not. But the realm needs *your* protection."

I inhale a deep breath, anger simmering in the depths of my mind. "I need you to tell me the truth, Father. All of it. I will not accept him until you tell me what the hell is going on. Why is it that everyone but me seemed aware that this proposal was coming, long before Thorne even...."

I still can't bring myself to say he died. Still can't accept it, after all these weeks.

Maybe that's why I can't begin to imagine accepting another man.

"Do you know why they call me the Shadow?" my father says, failing infuriatingly to answer my request.

"Rivenna told me it has to do with Soleia's death. That you became a shadow of your former self when she passed away. Then again, she didn't really die. So, I suppose my answer is no."

"Losing a person will do that to you—it will rob you of what you once were. You know it as well as anyone. But there are other reasons I'm called Shadow, and there are only a few who know the truth. If you accept Kith—if you trust me a little longer—then I promise you, I will tell you the entire truth. But you need to agree to be his, with every painful emotion that comes along with that acceptance. He needs to feel your sincerity when you say yes. Even your conflict and your sorrow. He must know you mean it."

"Why?"

"Because if you go to him with dishonesty in your heart, he'll see right through you—and he will choose another path."

"Kith isn't my tethered mate. I'm not meant to be with him."

"No," my father sighs. "You're *meant* to be with Thorne. You were fortunate to have the time you did with him, and he knew it. We are all fortunate if we find that one person... but the truth is, most don't. Most people find a way to be content with someone kind and loving. Someone protective. Kith will look after you. He will grant you everything you've ever wanted. That should be enough."

"Everything I ever wanted, except for Thorne. Except for love."

"Perhaps you will find love after you say yes."

"I very much doubt that," I murmur. "But I understand that this is what Thorne wanted, for some insane reason. For that reason alone, I'll consider it. I have nothing to lose at this point, after all."

"You have a great deal to gain, however. And I promise you—very soon, you'll understand what I mean by that."

I leave my father then, fully aware that he has asked the world of me—and I'm not sure I'm strong enough to give him or Kith what they want.

But the truth is, I'm not sure I even care anymore.

I am shattered and spent, and I have nothing left to give. Which means marrying Kith can't hurt me.

It can't bring me joy, either. I will simply continue to be, broken as I am.

But that's what confuses me most.

If I say yes, the day of my Pairing will come to pass.

But when it does, I cannot imagine feeling a single ounce of joy.

CHAPTER
FORTY-NINE

IT MAY BE a stroke of madness that compels me to head to the cells to seek out Tallin after I see my father.

I haven't spoken to him since the day before the hanging, when he asked for my forgiveness. But now, for some mad reason, I want his advice.

"I *must* be losing my mind," I mutter as I make my way to the high-security prison on the third sub-level.

~That would imply you had a mind to begin with, Maude counters.

The guards allow me through, unquestioning when I approach. I flush slightly when I see the one whose identity I stole all those weeks ago. So strange to think I've lived inside his body and borrowed his voice.

When I enter Tallin's cell, he leaps to his feet, a gleaming smile on his lips. "Shara," he beams. "To what do I owe this pleasure?"

The walls of the cell are covered in drawings—skilled charcoal renderings of the gardens surrounding the palace, the palace itself, and rolling hills and trees.

Alongside them are portraits of a pretty, dark-haired woman I've never encountered.

"I...wanted to speak to you about something," I say, pointing to one of the images. "That woman...is she..."

"My tethered mate," he replies with a nod. "Her name was Sarena. For a long time, I couldn't bear to picture her face in my mind's eye. But now...well. She keeps me company."

I stare at the image, wondering about the agony Tallin must have endured when she died and then was forced to relive the moment over and over again.

"May I ask you something?" I murmur as I stare at her face.

"Of course."

I turn his way. "Did you feel your tether break when she died?"

"Yes," he says, swallowing at the memory. "I felt it, like a snapping tendon. It was excruciating."

"The thing is, I didn't feel that when Thorne...*died.*" The word grates at my throat. "He sort of...faded away. But sometimes, I'm certain the tether is still there, like it's holding on for dear life. It feels like a blade in my chest, turning slowly, slowly, all the while knowing that one final turn might be the one to break us apart for good."

Tallin looks sympathetic when he says, "I suppose it varies from one person to the next. I don't think it's a thing many people talk about. Not the most pleasant subject in the world."

"No. I suppose not." I move slowly along the floor, taking in all the drawings as I go. "Did you ever meet Sarena in the Nether while she was alive?"

"Yes—sometimes, during the many days when my father kept us apart. It was..." He seals his eyes. "It was good."

"And after she died?"

"No more," he says softly. "But I didn't try. It was too painful to consider entering the Nether and finding it empty. But I suspect you've tried—am I right?"

I nod. "I'm convinced sometimes that I can still feel him when I close my eyes at night—still see him there. But then, I tell myself it's nothing more than a shadow. The merest version of him. It's all wishful thinking, I suppose."

"I'm so sorry," he tells me with a grim exhalation. "Really, I am. You didn't deserve that. Neither did Thorne. I didn't like the guy, and he wanted to tear my face off. But he was decent—and he loved the hell out of you. Fuck—what they did to you, Shara."

"It wasn't *they*," I retort. "It was the Magister's doing."

"Right. The Magister. Where is he, exactly?" Something tells me Tallin isn't simply asking a question.

He's trying to tell me something.

I shrug. "He's been ill, and I can't say I'm sad about it. I hope he dies, honestly."

The former prince lets out a laugh. "You'd best hope he's not listening in on this conversation."

"I don't care if he is. I despise that fucker."

"You once despised me, yet here you are, paying me a nice social visit."

At that, I manage a laugh. "You're one of the few people who knows my pain," I tell him. "And what makes you think I don't despise you anymore?"

"A hunch."

I bite my lip, unwilling to confirm or deny the accuracy of his theory.

"Kith asked me to marry him," I blurt out, turning to face him. "He wants a Pairing ceremony—a *wedding,* that is—and soon."

Tallin appears unconcerned when he says, "Ah. Will you say yes?"

"I don't know." I move to the wall again to study another drawing, though my mind isn't fully registering what it is. "I think I was hoping you'd tell me what to do."

"Me?" he laughs. "I'm the last person you should ask for advice."

"Something tells me you'll give it regardless."

"In that case," he says, "You should accept."

I pivot back to face him. "Why do you say that? You know I still love Thorne."

"Yes, and you always will. But I've met your Kith. He's an ambitious man. If he rises to any position of power—and I assume that's his goal, if he's looking to pair quickly with you—then a ceremony would benefit you, and this realm."

"Explain this to me, because I don't quite see how."

"Fine," Tallin says. "The vows exchanged during the Pairing protect you both, and grant each of you all the legal rights of the other. So, if Kith were to become, say, president, and something happened to him, you would be president in his stead. You're the Shadow's daughter—which means if Kith wins an election and something happens to him, someone he trusts would rule—and have the Shadow as their closest advisor. He sees you as a political strength, probably. You and your father would make for a formidable team—and by pairing with you, Kith would become a *part* of that team."

"You told me to go see the Lady," I say. "The day before... before the hanging."

"I remember."

"She told me I would have to make a choice. She advised me to say yes. I think *this* is the choice."

"You don't want to, then? Despite the fact that Kith is easy on the eyes and probably hung like a bear, you don't want him?"

I shake my head, refusing to be amused by his poor taste. "I haven't even begun to process my grief. How could I say yes without feeling like I'm betraying Thorne? How am I meant to move on? It's only been two months, Tallin."

He scratches his fingertips over a healthy dose of stubble on his jaw, focusing his dark eyes on me. "Tell me something. Do you see yourself feeling more inclined to marry Kith in two years' time?"

Without hesitation, I say, "No."

"Well, then, go for it," he replies with a casual shrug. "If it makes you feel any better, I never moved on, either. The truth is, our existence consists of taking one difficult step at a time until we're dead. That's what life is. You can choose to say no to Kith, or choose to say yes. It's that simple. But if the Lady told you to say yes...then I strongly advise you to do it."

I want to think he's right—that he simply *knows.* But there's one thing I still don't understand. "How do you even know her? Isn't she your arch-enemy or something?"

He moves over to the wall, pointing toward a picture of a pretty house with elegant gables set in its roof.

"I went to see her once, some time ago, when I was in the

Capitol. It was a silly thing to do, but I'd been told there was a remarkable Seer living in the city—one who could help guide me and free me of the pain I had suffered for so long. She told me there would come a day when I would make a choice—one that would impact Kravan's future. She said I needed to choose wisely, but that it might break me before it healed me. Sound familiar?"

I nod. "Mostly, yes."

"I made that choice," he says. "The day I killed my parents and set you free, Shara. The day you left the Isles and fled to the Capitol. I made the choice to take them down—to give you a chance to flee. Because the Lady had shown me something incredible." He lets out a laugh. "When I first met you, I thought you were a meddling, mischievous little twat who was trying to spy on me, or worse. But as time went on and I began to understand your mind, I realized you were far more than that. Thorne saw it. Kith probably sees it, too—and I know your father and the Lady see it when they look at you."

"See what?" I ask, almost afraid of what the answer will be.

"Isn't it obvious?" Tallin says with a smirk. "You, Shara, will save us all."

CHAPTER FIFTY

As promised, I decide to go see Kith the following afternoon. But first, I reread Thorne's letter for what feels like the thousandth time, searching for answers.

I've asked myself so many times why Thorne, of all people, would want me to accept a proposal from Kith or anyone, or how the proposal could possibly impact Kravan. All I can think is that Tallin is probably right. Kith wants the political strength of my father behind him, and pairing with me is the best way to secure it.

I tell myself there's nothing to do now but say *yes* and see what happens. To accept a man I don't love—but whom I like well enough. Besides, there are worse things than having a man around who can take away your pain whenever it becomes too great.

I'm about to leave for Kith's quarters when a knock sounds at the door.

"Who is it?" I call.

"Joy."

When I open the door, she holds out a small parcel wrapped in silver fabric.

"A gift from my mother," she says. "The day the four Starless sought you out—when you were in the city with Thorne—you saw a pendant with a dagger at its center."

Confused, I take the package and begin to unravel its wrapping. "I remember," I tell her. "I still have it."

"That dagger—that symbol—well, it exists for a reason. I told you once there were better ways to grant yourself another Tethered's powers. Swiping a little blood with your finger is one thing. But extracting a large amount and absorbing it into your veins will produce a long-lasting effect."

As she speaks, a silver dagger reveals itself among the mound of fabric. Its hilt is gold, and it looks almost like an elegant letter opener. Next to it lies a pretty, leather sheath.

When I pick the weapon up, I see that its tip is hollow, the blade ever so slightly rounded, as if its intended use is to collect the blood Joy is speaking of.

"In the coming days, you'll need to use it," Joy tells me. "But only on your worst enemies. The dagger will hurt them—even kill them—as it extracts their power. The name *Blade*—it comes from the days when those like Kith would steal powers in a similar manner. Each had a weapon customized for them. Over time, their powers evolved until they could steal the gifts with nothing more than their minds. But you are not a Blade—you're a Sapper. If you want to extract power and incapacitate your foe, use the dagger."

"Do I need to stab myself afterwards?" I ask. "That sounds...unpleasant."

"No. The dagger is imbued with powers of its own. It will

only work for *you*, and all you need to do is use it on the person whose powers you seek. Obviously, there are other ways to give yourself temporary gifts, such as the bracelet Thorne left for you."

I don't ask Joy how she knows about the secret gift—the one currently tucked away in a drawer. It seems she knows even the smallest details about my life.

"Why would I need a dagger, if I have Thorne's bracelet?"

"Because some powers are only obtainable through blood. Thorne's bracers are impressive, but they can only provide a limited number of gifts."

"Thank you, Joy," I reply, sheathing the dagger and tucking it into the drawer alongside the bracelet. "I really don't see myself needing this, though. I don't generally pick fights."

"You will," she says. "And soon. But now, I'll leave you to your business. Good luck today, Shara. I'm sure you'll make Kith a very happy man."

"Is there anything about me you don't know?" I ask.

She ponders that for a moment, narrowing her eyes. "Many things. But one thing I do know is that your life will only get better from here. Trust me on that."

I offer up a weak smile and thank her again, then watch her go.

Kith greets me with trepidation, his slight smile betraying nervousness.

He invites me into his quarters, which are laid out similarly to my own. A bed, a dresser, a bathroom. There's a leather chair and a small desk to one side, and he asks if I'd like to take a seat, but I refuse.

He doesn't touch me at first, almost as if he's afraid that, if he does, he'll know what I'm feeling. He'll know whether I'm about to reject him.

"You know why I'm here," I tell him. "So I'll make this as painless as I can."

I watch his jaw tense, disappointment already etching its way over his features.

"Kith," I say with a nervous chuckle, stepping toward him. I take his hand in mine, and his disappointment fades away instantly. "It's okay. I'm not here to ruin your life."

"Does this mean...Are you...accepting my proposal?" he says, breathless.

"I am—on one condition."

"Which is?"

"Be patient with me. I mean, when it comes to anything physical. I need a little more time. But yes. I am accepting you...that is, if you still want me."

I know from the tightening of his hand around mine that he feels the pain rising inside me as I utter the words—the betrayal I have just committed.

But he smiles all the same, and takes me in his arms, holding me to his chest.

"You've made me so happy," he whispers. "I can't tell you. I will do everything in my power to deserve this—and you."

I pull away, torn up inside in spite of his soothing touch. "I know." I peer into the swirling eyes that hide powers I don't even know about. So many gifts lurking inside him—so much strength that it almost frightens me.

"There's something else," he says. "Another part to this —if I may."

He slips over to the desk and opens a small drawer, extracting a velvet-covered box. When he opens it, two golden rings reveal themselves.

"We must wear these now," he says. "And on the day of our Pairing, they will connect to one another and bind us. What's mine will be yours, Shara. Always. We will share everything."

So, Tallin told me the truth. Will miracles never cease?

"I don't have much to offer you," I confess.

"You have plenty. You are gift enough."

We extract the rings from the box and slip them on. I expect some unseen power to reverberate through me, but to my relief, I feel nothing but the touch of metal on my skin.

"What's mine is yours," Kith says. "What's yours is mine."

I muster a smile, and he cups my cheek in his hand. "I know you're still sorrowful. But I will spend all my days striving to change that."

I'm suddenly exhausted, and want nothing more than to leave—to go back to my quarters and weep for all I've lost.

But Kith delays my departure.

"There's one last thing I want to show you. Something that may encourage you a little."

"Go ahead," I tell him weakly.

Instead of opening another drawer, he presses a hand to my collarbone and says, "Close your eyes."

I do, and a vision swirls through my mind. The same one he showed me long ago of my wedding day—the day I wear the golden gown and bliss courses through me. The happiest day of my life.

Only, this time, I see Kith looking down at me, my hands in his as he mouths the words, "I do."

When the scene comes to a close, I pull away, baffled.

"You will be happy," he says. "Once it's sunk in. I know it —I've seen it, and so have you."

I nod. "I'm sure you're right." I hesitate before adding, "When, exactly, is it to take place?"

"Soon." He offers up a strange, knowing smile, and adds, "When the time comes, I'll send your father for you. The ceremony will be quick and painless, I promise."

"I'm glad." Nausea twists inside me.

Kith presses forward and, taking my face in his hands, kisses me gently on the forehead.

I'm grateful when he doesn't make an attempt at my lips.

When he draws back, he says, "You still have the golden gown I bought you, don't you?"

I nod. "Of course I do. I've been saving it for this very occasion."

A lie—but I hope he doesn't manage to see through it.

"Good," Kith says. "God, Shara—there are so many things I wish I could tell you. But I promise, the moment we've pledged ourselves, you'll know everything."

This time, I mean it with all my heart when I reply, "I'm counting on it."

CHAPTER FIFTY-ONE

I've always assumed that brides-to-be are the happiest people in the world. Or, possibly, the most stressed out.

Yet here I am, about to wed...and I couldn't care less. The numbness in my heart runs so deep that I'm convinced a block of ice surrounds the organ.

All that resides inside me is the quiet acceptance of a fate I never asked for or wanted.

I lie on my bed, staring at the ceiling, wondering if I'll ever again know what it is to feel joy. Wondering why this ridiculous destiny has inflicted itself on me, and why I am seemingly at the center of a plot I can't begin to comprehend.

I'm still pondering it bitterly when I hear the door crack open. I gave Rivenna the code to the quarters long ago, and she has availed herself of it plenty of times over the last weeks—so I have little doubt that she's the one who's come to see me.

She knocks softly as she pushes the door open, and Berengar leaps in and onto the bed next to me. I stroke his fur, realizing with a pang of sadness that he does more to make me feel genuinely human than Kith's touch ever could.

Rivenna kicks gently at my foot, which is hanging over the edge of the bed.

"You look terrible," she says, eyeing the ring on my finger. "Happy engagement, by the way."

"You don't seem particularly surprised."

She shrugs. "I've told you before—there's not a lot in the world that surprises me. This is just another weird pothole in the road of life."

"Your metaphors are fucking horrible. You and Maude should team up and write greeting cards."

Rivenna snickers. "When's the big day?"

I hurl my arm over my eyes and moan, "All Kith said was 'soon.'"

"Ah." She plops down on the edge of the bed. "Well, here's some interesting trivia for you: Between the time someone accepts a proposal for a Pairing and the time of the actual ceremony, the two people involved aren't supposed to see one another. It's a cute little tradition."

My voice is hoarse when I reply, "Fine with me. I don't suppose Kith really wants to be around me in this state."

"You're unhappy, then."

"I'm...*nothing*. I am devoid of feeling—which I suppose is better than wanting to throw myself from the Tower. Only marginally, but still."

"Well, then," Rivenna says, slapping a hand onto my calf. "We'd better get a move on. There's a fuckload to do between now and your ceremony. It's time we put some feeling back into your cold heart, Shara, my friend."

"I'm not doing the whole *wedding* thing, Riv," I mutter. "I said yes because I was supposed to—not because I want some big affair with flowers and dresses and ridiculous amounts of food."

"I know," she says, her tone altering to something more earnest. "I know about the future. About the Lady. All of it."

I look her in the eye. "Joy told you about—?"

She rises to her feet, a strange smile on her lips, and reaches a hand out. "Come with me, you mopey monster. I have something for you. Call it an early wedding gift, if you like. Point is, I've been waiting for this day for far too long."

She pulls me off the bed, and I dress and follow her out of my quarters, curious and uncaring at once.

"Where are we going?"

"You'll see soon enough."

She and Berengar lead me out of the Citadel through the exit that Thorne and I took that first day we went exploring together—the exit that led to the pretty, residential street... and the discovery of our decrepit dream house.

I haven't been back to this street since, though I've thought of the house every day since I lost Thorne. All the wishes we'd shared for our future together.

One we'll never see.

"Riv. Why are we here?" I ask, stopping when I realize what I'm seeing. "This isn't funny."

Her face is expressionless. "I know. It's the farthest thing from funny. But trust me, okay? You're going to want to see this."

Too exhausted to argue, I trudge along behind her and Berengar until we come to a house with a white fence—a house that looks incredibly familiar, yet...

~It's your house, Maude says. *The dream house.*

I want to contradict her, except that she's...right.

The house has been repaired and painted. There are no more gaping holes in its roof, and its front window is no longer boarded up. The lawn is green and pretty, and on its porch is a perfect, cheerful swing large enough for two people to sit side by side.

My heart hurts to see it and think of what could have been.

"Welcome home," Rivenna says softly. "Well, not home officially. Let's just call it a temporary sort of thing."

I step up to the front porch and open the door, slipping inside. Glancing around, I see the very place where Thorne and I stood when we watched the drone attack.

I feel a shadow of him in this place, like the outline of an old picture on the wall—an echo of his presence, living in my mind and straining to release itself.

"Upstairs," Rivenna says with a nod. Berengar is already trotting up a flight of white-painted steps, and I follow, clutching the handrail nervously.

Something about this feels...dangerous.

I stop in the middle of the staircase and turn to look down at her.

"Are you going to kill me?"

She snickers. "Not today, no. I'm going to give you the life you've always wanted."

I almost ask whether she's giving me this house as a gift, but that seems absurd.

For one thing, it would have cost her a fortune.

For another, Thorne isn't here to enjoy it with me...so, it would be pointless.

A waste.

"Just go," Rivenna tells me. "Hurry. Turn right at the top of the stairs."

I obey wordlessly, following Berengar down a short hallway and into a large, bright bedroom.

The sun beams through a window on the opposite side of the room, highlighting a bed dressed in white linens.

Lying on the bed, his cheeks pale, breaths emerging in slow waves from his lips...is Thorne.

CHAPTER
FIFTY-TWO

"He's alive," I stammer, unwilling to take my eyes off Thorne as I stagger to his side, falling to my knees next to the bed. I reach for his hand, which is cold—*so* cold—to the touch.

But I can feel the life in him—see the rise and fall of his extraordinary chest.

I understand at long last why our tether never fully broke. Why I saw shadows of him in the Nether, and why I could never bring myself to release him from my heart or mind.

But I understand absolutely nothing else.

After months spent casting my pain aside out of sheer desperation, a sea of feeling swells inside me, mounting and swirling in a torrential wave.

"He is alive, yes," Rivenna says from the doorway. "Just barely. And it will be some time—and some effort—before we can bring him back."

A sudden shot of fury rouses some dormant part of my soul. I leap up, twist around, and lunge at her, not caring that she's a Reaper—that she could take my life in an instant. My arm shoots out, my palm slapping her hard across the cheek.

She accepts the blow with dignity, staring back at me with black eyes, expressionless.

"I know you think I deserved that. Believe me—I know."

"You *did* fucking deserve it. You knew he was here—alive—and you didn't tell me?" I shove her hard. My vision is red, my rage clouding every thought. "How could you? How could you do this to me, when you knew it was killing me?"

"Because I've seen the future," she says. "I've seen your wedding day and all it means, and I knew there was no way in hell you'd accept Kith's proposal if Thorne was still alive."

"Fuck, no!" I shout. "I would have fled with Thorne! I would have..." My voice trails off.

"Exactly. You would have tried to escape your fate, and you would have died. Not fake-died. *Really* died. And, given that you hold the keys to Kravan's entire future in your hands, it seemed like it would have been a bad idea to let that happen."

Moving back to the bed, I take Thorne's hand in mine again, pressing his palm to my face.

She knows, then. About the other future Thorne saw—the one where he held onto me as the life drained from me.

I want to believe there really was no other way. That this, here, is the only possible path Thorne and I could have taken. But to give fate that much power makes me want to tear the walls down with my screams.

"Why is he so cold? Why doesn't he wake up?"

"I had no choice. I had to make it convincing—I needed you to *believe* he'd died—to feel it with all the emotion you're capable of. It was the only way. I drew all the life out of him that I could."

"*You* had no choice?" I gawk at her as she moves around the bed. "You're telling me you did this to him? Come on, now—I saw the hanging, Rivenna. I was there. I know how it happened."

She looks sheepish when she says, "He was wearing a prosthetic—a brace of sorts—that kept the noose from strangling him or breaking his neck. There was a reason I didn't let you run up onto the gallows after the hanging. I'm a Reaper, Shara—and yes, I did this. I took every bit of life he could afford to lose, to make the act convincing."

"But...the executioner. He..."

"It was Joy." She bows her head. "The executioner was Joy."

My jaw drops open. It never occurred to me that Joy might have been at the hanging. I'd always assumed she'd stayed behind, in the Citadel.

It's no wonder Morphs are considered so dangerous.

"Remember," Riv adds, "I saw all of this unfold in nightmares, night after night. Thorne's hanging—his death. Long before I ever met him, I knew there was something off about it all—like I was *supposed* to help him. I always felt baffled, as if he was a puzzle I couldn't solve...until I realized what I had to do, and why. There was a reason I had been sent to find you in those tunnels. A reason everything has led us to here and now."

"Oh my God," I stammer, then stare at Thorne again. "You had this all planned out—this fucking torture that you inflicted on me."

"The plan was never to torture you. It was to save you and Thorne, both. And we did."

"We. You and Joy, you mean."

"Not exactly."

The words are uttered by a familiar, deep voice, and when I twist around, it's my father I see standing in the doorway, arms crossed.

I want to rush over and slap him, too. My rage is only moderated by my joy at finding Thorne breathing under my touch.

"I'm not doing it," I snarl at him between gritted teeth. "There's no way. I'm not pledging myself to Kith while Thorne is lying here like this."

"Listen to me," my father says. "Kith cannot know Thorne is alive. He needs to be under the absolute illusion that you're committed to him—that you're happy with your choice."

"Why?"

"Because marrying Kith will grant you a power you need in order to heal this land, Daughter. And not marrying him will lead to this realm's demise, once and for all. I'm sorry to say the weight of the world is literally on your shoulders."

I shake my head, my disbelief almost enough to make me howl with laughter.

"I could have pretended. I posed as Tallin's fiancée for weeks, for fuck's sake. I didn't need to think I'd lost Thorne to accept Kith!"

"Didn't you? Are you really telling me you would have said yes to a Pairing with another man, had you thought Thorne was alive?"

"I—"

~He raises a good point, you know, Maude says. *You would have run screaming into the sea before accepting Kith's proposal.*

I was hoping you'd keep your mouth shut.

~I have no mouth, you ignorant noodle loaf.

"This isn't a mere act, Shara," he says when I go mute. "More importantly, if you'd accepted on false pretenses, Kith would have seen right through it. You couldn't have fooled him. Almost no one can." My father lets out a rough breath. "Kith can read emotion like you or I would read the words on a page."

I want to argue—to scream.

But I know he's right.

"The moment he touches you," he continues, "he's aware of every flicker of joy, sadness, or confusion inside you. For someone who feels as deeply as you do, there is no tricking him. There is no actor in the world skilled enough to fake their way through to his mind. I know. I've watched people try, and I've watched them die for it. I was not willing to lose you—not now that I've finally found you."

"*You've* fooled Kith!" I snap. "You knew about Thorne. Clearly, it can be done."

My father looks as if I've just stabbed him in the heart.

He bows his head, shaking it, and says, "The only reason I can fool him is that a part of me is long dead. I am almost devoid of feeling, and have been for a long time. I learned long ago how important it was to erect a fortress around my heart—but I would never ask you to do the same. It is... impossible to hide grief in the face of death. I am so sorry to say it, truly—but I needed you to grieve. Every single day, I needed Kith to witness your pain. He needed to be convinced you were alone in the world."

I absorb his words like slow-working poison. "You needed me crushed so you could get your way," I hiss. "That's vile, and I hate you for it."

He shuts his eyes against my words, and an instant stab of regret assaults my heart.

"I knew the risk," he says. "I knew you might loathe me for letting you hurt. I made my choice. I must live with it. For the record, I have never wished for you to be with Kith. I have never trusted him." With a long breath, he adds, "When I first met him, I thought he was a promising young man with an extraordinary gift. But over time, I learned that he had taken to tracking Tethered, using the very implants I had developed. He hunted them then stole their powers to hoard them for himself. He has never had good intentions for this realm—as much as he pretends otherwise."

"So why the fuck would you want me to marry him?"

"Because you are the only one with the power to stop him. And by accepting him, you have made a sacred promise. You *must* pledge yourself to him now. All that remains is one final step."

"But Thorne could have *killed* him," I nearly shout. "Any number of people could! He's not invincible, is he?"

With pain in his eyes, he shakes his head. "I know it's hard to understand—but Kith needs to live to see his wedding to you. It's crucial. We can't simply *end* him."

"But if he's that powerful—that dangerous—then the Magister should—"

"The Magister is dead."

The words ring through my head like a reverberating bell.

"What? When did he die?"

"A week or so before Thorne's hanging."

I shake my head. "No—that's not possible. He ordered the hanging himself as punishment for the bombing."

"No. He didn't. But the guards were led to believe he did. Kith told them so."

"I hate to interrupt," Rivenna says, nodding toward Thorne. "But there is the small matter of reviving him."

"Reviving?" I blurt out. "But he's already alive!"

"Yes—he's still in there, somewhere. He knows the truth, Shara. He'll tell you everything. But first, you need to help him. He must be brought back from the brink."

A fist pounds at my heart like a wild beast. Sensing it, Berengar slips over and presses himself against me in a show of support.

"What do you mean, the *brink?*"

"In order to convince you Thorne was really gone—to slow his heart enough that you were certain he'd died—I had to steal almost all the life from him. Years' worth. I've given it back, of course. But what happens when a Reaper steals that much life at once is that the mind shuts itself off, as if a switch has been flicked. Thorne is comatose—and there's only one way to help him."

My mind veers to one sentence in Thorne's letter—words I never stopped to think too hard about.

The reaper comes for us all.

He told me what had happened. He said it in plain language, and I still missed it.

"How do we do that?"

It's my father who answers. "You are going to need to borrow the gift of a powerful Mind-bender. And I can think of only one who's strong enough to wake him."

My jaw drops open. "You don't mean—"

With a nod, he says, "Ellion Graystone—unofficial king of Kravan. I believe Thorne left you a silver wrist piece—did he not? One that looks like a bracelet."

"Yes," I reply, my heart racing. "It's in my suite."

"Use it to port to the Graystone home. You need to acquire Ellion's power and use it on Thorne to bring him back—slowly and carefully."

"Ellion will kill me the second he sees me."

"He cannot control *your* mind, can he? You're the one person he has never been able to manipulate."

"How do you know..." I seal my mouth shut. There's no point in asking. As usual, he simply knows.

I remember something Tallin said then—about Ellion's lust for beautiful women. "Given that he hates me, I'll be more likely to succeed if I show up looking like someone other than myself."

"Hence the bracelet," my father says again. "Thorne knew this day was coming—which means he was prepared. Obviously, mind control is beyond the bracelet's capacity. But morphing is not. Go—take Ellion's power from him. And while you're there, Shara...put an end to his reign before it begins."

Many days ago, my father told me I should find a way to end Ellion. I had convinced myself I'd imagined those words—that he would never suggest anything so gruesome.

I try to read his expression, but as always, he is a mystery. Rivenna, on the other hand, looks hopeful, almost giddy—if Rivenna is even capable of giddiness.

"You know what you have to do," she says. "And trust me—you'll be fine, Shara. You're a badass if ever there was one."

CHAPTER
FIFTY-THREE

WITH A KISS to Thorne's brow and a promise to return to him as soon as I possibly can, I run back to the Citadel, sprinting my way through the labyrinthine corridors until I reach my quarters.

As angry and betrayed as I feel, I'm grateful that Rivenna has Thorne hidden away—clearly with my father's help. I don't know how they're keeping the knowledge from Kith, but as long as Thorne remains safe, I don't care.

When I'm back in the suite, I dig through the dresser until I find the sheathed dagger that the Lady gave me.

"What do I do, Maude?" I ask.

~You need to get to Ellion. Which means you need to become a Porter temporarily. But you also need to disguise yourself—which means taking on the powers of a Morph. I assume the bracelet can give you both those skills at once.

"Is there anything I haven't thought of?" I ask.

~Just...don't fuck this up.

"Thanks for that vote of confidence, Maude."

I slip the bracer onto my wrist, hoping that when the

time comes, it will help me achieve my goal—whatever that is.

"What do you think is going to happen at the wedding? What is the big, momentous event that's going to change Kravan?"

~I'm not certain. But I would look to the messages sprayed across the Capitol's walls for answers. The Rebellion is a lie. The heir will bring ruin on us all. The queen will save us.

"Maybe Ellion has found his queen," I mutter. "But somehow, I doubt it. Who the hell would consent to marry him?"

~Someone equally cruel, perhaps?

I change into an outfit of dark pants, knee-high leather boots and a black sweater. When I'm fully dressed and have slipped the dagger into the back of my pants, I look into the bathroom's full-length mirror and press a finger to the wolf on the bracer, picturing Rivenna's face and body.

I seal my eyes shut, willing the device to work, and a jolt of unease assaults me, as if my organs are moving around my torso.

I open my eyes to see Rivenna staring back at me, complete with the elegant scars running down her cheek. My hair has turned blond, my stature a few inches taller.

"That was...interesting," I whisper.

Once again I morph, shifting into an uninteresting-looking man in a Royal Guard uniform, then slide my finger over the arrow, willing myself to port to my old bedroom at the palace.

My borrowed body lurches uncontrollably over a great distance—the strangest sensation I've ever experienced. When the nausea settles and I find myself staring at a familiar but horrifying bedroom, I remind myself that I'm here to help Thorne. Whatever is about to unfold will be worthwhile, so long as I can wake him when all this is done.

I'm about to walk up to Ellion Graystone and pray he doesn't try to dig around enough in my mind to realize who I really am.

I slip out of the room and stride past a few other guards, who glance at me only briefly before moving on.

I know from experience that the turnover of Royal Guard is quick and frantic, and given that the king has been replaced twice in the last few months, it's no surprise that those who patrol the palace would barely raise an eyebrow when they see a new face.

I stride confidently through the palace until I reach the dining chamber, where a solitary female Guard stands at attention.

"Have you seen the—king?" I ask her, unsure whether the Royal Guard refer to Ellion by the official title.

"In there," she says, nodding to the door. "Having brunch."

"Is he alone?"

She shrugs. "Last I checked. I'm about to go off duty, honestly, so my mind's a bit addled. Been standing here for eight fucking hours."

"I can take over," I tell her. "Why don't you get some sleep?"

She nods once, asks no questions, and takes off, leaving me alone in the hallway.

When she's disappeared around the corner, I shift into Rivenna's form once again.

~*Wouldn't it be more sensible to approach Ellion as a Royal Guard?* Maude asks.

Probably, I tell her. *But I suspect Ellion will be far more intrigued by Rivenna than one of his servants.*

I turn the door's knob and let myself into the dining room, only to see Ellion sitting at the table where I used to eat breakfast with Tallin and the king.

If they could see me now, I think. *Tallin would laugh his ass off to know what I'm up to.*

"Your Grace," I say when Ellion's eyes shoot to mine.

Pushing himself to his feet, he calls out, "Who the fuck are you?"

"My name is...Marsilla," I tell him in Rivenna's sultriest tone. My hand slips to the hilt of the dagger at my back when I say, "I'm here to warn you about a conspiracy by those who live in the Capitol."

He scoffs. "I know all about the Magister's plans already," he says, eyeing me warily. "And I have no intention of allowing an election. Even now, my Royal Guard are preparing to storm the Citadel."

"That's just the thing," I say, taking a cautious step forward. I can feel him digging at my mind, trying and failing to work his way inside my thoughts. "I came to warn you about the need to move quickly. But also to let you know there are some among us in the Capitol who have been enjoying a certain amount of privilege since the king's death. Mercenaries like me, for instance."

"A mercenary," Ellion says, easing toward me, his eyes moving from my face down my body, then back to my face. He smiles, impressed. "Tell me more. What are you, exactly?"

"A Reaper," I reply.

"Fascinating," he says, admiring me a little too intently. "I never thought the day would come when I would enjoy the privilege of meeting such a woman."

~Leave it to Ellion Graystone to find himself aroused by a woman who can suck life from him like she's downing a milk-shake, Maude sneers.

I almost laugh, but manage to contain myself.

"I suppose it explains why I can't find my way into your mind," Ellion says, tilting his head. "A Mind-Bender controlling a Reaper would be too powerful a monster."

"Perhaps," I tell him with a sly smile. *This is easier than I expected. Thank God Ellion is so twisted.* "Or perhaps we could combine our power and work together, your Grace."

He slips closer still, delight igniting behind his eyes. "What is it that you're proposing, exactly?"

I lean forward and whisper, "A Pairing between two of the most powerful Tethered in Kravan. I've heard you're looking for your queen."

Ellion pulls back, staring at me in wonder. There's a split-second when I'm convinced he knows I'm lying. But instead of calling for his Guard, he smiles.

"You came here from the Capitol—no doubt through filthy tunnels—to propose to me?"

"I suppose I did."

"What a woman." He slips forward, laying a hand on my cheek and pushing his face into my neck. He inhales deeply, taking in my scent, and I wonder for a moment whether he recognizes it.

With my right hand, I reach behind my back and slowly extract the blade from its hiding place.

"Your scent," Ellion says. "It's so familiar...yet I can't quite place it."

With a forced giggle, I reply, "It's one I borrowed...from a friend."

With the last word, I move quickly, ramming the dagger into his chest and twisting the hilt as it draws the blood and power from him, all at once.

Ellion's skin goes gray, his eyes bloodshot, and he gasps horrifically as the life leaves his body.

"Some already call me *Regent Killer*," I whisper. "I suppose I may as well live up to the name."

When I back away, Ellion tumbles to the floor, landing hard on his knees then crashing face-first into hard stone. I watch, cold-hearted, as a lake of blood pools around him.

I *could* heal him.

I could save Kravan's would-be king.

But he is one of the most odious men I've ever met, and I feel nothing as I watch the life desert him. Nothing, as I look down at the blade coated in his blood—a blade that has extracted enough of it to grant me his powers long enough for me to heal Thorne.

"Thank you, Ellion," I say. "Your gift is going to save the man I love."

Sheathing the blade carefully so that I don't spill its precious contents, I slip my finger over the bracelet once more, and flee the palace for the last time.

CHAPTER FIFTY-FOUR

Leaving Ellion behind, I port to the room where Rivenna is guarding Thorne.

Some Royal Guard or other will find him eventually, and word will spread of a murder...by another Royal Guard.

One with no name and an unmemorable face.

But I don't care about any of that. Not anymore.

I leap over to Thorne's bedside, extracting the blood-stained blade from its sheath...only to see Rivenna staring at me, wide-eyed, from across the room.

"You're...*me*," she says.

Shit.

I swipe my finger over the bracelet again, pulling myself back into my own face and body.

"You really did it," she says. "You killed the would-be king."

"If you want to call him that, yes. He's dead."

"You murdered him *as me*."

"I wasn't trying to frame you, for the record," I tell her,

locking my eyes on Thorne. "I just wanted to feel what it's like to live inside your skin."

"And?"

"It's pretty awesome," I say with a smile. "You're beautiful, damn you. Ellion would absolutely have married you. To be fair, then he would probably have murdered you in your sleep or fed you to his pet ferret, or something."

"You're beautiful too, you know. And *Healer* is a nobler title than Reaper any day of the week, so you have that on me."

She moves closer, watching as I hold the dagger, tip facing the ceiling, its blade pressed flat against my chest.

"Please work," I whisper.

"How do you know what to do?"

"I'm not sure. I just...do. The Lady said this blade was made for me, so I suppose I was made for it, too."

When a surge of Ellion's mind-bending power assaults me, I feel my mind explode with Rivenna's thoughts. They collide with my own, uncontrolled and overwhelming. I drop the blade and press my hands to my temples, willing away the cacophony until I've found a way to disengage from her mind.

"Sorry," I gasp, struggling to gain control. "I didn't mean to pry."

"Doesn't matter. There's not much in there, anyhow."

She's joking, of course. Her head was reeling with hope, with expectation—and with a multitude of musings far too personal for me to delve into.

When I take a deep breath and collect myself, I press a gentle hand to Thorne's forehead. Instantly, I feel a series of delicate electrical charges sparking inside his mind. There's a quiet stirring inside him, a desire to wake—yet he's just beyond the point where he can come back without a little help.

"I don't know how much time I have to do this—how long it will take."

"Don't rush," Rivenna warns. "You don't want to mess this up. Just...do what feels right."

I press one hand to Thorne's cheek, as if I'm about to heal him. But instead, I close my eyes and call to his mind, feeling it inside my own as the delicate sparks ignite into flame inside him.

With heat spreading from my palm, I feel his mind awaken. With a shock of horror, I'm confronted with the last memory before his so-called death.

My face in the crowd, terrified. Distraught.

Heartbroken.

Thorne's words tear their way through my soul.

I will love you until my last day in this world...and beyond.

And then...

His eyes open, and a deep, desperate gasp erupts from his lungs.

I press my palms to his chest, calming his heart, which has begun to race frantically.

"Shara!" he calls out, his eyes fixed on the distance, as if he can still see me out there in the crowd somewhere.

"I'm here," I tell him, pulling his face to mine. "I'm with you. It's all right—you're back."

He focuses on my eyes, then thrusts himself upward, his arms coiling around me like the roots of a powerful tree.

"You're back," I say again, tears stinging my eyes as my

arms lock around his body. "And if you ever die again, I promise I will murder you."

He laughs against my neck, my hair, then pulls back and looks me up and down, eyeing my clothing with confusion.

"Why are you dressed like a cat burglar?"

I point to the silver bracelet, and understanding stalks into his expression. "You went to Ellion. You..."

"*I* killed him," Rivenna says, stepping forward. "Stabbed him in the chest."

"Rivenna! You don't have to—"

"It's all right," she tells me with a shrug. "I like when people think I'm a scary bitch." With a nod to us both, she adds, "I'm going to leave you two alone. But don't forget, Shara—if you stay here too long, Kith will probably find out you're not in the Citadel."

I nod thanks and watch her leave, grateful when the door seals behind her.

"You brought me back from the brink," Thorne says, kissing my hand.

"I did. And one day soon, you're going to need to explain to me why all this secrecy was necessary. Because honestly, I'm so pissed off at you right now. If I weren't so happy, I would find a way to punish the hell out of you."

~*As would I,* Maude says out loud.

"See? You've even made Maude angry."

"I'd be upset if you *weren't* enraged," Thorne chuckles. "God, I'm so sorry. I never wanted to do that to you."

"Why didn't you just tell me, Thorne? You didn't need to confess. The Magister might have let you go. He had no evidence—Kith told me—"

"Kith was lying. He's the one who killed the Magister."

I stare blankly at him, then shake my head. "No—the Magister was ill for a long time. He..."

I ask myself if I ever saw Brant with my own eyes during the period when he was allegedly under the weather. But the answer is no. I've only ever encountered him a few times, and he was in perfect health.

"Why would Kith do that?"

Thorne holds my hand tightly. "You brought me back, which means you and he are engaged." He glances down at the gold ring. "That's good."

"You just told me he killed the Magister. How the hell is it a good thing that I'm..." I stop for a moment, the realization clobbering me in the gut. "Oh, *God.* I'm engaged. We're supposed to pledge ourselves to one another, Thorne."

"Yes. And you must go through with it."

I try to pull my hand away, but he won't let me go.

"Why would you want me to marry someone else? You're here now. We can start our lives. This house—Thorne...this is *our* house. I can't possibly—"

"I know," he laughs, weaving his fingers between mine. "I love you so much, and I can't wait to start living our lives together here, in this very house. But in the meantime, you *need* to marry Kith."

"That is the absolute worst thing you've ever said to me."

I don't find any of this funny in the slightest, and I'm starting to wonder if I'm in the midst of one of Rivenna's nightmares.

"Let me explain," Thorne says. "Actually, no. It's best if Mercutio does it. Do you have him with you?"

I slip a hand into my pocket. "For a long time, he was going off on solo treks through the Citadel. You remember," I say, extracting the tiny mouse. "But lately, I've kept him by my side for comfort. He's felt like a piece of you. I don't see what part he has to play in all this, though."

"Ah," Thorne replies when I pull the mouse out and hand him over. Mercutio rises to his hind feet and fixes his shining eyes on one of us, then the other. "I programmed him to watch over you, and he's done just that. He has protected you and this realm. Inside him lie secrets that will bring a leader to his knees."

"Leader? Magister Brant is dead. So is Ellion—and Tallin is locked in a cell."

Thorne grins, looks at the mouse, then says, "Show her."

Mercutio scrambles onto the nightstand and faces the white wall next to Thorne, his dark eyes illuminating brightly. A scene projects itself against the wall, and then another, and another, each more shocking than the last.

And then, he shows us a dark, forbidding chamber—one I've only seen once in my life, in the vision that warned me Thorne would be taken by a group of men in masks.

Only, the chamber isn't in some remote corner of the Capitol or some tunnel where the Starless conceal themselves.

It lies inside the Citadel itself.

"The men who took you on that first day," I say, staring at the scene. "They weren't Starless."

"No," Thorne tells me. "They weren't. Kith wanted to put on an act—to convince you and me both that he'd heroically rescued me from a group of dangerous enemies. He wanted us thinking he was our trusted ally, that he had our best interests at heart, and that the Lady of the Starless was our foe, when the opposite was true. He staged it all in a remote wing of the Citadel—one that no one uses."

"But why would he—?"

Thorne nods toward Mercutio again, and the small mouse shows me another scene.

I see Kith speaking to my father.

Mercutio must have concealed himself in an air vent above them, because the two men are some distance below, staring at the open pages of a book. At first, the pages are unclear...

But as Mercutio's vision zooms in, I begin to piece together exactly what it is they're looking at. And for the first time, I understand why all this has happened—why fate has led us to this exact moment. I understand that the future of our entire realm lies in my hands, and my hands alone.

All of a sudden, I can't wait to pledge my undying loyalty to a man that I have come to despise.

A man who has made the greatest mistake of his life by asking me, of all people, to be his wife.

CHAPTER

FIFTY-FIVE

SPENDING the night in my quarters feels like a whole new kind of torture. Thorne is alive—yet after all this time, I am separated from him again.

Part of me wants to be angry at him, but I simply can't find it in myself to waste needless emotion. My relief at finding him alive is so great that it's almost inconceivable that I could feel anything but happiness and love.

Besides, now that I've seen what I have and I understand the gravity of what I must do, there's no room for anger.

I only hope that, when the time comes, I'm able to do it.

MY FATHER COMES to see me first thing in the morning. When I open the door, he tells me simply, "I came to let you know the Pairing is happening today."

"Today?" Shock jolts my heart into a wild sprint.

With a knowing smirk, he replies, "Word has gotten out that Ellion was found dead in his dining chamber. Some

Royal Guard, out for revenge, apparently. The bizarre thing is that no one knows who he is—nor can they find any trace of him."

"How strange."

"Truly odd." He steps into the room and walks over to the small dresser, picking up the silver bracelet Thorne gave me. "Do you know—there's a reason we haven't called an election in all this time. A reason we never simply murdered King Tomas and took power."

"He was surrounded by Royal Guard. I always assumed that was why."

"That was part of it." He pivots to lock eyes with me. "Another is a rule that King Julian Quinton put in place long ago. A rule that I only uncovered recently—but one that protected Tomas."

"Which was?"

"Only a monarch can abolish the monarchy." He doesn't give me time to process the meaning behind those words before adding, "Now, get ready, Shara. We have a wedding to attend."

I open the closet and extract the golden gown that has been such a cause of torment for me over the last months. More than once, I've considered taking a blade to it, shredding it into ribbons.

Now, I'm glad I didn't.

~It wouldn't do to get married naked, Maude tells me. *Though I suspect Kith would enjoy it.*

I shudder with disgust at the thought. *Kith will never, ever see me naked. I promise you that.*

Something occurs to me, and I turn back to my father.

"Thorne," I say. "He doesn't know the Pairing is taking place today, does he?"

He reads my expression. "Everything is looked after. You know what you have to do, don't you?"

I nod, chewing my lip apprehensively. "Yes. I do."

My father steps over and cups my face in his hands. "Shara—everything that needs to happen will happen. I've seen it all, thanks to the Lady. But I want to tell you now..." He clears his throat and pulls away, turning his eyes to the opposite wall, as if this is difficult for him. "I want to say how proud I am of you. I know you've been through hell. Believe it or not, I have some idea how that feels."

I want to tell him he can't know—that he's never lost someone he loves. But we both know that's not true.

"I've never broken my promise to you," I say. "I've never told Thorne about my sister—that she's alive. But I know how hard it was for you to send her away. To protect her. I know it was a terrible loss."

"For many years," he says with a nod, "I've lived a life of lies I never wished to tell. I've gone without Soleia. Without you—all because of the tyrannical bastards ruling this realm. I have made sacrifices, and it has been a lonely existence. I may seem hard-edged and cold, but trust me when I say it's nothing more than a shield I hold before me to fight off emotion, because feeling too deeply would inevitably have led me to ruin."

With a deep sigh, he turns back to look me in the eye. "I put you in a position that I know was unforgivable. Believe it or not, I couldn't bear to see you hurt. It's why I couldn't come check in on you each day. I would have broken down and revealed the truth to you—and when Kith proposed, he would have felt it in your heart."

He nods down to the gold ring on my finger.

"Now, thanks to that ring and his, he can't back out of the Pairing, and neither can you. The realm is saved—provided today plays out as it's supposed to. I just hope that one day, you can forgive me for allowing you to be so deeply hurt for so long."

It feels like the first time my father has ever admitted he has a heart, and tears sting my eyes as he speaks. I want to forgive him—I do. But the hurt is still raw. It's still there. I was in hell, and he could have pulled me out.

No amount of understanding can take that pain from me.

But time might help me to heal. If I can forgive Rivenna, then I can find it in my heart to forgive him, too.

I'm about to tell him so when the door opens and Joy enters.

"I'm really sorry, but it's time. Shara, you need to get dressed."

An hour later, I find myself standing on the sprawling lawn outside the Tower for the first time since the day of the hanging.

The enormous tree that shaded the gallows now lords over a small arbor covered in white roses. As I look around at a series of newly planted gardens, I know this is the very spot I saw in Kith's vision of the future. The place where we will pledge ourselves to one another.

Chilly though the day is, I don't feel the bite of cold nipping at my bare skin. All I feel is energized. Nervous. Happy. Excited. It's as though a part of me has woken that I thought had died...and I suppose that's exactly what happened.

A few guests mill about, most of whom I don't know. I spot Terrence, the unpleasant man I met on my first day in the Citadel. Joy is here, as well as a few guards.

One of them is a tall, blond man I've never seen before. His jaw is chiseled, his shoulders broad. His presence is formidable, and I find myself wondering where the hell he came from.

Rivenna steps over to me with Berengar by her side, looks me up and down, and says, "That's a beautiful dress. You look incredible."

"Thank you," I tell her, my eyes darting left and right. "I wish I could see Thorne," I whisper. "I'm not sure I can do this without him."

"Don't worry," she replies. "He'll be here. You can sense him close by, can't you?"

She's right. I can feel his heart beating next to mine for the first time in far too long.

"I can," I say.

"You'll need courage today. But whatever happens—I'm in your corner. I won't let this end badly."

I nod, distracted by a flurry of movement behind her.

"What the hell?" I mutter, watching as row upon row of uniformed guards line up near the Tower's doors. "What are they doing here?"

"Kith wanted to make a show of strength," Rivenna says with a roll of her eyes. "Ironically, *those* are Thorne's trainees.

The ones with the bracers. They wouldn't be here, all disciplined and organized, if it weren't for Thorne."

I glance over to see that, sure enough, each of them has a silver device secured around their wrist. Each bracer is programmed with a power that Thorne chose for its particular trainee.

Fear creeps along my flesh to know how easily any one of those fighters could kill me, if their leader commanded it.

Joy, who's wearing a pretty blue dress, steps over to us and smiles. "My mother says to wish you all the best today, Shara. She says not to worry—that all will go exactly as it should."

"Thank you, I think," I reply, glancing warily at Rivenna. I'm not sure whether she knows yet that the Lady is Joy's mother. If not, I'm sure she's piecing it together as we speak.

"It's all right," Riv tells me. "Joy's filled me in on everything. And yes, I feel like an absolute ass."

"What do you mean?"

She looks irritated with herself when she moans, "I bought into all the Starless lies. All the bullshit. I may be old and wise, but I still thought the Lady was some harpy who feasted on the blood of children, or worse. I had no idea who she really was—that she and your father..."

My eyes go wide as Joy elbows Rivenna in the ribs. "Oh, shit," Rivenna snorts. "I'm sorry. I thought you already knew."

I glance over at my father, who's standing some distance away, arms crossed, talking to Terrence and Kith.

"My father and Joy's mother..." I say under my breath. "Really?"

Then again, he *did* once tell me he had feelings for someone other than my mother.

"They've been conspiring together for years," Joy says with a quiet chuckle. "Ever since the implant system started being used to hurt Starless. I suppose it's natural that they fell in love. Some say they're tethered mates."

Tempting though it is to pry deeper into the subject, I shake off the urge and say, "I brought it, you know. Your mother's gift. It's hidden—but it's here, in case I need it."

Joy nods. "I know."

"I'm going to show everyone the truth." I hold up the little gold clutch I've been carrying, to reveal Mercutio's head peeking out. I whisper a few words to him and he leaps down, scampering off to do the job I've assigned him.

"Are you sure you're okay with this?" Rivenna asks. "You have to say *I do,* you realize. This is for real."

"I know, and I'd be lying to say it doesn't feel like I'm betraying Thorne. But to be fair, he *did* fake his own death and let me suffer the agony of the damned for two fucking months, so I'd say we're even."

"Fair enough."

With a nod to someone behind me, Rivenna steps away to stand next to the oak tree with Berengar.

"Shara."

My eyes seal against the voice calling my name, but I manage to turn around with a smile on my lips to greet my fiancé.

"Kith."

"My God, you look beautiful," he tells me, pressing in for a kiss, but I shake my head.

"Not until we're pledged to one another," I tell him with

a sly grin, avoiding physical contact for fear that one touch from him will be enough to reveal every lie swarming through my mind.

He can't read your thoughts, I remind myself. *Only your emotions.*

He laughs. "I can accept that—but only because the ceremony is about to start, so it won't be long now." Nodding toward the tree, he draws my gaze to my father, who is standing under a large, sprawling limb, holding a leather-bound book in his hands. "He's officiating, you know."

"Really?" I ask, wondering why my father never told me as much. Knowing he'll be so close by offers me a renewed dose of courage, and I manage a broad smile. "Then I think we should get on with it."

Kith lets out a laugh—one that I would have found charming a few months ago. But now, it rings hollow, bordering on cold.

"I don't know what's changed," he says, "but my heart is full to see joy in your eyes again."

What heart might that be? The one that allows you to kill without mercy and steal powers from so many? The one that told you to propose to a woman who was grieving the love of her life?

The one that is about to betray this realm for your own selfish reasons?

"Oh, there's definitely joy," I say, slipping a hand onto his cheek to prove it. There's no lie in my words. I *am* genuinely happy—because what I'm about to do will destroy him.

Today, Kravan will be freed from its shackles...and Kith will be brought to his knees.

CHAPTER FIFTY-SIX

THERE ARE NO FLOWER GIRLS. No musicians. No pomp and circumstance.

Kith and I simply make our way over to my father as the small crowd gathers around us. The guards are still amassed twenty or so feet away, the Magister's mark prominent on the left side of their chests.

I glance over at Rivenna, who's standing with Joy and Berengar, their expressions muted.

There is tension behind her black eyes—a focus to the set of her jaw that almost frightens me.

Joy, on the other hand, looks perfectly at peace, as if she's attending a pleasant garden party.

A few feet behind Kith stands the tall, blond guard I spotted earlier.

"Who is that man?" I whisper, nodding toward him. "I've never seen him."

"Calv, you mean? He's my secret weapon," Kith tells me with a wink. "He's the Stealther who has brought us so much information over the years from the palace and elsewhere. He keeps a low profile, as you can imagine."

Which means that, at any given moment, he could have watched me conspiring with my father. With Rivenna.

Oh, shit.

A heavy stone settles in my gut.

He could know about Thorne.

My heart slams staccato beats against my ribcage as fear tears at me, but I force the feeling away and smile, hoping my act will be sufficient to convince Kith I'm not going into a full-on panic.

I turn my attention to my father, who offers up a slight shake of his head, signaling me not to give myself away.

"Are you both ready?" he asks. "If so, we'll begin."

The truth is, I'm *not* anymore. I want to run to the house—*our* house—and make sure Thorne is all right. Fear is gestating inside me, a cruel, cloying voice insisting that something terrible is about to happen.

But even as I contemplate sprinting away from this place, I feel the powerful pulse of Thorne's heart beating in synchronicity with mine. I look around, searching the grounds for him, but I see no sign of him.

Still, he *must* be close, as Rivenna said. He'll be here when the time is right.

With a deep breath, I nod to my father. "I'm ready."

"As am I," Kith says, taking my hands in his.

I lift my chin to look into his eyes, wondering if he can feel the quiet fear lingering inside me.

~*Shara,* Maude whispers.

Yes?

~*Good luck. Don't do anything stupid on your special day.*

Thanks, Maude. You're a gem.

My father clears his throat and speaks loudly enough for the crowd to hear.

"Let the Pairing ceremony begin."

I look into Kith's eyes, fighting back thoughts of Thorne, of the life I had always dreamed of.

A few minutes, I tell myself. *That's all it will take, and then, it'll all be over.*

"You, Kith," my father says, "and you, Shara, are each invited now to pledge yourselves to one another. The rings you wear on your fingers already bind you, but it is the words you speak today that will create an everlasting Pairing—one that can only be broken by death. Any possessions, property, or titles will be shared. In the event that one of you should die, the other will retain all responsibilities, titles, and possessions of the other. Is that understood?"

"Yes," Kith and I both reply. "It is."

"Kith," my father says. "I believe there is something you wish to share with my daughter and everyone present. Is that right?"

"It is."

"Then you have my blessing to do so."

My father hands him the leather-bound tome he's been holding and Kith takes it in hand, positioning it between us.

"Shara," he says. "When I was a child living on the Capitol's streets, an old woman gave me this book, its pages stained and torn. She told me it was the only one of its kind—a secret history meant for my eyes only. I was to hold onto it, and to keep its contents to myself until the day of my Pairing came near. I showed it to your father some time ago, when I was seeking his approval to propose to you. And now, here before everyone else, I wish to show it to you at long last."

He hands me the book. "Open it to the first page."

I do as he asks, only to see a drawing of a tree with sprawling limbs like those of the oak that shades us now. Names of various people are scrawled on its multitude of branches.

I feign surprise as my eyes land on the same image I saw in the projection Mercutio revealed to me yesterday. It seems the mouse's adventures in the Citadel were about more than mere curiosity. The little mouse was gathering evidence.

And it's only now, because of him, that I've come to understand the extraordinary intricacy of my fate.

There is a reason I met Thorne in the Tower and that he steered me toward a position in the Verdan house. There, he gifted me an electronic mouse, custom-designed to protect me, to watch for threats—and ultimately, to help me to save our land.

As terrible as it was to endure, there is even a reason my heart needed to break.

And now, I stare down at the drawing, smiling to myself at the absurdity of it all.

Scrawled at the tree's peak is a name I learned the day I met the Storian.

A name few now living have ever heard.

CHAPTER FIFTY-SEVEN

I LEARNED about family trees from a book in the Tower.

Usually, they consist of a series of leafless branches reaching out from a tree's trunk, each accented by names of people descended from one common ancestor.

None of us had families, of course—and none of us was ever meant to know our parents, our surnames, or anything else about ourselves.

The tree Kith is showing me has nothing to do with my own ancestry. My father's surname will forever remain a mystery to me. But soon—very soon—I will take on the name of the greatest traitor this realm has ever known.

Mercutio showed me a great deal of evidence yesterday. Conspiracies. Lies. Treachery. Cruelty.

Thanks to the little mouse, I learned at last what kind of man Kith is—and how deep his lies go.

But it is the image in the leather-bound book that tells me why it was so important for me to accept his proposal.

I scan the names on the page, taking each in.

At the top, I see:

Julian Quinton,
First King of Kravan.

His wife, Georgiana, is listed next to him.

Their children and grandchildren, and so on...all the way down to one solitary name at the bottom.

Beckwith Quinton.

"Beckwith," I read out loud.

Kith nods. "When I was young, I couldn't pronounce it properly. I called myself Beh-kith."

He chuckles as if he's recounting some cute little story instead of revealing a lifetime of lies. "Over time, it just became..."

"*Kith*," I say, struggling to keep my voice steady as I strain my lips into a grin. "You are Beckwith Quinton. Which means..."

I pause, fixing my eyes on his.

Say it.

Now.

I want to hear it from his lips.

I want the truth. All of it.

"I'm Quinton's only living heir. I am rightful king of this land."

He turns to the gathered guests and announces, "Julian Quinton was the first king of Kravan—the man who established the throne and built the palace. He was a great leader, though he made some terrible choices. But I intend to right his wrongs."

I smile and tilt my head, my brow furrowing as I play the role of confused wife-to-be. "But...when you said you were considering leadership, I assumed you were running for president."

"I can do far more from the throne than I could ever do with the constraints of an elected figure," he laughs. "In a few minutes, thanks to you, I will be the new king."

He takes the book from me and hands it back to my father.

Rage simmers inside me, threatening to erupt—but I swallow it down.

Soon, I think. *Patience. I only need to last a few minutes, until the vows have been exchanged.*

All emotions are banished from my heart—except for those associated with a future in which Kravan is freed at last from men like Kith.

"You will be my queen," he tells me, as if it should be the greatest news I've ever received. "Ellion Graystone is dead, Shara. There is no one to stand in our way. No one to challenge us. We are free to mold this land in any way we choose, with Ellion gone and Tallin unseated."

"And, of course, the Magister is dead," I say, pulling my hands away and forcing a smile onto my lips. "Isn't he?"

"Yes," Kith says, bowing his head in mock-grief. "Such a shame about Brant. He would have made an excellent advisor."

"I am heir to the first king!" he cries, inspiring a swell of confused murmurs from guests and guards alike. "Kravan is about to see a new dawn at long last!"

On cue, the soldiers in their rows reach for the Magister's symbols on their chests and tear them off, throwing them to the ground. In their place appears a golden crown—a symbol I've seen once before...branded into the flesh of the Starless woman who was held prisoner in the Citadel before being hanged for her allegiances.

"As of today, you are officially named King's Guard," Kith calls to his loyal soldiers. "You have a new leader to protect!"

The guards nod in unison, and bile rises in my throat.

The large blond guard behind Kith—the Stealther—looks uneasy for a moment, then raises his chin in solidarity.

At Rivenna's side, Berengar stiffens, but she lays a hand on his head, warning him to stay quiet.

I came here today with confidence in my heart that I would know how to react when the time came—that I knew exactly what I needed to do.

But now that it's happening, my confidence has begun to wane.

"There is a law," my father announces, "put in place recently by King Tallin, during his short reign—that no man may be named king unless he first takes a wife. He felt that a king and queen on Kravan's throne would bring more stability to the realm than a king alone."

My eyes move to Kith's smiling features. *Which is why you wanted to marry me.*

My father looks around at the guards and the guests, and then his gaze lands on me.

"By pledging yourself to Kith, Shara, you will be crowned queen on this day. You will share your husband's power as an equal, according to the new law." He pauses briefly, then quietly adds, "And in the event that he should die, you will be the sole reigning monarch in all of Kravan."

In my father's words are clear instructions.

My eyes move to Joy's as I try to assess whether she knew this was about to happen. *You've known all along, haven't you?*

She smiles and silently mouths two sentences.

The heir will bring ruin on us all.

But the queen...will save us.

My father lets out a quiet cough then continues. "Since you have already exchanged rings, it is time for you to pledge your loyalty to one another."

I stiffen, nodding once, my mind reeling. My eyes dart over to the guards, the gold crown of the King's Guard gleaming on their chests. My gaze shifts to the Tower, looming dark and gruesome above us, its windowless exterior like a vile skin concealing innumerable innocent children stolen from their parents by cruel monsters.

"What will happen to them?" I ask softly.

~*Now is not the time,* Maude warns. *Shara—you're so close. Just wait.*

Kith pulls his eyes to the Tower, then smiles. "You'll see soon, my love."

I nod and force another smile despite the horror churning inside me. He must feel it. He must know.

~*He also feels your hope,* Maude insists. *And, given his arrogance, he's probably convinced it has something to do with his coming reign.*

"Kith," my father says while I struggle to keep from hyperventilating, "do you declare before everyone present that you dedicate yourself to Shara for all your life, vowing to be true to her, to protect her, and to share your possessions, titles, and life with her?"

"I do." Kith's voice is giddy, and I have to fight back the urge to run from him as fast as my legs will carry me.

My father asks me the same question. "Shara, do you declare before everyone present that you dedicate yourself to

Kith for all your life, vowing to be true to him, to protect him, and to share your possessions, titles, and life with him?"

I take a deep breath, seeking out Thorne's powerful heartbeat.

I can't. I won't. I...

But when I feel it again, hammering alongside mine, I swallow hard, nod, and say, "I do."

Easily the two most terrifying words I've ever uttered.

My father pulls his eyes to the blond guard. "It's time," he says. "The crowns, if you please."

The guard moves to a square table set up in the shade of the oak tree. A black cloth is draped over the table, and he removes it to reveal two elegant golden crowns. He picks both of them up and brings them over, handing the smaller one to my father.

The Shadow turns to me. "Shara, with your pledge, I declare you bound with Kith—which means you are now his queen. You hold in your hands the fate of a realm, Queen Shara of Kravan."

He lays the crown on my head and I force myself to hold onto the cruel smile on my lips, the muscles in my face twitching in retaliation.

I want to scream. To run. Anything but stare lovingly at the man I thought was my friend—a man who has betrayed our realm just as his ancestor did.

"Kith," my father says, taking the other crown in hand. "You have taken a wife. As heir to King Julian Quinton, you are now king of this realm. *Long live King Beckwith Quinton.*"

Speaking the words softly, he lays the crown on Kith's head.

I'm convinced I hear strain in my father's voice when he

says, "You have pledged yourselves to one another. You wear Kravan's golden crowns. And now that your bond is official, your Grace—you may kiss your bride."

Kith steps forward, cupping my face in his hands. He presses his lips to mine...

Then pulls back with a violent jerk of his head, as though my touch has stung him. And then, I see it—a deep, wretched understanding sinking into his soul like a rock in a deep sea.

~*He knows,* Maude whispers.

Yes. He does. But it's too late. I am queen now.

"Shara," Kith breathes.

"I believe you're supposed to call me *your Grace.*"

He presses a hand to my cheek, absorbing the cocktail of emotions swirling inside me.

Rage. Joy. Hatred. Disgust. Bliss.

"I do love you," he says, his voice coarse like it's been dragged over jagged stone. "You may not believe it, but I do. I want to spend my life with you."

"Oh, I believe you," I tell him, raising my chin alongside my own voice. "And because you love me, I know you won't lie to me when I ask you a question that's been eating away at me for a long time now."

Kith turns to the guests, laughing awkwardly when he sees the baffled looks on their faces. "What question is that, my darling wife?"

I raise my chin, rage-fueled flames scalding my heart. "Why the fuck did you bomb Magister's Row?"

CHAPTER FIFTY-EIGHT

Kith's brow crumples like a linen shirt.

He lets out a too-loud laugh, clearly intended to win over the crowd after my hilarious joke.

"You know who was responsible for the bombing. Thorne *confessed,* my love. He was hanged for the crime—or have you forgotten?"

"And the Magister?" I ask, venom seeping through the words. "What about him?"

Kith turns to my father, commanding him with a silent look to keep his daughter in check.

"The Magister was ill," Kith insists. "Everyone knew it."

"I see." I step away from him, turning to face the Tower and the small force of dangerous fighters gathered before its doors. "I'm not sure everyone *else* knows the truth, however."

On cue, a projection appears on the Tower's outer wall, large and bright enough to be seen from a mile away, even in the light of day. I don't know how Mercutio is managing it—only that Thorne said he would know what to do when the time came to reveal the truth to the world.

"I'm not the only one who can harness the power of electronic devices," he told me with a smile.

Kith's face fills the screen, then the image pulls back to reveal him standing over the Magister, a hand pressed to Brant's chest. He draws back, leaving a gaping hole behind—the same power he used to kill the Starless the day we went to see the Bonesmith.

"What is this?" Kith asks, frantic as he stares at the Tower, then looks around, seeking out the source of the projection. "Who is responsible for this bullshit?"

Another scene crops up of Kith speaking to a man in uniform—one I know as a drone controller inside the Citadel. Kith's recorded voice blasts through a series of speakers surrounding the Tower. "Take down as many civilians as you can. I'll reward you with a suite in the palace when the time comes."

More scenes flash by, each more incriminating than the last. Kith, killing innocent Tethered in the city. Conspiring with others to murder and extract powers for his own use.

Telling Thorne that if he doesn't confess, Kith will kill me.

The final projection shows Kith giving an order to his new army. "You will empty the Tower of the oldest of the Tethered who are being held there. But first, I will assess them and strip the powers from any Elites. As thanks for your loyalty, I will grant those powers to a lucky few of you."

What Kith is proposing is monstrous.

Worse, even, than what's been done to every Tower Orphan ever imprisoned.

As awful as our lives were inside the Tower, no one ever

threatened to tear out the one piece of us that gave us strength and made us whole.

The projections start over, cycling through in a grim montage. By now, the Capitol's residents—Normals and Tethered alike—have begun to gather around the Tower, their eyes cast on the images flickering over its dark surface.

"What is this shit?" Kith hisses, grabbing my arm. "Where the fuck did you get this footage?"

"A little friend gave it to me," I say with a smile, "and a hundred more scenes just like these. It seems you've been busy." I nod toward the growing crowd of spectators. "I thought they should know who you really are...*Beckwith*. Murders of countless innocent people on the streets, including the bombing of four Starless who came to talk to Thorne and me. Forced branding with your vile crown."

His jaw grinds so violently that I can almost hear it. He has no defense. No excuse to make.

This has been his plan for years—to work his way up in the ranks and form alliances with the Magister and my father.

Marrying the Shadow's eldest daughter is the final touch for his plan to become the most powerful man in Kravan.

"They call you the Hunter now, don't they?" I snarl. "*That's* what the woman in the cell meant when she told me who had scalded a crown into her flesh. You hunt them for their powers and hoard those gifts for yourself. You're nothing but a glorified serial killer."

"If we didn't have so many witnesses, I swear to God," Kith growls under his breath. "I would tear you to pieces here and now."

I laugh. "You already killed me, Kith—when you ordered Thorne hanged."

"*That* was the Magister's doing."

"Oh, come on." I nod toward the Tower. The projections are still cycling, Kith's sins still being transmitted to thousands of people. "The Magister had been dead for days before the hanging occurred. You're a fucking liar. You wanted him gone, all because a Seer showed you your fate long ago. You never wanted me, Kith. You never gave a shit about me—you just wanted to become an official tyrant, like all the rest of them—and the only way to do it was to take a wife."

He lets me go and backs away, and in his eyes I see fire raging as he contemplates his next move. "I'm still the fucking king," he growls, gesturing to the Tower. "Whether I did those things or not. I am immune from prosecution. It doesn't matter that I'm a killer—*every* fucking king is a killer."

He looks like he's about to spew more lies.

But instead, he says, "The Tethered may be powerful, but we're also vicious animals. I seek only to keep our kind in check. As their king—as the heir of the *first* of Kravan's kings—it is my right to decide how our society should run."

"And what of the Normals who don't want powers forced upon them?" I spit.

Before he can help himself, Kith's eyes veer to the Tower again.

"It's all right," I tell him. "I already know you intend to imprison them—but not forever."

"No, not forever."

The voice is my father's. He steps up beside me, staring Kith down.

"He intends to kill them."

"There are too many of them," Kith protests. "Too many Starless. Too many naysayers who want me dead. As king, I will punish those who don't support me—just as anyone would."

"*King,*" my father scoffs. "You're no more king than a certain mouse I know."

"I am Quinton's heir!" Kith shrieks, the crown juddering on his head and threatening to crash to the ground.

"You are nothing more than the descendant of a traitor. A liar, who pretended for years to support a president in the making, and then murdered him. You're a fraud, Kith. But you have given Kravan one gift that it will cherish, I promise you. You *have* saved this realm."

Kith snarls, "What gift is that, exactly?"

My father lays a hand on my shoulder. "You have given us a queen. You wed her—and now she holds every power that you do. For that, we thank you."

A grim understanding settles on Kith's features. I watch him rifling through his vast catalog of powers, searching for the one he'll use to end me.

"I believed you cared for me," he snarls, raising a hand into the air. "I truly did."

"Well, as someone once told me, I'm a decent liar," I say, offering up a smile in Rivenna's direction. "I care for Kravan. I have wanted this realm healed ever since I was a child. I want to reopen shipping channels and communicate with other lands. I want to empty the Tower of every person trapped within its walls and burn it to the ground. But most of all," I sneer, my eyes locking on the blond behemoth hovering over Kith, "I want my tethered mate back."

"Calvar," Kith says, addressing the Stealther.

It's only a moment ago that I noticed the giant of a man is wearing one of Thorne's silver bracers—which means he has more than his own power at his disposal.

The question is, what else can he do?

"Take her to the cells," Kith sneers. "Clamp a cilice tightly onto her arm. I'll decide later what punishment she deserves for this."

The large, blond guard takes a step toward me, reaching a hand out to grab me by the throat. He pulls me close, a snarl crawling its way over his lips.

When his face is a mere inch from mine, he whispers, "Hi, Beautiful."

"I was hoping that was you," I whisper back. "Hi."

He sets me down gently, then turns back to Kith, who's suddenly frozen in place.

His eyes have turned wild, panicked. He attempts to speak, but at first, the sound is nothing more than a wretched choke.

Every guard in his small army is also frozen in place—statues, as hard and stiff as stone.

The blond man slips a finger over the bracer on his wrist, his face altering instantly.

He runs a hand through his hair, his eyes landing on my father's.

"A wise man once said that a skilled Courser can control minds as well as a Bender can. He said taking control of electrical impulses in the brain is enough to take hold of someone's entire body."

He shifts his gaze to Kith, whose terror has deepened now, the whites of his eyes prominent as his crown slides comically sideways.

"I've been working on the skill for weeks," Thorne adds. "In my training sessions with your little soldiers. Here and there, I would cause someone's arm to jerk sideways, or a leg to give out under him. Nothing serious—just enough to know I could do it. Eventually, I learned to paralyze them temporarily. That always freaked them out a little—but I always let them go after a few seconds. I *also* learned to disable every one of their bracers at once. Which means you now have an army of useless duds at your disposal, *King*."

When Thorne extends a hand toward the fighters, their bracers drop to the ground. The army remains frozen in place, still helpless.

I raise my chin and step toward the men in uniform.

"You're all free," I tell them. "Free to live, to love, to work. To do anything you like except serve any monarch, ever again. I intend to abolish the monarchy. Once and for all."

Thorne releases the men from his power while maintaining his grip on Kith's mind. The soldiers gasp and double over, inhaling deep breaths as they reach for their throats.

I gesture with my hand, and the projections on the Tower's wall cease at last.

"I hereby call for an election in Kravan!" I call out to the masses of people now gathered around us. "Every individual—Tethered or Normal—will be entitled to an equal vote. No more will kings, or queens, or Nobles, be allowed to tear this realm apart and mine it for their own purposes. No more will Tethered be imprisoned in the Tower. Every child locked up in that wretched structure is free, as of today. Every warden and fight trainer will be granted a trial in criminal court. And every single person who has enabled this cruel system will be tried alongside them."

The Capitol's citizens move closer, listening intently. Among the crowd, I spot a few Starless stepping forward.

As I speak, they pull the gray masks from their faces, raising them into the air then dropping them to the ground.

"There will be no more bombings," I call. "All drones will be stripped of weapons. This city will be rebuilt—and if anyone *ever* tries claiming the throne again, they will suffer for it. Nobles in the Isles who have mistreated or murdered their Tethered servants will pay for their crimes—but those who have been kind will be given a chance at freedom. However, they will live by the same set of rules as all of you."

A shout of "The queen will save us!" erupts from somewhere in the crowd, but I raise a hand to quiet it.

"I am no queen!" I shout. "I'm just one of you. I always have been. Kravan belongs to its people!"

As my words echo off the Tower, a gut-wrenching scream tears at the air.

All of a sudden, a set of powerful hands is throwing me hard to the ground.

The air bursts from my lungs, my head spinning. I twist around, gasping for breath, to see Kith leaping at me, frantic—a wild animal seeking to kill his prey. He has fought off Thorne's power—shaken off the control my tethered mate was exerting over him.

Kith thrusts a hand toward my chest and heat rages inside me—a gruesome pyre bursting to life and singeing my heart, vicious and inexorable. At first, I'm convinced I'm burning from the inside out.

But when I begin to feel a part of me tear itself away like flesh from bone, the ghastly truth comes to me.

He's taking my gifts.

He's robbing me of the ability to heal myself.

He's killing me.

And then Thorne is on him, pulling him off me and hurling him aside with a feral brutality I've never seen in anyone—not even Tallin in the depths of his darkest rage.

Kith goes flying, slamming into the ground several feet from where Thorne stands. He rises to his feet and storms back toward me, his eyes twisting with untold power.

But Thorne, too, is powerful. He twists through the air with the speed of the fastest Velor, but Kith only matches his speed.

It's impossible at first to decipher whose limbs are tearing at whom—to see who's winning this horrible match, and who is losing. Cries rip through the air, echoing off the Tower's broad walls. Blood splashes the ground and snarls claw at my soul.

My father's hands are on me then, protective and strong. Berengar stands by, not wanting to unleash an attack until he's certain his teeth will sink into his enemy and not Thorne.

The distant crowd gasps with horror as they watch the fight between their new traitor of a king and a man willing to die to stop him killing his queen.

And then, Kith is on me again, shoving my father brutally backward and hurling me to the ground for the second time.

"I am the fucking *king*!" he snarls, ramming his hand at my chest. "I will rule alone if I must—but I will rule!"

But just as the agonizing heat rises inside me again, Kith

stiffens and staggers away, one arm twisting unnaturally at his side. It bends horrifically backward, the sound of snapping bone attacking the air.

With a scream, Kith crashes to his knees.

Behind him, Rivenna and Thorne stand side by side, their eyes locked on the king. Thorne's arm and chest are bloody—but I'm not certain it's his own blood.

Kith's other arm bends horribly—another manipulation of his mind by Thorne—then his skin goes ghastly white.

The swirling color in his irises slows as a hideous gasp hangs in the air between us.

Silently, Rivenna has unleashed the full extent of her powers, drawing life painfully and methodically from the Blade—and for all Kith's arsenal of powers, he is helpless against the might of the Reaper.

"Rivenna!" I cry. "Stop! We'll imprison him—we'll put him on trial!"

"While he lives, he's still king. We all know that's too much power for any asshole to have."

She strides forward to wrap a fist tightly around Kith's throat, and he stares at her, helpless.

"I trusted this asshole," Rivenna growls. "I let him get close to you—and he nearly broke you, Shara."

I step toward her, reaching a hand out. "It's all right, Riv. It's over now. You can let him go."

"No!" she says with a wild shake of her blond hair, black eyes fixed on Kith as her grip tightens. "It's not over."

A strange, terrible wail emerges from Kith's chest as she stares him down. The crowd is silent now, their eyes locked on a king who has been brought down within minutes of his coronation.

"Rivenna! Stop!" I shout, grabbing her shoulders and trying to yank her away. But Thorne takes hold of my arms, pulling me back.

My father looks on, his chin high, cold satisfaction in his eyes—as if he foresaw this exact moment.

"While Kith lives, he rules," Thorne whispers. "Even from a cell. Rivenna is right. He is too powerful—and no trial will keep him in check. A king can override all laws in this land. While he lives, there is no prison that can hold him."

I watch in horror as Kith's skin turns translucent, his eyes going gray-white as Rivenna extracts the life from him, minute by minute, second by second. He withers and cracks like a leaf robbed of all moisture, and at last, he tumbles to his knees and lands hard, his legs crumpling beneath him.

"I've had it with kings." Rivenna says, wiping the sweat from her brow and turning to me. She steps over, takes my hand, and raises it into the air, shouting, *"Long live the fucking queen!"*

CHAPTER
FIFTY-NINE

One Month Later

Over the weeks, the memory of the Pairing ceremony fades into little more than a distant, hazy dream.

As I promised, the Tower emptied of Tethered that day. Every single Tower Orphan was reunited with their parents. Every Tethered Domestic and Guard was freed from servitude in the Isles.

Everyone else—wardens, fight trainers, and administrators—was driven out of the Tower within a week by Thorne, Rivenna, Berengar, and a number of Starless who offered to use their powers to ensure that no guilty party escaped potential prosecution.

Now, a month later, I am still queen—*officially* speaking. But I have no intention of holding onto the title any longer than I have to. I told our people I would abdicate and abolish the monarchy the second an election date had been named, and I intend to hold to that promise.

As queen, I have issued only a few orders.

One of the last of them was that the Tower be razed to the ground within a week of its emptying.

"The land where the Tower stood will be a vast public garden," I decreed in a public announcement broadcast to the Capitol's population via the now-disarmed drones that fly over the city on rare occasions. "At its center will be a monument in tribute to those who suffered between its walls for generations. We must never forget what was done to our people—and we must ensure it never happens again."

I leave it to Kravan's future leaders to keep that promise.

It's on a cold, late autumn day that snow begins to fall—the first snow I've ever seen.

I absorb the astonishing peacefulness of the silent flakes as they dance lazily to the ground. Every branch of every tree, every roof and sidewalk is coated in a soft, white blanket, and I watch from under a set of blankets on the porch of our small dream house.

Our little house is not exactly the domicile anyone ever pictured for a monarch. But as far as I'm concerned, it's the greatest palace that ever was.

Thorne brings me a cup of hot chocolate and hands it to me, a scarf wrapped around his neck.

"Seven marshmallows," he tells me. "A beverage fit for a—"

"Don't say it," I laugh. "Please. I beg of you."

He takes a seat next to me on the porch swing, and I rest my head on his shoulder.

We have no Royal Guard. No servants. We do, however, have a good deal of money left to us by a certain descendant of a king who was my husband for all of fifteen minutes one day. The Pairing ensured that his fortune became legally mine, and by extension, Thorne's.

I've considered using it to purchase a shop on Magister's Row and work there, selling handmade, cozy wares. But I suspect some of the money will go to another use—depending on what my father and the Lady say to us today.

"They'll be here soon," Thorne tells me, taking a sip of his hot chocolate. "What do you suppose the verdict will be?"

"Impossible to know. But I can't imagine she'll throw a death sentence at us."

Thorne shrugs. "No. Probably not. Then again, you can override anything she suggests—so..."

"I know. I still want to see what she's intending. We both know the Lady never makes plans without good reason."

"As long as neither of us has to die," Thorne chuckles, and I offer up a playful glare.

"Don't even joke about that."

"Sorry, Beautiful. I couldn't help it."

I named Lady Allegra to the role of Kravan's interim leader on my second day, with my father as her advisor. I figure a Seer who knows the future might be the ideal person to run a realm that's been decimated by tyrants and liars over the course of generations.

At first, I expected pushback from Kravan's population. For so long, the Starless had been feared and maligned in the Capitol, after all.

But as it turned out, the moment the bombings stopped for good—the moment I told Kravan's citizens that the Lady was instrumental in that positive change—suspicion shifted instantly to support.

She has now grown popular among Tethered and Normals alike. No Starless wears a mask these days—and no one slices into their brands anymore. All implants have been disabled, and my father—and I—are no longer interested in hunting Tethered.

Thorne elbows me gently when my father and the Lady appear some distance down the street, walking arm in arm as they approach the house.

"They're pretty cute, I'll admit," Thorne murmurs.

I allow myself a smile, but there's sadness eating away at me somewhere deep inside—a question lingering as to whether my parents might have stayed together, had circumstances been different.

My mother did come to see me a few weeks back to let me know she was enjoying her position with the Verdans and that she had chosen to remain there to help Devorah and Pippa along. I was a little shocked, to say the least. But I suppose she has found her equivalent of two daughters at last.

"You two gave this land its life back," the Lady says when she and my father have joined us on the porch. "You sacrificed so much for Kravan, and we will never forget it."

My father adds, "But there's something we need to tell you both."

Thorne wraps an arm around me. "Whatever it is, it had better be good. Shara is still queen, remember."

The Lady smiles, and my father chuckles. "The thing is, Shara," he says, "you are also a king killer. You murdered Ellion Graystone."

"I did," I say, my jaw tight. "I can't say I regret it, but yes. I did kill him."

"Still, you are the queen, as Thorne says." The Lady's gaze moves toward the distant horizon, beyond the place where the Tower once stood. "Your friend Rivenna killed a king, too."

"I pardoned her."

"I know," she replies, turning back to me with a smile.

"Yes, of course you do."

"What punishment do you have planned for Shara?" Thorne asks, protective menace in his tone.

"Well." The Lady pulls her eyes to his, then mine. "I was wondering how you two would feel about exile."

"Exile?" My brows shoot upward. This is not what I'd expected. "Meaning what, exactly?"

"Meaning," my father says, "that when a ship arrives in Kravan's harbor in twelve months' time, you will go off in search of your sister, Soleia, wherever she may be. You may return here after five years, if you wish—but not before then."

Thorne reaches for my hand. By now, he knows all about Soleia—that she's alive and living in some distant land.

We've spoken of her often over the weeks, wondering where she might have ended up all those years ago. I've expressed my desire to find her, but have never known how or where to start.

Part of me leaps with excitement at the idea of heading out on the ocean to seek new lands. But other parts yearn for the rest we so sorely need, and the healing our little house provides.

"We would stay here for a year, you say," Thorne replies slowly. "Before the exile would begin."

The Lady nods. "A year in this house. Your sentence would only begin when you step onto the ship."

"We'll discuss it," I say, squeezing Thorne's hand. "But you're right—I would like to find my sister. To get to know her. And...I suspect you've seen a future where we meet."

"I'm saying nothing," Lady Allegra replies. "Only that I want you both to be happy. You deserve it, after everything."

"The truth is," my father explains, "Neither of us knows exactly where Soleia is. You two will have a hunt on your hands, if you're up for it."

"She lives near mountains," the Lady adds. "That's all I can tell you. Go speak to Rivenna when you can. She has information that will help you prepare for your journey."

"We will." I nod. "But—there's one other matter I haven't discussed with you yet. Before we decide our fates, I'd like to see it resolved."

"Which matter might that be?" my father asks.

"Tallin."

Thorne side-eyes me with mild shock but says nothing.

"What, exactly, do you want resolved where the former prince is concerned?"

"He helped us. He set me free and killed his parents, knowing all he would lose. He's no longer a Cendiary. He's a harmless Normal, and I think he should be set free."

"Free?" Thorne's surprise paints itself vividly on the word. "Shara—are you sure about that?"

"I know you despise him, and I'm the first to admit he's not the best person in the world. But he's not ambitious. He won't seek power. And there are hundreds of Tethered in the

Capitol alone who could destroy him. He's lived in pain for so long—can't we call those years time served?"

"If you wish to set him free, you may do it. You are still the queen, after all," my father says. "You hold the power here."

"I don't want his liberation to come from me. He respects *you*, Lady Allegra. Let it come from you."

"Very well." She lets out a long sigh, as if she's as exhausted as the rest of us, and takes my father's arm again. "I'll make sure he is released from his cell. In the meantime, speak to Rivenna. She has a little surprise for you."

"Ugh," I laugh. "I'm not sure I can take any more of Rivenna's little surprises."

"Oh...I think you'll like this one."

I look into her eyes for a moment, then say, "May I ask you something?"

"Of course."

The question is one I've pondered for a long time, and I'm fairly certain I already know the answer. Still, I want to hear it from her lips.

"The fortune teller Kith spoke to years ago—the 'old lady' who showed him his coronation. The one who gave him the book with the Quinton family history..."

"You'd like to know whether it was me."

"You're not an old lady...but yes. I'm curious."

She offers up a mysterious grin and nods once. "It was my mother. She set all of this in motion—this series of dominoes that needed to fall in exactly the right manner in order to bring us to *now*. She showed Kith just enough to tease him and excite him—his wedding to the Shadow's daughter, and his coronation."

"But not the end of his life."

With a shake of her head, she says, "A Seer never divulges a client's death. It would be bad form."

"She must have known, though—didn't she?"

Lady Allegra bows her head once, sighs, and says, "She knew."

"On that note," my father interjects. "We should be on our way, I think. We'll see you two soon, yes?"

Thorne and I both nod and agree to meet up in a week's time for dinner.

They're about to leave when I say, "Father—one last thing."

The Shadow turns back to me. "Yes?"

"You told me once we could choose our own surname. I was wondering if you had given it any more thought."

"Every day," he admits. "But I've never really come up with anything suitable." Raising his brows, he adds, "Something tells me you might have something in mind, however."

"I do." I take Thorne's hand in mine. "Back in the day, people were named for their professions. Smith, Carter, Milliner...that sort of thing. So, I was thinking *Laurence Hunter* sounded like an excellent name. A fitting one—and one you and I both deserve to wear with pride...despite the fact that our hunting days are over."

"*My* hunting days are over," he replies with a shake of his head. "But yours are just beginning. *Shara Hunter* is a perfect name. Perhaps you could tell your sister when you find her. She might like to know her full name."

"Yes," I say. "I think she will."

CHAPTER SIXTY

Rivenna has been living in a house only a few blocks from ours—a small bungalow with a sunroom and a large back garden.

It's not the type of home I would have envisioned for her, given that I associate her with windowless rooms, tunnels, and eyes as black as the deepest night.

But she's stopped wearing her dark contact lenses, and even stopped dressing in black. When Thorne and I arrive, she's dressed in gray trousers and a white sweater, her hair pulled back into a high ponytail.

For the first time, her surname, Sterling, seems to suit her perfectly.

Berengar wags his tail enthusiastically when we arrive, and as always, I offer up a pat on his head before Rivenna invites us in.

"The Lady told you to come by," she says. "Didn't she?"

"She didn't tell us much. Only that you have a little surprise for us."

"Two, actually."

"Two?"

"We're screwed," Thorne mutters.

Rivenna lets out a dastardly laugh and leads us into a small office with a desk at its center.

On a shelf along one wall is a series of tattered old books. Rivenna steps over and fingers her way through their spines until she comes to one in particular, which she pulls off the shelf.

She opens it and holds it up to show us, but all I see is a series of numbers and a few words—*names*—I don't recognize.

"I don't know what this is," I tell her.

"It's a log," Thorne says.

With a nod, Rivenna replies, "These are the names of ships that used to move between Kravan and other realms. The numbers are dates and times. Once a year, a ship arrives carrying supplies that we don't have access to—precious metals, seeds, that sort of thing."

Thorne and I exchange a look, but neither of us is quite willing to express our hopes.

Riv flips through to one specific page, displaying it for us again. "The night your sister allegedly died—the night she vanished, I mean—a ship left Kravan, bound for the western realms."

"Do you know exactly where it went?" I ask.

"Sort of. The bad news is, it docked at about fifteen different ports in various realms after it left here. Your sister could be in any of those realms—or none of them."

I turn to the shelf, pulling one book then another down to leaf through them. "Are there maps?" I ask. "Any indication of a land with mountains?"

"Quite a few have mountains," Rivenna replies, reaching for one tome in particular, which she hands me. "You're going to have your work cut out for you."

"Well...we do have a year." I set the books down and take Thorne's hand. "A year to make things right in this place before we go anywhere."

"Then use me." She nods to the bookshelf. "Any time you want to do some research, come on over. I stole these from the Citadel's store room. I'm sure no one will miss them. That whole place should be turned into an underground lake or something. It's a grim dungeon filled with cruel ghosts."

"Maybe flooding it will be my last official order before I melt my crown." I laugh, then look around, pursing my lips. "You said you had two surprises, didn't you?"

"Oh...right." Rivenna lets out a sigh. "The thing is, a few weeks ago, I met someone. A liberated Tethered who had made her way to the Capitol to look for work. She seemed pretty cool, and we struck up a friendship. Well...*more* than a friendship."

"Riv!" Thorne says with a smile. "I'm happy for you."

"Me, too," I say, tilting my head and narrowing my eyes. "But something tells me there's more to this than you're letting on."

"There's a *lot* more to it, actually."

The words come at us from the doorway behind us, like something out of a long-forgotten dream.

I spin around, let out a laugh, and hurl myself at the Porter standing a few feet away.

"Nev!" I cry, squeezing her tight. "Holy shit."

It feels so good to hug my old friend—to know that no

one will ever again tell us we're not allowed to touch one another.

"*You've* been busy," she laughs when I draw back, moving her eyes to Thorne. "Both of you."

"I can't imagine what you've heard, but yes. A little busy."

"I heard you became queen, for one thing. A Tower Orphan—queen of all Kravan. Isn't there some law about Tethered being crowned?"

"Tallin is a Tethered, and he became king. The laws are looser in this damned place than we ever knew when we were growing up. They'll throw a crown on anything that breathes, apparently."

Nev laughs. "The Isles were all aflutter with gossip. The Prefect and his wife got into screaming matches about you—they were terrified for a while that they might be arrested for all their shitty behavior."

"And then they were," Rivenna replies, sidling up next to Nev. She towers over her, a blond goddess with explosive eyes next to my childhood best friend.

What a world we've built.

"So, you two..." Thorne says, pointing from one to the other. "Is this...fate?"

"Hell, no," Rivenna says, slipping an arm around Nev's shoulders. "Not fate. Just...perfection."

EPILOGUE

One Year Later

The election took place six months ago.

Unchallenged, the Lady was officially named President of Kravan a week after the last ballot was cast.

As promised, I abdicated and announced the dissolution of the monarchy within hours of the announcement. I had my crown and Kith's melted down, the gold distributed to the families of Tower Orphans in need of help.

It has proven bittersweet to think of leaving our home behind for five years, but my father assured me that it will be waiting for us when we return.

He is now the Lady's top advisor. She has surrounded herself with capable Tethered and Normals, all of whom strive daily to make sure Kravan treats its people well.

Those who live in the Capitol are allowed to travel to the Isles, whether via the now refurbished tunnels or by small craft. Some people have even begun building houses on plots of land on the various islands, much to the former Nobles' horror.

The palace has been turned into a museum, open for free to visitors of all ages.

One of Thorne's and my final excursions before our exile begins is to wander its grounds as tourists.

"I really hate this place," I whisper as we trudge along, taking in every bit of opulence that tormented us as servants to the Royals, from portraits of Tomas and Tallin to busts of former kings and queens, to the arena where so many of our kind were murdered over the years.

"Me, too," Thorne says, then pulls me close and kisses me deeply in front of a tour group made up entirely of Normals —who don't pay attention to us for even a second.

Never have I felt more free or more empowered than I do at this moment.

A few feet away, someone clears his throat, drawing us apart.

Thorne and I glance over to see Tallin staring at us.

He's dressed in gray pants and a light-colored shirt, and like us, he's visiting the palace as nothing more than a tourist.

He looks strong—happy, too.

"I've taken a job in the Capitol," he tells us when we've greeted one another. "Working in a coffee shop."

The image of it is enough to make me stifle a snort. Tallin, of all people—the vile prince I met at the ball so long ago—serving coffee to Normals and Tethered.

"I am happy for you," I tell him. "Truly."

"I know you are." He shakes Thorne's hand and apologizes profusely for everything he's done. "You two are the reason I'm free," he says. "I won't forget what you've given me."

"In a strange way," I tell him, "you're the reason we're free, too...so, let's call it even."

"Agreed," Thorne says. "I mean, I won't be inviting you over to join our book club or anything, but..."

Tallin offers up a tight-lipped smile, nods once, then heads off to take in the sights.

"I've experienced a lot of things," Thorne tells me with a kiss to the top of my head. "But that, right there, might just have been the weirdest of them."

"Seeing him in casual street clothes is weird, for sure. He looks...*normal.*"

"I don't mean that," he chuckles. "I'm talking about how strange is is that I just talked to the former prince, and for once, I didn't feel the urge to murder him."

TODAY, we leave Kravan for unknown lands.

Thorne and I have already said goodbye to my father, the Lady, Joy, and Rivenna and Nev, who are now living under the same roof.

We're not bringing much with us on our journey—only a couple of suitcases filled with clothing, a couple of maps, and a few other items.

As we step onto the ramp that will lead us onto the massive ship whose name is the *Moirai*, Mercutio scampers ahead of us, turning occasionally as if to remind us he's there.

~He wants to make sure you're coming with him, Maude says out loud.

"How do you know that?"

~Maude's intuition.

She sounds a little down. Come to think of it, she's sounded maudlin for days now. I've been assuming she's upset to be leaving Kravan, but I'm beginning to suspect it's something else entirely.

"Are you all right, Maude?" Thorne asks. "You seem worried."

~It's just...I have a suspicion Maude units aren't so common in other realms. I've been wondering whether you two plan to...

"Kill you?" I say with a look at Thorne.

~Yes.

"Wait." I have to stifle a laugh. "Is that seriously why you've been so quiet lately?"

~Possibly.

I roll my eyes. "Maude, don't get me wrong—you're an irritating jackass. But I love you. You're part of me. And as long as you promise not to give me running commentary while Thorne and I are in bed tonight, I have absolutely no intention of ending you."

She goes silent for a few seconds, then says, *~Deal.*

The Thrall Series Continues with Bound.

THRALL, BOOK FOUR: BOUND

Bound begins a new story arc in the Thrall series and follows Shara's sister, Soleia. Based loosely on *Jane Eyre,* Soleia's story is one of slow-burn love, fast-burn betrayals, and everything in between.

Most Tethered and Powerless live free in the Peaks. Only one kind of human is hunted for their power.

Those known as Blades.

Ever since her childhood arrival in the land known as the Peaks, Soleia has been raised among a loving family of Powerless. Their home in a small village is idyllic, calm, and peaceful. Her nineteenth birthday has come and gone and at long last, she's confident that—unlike the father she left behind years ago—she is no Tethered.

But when she encounters a thief one awful day, a terrible truth rears its head, and Soleia quickly realizes she will endanger her family if she remains under their roof.

Her only choice is to go into hiding or turn herself in and suffer a wretched fate. She chooses to run, leaving her family behind to find a job in a remote, stately home in the mountains, owned by a powerful, mysterious young man named Rowland Fairfax.

At first, Soleia's life seems perfect once again. She rarely sees the imposing businessman who owns the property. She rides horses daily, ventures into the mountains as she pleases, and spends the rest of her time entranced by her employer's massive library. Occasionally, mysterious letters arrive for her via mechanical birds that claim to come from a long-lost sister.

Over the days and weeks, Soleia begins to hope she may find a life beyond the high mountains that hold her prisoner.

But when Fairfax begins to spend more time in his mountain home, Soleia comes to realize she's living inside a trap that could end her...or it could prove the beginning of a new life for both of them.

Loosely based on the novel Jane Eyre, Bound begins the next story arc of the exciting Thrall series!

THRALL, BOOK FOUR: BOUND

Acknowledgments

Normally, when I write acknowledgments, it's because something has come to an end. This time, though, I want to take a moment to thank a few people for their inspiration and support as I begin to work on ***Bound.***

I'm not going to name names—not because the people I'd like to thank don't deserve it, but because I don't want to forget anyone.

With that in mind...

To everyone who has ever sent me a message to yell at me for what I've done to their beloved characters: Thank you.

To everyone who's ever messaged me to thank me for entertaining them: Thank you.

To everyone's who's ever gone on a late-night rant in my DMs to scream obscenities at me for any hilarious reason: Thank you.

I mean it.

Writing can be a solitary pursuit, and while I have an amazing set of real-life family and friends who support me daily, I couldn't do what I do without the readers who keep me energized and excited.

Creating worlds is the most fun I've ever had, but it's exhausting, and the last few months have been more tiring than most (IYKYK).

Your words keep my words flowing.

So....thank you to ***all*** of you.

And an extra thank you to Mandy for Rivenna.

I hope, Mandy, that you didn't get extremely angry with me in the middle of this novel (again, IYKYK). ;)

xo,

K. A.

ALSO BY K. A. RILEY

If you're enjoying K. A. Riley's books, please consider leaving a review on Amazon or Goodreads to let your fellow book-lovers know!

Here is K. A. Riley's full catalogue of YA and Adult Dystopian and Fantasy novels!

READING ORDER FOR THE 5 TRILOGIES OF THE 15-PART *CONSPIRACY CHRONICLES*:

I. THE RESISTANCE TRILOGY

1. *RECRUITMENT*
2. *RENDER*
3. *REBELLION*

II. THE EMERGENTS TRILOGY

1. *SURVIVAL*
2. *SACRIFICE*
3. *SYNTHESIS*

III. THE TRANSCENDENT TRILOGY

1. *TRAVELERS*
2. *TRANSFIGURED*
3. *TERMINUS*

IV. The Academy of the Apocalypse

1. *Emergents Academy*

2. *Cult of the Devoted*

3. *Army of the Unsettled*

V. The Ravenmaster Chronicles

1. *Arise*

2. *Banished*

3. *Crusade*

* * *

The Cure Chronicles

The Cure | Awaken | Ascend | Fallen | Reign

* * *

The Thrall Series

Thrall | Broken | Queen

* * *

The Amnesty Games

The Amnesty Games | Middlegame | Endgame

* * *

Viral High Trilogy

Apocalypchix | Lockdown | Final Exam

* * *

Athena's Law

Rise of the Inciters | Into an Unholy Land | No Man's Land

* * *

Fae of Tíria Series

A Kingdom Scarred | A Crown Broken | Of Flame and Fury

* * *

Seeker's Series

Seeker's World |Seeker's Quest | Seeker's Fate | Seeker's Promise
|Seeker's Hunt | Seeker's Prophecy

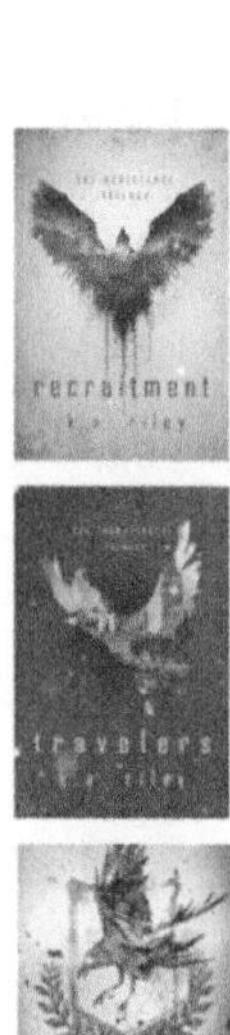
recruitment
k.a. riley
travelers
k.a. riley

render
k.a. riley

rebellion
k.a. riley

survival
k.a. riley

sacrifice
k.a. riley

synthesis
k.a. riley

transfigured
k.a. riley
terminus
k.a. riley

arise
K.A. RILEY

banished
K.A. RILEY

crusade
K.A. RILEY

emergents academy
K.A. RILEY

cult of the devoted
K.A. RILEY

army of the unsettled
K.A. RILEY

KINGDOM SCARRED
K.A. RILEY

K.A. RILEY
A CROWN BROKEN

OF FLAME AND FURY
K.A. RILEY

SEEKER'S WORLD
K.A. RILEY

SEEKER'S QUEST
K.A. RILEY

SEEKER'S FATE
K.A. RILEY

SEEKER'S PROMISE
K.A. RILEY

SEEKER'S HUNT
K.A. RILEY

SEEKER'S PROPHECY
K.A. RILEY

thrall
K.A. RILEY

broken
K.A. RILEY

queen
K.A. RILEY

THE AMNESTY GAMES
K.A. RILEY

MIDDLEGAME
K.A. RILEY

ENDGAME
K.A. RILEY

RISE OF THE INCITERS
K.A. RILEY

INTO AN UNHOLY LAND
K.A. RILEY

NO MAN'S LAND
K.A. RILEY

APOCALYPCHIX
K.A. RILEY

LOCK DOWN
K.A. RILEY

FINAL EXAM
K.A. RILEY

THE CURE
K.A. RILEY

AWAKEN
K.A. RILEY

ASCEND
K.A. RILEY

FALLEN
K.A. RILEY

REIGN
K.A. RILEY

K. A.
RILEY

ABOUT THE AUTHOR

K. A. RILEY is a full-time writer of YA and New Adult Dystopian Fantasy and Science Fiction. Riley is dedicated to creating worlds just different enough from our own to be entertaining, intriguing, and a little frightening all at once.

She lives in the Niagara Region with her slobbery golden retriever and her combative cat. Riley is fluent in French, is an experienced equestrian, and suffers from a major but manageable addiction to Wordle, white wine, and Reality TV.

She loves to travel and often incorporates elements of the places she's visited in her fiction. She has written half of her books in the vineyards of the French countryside, half while strolling the streets of London, and half at home. (That's three halves, but she's a writer not a mathematician.)

In addition to being a successful author, Riley is a classically trained violinist and violist who has performed professionally alongside big names such as Michael Bublé, Andrea Bocelli, and Tom Cochrane as well as in various quartets and orchestras for over thirty years.

* * *

Stay in touch with K. A. Riley

Website: https://karileywrites.org/

K.A. Riley's Bookbub Author Page

K.A. Riley on Amazon.com

K.A. Riley on Goodreads.com

on TikTok: @karileywrites

To be informed of future releases, and for occasional chances to win free swag, books, and other goodies, please sign up here:

https://karileywrites.org/#subscribe

Made in the USA
Las Vegas, NV
27 November 2024